MAY 17th 199?
2230 hrs

"SUBARU"

DEAR TJ + Tom + Patty :

THAT WAS A NIGHT I WILL
NEVER FORGET.

   THE FIRE WAS THE END OF THE
"SUBARU" BUT HER LEGACY LIVES
ON.
   REMEMBER ALL THE GOOD TIMES
WE SHARED!

        LOVE
          DAD
           AK.A.
             CAPT. BLIGH   21 MAY 2001

DROPBACK

A Story of the Intrigue and Villainy
behind the Cocaine Trade

PIET VAN ALDER

The Palancar Company Limited

For information
about permission
to reproduce or adapt
selections from this book
or permission
to transmit in any form
including any electronic transmittal
or recording system,
write to:

THE PALANCAR COMPANY LIMITED
The Courtyard, 12 Hill Street, St. Helier, Jersey JE4 9NU
E-mail: Twolowns@aol.com

Library of Congress Catalogue Card Number 00-130344

ISBN 0-9643256-7-5

For Anne, my Mom, who passed away in 1982

Author's Note

It takes a great deal of effort to turn a good story into an even better book, and I'd like to take this opportuntity to thank my publishers, The Palancar Company and, specifically, David and Patricia Lown, who saw talent in a new writer with an overactive yet unrefined imagination. Without their support, guidance and keen editorial eye, this book might have remained just a story, swimming around with the countless others in my mind.

I'd also like to thank my father and everyone else who believed I could write this book. You all spurred me on, gave me input and pointed to the light at the end of the tunnel, which I have finally reached.

Everyone has his own story about "the big one that got away". That's probably why the fish was so big in the first place. But once you kill him, that is the end of your story, and his. Billfish are really cool. There is really no good reason to kill one, and that's why I practice catch and release. If we all do the same, fishing can only get better. And bottom line, isn't that what we all really want?

Piet van Alder, February 2000

Prologue

Ciudad Juarez, Mexico   32°11.46"N   106°37.72"W
March 3, 1996 2317 Local Time (0117 EDT)

The final stage of the assault began just after dark. No one, not even the Administrator himself, knew they were there. And they'd already been across the border way too long.

The Mexican sentry paraded back and forth in front of the warehouse with the tired, erratic gait of a weary foot soldier. Special agent Wes Gates studied him closely through his night-vision goggles. The man lazily carried what appeared to be an AK-47, the weapon of choice for most of the *traficantes*. Even through the green and black field of vision, the Special Forces veteran could see the Mexican's expression. A victim of routine, the *traficante* plodded along, studying the ground. Wishing he was somewhere else.

"You think he's in there?" Gates partner whispered in the darkness. He was one of seven other DEA agents concealed in the underbrush surrounding the rusted metal structure. The assault team had crossed the border from El Paso, Texas more than an hour earlier.

"Carrillo?" Gates responded. "I don't know. Take a look at this character." He handed T.J. the special scope. Ty Jefferson was the only black man on the team. He'd never been to Mexico before—what the agents called "in country"—and Gates knew he was scared.

5

The man they were after was Amado Carrillo Fuentes, leader of the powerful Juarez cartel. Kingpin. Drug lord. There were all kinds of names...

"Well there's somethin' in there," T.J. said. "Here comes another guy." He, too, was armed and more alert than the first man they had seen. "Where'd the intel come from?"

"We're not sure," Gates told him.

"Not sure?" T.J. stressed. "Is it solid?"

"Yeah. It came from high up. Some government official, supposedly. Said it was a big load. Said Carrillo would definitely be here to check it." A tiny stream of sweat seeped into Gates' left eye and blurred his incredibly sharp vision. He blinked away the sting, took a deep breath and relaxed his finger on the trigger of his own weapon.

"You think everybody's in place?" T.J. asked.

"They should be," Gates whispered back. Staging from an area more than a mile away, the team had broken into four groups of two. They had approached the warehouse from different directions and that was the last he'd seen of his men. The necessary separation of the eight-man unit bothered Gates, and he pulled down hard at the deep tracks carved into the corners of his mouth, feeling the grooves through the thick layers of a heavy mustache.

A big man at six-four, Gates was a rugged-looking character, not an old man, but with a face that was old before its time. Weathered by a life that, so far, had been anything but easy, permanent emotional scars mixed with those of battle. He was a serious "operator", the only man in the team who had seen action—the only one who had been wounded before and had watched his friends and enemies die. And so it was with great apprehension that he led these men into danger, knowing that they looked to him for guidance and also knowing that real-life danger was the only training that would do them any good.

Gates brought the tiny mike of his voice-operated transmitter to his lips. "One in position, Northeast secure." The response was instantaneous as the others began to check in. The four teams were all in place, covering the four corners of the warehouse, and each team could see two sides. Now all they had to do was wait.

Cocking his head, Gates could hear voices coming from inside the building. His pulse raced. Soft light was visible from a crack under the sliding metal doors; it appeared through the goggles as a thin green line. Uncomfortably crouched, he shifted his weight onto one knee. He swatted a mosquito on his neck and wiped sweat from his forehead. The heavy humidity and weight of his Kevlar vest made him sweat like an inmate on his way to the chair. He looked over at T.J. and could see he was faring no better. The infiltration through the bush had been difficult. They carried automatic rifles, semi-automatic handguns, grenades, ammunition—and water. Had to have water. He took a sip from his canteen and passed it to T.J.

"We waitin' for back-up or somethin'?" T.J. asked, handing the water back. It took a few seconds for Gates to respond. "There's not going to be any back-up."
"Aw, shit, man, you're not s'posed to tell me that. I got kids." He was really alarmed now.

And Gates couldn't blame him. It was against the law for American agents to make an arrest in a foreign country without the presence of local authorities. They couldn't use force—hell, in Mexico, they weren't even supposed to carry guns! And every time they passed on intelligence to the Mexican authorities, their attempts to capture a cartel leader failed. It was total bullshit, and Gates wasn't the only one who knew it. "Sorry, T.J.," he told his friend, "We're on our own."

"Well goddamn, Wes!" T.J. said, trying to keep his voice down. "I'm telling you, man, I got a bad feeling on this one..." He turned away, anxious and ashamed.
"You just hang in there, brother. We've got the men, the training, and the firepower. And I'll be right next to you the whole time." Gates grabbed him by the arm and squeezed it tightly. "Right here." They crouched for a moment in awkward silence.
"I know, man, but I can't help it," he told Gates, his voice strained, nervous. "I'm scared."

And Gates knew he wasn't lying. He could actually smell the man. And now the smell was more obvious, jammed up his nose with its source written all over it. The smell of fear was unlike any other, and it couldn't be masked or washed away. And the faces of the men went with it: wide eyes, like scared animals trapped in the headlights, their eyes looked deep inside you, penetrating, pleading for help, boring through your brain into the back of your skull. Gates couldn't see T.J.'s eyes, but he knew how they looked. Like the eyes of his men that first night in Kafji, surrounded and unsure of themselves: far away in the Arab land, and thousands of miles from their homes. And the memory was painful. The confidence had seeped out of his men that night in Iraq, right along with their blood. And good men had died. The unit, the weapon—had broken down. Because he'd allowed them to lose their nerve. Because of the fear.

"Three has visual on one sentry along the south side of the building. Appears to be armed with an AK-47 and is patrolling east and west, not spending much time looking down sides, over." The transmission startled Gates, but made him feel good. At least the other two-man teams were paying attention and using their goggles to the best advantage.

"Roger that, One also has visual, one sentry, also armed, patrolling north side of building," Gates told the other units. "What about the east and west sides?"

"Affirmative, we've got another local returning towards the west side from the tree line. Must've been taking a leak. Also armed." The agent failed to give his team number and Gates could tell from his voice that he was nervous.

"Who's that?" Gates asked.

"Two," came the response.

"Okay, everybody just stay cool," Gates warned. "Wait for the signal."

A sudden movement out of the corner of his eye caught Gates attention and he turned to see a sentry come from around the west side of the warehouse. He joined the other *traficante*.

"Two, is that the guy from the west side?" Gates asked. They must have seen the movement.

"Roger that," Two replied. There was a flash of light and the men of both teams immediately looked away. When Gates looked back, the goggles were still working. Just a cigarette. Watching the sentries smoke and talk, he wondered at their lack of professionalism. Maybe it was a good sign.

"West sentry is now together with north sentry on north side," Gates said into his mike.

"Four still has visual. One man, south side."

"Copy that." But something in Gates' mind cried out. There was one man missing.

Jefferson nudged Gates to get his attention. The man pointed to the sky but Gates did not understand what he had seen or heard. He looked up and strained to hear in the dense underbrush. But it was the lack of any sound that Jefferson had noticed. The evening had become still. He nodded at T.J. to show that he also was aware of the silence, and a branch cracked a few feet from their position. Looking into the darkness, he could see the outline of an armed man, apparently staring at the two DEA agents crouched in the bushes. And it wasn't one of his men.

Gates held up his hand in front of his partner, silently telling him not to move, and touched the ground to steady his legs. Realizing he had stopped breathing, he exhaled as quietly as he could as the man continued walking towards the warehouse.

Seconds later, Gates heard the unmistakable "klatch" sound of the safety being flicked off an AK-47. Acting on instinct alone, he slid his Kaybar killing knife from its worn leather scabbard. The attack would need to be swift.

Before he could act, the stillness was shattered as the man unleashed a burst from his automatic weapon into the bushes where Gates and Jefferson were hiding. T.J. cried out as they dove to the ground. With bits of leaves, twigs, and dirt flying all around them, Gates returned fire and blew the man off his feet, killing him.

The other sentries let loose with their AK-47s on full automatic, firing without targets into the tree line surrounding the warehouse. Lacking the advantage of the Americans' night-vision, they were taken out by the other teams. The gunfire was relentless—the locals must have thought all hell was breaking loose south of the border.

Gates moved over to where T.J. lay on the ground. "How bad you hit?" he shouted.

"I don't know, man. It's my shoulder."

Gates reached out and probed the wound. T.J. gasped as his partner ran his fingers along a two-inch groove. They came back warm, sticky. "Can you move it?"

"Yeah, a little."

"Then let's move," he ordered, and they were off.

"Prepare to attack through the north side," Gates radioed the other teams. He was still speaking when Team Four came out of the southeast tree line and began running towards the front of the warehouse. Gates and his partner split, and took up positions on each side of the giant steel doors.

The doors began to slide open. Seeing that the interior of the warehouse was well lit, both Gates and Jefferson whipped off their goggles and each hurled a flash-bang grenade inside. They charged through the door and dived to the hard dirt floor. Inside, chaos ruled: there was shouting, screaming and smoke. And Mexicans scattering in all directions, like nervous insects seeking sanctuary from a superior intruder. An engine revved, and Gates and Jefferson rolled out of the way as a vehicle roared past with an automatic weapon firing indiscriminately. To Gates it sounded big, maybe .50 caliber.

Outside, the other agents dove to the ground as the jeep appeared. A mounted machine gun blazed away at anything that moved. Two agents were raked by a stream of bullets but the others' M16's found their mark, killing the jeep's driver and wounding the gunner. In a cloud of dust, the vehicle veered to the right and flipped over onto its left side.

Inside the warehouse, the smoke had begun to clear. Gates and Jefferson used their weapons to round up seven men, miraculously killing no one in the process. Now the prisoners stood huddled together with their hands up. They were terrified and some were even praying. Gates nodded and T.J. checked the men for hidden weapons. Finding nothing, he stepped back. Gates yelled "Clear!" and two of the other agents darted inside.

"Wow," one of them said. And he was right.

The men were surrounded by stacks of cocaine. Thousands of individually wrapped kilo-packages. More than Gates had seen in a long time. He stepped forward and screamed at the men, inches from their faces.

"Where's Carrillo?!" he demanded. "Where's the boss?!" The Mexicans just shook their heads back and forth, and he repeated the question in Spanish. But he didn't see anyone who looked like the cartel leader. Although intelligence on Carrillo was sparse, the few photos he had seen did not resemble any of the men in the warehouse.

"He's got to be in here..." Gates mumbled. "You." He pointed at one of the black-clad agents. Beneath the camouflage face paint and assault gear, he couldn't even tell who it was. "Watch these guys."

Together, the other three agents swept the interior of the building, weapons held at hip level, ready for an ambush. Five minutes later, they had come up dry.

"T.J.—check the jeep," Gates told his partner. "See if he might be out there."

The agent returned in less than a minute. "Negative. Sorry, Wes," he said.

"Goddammit!" Gates snarled, but stifled his anger quickly and asked about his men.

"Adams got hit in the leg, but it doesn't look too bad. Everyone else is O.K."

"What about you?" Gates asked T.J., motioning towards his blood-soaked shoulder.

"Scared me at first, but I guess I'll live. Give me something to tell my kids about." He smiled at Gates, a look of relief on his face.

"Get a field dressing on that."

"Yeah, I will. What do you want to do with these clowns? And what about all the stuff?" he asked Gates.

Gates had to think. He hadn't planned on taking anyone but Carrillo. "Tie them up. We'll have to leave them." Once back on American soil, he would alert the proper Mexican authorities and later deny any involvement.

After restraining the survivors of the raid, the agents turned off the lights and closed the doors to the warehouse with the smugglers inside.

The dead were left where they had fallen. The other members of the team had managed to flip the jeep back over and it appeared to be functional. Loading the wounded man in the back, the agents crammed into the jeep. It was time to haul ass.

The road was rocky and overgrown, hardly a road at all. But they covered the first mile quickly, and continued towards the extraction point in silence. And then they saw the lights.

The agents were out of the jeep in a flash. With Gates carrying the wounded man, they took up positions in the tall brush along both sides of the narrow drive. There was no time to hide the jeep.

Up ahead, the oncoming vehicle had also stopped. Figures were scurrying about in the darkness. Heavily armed figures. They deployed in a classic battle position. For a moment, the only sound was heavy breathing.

A voice ruined the silence as a man in uniform stepped forward and identified himself as the *comandante* of the local Mexican Federal Judicial Police—the *Federales*.

For Gates, things couldn't get much worse. "Gentlemen, I think the shit just hit the fan," he told the other agents. "We've been set up." Placing his weapon on the ground, he stepped out into the dirt road to confront the *comandante*.

"*Somos Americanos*," Gates said. "D-E-A." Behind him his men began to filter out of the brush.

The *comandante* greeted him with a stare. "Drop your weapons and get on the ground!" he barked in English.

The team members looked at each other nervously. Gates was right. They were in deep shit.

1

Buccaneer Marina, Singer Island, Florida 26°46.72"N 80°02.41"W
March 4, 1996 0845 EDT

Slowly opening his eyes to search for the source of the annoying
sound that had awakened him, Captain Dan Larsen realized he had
slept on the boat again. As he reached for his jeans from the floor,
Larsen was aware that he had not spent the night alone. Asleep in the
bed next to him, the blonde he had met in the marina bar lay on her
back, naked, with the pillow squashed around her head and ears. He
fished the beeper out of the pocket of his pants and admired the sight
of her round, full breasts tanned to an attractive deep brown. Maybe,
with a little effort, he might even be able to come up with her name.
Glancing at the number in the tiny digital display, he sat up slowly and
swung his legs over the side of the bed. The pain that surged into his
severely hung-over brain made his head feel as though it was about to
explode.

The woman felt the bed move and watched as Larsen crossed the
room.
"Where are you going so early?"
Larsen grabbed his shirt and boxers off the floor and padded towards
the head.
"It's not early," he answered, without looking back. Slipping into the
small shower, Larsen turned the water to a comfortable setting and

doused his strong lean body the best he could. Then he stuck his head under the spigot and turned off the hot water, letting ice-cold water beat on the back of his throbbing head. Finally, as he washed away the last of the smell of bar smoke and sweat he had absorbed during the previous night's sex, he tried to remember the experience. Most of it was a blur.

Picking up women in the bar was like taking candy from a baby when you had a sixty-five foot sportfishing yacht docked right outside. But in the morning, he always felt the same. Gone were the feelings of the previous evening, the lust and desire and drunken flirtation, as he tried to snake them back to the boat. Instead, Larsen always felt rather hollow and lonely, knowing that it would all be just another one-night-stand. Then came the phone calls, the desperate attempts to make something more out of what was usually just another one of his drunken mistakes. This wasn't the first time and Larsen was sure it wouldn't be the last. Florida was filled with gold-diggers from around the country and chasing cash was what most of these bimbos did best.

Toweling himself off in the tight confines of the bathroom, Larsen looked into the mirror to see what kind of destruction the previous night's behavior had caused. Besides being a little bloodshot, the deep-set, kind, brown eyes were clear and not too swollen. His well-tanned face looked younger than his thirty-three years and the dark stubble of a two-day beard contrasted with his sun-bleached, shoulder-length blond hair, even though it was wet. With just the beginning of crow's feet around the eyes and small creases at the corner of the mouth from years of smiling and laughing, the face that looked out at him seemed that of a surfer or lifeguard. And that, along with his job as captain aboard the private sportfisher, was the perfect cover for Dan Larsen, special agent of the DEA.

When he opened the bathroom door, the blonde was sitting up in bed, still naked. "You aren't in that big a hurry are you?" she teased, getting off the bed and coming over to him. She stood on her tiptoes as she wrapped her arms around his neck and kissed him. Her clever hands wandered to Larsen's crotch, massaging him gently through the towel that he had wrapped around his waist. Larsen's own hands slipped around her back and glided down the smooth curves of her buttocks. Feeling himself getting hard, he grasped the cheeks of her ass and ground his pelvis into hers, and gently lay her down on the bed.

"I really want to do this," he said. "But let me answer that page. It's important and I'm not sure if or when I'll be back."

The blonde reached out for him and he backed away. "There's a towel under the sink if you want to take a shower," he told her.

"When can I see you again?"

"I don't know. Leave your number on the table." Larsen pulled his t-shirt over his head and bent over and kissed her. The blonde made a sad puppy-dog face, but she knew the game and she knew he would never call. Feeling a twinge of guilt, he disappeared up into the salon. "Don't worry about locking it," he shouted down and headed out the door.

Larsen crossed the cockpit and stepped onto the dock. Looking up at the overcast sky, he noticed the wind was coming from the west, an off-shore breeze that wasn't great for fishing. Most of the other boats in the marina remained in their slips, their captains and crews taking the day off, cleaning their vessels and doing routine maintenance.

Not stopping to chat, Larsen headed for the pay phone outside the bar to return the page. He knew that number by heart and it seemed that whenever he called it, something bad always happened.

Central Intelligence Agency
Langley, Virginia 38°50.06"N 77°08.92"W
March 4, 1996 0843 EDT

John Macki, Director of the CIA's Office of Narcotics Intelligence laughed softly and hung up the phone. The calls had been coming for nearly an hour now, from the moment he'd set foot inside his office, his think tank, his sanctuary. Lately it seemed he spent more time inside than out, but it didn't matter. He was single, divorced actually, and it wasn't like he was missing anything at home. His failed marriage was a memory now; she'd given him the ultimatum—the job or me—and he hadn't really missed her.

The fact that two agents of the DEA had been wounded in a shootout with the Juarez cartel concerned him, but there were other reasons, politically explosive, and far more serious, that troubled him more. Someone had tipped off the bad guys and, most likely, tipped off the *Federales* as well. Stateside, the resulting shitstorm was quickly gaining momentum. And, like always, the true target of the raid was nowhere to be found. Amado Carrillo Fuentes was good. Real good.

"So he slips away again," Macki said to his empty office. Rubbing his ear, he took a deep breath and pressed the intercom button which connected him to his secretary in the outer office. The wheels of his mind had been working all morning on a plan. It was time to get to work.

"Carla, would you beep Dan Larsen for me please? His number should be in the computer."

There was no response for a moment. "Umm...sure," she finally said, and he sensed a bit of tension in her voice. As a secretary, Carla Deering was more than he could ever ask for. Smart as a whip, she'd graduated from Brown and gone on to get a masters in political affairs. Young, somewhere around twenty-five, she could hold her own against any of the current affairs wizards and Macki was sure that she wouldn't be sitting outside his office for long. She was a looker, too, and he sometimes had difficulty remembering the old adage about not shitting where you eat.

Macki made a few more calls and was mulling over what could have gone wrong with the previous night's raid when his intercom buzzed and snapped him back to reality.

"Dan Larsen on the line, John."
"Put him through," he told her and pushed the right button. "Good morning, Captain."
"Is it?" the voice asked him.
"Well, maybe for you, Dan, but definitely not for me. How are the kids?"
"Don't have any yet."
"How's the wife?"

"I'm afraid I've struck out in that department, too. Listen, John, my head's about three times too big right now, and I couldn't find the fuckin' Advil. What's up?"

Macki decided to hit him directly with it. "Everything secure?" he asked him first, checking to be sure Larsen was on a pay phone.

"Yeah. Tell me."

"All right, Dan. Some bad shit went down last night in Juarez. A big shootout between the druggies and the DEA."

"So what else is new?" Larsen interrupted.

"Couple of your boys got whacked."

"Killed?"

"No, but I'm getting conflicting reports as to how bad they were hit. They were after Carrillo. He's under indictment in both Dallas and Miami, you know. That's your neck of the woods."

"So what's the big deal?" Larsen asked. "Did they get him?"

"No."

"Well it's not the first time they missed." Larsen said.

"Yeah, I know. But they fucked up. Bad. They were alone."

"Huh?"

"No Mexican escorts," Macki whispered. As if someone listening in might hear.

"Really."

"And they got caught." Still whispering.

"No shit..." Larsen was beginning to understand the situation.

Macki let it sink in for a few seconds and then said, "Some heads are gonna roll on this one, my friend."

"You can say that again."

"I just got word from the top," Macki said, all serious now. "They want something done and get this—they've dumped it all on me."

"Well, they couldn't have picked a better man. John Macki. Mister Intelligence-the drug smuggler's worst nightmare."

"Let's get serious, Dan. I need your help. We need to talk. When can you get up here?"

"When can I get up there?" he repeated. It was obvious from his voice that he had no such intention. "I've got shit to do, John." On the defensive now. "I'm going to Cancun in less than two weeks!"

"I know that. That's why we need to talk. As a favor to an old friend..."
Macki knew that one would get him.

"All right. But I've got a few things to take care of first. Maybe near the end of the week...I'll have to get back to you. Shit," he said and the line went dead.

The intercom buzzed again. "A Miz Brockman to see you, John." Carla emphasized the Miz.

"Thanks, Carla. Send her in."

His door opened and a forty-something brunette with her hair piled up in a bun entered the office. She clutched a briefcase like it was filled with secrets. Really wasn't bad looking, he thought. Nice body, great eyes. Definitely needed to lose the horn-rimmed glasses.

"Hello, John. You wanted to see me?"

Macki stood, and extended his hand. "Hi Liz. Thanks for coming. Have a seat." He was always amazed by the firmness of her grip, not limp and frail like many of the women he met.

"It's Elizabeth."

"Oh. Sorry." He'd forgotten what a tight-ass she could be. A real 90's woman. Gloria Steinem would be proud.

"What can I do for you, John?" Right to the point, as usual. No time for pleasantries. He knew she was impatient, but she had to be. As a staff psychoanalyst, Elizabeth Brockman was a busy lady, a woman in demand throughout the Agency.

"I need to ask your advice on something," he began. She was tapping her pen on the desk like she couldn't wait for him to get on with it. "Last night two DEA agents were wounded in a shootout with some drug dealers in Juarez, Mexico."

Before he could elaborate, she cut him off. "And Amado Carrillo wasn't anywhere around."

"Jesus Christ! The whole world knows!"

"It was on CNN, John," she said dryly. Like he should have realized.

"How in hell did they find out?"

"Good question. How do they ever find out? Maybe they have a mole within the organization," she joked.

"That's not even funny." Macki knew it had happened before and would probably happen again. The newsies had no conscience when it came to breaking a story. "Somebody tipped them off, Elizabeth."

"Somebody within the Agency?" she asked.

"Too early to tell. Anyway, I'm thinking of bringing in a special guy on this case. DEA. I want you to take a look at him. See what you think. Tell me if I've got the right man for the job".

"I don't know, John. That's not exactly what I do." She was on the defensive now, slightly flustered. "I'm used to psychoanalyzing the bad guys, you know, murderers, foreign operatives, double-agents..."

"Couldn't you just take a quick look? Please?" He had her now, and he put on his best little-boy pout.

"All right. You have file or something?"

"Yeah. C'mon around here," he said as he motioned her to his side of the plain, steel desk. As she came around, he got a good look at her out-fit. One of those severe, no-nonsense, long skirts, with a matching suit-jacket buttoned tight. Jet black—like she was on her way to a funeral.

"Nice outfit," he lied.

"Save it, John." She gave him one of those disapproving looks over the top of her specs, the librarian silently chastising the rambunctious pupil.

He began tapping on the keyboard in front of the small personal com-puter. Everything was digital, nowadays. Cut down on the need for paper-work, they said, but it took just as long to enter the goddamn computer-work.

A few seconds later the file appeared on the screen. With a click of the mouse, he opened it. Clicked again, and the image of Dan Larsen slowly took form, top to bottom, in the upper right hand corner of the screen. All blond hair and tan—looked like he'd just come from the beach.

"Hey, dude, surf's up," she said in her best surfspeak. Slow and stoney. Not a bad impression.

"Don't be fooled," Macki warned her. "I've worked with this guy. He's good."

"Looks like he'd rather be dropping in on a nice wave. Is he from California?"

"Yeah. Southern Cal. Near San Diego."

"Navy brat?"

"Yep."

"Any service record?"

"None. Spent most of his life in upstate New York."

"Poor guy," she said. "He must have been lost up there. Landlocked, I mean. They say most people born near the water tend to stay there or eventually gravitate to it."

"That makes sense. He lives in Florida now. East Coast. North of Miami."

"And you say he's with DEA down there?"

"That's right. Works out of the West Palm Beach office, but he's undercover. Drives one of those big fishing boats. But not the ones that take all the people out. One of those sleek, private jobs."

"Let's backtrack for a second. Family?"

"One older brother in Hawaii and one younger sister, deceased."

"Cause of death?"

"Not sure," he lied. "Sudden death. We didn't feel the need to poke into it." But he could see her brain working on that one.

"A middle child," she observed.

"That mean anything?"

"Well, often the middle child gets lost in between. They tend to become very strong, independent. Bear the weight of the world on their shoulders, you know?"

"Yeah. This guy is like that," he told her.

"Where'd he go to school? Or did he?" she asked.

"Back in New York. State University at Albany. Graduated in eighty-five. Studied Russian."

"Russian?" As if she couldn't believe it.

"Yeah. Now here's the good part. Remember that big intelligence fiasco in Moscow about ten years ago?"

"You mean the one with the new embassy being bugged and all that?"

"That's the one. It seems my man Larsen was studying over there at that time. Exchange student at some foreign language institute. Spent a lot of time at the embassy. On Friday and Saturday nights they'd turn the compound snack bar into a disco. Cold Budweiser, cheeseburgers, pizza—you know, the works. Anyway, as you know, like all our embassies, the one in Moscow was guarded by a contingent of U.S. Marines. So our man Larsen buddies up with these guys and starts hanging out at the after-hour parties."

"And what happened at such after-hour fiestas?" she asked, raising one eyebrow in amusement. "I think it's coming back to me now."

"The marines would invite several members of the opposite sex in for some late night activity. Russians, East Germans, Poles..."

"Sex for secrets," she said, remembering now.

"Exactly. And thanks be to God, our man Larsen was one hell of a patriot."

"What happened?"

Macki turned away from the screen to face her. "After he got back, the Agency was holding interviews on his campus in Albany. He marched right in there and blew their minds with his information. One of the biggest security breaches in U.S. history!"

"Wow." For a moment she was speechless. "This guy?"

"This guy." He paused for effect. "But get this! The Agency tries to recruit him on the spot and he refuses!"

"Really! So how did he wind up with DEA?"

"Less than a year after he got back from Russia, he high-tails it to Florida. Moved there right after he graduated. Like he was trying to get away from it all. Hooked up with the DEA two years later. But he didn't get busted or anything like that. We looked into it. Just signed up, went through the training in Quantico, and finished in the top of his class. Insisted on being undercover. Kinda weird, huh?"

"Yeah, but it fits. Sometimes it takes a shock to make somebody get involved. Like a kid who gets killed in a car accident where alcohol is involved and the mother joins Mothers Against Drunk Drivers. Right after my grandmother died, I joined the American Cancer Society. You know what I mean? Something motivated him."

"Yeah. I wonder what made him agree to help me? We've been working together, on and off, for about five years now."

"Maybe for some strange reason he likes you, John," she snipped, checking the time on her watch. She never left without a zinger like that, and that's what kept his interest. "Maybe he likes the money. I've really got to get going." She got up and made for the door.

But Macki knew it was more than that, more than just the money. "So what do you think? Is he the right man for the job?" he shouted at her back.

"Well, from what I've seen, he's certainly inconspicuous, loves his country and seems to be driven by something."

"So you think he'd be useful in tracking down Carrillo?" he asked.

"I think he's perfect." And then she was gone.

Drug Enforcement Administration   El Paso, Texas
Same Day 1143 CT

When special agent Wes Gates looked up at the door to his tiny office, the last person he expected to see was Bob Constance, Administrator of the DEA, in the flesh, right there in El Paso.

Gates jumped up from behind his desk and stopped his arm just shy of a salute.

"Mr. Gates?" the man asked.

"Y-yes sir. Pleased to meet you, sir." He stood paralyzed as Constance strode across the room and extended his hand. Gates had seen pictures of the man, all over the papers and the TV news, yet they had never met. Goddamn he was a big mother and right now he didn't look happy. When their hands met, Gates gave it his best shot and Constance matched it with a look in his eyes that said 'don't mess with me'.

"Please. Sit," Constance told him. An order, not a suggestion. He grabbed a chair from against the wall and dragged it across the polished marble floor. Gates winced at the sound. "Quite an office you've got here." He looked around. The walls were bare, the place antiseptic.

"I spend most of my time in the field, sir. Hardly need an office."

Constance took a deep breath and exhaled loudly. "Let me get right to it. A lot of people are after my ass this morning, Mr. Gates."

"I can understand that, sir."

"Would you like to tell me just what in hell happened last night? I've already spoken with your supervisor. I'd like to hear your version." The angry grey eyes burned into the agent.

"Well, sir," he began. He tugged at his mustache and his right leg bounced up and down underneath the desk.

"Stop calling me sir."

"Sorry." Gates took a deep breath of his own. "It was like this. One of our informants in Juarez, a reliable one, gave us the exact location of a warehouse on the west edge of town. Said Carrillo was definitely gonna be there, making a final inspection of a load that was supposed to come across the border this morning. I saw it. It was a big one. Probably a couple of tons. The assault element consisted of eight men, four two-man units. It was a perfect opportunity. A textbook raid."

"What the fuck happened?" A little louder now, but trying to control himself.

"They knew we were coming, sir." Constance let that one slide. "It was like they were waiting for us."

"And you were unescorted."

"That's right." He waited for the reprimand but it never came.

"How long have you been out of the army, Gates?"

"Five years. My recon platoon got shot all to hell. Up in Kafji." Gates could tell that Constance knew where that was.

"Why'd you get out?"

"Well, when I got back home, and got out of the hospital, it just didn't seem to make sense. You know, being over in Iraq. Turns out it was all about oil, anyway."

"Where you from, Gates?"

"Here."

"You don't have much of an accent."

"My father was in the service. I spent quite a few years overseas. And I've worked pretty hard at losing it. In this business, a Texas twang can be a dead giveaway."

"Good point," Constance told him. He seemed to be losing a bit of the hostility. "What made you join DEA?"

"When I came back from the war, I really began to see what's been happening around here. Violence in the streets, murders every night. All the new building going on is drug money. We don't even own this town anymore."

Constance stared at him in silence, and ran his fingers through his short, peppercorn buzzcut. He looked ill at ease in his fancy charcoal suit. A pair of fatigues would have done much better. Gates had the feeling he had seen action, but now was not the time to ask. Finally, he spoke.

"I want you to know I sympathize with you, Mr. Gates. But there's certain ways things need to be done around here. The Southwest Border Project has done more than we could ever dream of." The great effort by the Justice Department, DEA and FBI got hundreds of supervisors, agents, and law enforcement officers involved. These were guys who were trying to break major cases that would undermine the Mexican cartels' U.S. distribution cells as well as their command and control structures here in the States.

"We've seized tons of cocaine and made hundreds of arrests, but it's still not enough. The latest statistics show that 70 percent of the coke entering the U.S. is coming over the border between here and California. The alliance between the Colombians and the Mexicans is stronger than ever. We need to smash the Mexican Federation."

"And how are we gonna do that?" Gates asked.

"That's just it. Because however we do it, we have to do it legally. Which isn't necessarily the best way, as you well know."

"We're losing the war on drugs, aren't we?" Gates question was more of a statement.

"Yes, you could sat that, but it's not really a war. As a former soldier, you should know that. In a war, you win a few battles, grab a little more land, and you're on your way to victory. But this is different. This drug smuggling is like a cancer gnawing away at the very heart of the country. There is no cure, no vaccine. No one's going to ride in and make it go away with a silver bullet." He was getting angry again.

"The way I see it, we reduce the demand, they'll reduce the supply," Gates told him.

"Damn straight! But that's never going to happen. I've been with this administration for twenty-three years! Since its fucking inception!" Getting real mad now. "I've seen the country go from pot to coke to heroin, then back to coke. It's never gonna change! But in the meantime, we can try, we can make a dent by nailing this Carrillo fucker."

"We've been trying..."

"I know, I appreciate your efforts. But it's out of our hands now..." Constance looked like a man suddenly deflated.

"Out of our hands!" Gates couldn't believe it.

"Just like that." Constance snapped his huge fingers. "They've turned the whole thing over to the CIA. The special narcotics intelligence outfit. I'm sorry, Mr. Gates."

Gates anger had him nearly speechless. "I'm sorry too, sir." He stood as Constance got up to leave. Their eyes met once more.

"I'm sure we haven't heard the end of this."

"No, sir."

"And Gates?"

"Sir?"

"You're not in the army anymore. You're a civilian. Stop acting like a fucking soldier."

CIA Headquarters
March 8, 1996 1036 EDT

On his way from the airport to CIA headquarters at Langley, Larsen was reminded just how much he despised big city life. Not only the traffic bothered him, but the series of security checkpoints once inside the complex made him feel like a criminal trying to do something or go somewhere that he wasn't supposed to.

Ignoring the furtive glances of the other employees as well as their snide remarks about his casual dress, Larsen thought to himself how lucky not to be part of this rat race. Long ago he'd realized that a nine-to-five job behind a desk was not for him.

Opening the door to Macki's office, Larsen was greeted by the lovely sight of Carla Deering, who was busy typing something into her personal computer. She turned as if surprised.

"Hello Dan." A solemn greeting, as he had expected.

"Carla." He searched for the right words, but they would not come, and after their eyes met, he could see she was uncomfortable too, and she looked away.

They'd been on two dates together the last time he was in town, and Carla had quickly let it be known that she was no easy lay, no one-night stand. And he hadn't called her again, not because she didn't put out, but because he didn't want to waste her time. She was attractive, no doubt about that, but she was also one of the smartest girls he had ever met. She loved her job, loved the whole scene, and he knew damned well she wasn't going anywhere. She'd misread him, misunderstood his intentions, and it was probably better for the both of them. No need to lengthen the trail of broken hearts.

"Nice shirt," she told him.

"Thanks," he said, but he wondered if she meant it. It was one of his favorites, a blue and white, aloha-style with a pattern of blue marlins. Larsen was one of the few people who dared enter the building in such casual attire. But fuck them. They were lucky he'd even bothered to tuck it in. His light-blue shorts and off-white Sperry docksiders only emphasised that he was not a regular employee. And that was just the way he wanted it.

"Your hair's longer," she tried. "Blonder, too." But the wall between them had already been built.

"Yeah, well, you know how it is for a man of the sea." Only separating them further.

"John's been waiting for you. You better get in there before he has a baby." Her phony smile pushed the daggers of guilt deeper into his heart. He turned the handle and walked into Macki's office.

"Well goddamn, Captain," Macki said, rising from behind his desk. "It's good to see you, Dan." He grabbed Larsen's outstretched hand with both of his own, in the old surf-style that had practically disappeared.

"You too," Larsen told him, and it was true. The CIA man hadn't changed a bit. Same white, short-sleeved shirt, starched crisp, and solid-color tie. Today it was blood red. Hair cut short, but out of control. Maybe a tad more gray.

Without asking, Larsen took a seat and Macki did the same.

"Good trip?"

"Yep. Let's cut the small talk, John." He was a fish out of water and he knew that Macki knew it.

"Right. Well then, like I told you already, the pressure is really on to nab this guy Carrillo. DEA already had their shot and once again, they blew it. No offense."

"None taken." Larsen had heard all about the botched raid for several days, both on the news and in the papers. He knew the finger pointing was inevitable.

"It's simply a matter of too many people being involved in one operation," Macki continued. "Somewhere along the line somebody spilled the beans and look what happened. Anyway, this motherfucker has to go down. Pardon my French. The word's come down from the top, and I'm sure it can be traced all the way from the Director of the Agency to the President himself. This is an election year, my friend, so I don't have to tell you how important it is for them to show some results in their little war on drugs." He stopped to let that sink in.

"Why do I get the feeling you think I'm gonna help you take him down? I thought I told you I was done with this kind of shit!"

"Because I know you, Dan. This is right up your alley. A chance to put away the guy responsible for more than half the cocaine that comes into this country." And he saw that he was finally getting to him.

"But I don't know shit about him, John. Nobody does. All I know is what I've seen on CNN, and in the papers. Most of it's guesswork."

"Yeah, but we know enough. This guy Carrillo's rise to the top was amazing. He grew up in the mid-sixties in a little village just outside of Culiacan, the capital of Sinaloa, on the Pacific coast. Fields and fields of opium and marijuana. This is where we found the beginnings of the Mexican drug trafficking: The Federation."

"Thirty years ago? I was three years old."

"Right. Carrillo wasn't much older. The godfather of the Federation was a guy named Pedro Aviles Perez. His bookkeeper was Ernesto Fonseca Carrillo, Amado's uncle. They taught him all about smuggling and he started at the bottom, smuggling pot in donkey carts.

"But here's the important thing. Pedro Aviles was the first to get hooked up with the Colombians. We're talking middle to late seventies now."

"So how did Carrillo get hooked up with the Colombians?" Larsen asked.

"Aviles gets zapped in 1978 by the Mexican Federal Judicial Police."

"The *Federales*." Larsen knew all about them and their corruption.

"Right. And who was Aviles' bookkeeper? Fonseca, Amado Carrillo's uncle."

"Gotcha. So now Carrillo's hooked up too."

"In the eighties, uncle Fonseca introduces Carrillo to the Herreras in Durango, right next door to Sinaloa."

"Wait a minute," Larsen interrupted. "Weren't they famous for smuggling heroin?"

"Very good, Dan!" Macki was getting more animated by the minute, leaning forward, bugged-out eyes, a little boy with a big secret to tell. "The Herreras were the last of a dying breed. Their operation was strictly family. They controlled every aspect of their operation, from the planting of the seeds to the harvest, delivery and distribution of the shit in the U.S.. They took a liking to Carrillo and put him to work, teaching him more about the biz. Carrillo starts hanging out with Jaime Herrera Junior and Rafael Caro Quintero—poster boys for the new-age trafficker."

"New-age trafficker?" Larsen was confused. "I thought new-age was some type of shitty music that I don't like."

"You know, the internationalist. Thousand dollar boots, gold chains, zipping around on the Concorde and all that bullshit. Spending their money on the American side of the border. Buying up the mansions, racehorses, yachts: the works. And all the time Carrillo is hanging out with these idiots, he's gaining experience and making new contacts. And watching what they do right and what they do wrong.

"But how does he get to the top? When does he get the power?" Larsen interrupted.

"Will you relax? I'm getting to that." He took a sip from his third cup of coffee and continued. "Caro Quintero hooks up Carrillo with Pablo Acosta Villarreal, another one of the jet-setting drug lords from Chihuahua in the north. Carrillo becomes his lieutenant. And believe me, they were tight. High as kites most of the time from freebasing coke."

"I thought the rule was 'never get high on your own supply'."

"That was Scarface. And that was a movie, Dan. Anyway, Acosta taught him everything. How to move the stuff, how to time a delivery, who to bribe, who to trust—everything."

"And what happened to him?"

"Killed in a shootout with the police in 1987."

"How do you know all this shit? How do you remember it?"

"It's my job, Dan. I'm in the intelligence biz."

"I guess there's still a lot more about him we don't know."

"Right again, my friend. You see, even though he hung out with them for a little while, Carrillo never bought into that flamboyant trafficker crap. Always kept a low profile. Built up his contacts quietly and learned from everybody else's mistakes. He can handle an automatic pretty good, but he tends to leave the dirty work to his *pistoleros*. Don't get me wrong, he's done his share of the killing."

"How did he become so powerful in Juarez?"

"Remember when Kiki Camerena was murdered in 1985?"

"Of course I do. Tortured first. Then murdered." Larsen's face took on a mean look. The eyes narrowed, lips curled in tight. The murder of the DEA agent hit close to home. "I was just getting out of college," he added.

"In the years after the murder hundreds of members of the all the organizations were arrested. Fonseca, Gallardo, Quintero. They all went down. The warring between different families blew the Mexican Federation apart."

"And Carrillo slithered right on in."

"Just like a snake," Macki said. "Experienced, contacts with the Colombians, it was easy. Once in, he reunited the remaining drug lords and convinced them to let him set up the deals with his contacts in the Cali cartel. The trafficking network he set up was amazing—from Tijuana to the western lip of the Gulf.

"When the Colombians started flying larger loads into Mexico, Carrillo moved it into the U.S. without missing a beat. Bigger airstrips, more smuggling vehicles and, Christ, hundreds of people who just drove the fucking blow across!"

"I heard the Colombians have been flying it in with 727's and French Caravelles!" Larsen added.

"It's true!" Macki nearly shouted. "No wonder they call him the fucking "Lord of the Skies."

Just then Macki's intercom buzzed.

"Bob Constance on the line for you, John."

"Thanks, Carla. Tell him I'll get back to him in a few minutes." As he looked back at Larsen, a smile spread across his face. "Still got the hots for her, Dan?"

"No comment." He was fidgety now and slightly claustrophobic. He searched for a window to crack, but there were none. It was time to go. "So what's your angle on all this, John? What's your plan?" The million-dollar-question.

"Hold on a minute and I'll explain. First of all, my instructions are to take Carrillo down A-S-A-P and by whatever means necessary. They emphasized 'by whatever means necessary', you got me?" Macki paused and stared at Larsen to see if he was following him.

"Sounds like they don't care if we kill the bastard," Larsen said. "And they probably expect you to coordinate with every agency known to man; your office, DEA, FBI, Customs, Justice...."

"That's right! And we both know what happens then," Macki said loudly. "We spend all kinds of money and manpower and still come out the same—empty handed."

"Well, what did you have in mind?"

Macki leaned forward again and lowered his voice as if they weren't alone. "I think we need a nice, small, covert operation. No more than ten people involved. Informants and some of my other sources tell us that in the last few months, Carrillo has been making some shipments into Florida by way of Cancun, which doesn't surprise me. The Southwest Border Project has really put the heat on Carrillo's routes into El Paso. I think we're going to see a big shift in loads from the western border back to the East. Florida is ripe for the picking right now. You know as well as anyone that there are more drugs coming into Florida than ever. And we know that Carrillo is in bed with the Colombians. Right now we're tracking some forty different Cali factions that have moved into South Florida. Forty!

"Carrillo's ready to make a move, I know it. You told me that you spend a couple of months down there every spring. Fishing, right? All I want you to do is a little fishing. See if it's true. See if Carrillo is setting up shop in Cancun."

Larsen didn't say a word, deep in thought about the possible ramifications of what he'd been asked to do.

"Of course you'll never find Carrillo himself," Macki continued. "You'll never get that close. He's smarter than that. No, Carrillo won't be there. But someone else—someone tied into him will be."

"And what then?" Larsen asked.

"You just leave that to me, Captain."

Larsen could feel the walls closing in, forcing him to commit.

"I'll have to take a leave of absence. My people won't like that."

"I'll handle the paperwork," Macki told him. "Besides, they'll be happy to get you off their payroll and I know you don't mind being on ours."

But it wasn't the money. Dan took a deep breath. Definitely needed some fresh air.

"When can you leave?"

"Next week." Committed now.

Larsen got up and opened the door. Carla Deering was nowhere in sight. Thank God. He turned back to Macki. "I'll be in touch. But let me ask you one last thing, John."

"Shoot."

"How can you stay in here all day with no sunlight, no windows?"

"I don't know, Dan. You get used to it, I guess."

Larsen left the office without another word. So Macki had gotten used to it. Poor bastard.

2

Vera Cruz, Mexico 19°04.35"N 96°12.66"W
March 6, 1996 1513 Local Time

Six hundred miles west of Cancun, Amado Carrillo Fuentes stood close to the edge of a huge cliff overlooking the Bay of Campeche, part of the Gulf of Mexico. Swaying back and forth as the result of several shots of tequila, he drunkenly raised the AK-47 automatic rifle to hip level and gently squeezed the trigger. Waving the weapon left and right, Carrillo smiled with pleasure at the sight of a dozen empty Corona beer bottles disappearing in an explosive shower of dirt and clear glass.

"You see, not bad for an old man!" Carrillo shouted, his words slurred and almost unintelligible. He staggered back and tilted the bottle to his lips once more.

Sensing disaster, Paco Herrera Tejeda, lieutenant and chief assassin for the Juarez cartel as well as Carrillo's right-hand man, rushed towards him and grabbed both the bottle and rifle from the drunken kingpin's hands. Throwing the bottle over the cliff, Herrera turned back and faced Carrillo.

"Shit, Amado, look at yourself." He pushed Carrillo's greasy, black hair out of his grimy, pudgy face. "You need to get it together!" He tried to straighten him up, grabbing him by the shoulders, tugging at the ragged, brown shirt that was plastered to the cartel leader's body in huge, sweaty stains. "Just look at you. Forgive me, but you look like a fucking peasant!"

"You call me a peasant?" he sputtered, with squinty eyes to show his displeasure.

"Oh, come on, Amado. If you keep up like this, you won't be able to piss into the damn toilet." It had been three days since the two of them had fled the warehouse in Juarez. If it hadn't been for a phone call three hours before the DEA's storming of the warehouse, both Carrillo and Herrera would probably be dead.

Arriving at their new hideout, a huge mansion perched on the cliffs thirty miles north of Vera Cruz and just northeast of the town of Jalapa, Carrillo had spent most of the time in a drunken stupor, bitching about their brush with death and raving about the certain existence of an informant within his organization.

"You realize they would have killed us," Carrillo said yet again. "Fucking DEA. They're not playing the game anymore. They would have killed us..." His voice trailed off and his glazed eyes took on a lost vacant look.

"I know you are upset about what happened in Juarez," Herrera told him, putting his arm around him and guiding the intoxicated Carrillo back to the mansion. "You should be." Patronizing him. "But you'll be safe here. We will find the rat in our midst, and he will be punished."

"I won't be safe until we finish this place. I will build a fucking fortress here, Paco. But it has to happen now! We're running out of time."

"But when will we go back?" Herrera asked.

"Mother of God, man, don't you understand?" Carrillo shouted, spitting into the younger man's face. And Herrera knew he was really pissed. Taking the name of the Virgin in vain. It was almost unheard of among Mexicans, no matter how drunk.

"We can never go back," Carrillo continued. "They're closing in. DEA, FBI...and others! It's getting too hot along the border, Paco. We need to regroup. It's time to shift our priorities, expand our territory."

"Yes, yes," Herrera told him. "Now I hear the old Carrillo talking."

"This...this will be our new territory," he proclaimed, turning around and waving his arm back and forth at the water. Herrera could see him sobering a little. See him fighting it, see the clarity coming back into the eyes. "The Americans call me Lord of the Skies. Fucking stupid *gringos*. Soon they will call me Neptune, King of the Seas. Am I right, Paco? Isn't it the truth?" He was shouting again, and Herrera looked around as if embarrassed.

"Yes, Amado."

"And you, Paco, you will lead us there!" He stood a step back, as if seeing Herrera for the first time. "But look at you, Paco." He reached out and grabbed Herrera's long black hair, tugging harshly on his ponytail. "These horses' tails...they are for women. And the gold..." Grabbing the chains around his neck. "What about this?" Carrillo asked, tugging at the soft fabric of Paco's sleeve. "I don't even own a silk shirt!"

Paco's eyes narrowed into slits at the reprimand. "Maybe you should."

"Listen to me Paco. You are my number one man. I was in your position once. I watched. I listened. I learned. Right now is your big chance. If we do this right, we can control the entire east coast of the Yucatan. The routes into South Florida are wide open."

"And we will be the ones to seize them," Herrera said.

"Right. But you need to keep a low profile, Paco. You need to be a chameleon, blend in with your surroundings. I've seen what happens when you don't."

"Yes," Herrera agreed. But he knew that Carrillo was missing it. Paco knew that he would fit right into the scene in Cancun, one of the biggest resort cities in the world.

Carrillo heaved a sigh, and turned away from the water, looking towards the building which to him seemed a hundred miles away.

"I need to get some rest, Paco," he said. "I'm just so fucking tired." As if he'd resigned himself to defeat.

"Yes, Amado. Rest is all you need." He grabbed his boss around the shoulder, and ran his free hand through Carrillo's hair. "You're going gray."

"Fuck your mother," Carrillo told him, and he couldn't see the venom that sprang into Paco's eyes.

Paco led him up the long stairway, past the Olympic-sized swimming pool and into the huge mansion. There he left him. Once outside, he looked back and gazed out to sea. Several small boats dotted the horizon. An afternoon breeze had picked up and small whitecaps were beginning to appear on the surface of the water. So it would be back to the sea. He'd done it before, and done it successfully. Smuggling by water was the same as by land; a vehicle and a route, only farther. He knew Cancun better than some of its natives, better than most of the people who now lived in the relatively new mega-resort. From its colossal hotels to its dark, dangerous alleys, Herrera was able to move like a snake. With confidence, he would slide right on in. And with the power and fear of the Juarez cartel behind him, he knew that finding and developing new waterways between Mexico and the U.S. wouldn't be too hard. The time had come to make his move.

Buccaneer Marina, Singer Island
March 9, 1996 1415 EDT

Pulling into the parking lot a little faster than was necessary, Dan Larsen slid his beat-up cruiser in between a buffed-out, jacked-up, Nissan Pathfinder and a new Dodge Ram pick-up. The Pathfinder belonged to his mate, Kurt, and Larsen was pleased to see it. The fishing maniac hadn't missed a day of work since he'd hired him. Larsen hadn't even told him he was leaving town. Opening the door with a horrible wrenching sound, Larsen was just able to squeeze himself out. Glancing at the two vehicles, he couldn't help but wonder if he should upgrade his own means of transportation. His cream colored four-door sedan looked horribly outdated next to the others, but it was paid for, was cheap to insure, and it got him from point A to point B with no problems. Although he could afford to buy a whole fleet of new vehicles, his trusty Chrysler was the perfect ride for an undercover DEA field agent, an unremarkable car that attracted little attention.

He headed through the archway, past the rental efficiency units, and down to the dock. Walking past the other sportfishing yachts and towards the end slip where the *Predator* was docked, he suddenly remembered that the Dodge belonged to his good friend Rob Masters. Masters had been the first mate on the *Pelican*, a forty-five foot Viking sportfisher on which Larsen had learned to fish in the late eighties. Now Masters was captain of a boat called the *Slammer*, a sixty-one foot Buddy Davis based at the Sailfish Marina next door. Last thing he had heard, Masters was in

35

Venezuela: slaying the billfish, as always. Maybe a little jealousy there, but they were still tight, and it would be good to see him.

Approaching the *Predator*, his pride and joy for close to three years, Larsen looked up and saw that Kurt and Rob were up in the tower, the helm station located above the flybridge, almost forty feet above the water. With a length of sixty-five feet and an eighteen foot beam, The Hatteras Convertible sportfisher was bigger than most and had a price tag to match. Fully outfitted for fishing with all the latest electronics, she came in at just under two million dollars. Unlike most of the other sport-fishers, the sixty-five foot Hatteras incorporated an enclosed flybridge complete with air-conditioning and carpeting. Inside the flybridge, the instrument console stretched some eight feet across and contained a vast array of electronics and gauges, making it look more like the cockpit of an airliner than of a fishing boat. The huge tinted windshield and dark, wrap-around side windows added to the effect.

Larsen stepped onto the gunwale and thumped down into the cockpit. Up above, his friends felt the vibration and carefully scurrying down the slippery, aluminum tower legs, made their way to the back of the bridge and down the ladder to join him.

"Gentlemen," Larsen said.

"Well look who's here," Kurt said. "I thought you were dead."

He adjusted his dirty, white visor, and brushed his light-brown, curly hair out of his eyes.

"Not yet, my friend." Larsen reached out to shake Masters hand and the other captain clamped down on it with a paw that was bigger by half. "How was Venezuela?" Larsen asked.

"Awesome. Didn't want to leave. Reminded me why I hate fishin' here, where it sucks."

"Now hold on there a second," Kurt told him. "Six hundred, thirty-two fish caught in the Buc. Thirty-seven boats. That's more than seven-teen fish per boat," he boasted. "And most of those were caught on the first day," he added.

The Buccaneer Cup, a tournament about a month earlier, had really been incredible. The ocean was a washing machine, and along with the piercing, cold wind that swept spray across the swells, packs of sailfish tailed downsea, sucking down the live goggle-eye baits with a fury Larsen had never seen.

"Yeah, well down in Venezuela we do that every day," Masters bragged.

"Bullshit," Kurt told him.

Larsen couldn't help but smile as he watched the exchange. Kurt, the mate, with his deep, reddish-brown tan, freckled face and bare feet versus Masters, the captain, short hair, polo shirt with boat name, dress shorts and docksiders, new ones that looked like they'd never been wet.

"When did you get back?" Larsen asked Masters, diffusing the situation. But he knew they weren't serious. Masters was a big bastard, a linebacker who'd decided to fish instead, and Kurt knew better than to truly mess with him.

"Came across yesterday from Nassau," Masters told him. "The Gulf Stream was pretty fuckin' big, too."

"Yeah, well, it's been blowing here for about a week," Larsen said. He opened the door and the three men went inside.

"Anybody call?" Larsen asked Kurt, who was busying himself cleaning off the counter in the galley. "Irv called yesterday. He wanted to know how everything was going with getting the boat ready and all that," Kurt said. Irving Mendel, the owner of the *Predator*, lived up in Jersey and except for long weekends, occasional trips to the Bahamas, and the yearly trip to Mexico, Larsen rarely saw him. "He asked me where you were and I told him you were probably running around getting something at the Home Depot or Boat Owners."

Masters zapped the dark television with the remote and the tube sprang to life. Larsen shot a look at the screen. CNN, but nothing about the raid. As if there would be: several days had passed and yesterday's news was dead as far as TV news was concerned.

"Where were you, anyway?" Kurt asked, but he could tell his captain's mind was elsewhere.

"What's that?"

"I asked where you were," he repeated.

"Just out and about," Larsen lied, and he felt guilty because he didn't like keeping his mate in the dark. And Kurt didn't ask again, because he knew better. Larsen disappeared sometimes, and if he wanted Kurt to know where he was, he would tell him. A strange kind of mutual trust.

"You guys seen Terry?" Larsen asked, changing the subject. Terry Stanton, another captain at the Sailfish Marina, also spent the spring in the same marina in Mexico. Larsen was in love with Stanton's new boat, a 58 foot Monterey, the *Tempest*.

"I went over and looked for him yesterday, but he wasn't there," Kurt said. "There was some new kid cleaning the teak. Never seen him before. Said Terry was at the dentist."

"Terry hates dentists."

"I know," Kurt agreed. "I'll bet he was over at his other job."

"Other job?" Larsen knew nothing about it, and he'd thought that he and Stanton were close. "He's double-dipping?"

"Yeah, but don't say anything." Kurt said.

"You know me better than that."

Kurt was already sorry he'd said it. "I know, man, but Terry told me not to tell anyone. He said he really needs the cash. I don't know why."

Larsen didn't either, but he'd find out. He looked over at Masters who was lost on the beach somewhere in the program he was watching: the shooting of the swimsuit edition of "Sports Illustrated".

"What's your plan, Rob?"

"Huh?" To make Larsen repeat himself, give him a second to process the question, formulate a response. While he checked out the hot bikinis.

"You guys still going to Mexico?"

"Yeah..."

"When?" Larsen prodded.

"Uh...next week..." But he was gone, back in the Seychelles or wherever the swimsuit girls were.

Slightly frustrated, Larsen turned his attention back to Kurt.

"Well, I guess we'll all run together, then. I already told Terry."

"That's cool. The more, the better." Not only for a sense of camaraderie, but for safety reasons as well. Mechanical breakdowns on long journeys happened now and then, and it wasn't unusual to see one of the large sportfishers towing another.

"We've got a lot of work to do," Larsen said.

"I hear that. I'm gonna finish waxing the tower."

"I got some shit to do in the engine room. Come on, Rob."

Reluctantly, Masters got to his feet.

Larsen opened the door and the fishermen stepped outside. Immediately blinded by the glare of the stark, white cockpit, all three quickly donned their polarized shades. As Kurt climbed back towards the tower, Masters got up onto the dock and headed for his truck.

"I'll see you later," Masters said.

"Yeah, later," Larsen told his friend. And he wondered if he would ever have the chance to tell the two men where he had gone and why.

On his way home, Larsen stopped by the beach to check the surf. From the bluff where he stood, the ocean looked confused. Like his mind.

A strong nor'easter had whipped up the waves. They were almost double over-head, marching in to the beach from all directions, closing out all the way across. There were a few guys out paddling around on their boards, trying to get a ride, but really just trying to survive. Larsen knew the feeling.

And he knew that where there were guys surfing, there were girls, and he spotted three of them sitting together about fifty feet from the edge of the frothy whitewater. As if she could feel his presence, one of them turned around and looked up at him, frowning just a bit and smiling as if she knew him from somewhere. But he was sure she didn't. He was at least twice her age. She kept staring, and her long hair hovered in the wind the way his little sister's always did.

Larsen would never forget the night he dropped her off at the party. The arrogant colonial house with its perfect landscaping. The rich kids driving up in their parents' fancy cars. He knew he had to get out of upstate New York, and when she graduated in the spring, he would take her with him.

"I'm nervous," she told him. Twirling her hair around her finger.

"Don't be nervous. It's a party. Parties are supposed to be fun."

"I know, but I'm not as cool as some of the other kids."

"Sure you are," he told her. "Anyway, you don't need to be cool. Just be yourself." Larsen had been to his share of the keg parties when he was in high school. He remembered the peer pressure. And the drugs. "Don't do anything you don't want to do," he warned her. "Be smart."

"I will." She leaned across the car seat to kiss him good-bye. "That's what I love about you, Dan. You're always there to watch over me." He could feel himself blushing.

"Get out of here. Have a good time," he said. She looked in the visor mirror one last time, then got out. She leaned in the window.

"Don't worry," she said, and blew him another kiss.

"I won't," he lied, and he watched her until she reached the door.

Four hours later she hadn't called, and he was back at the house in a panic. Most of the kids were wasted and didn't seem to care where some older guy's sister was.

He finally found her in the garage. Lying there on the floor like she was sleeping. But he already knew she was dead. And he tried and tried to breathe the life back into her, but her little nervous heart had already given up.

He held her for what seemed like hours while her stupid friends stood there gawking and crying. And then the paramedics were there, prying his protective arms from her fragile, pale body.

He hadn't protected her at all. The cocaine had stolen her life. And ripped his fucking heart out.

Almost ten years later he still felt the pain. The other two girls turned to look at him and they all giggled at a private joke. Ashamed, Larsen turned away with his eyes full. He walked to his car and shut the door, feeling very alone. And the tears flowed.

The Mansion in Vera Cruz
That Same Day

Behind the compound that had become Carrillo's new hideout, the two Mexican sentries gazed down into the valley at the approaching convoy of trucks. They could barely make out the sounds of the trucks' laboring engines as they watched the trail of dust snake its way slowly up the winding, dirt road towards their position. For the past week, a never-ending stream of trucks, men, and supplies had made its way from the nearby towns of Jalapa and Vera Cruz up to the huge stone mansion that Carrillo was slowly transforming from a residence into a fortress.

Rounding the final bend of the road and approaching the almost finished rear walls of the compound, the trucks—most of them carrying loads of mortar, bricks, or cinder blocks—came screeching to a halt in a cloud of dust and exhaust fumes. The sentries, one armed with an AK-47 assault rifle and the other with an Israeli-made 9mm Uzi submachine gun, cautiously approached the lead vehicle and ordered the driver and passenger to get out. Nervously climbing out of the cab, the driver identified his cargo to the sentry with the AK-47, while the man with the Uzi searched under and behind the seats of the truck. Most of the men delivering the materials, and the laborers accompanying them, were *campesinos*, peasants from nearby towns and farms. They had been offered ridiculous sums of money to drop what they were doing, obtain the needed supplies and manpower and make their way up the long, narrow roadway to the mansion they had all heard about but most had never seen. The *campesinos* had quickly agreed. They knew better than to ask any questions.

After inspecting each truck, as well as its load and occupants, the sentries waved the convoy to pass into the compound, not failing to glare menacingly at the drivers and laborers as they drove by. Their job done the sentries, two of many of Carrillo's *pistoleros* imported from Juarez, lit cigarettes and trudged back towards their position.

Built on the highest cliff overlooking the water, the mansion was surrounded on three sides by a wall, two feet thick and thirty feet high. With the construction of the wall nearly completed, work had already begun on an additional barrier of razor-sharp concertina wire, placed atop the wall and making penetration nearly impossible. A series of dual-technology infrared/motion detectors had been placed inside and outside the perimeter of the walled compound and sixteen video surveillance cameras, also with infrared technology, swept back and forth throughout the compound, making undetected entry onto the grounds inconceivable. All the electronics were interfaced with a central computer and a bank of video monitors inside the mansion. This command post was manned by two of Carrillo's bodyguards, twenty-four hours a day. As if all that wasn't enough, a 20mm anti-aircraft artillery gun was mounted in the back of the mansion, surrounded by sandbags and ready to protect against any assault from the air.

Suddenly appearing from the side of the huge stucco mansion, Carrillo made his way towards Herrera, who stood conversing with three *pistoleros* near the anti-aircraft gun in the middle of the compound. Herrera had a rifle slung over his shoulder like it was nothing more than a backpack. Like it belonged there.

Dressed in a navy-blue blazer with tan slacks and shiny black shoes, Carrillo once again portrayed the image of cartel-leader, the way he saw himself—a confident businessman, not a reckless, cocky hotshot.

Herrera heard the scrape of gravel behind him and spun, startled and almost instinctively reached for his weapon.

"Ah, Amado. I wasn't expecting you," Herrera stammered. Embarrassed, like he'd been caught pissing in the bushes.

"Jumpy, Paco?"

"Just careful," he said. "You look great, Amado. Like a million dollars." Really buttering him up. And then, "It looks like my babysitting is over." A brash remark, testing the cartel leader.

And Carrillo noticed it, but said nothing for a moment. "I'm sorry about all that, Paco," he finally began, "but it was the alcohol. It nearly ruined me. I am through with it." And Carrillo hoped it was true.

"As you can see, the wall is nearly finished." Herrera said. He grabbed Carrillo by the arm and began leading him around the compound. "One, maybe two more days. And the security system will be online within hours. It will take an army to get in here."

"You have done good work, Paco. You will be rewarded."

"Thank you, Amado. It has not been easy. But now I must go. I need to go to Cancun and the other towns along the Yucatan coast. I need to make contacts—they do not happen overnight."

"This is true, Paco. I know some people, but some of my old ties need to be re-established. We need to come up with new ways of moving our product. Get into the ports, the marinas."

"We'll need to pay some people off," Paco added. "Threaten the ones who won't listen. Deal with anyone who gets in our way, right?"

"Right," Carrillo agreed. "I'll see you have plenty of money. Take whatever weapons you need. I'm sure you won't have any problems convincing anyone of our good intentions," he said, and they both laughed. Together the men walked, formulating a new game plan, plotting a new course in their journey to control the drug routes into South Florida, with or without the help of the Colombians.

They came upon a group of *campesinos* who were chattering back and forth while a wheelbarrow of cement hardened nearby.

"What are you doing?" Carrillo screamed. "Get to work! If this isn't done today, you will all be shot!" Herrera stood by while Carrillo took a shovel and smacked one of the men in the ass. They got back to work with renewed enthusiasm, eyeballing their tormentor in the sportcoat curiously, but carefully. They could tell he was a man of great importance, but none had seen him before and all knew better than to ask questions or be caught staring. With all the *pistoleros* walking around and the heavy armament on display, the *campesinos* were sure this man was one of the great *traficantes*, the only question was which one. For them, it didn't really matter. Between the money and the threats they received, their silence about what they had seen or heard was guaranteed.

Approaching slowly from the distance, the deep beating of helicopter blades interrupted the afternoon routine. The *campesinos* stopped what they were doing and looked skyward and south. Within a minute, the large black chopper loomed into view. It descended and hovered just above the wall, preparing to land inside the compound.

43

"Keep working!" Herrera shouted at the frightened laborers, but it was useless. The roar and pressure of the air being forced downward by the blades was intense. The *campesinos* scattered, grabbing for their straw hats and screaming incoherently, bewildered by the arrival of the giant flying beast. Carrillo bent down and shielded his eyes from the dust and debris, turning towards Herrera for an explanation.

"I don't like this, Paco," Carrillo shouted nervously, barely audible above the sound of the chopper now touching down less than twenty meters away. "What kind of shit is this?"

"Just something to help us sleep a little better," Herrera reassured him. "There is no question that there is a traitor among us. Today we will find out who he is."

With its blades still turning, the aircraft disgorged six men—two of them armed with AK-47s and four others who were blindfolded. All six remained crouched as the pilot of the helicopter increased power to the engines, slowly lifted off, and in another shower of wind, dust, and small rocks, flew up and out of the compound. Within seconds, the chopper had disappeared. The sound of the blades faded away down the coast.

The two men from the chopper prodded their blindfolded prisoners towards Herrera and Carrillo.

"As requested," the taller of the two men said. He was one of Carrillo's best *pistoleros*. He was unshaven and dirty, and Carrillo wondered whether he had been at the warehouse.

"I did not request this," Carrillo explained, angry now.

"No, sir, you did not." The *pistolero* said. He looked at Herrera and motioned towards the prisoners with the barrel of his weapon. A smile spread across his lips. "Paco did."

Facing Herrera, Carrillo's displeasure was obvious. But before he could speak, Paco began to explain.

"Eight men were arrested at the warehouse. Five were killed. These four are the only others who could have known we would be there that night," Herrera said, looking at Carrillo and waiting for a signal of understanding. But all he got was an angry stare. "Unless there may have been someone else" he continued, and he looked back at the *pistolero*, challenging him.

"I wasn't even there!" the man insisted, looking back at Carrillo and nervously shifting his feet.

44

"That's enough, Paco!" Carrillo exploded. "What about the other eight?"

"The eight in jail will be taken care of, but I can hardly believe they would call in a raid on themselves," Paco continued. "But these men may be smarter. They may tell us the truth and live to see their wives and families." Herrera's words had a sinister quality. Nonchalant, as if he were talking about the blindfolded men's chances for promotion, not their lives or deaths.

And then it was Carrillo's turn. "Who betrayed me?" he demanded. He stepped forward and spat his words at the first blindfolded man. "Tell me!"

The man shook his head back and forth, whimpering and proclaiming his innocence. Carrillo nodded at Herrera, who unshouldered his rifle and promptly shot the man in the left kneecap. He collapsed to the ground, clutching his bloody, shattered knee and screaming in agony. "Next," Carrillo said.

The other three men began babbling incoherently, begging for their lives. Two of the men had urinated on themselves, and their suddenly dark crotches spread the stink of ammonia. Herrera felt no remorse.

Carrillo reached out and shoved the second man. "Surely you will tell me! It makes no sense to die like a dog while protecting someone else. Think of your family!" Like he was pleading for the man to say something, anything. Then to the *pistolero* he said, "Take off his blindfold!" The *pistolero* stepped forward and looking nervously at Herrera, did as he was told and quickly stepped back. "I will ask you one more time," Carrillo said sternly. He looked into the man's frightened, watering eyes. But the man just stood there and said nothing, lips quivering. "Who tipped off the authorities? You must have heard something..." Really raising his voice now. Carrillo nodded at Herrera again.

The man lurched forward and crouched at Carrillo's feet. Crying hysterically now, but without sound. "Please...please," he managed in between the sobs. "Don't kill me. I swear to God, I don't know who told the police. No one knows. Maybe I can find out." His eyes met Carrillo's once more. They were scared, honest, full of truth. "Please," he begged.

Without warning, Herrera stepped forward and pulling an automatic pistol from his waist band, shot the begging man in the back of the head. Bits of hair, bone fragments and blood sprayed onto himself, Carrillo and the *pistoleros*. They stared at Herrera in horror.

"Jesus, Paco," Carrillo shouted, his voice filled with shock. He wiped away the bits of sickening gore like he'd be permanently scared.

"He was lying!" Herrera shot back. "They're all lying!" He was a wild-man now, losing control. Out of the corner of his eye, Herrera caught movement. The third man had somehow torn off his blindfold, and he lunged for the *pistolero*'s AK-47. Herrera spun and before the condemned man could grasp the trigger, Herrera shot him in the face, spewing blood on the other *pistolero*. Eyes wide with fear, the two *pistoleros* ran from the spot and headed towards the safety of the side of the mansion. Herrera watched them go, listening to their obscenities with amusement. "Fucking cowards," he said to Carrillo, but the cartel leader was already walking slowly towards the mansion, shaking his head and mumbling something which Herrera couldn't make out.

A shout brought Herrera's attention back to the fourth prisoner. He'd already removed his blindfold and was gesturing wildly, pointing at the third man's corpse.

"You see? You see?" he screamed. "It was him! Look what he tried to do! It must have been him!" he repeated. "He's the guilty one..."

Herrera considered it, appraising the man while his mind worked it over. This prisoner was older, wiser.

"Maybe you're right," Herrera said. Raising his weapon, he switched it to automatic and sprayed the first three men with bullets until the clip was empty. Their bodies jumped and twitched.

Around the compound, everyone else had disappeared. The silence of death hung humid in the air.

"Thank you, oh God, thank you," the surviving prisoner whimpered. He was on the ground, hugging his knees, rocking back and forth with tear-filled eyes.

"Don't mention it, it's nothing," Herrera said. The evil smile still there. And then he calmly shot the man in the face.

3

Cancun, Mexico 21°12.20"N 86°48.00"W
March 12, 1996 0743 Local Time

Every spring, huge numbers of sailfish, marlin and other species of billfish begin their annual migration north through the Yucatan Channel to the lower part of the Campeche Bank. At the same time, hundreds of sportfishing yachts make their way to Mexico from Texas, Florida, the East Coast of the U.S. and other parts of the Caribbean. The "season" lasts two or three months and these slick high-dollar machines, with their owners and crews, make their way hundreds and even thousands of miles with a single purpose; catching billfish.

As Larsen had hoped, both Terry Stanton and Rob Masters had been able to make the trip at the same time and they followed him from Singer Island all the way to Cancun. After spending a night in Key West, the three boats had made the crossing to Mexico in just under twenty-two hours. They left Florida early in the morning and arrived at the Marina Hacienda del Mar the next day. The seas were fairly calm and there had been no problems. The careful monitoring of distance and fuel consumption had taken them nearly four hundred miles.

Larsen and the others cleared customs, and then cleaned up their rigs. After a much-needed nap, the captains and their mates set off for a night of partying in Cancun.

With Spring Break in full swing, the hotel zone was packed with college kids, most of whom seemed hell bent on either screwing or drinking themselves to death. They swarmed the bars and restaurants by the thousands, grossly misbehaving in the foreign land, as if there were no laws against it.

Hitting up several different bars themselves, Larsen, Kurt and the others partied into the early hours of the morning. From experience, and knowing he had to take the *Predator* south the next day, Larsen stuck to drinking beer. Stanton and Masters also knew better and did the same. But their mates unfortunately felt the need to join the Spring Breakers and they consumed absurd amounts of the rotgut tequila that was served for free in most of the bars. Tilting their heads back to catch the multi-colored streams like they weren't going to make it anymore. Liquid courage. Nectar of the Mayan Gods.

In the morning they paid for it; with pain. Severely hung over, Kurt and the new mate on Stanton's boat were horrified to find that the girls they had picked up were not the same "perfect ten" supermodels they had brought back to the boat just hours before. Not "babes". Not "hotties". More like flies with their wings ripped off, was the way Kurt put it. Larsen just shook his head. Eventually they would learn, just like he had.

Cruising in the *Predator* at twenty-five knots just off the tip of the Cancun peninsula, Larsen and Kurt were riding in the tower and gazing in awe at the number of hotels lining the shore. Prime real estate. Huge dollars. The hotel zone stretched thirteen miles from Punta Nizuc up and around the point of Cancun. The once barren land was obscured by the monsters of construction. And the builders called them works of art, gold mines. It was Las Vegas in Mexico and gambling was supposedly on its way.

"It's hard to believe that twenty-five years ago, there was nothing here," Larsen shouted over the wind. He almost lost his cap and turned it around backwards.

"I know," Kurt said, "But I can see why it got so big so fast. Look at that water!"

It really was beautiful. Nowhere but in Mexico had Larsen seen such a collection of different blues and greens. "Look at how clear the water is," Larsen told him, "We're in a hundred feet." And they could see the bottom. Staring at the shoreline, with its white sand beaches and giant palm trees, it was easy to see how Cancun had become one of the most popular tourist destinations in the world.

"You want to check that engine room?" he asked Kurt, wanting to make sure everything was all right down below. "Check inside, too."

"Sure," Kurt said and disappeared down the tower ladder.

Behind him, Larsen could see the *Tempest* following in his wake. Stanton at the helm, standing tall, proud of his new rig. And way back there, Masters and the *Slammer*.

Larsen checked the compass bearing and looked at his watch. Less than three hours. He climbed down and went into the flybridge.

Continuing south, he watched the hotel zone slowly disappear. The landscape had turned into a low-lying thick brush, with small trees and an occasional stand of palms. Most of the Yucatan was covered by dense dry jungle, with few hills and only one main road heading south towards Belize. The road was inland and, most places, you couldn't see it from the water.

They passed the port town of Puerto Morelos and Larsen steered the *Predator* along the shoreline, approaching the town of Playa del Carmen. Considered by many to be the next Cancun, "Playa", as it was called, was enjoying an explosion of growth, with new businesses and buildings popping up daily. With its beautiful beaches and resorts, and hundreds of inexpensive places to stay, Playa was becoming quite popular with the foreigners, especially the Europeans.

A beat-up, mid-sized passenger ship cut across the *Predator*'s path, and Larsen slowed down a few knots. It was the hourly ferry to Cozumel, twelve miles away. Then he bumped her back up and a few minutes later, Playa was gone. Twelve miles to go.

Ten minutes later, the outline of Puerto Aventuras appeared in the distance. Larsen could see the red tile roof-tops of the condominiums and small houses as well as the outline of the mammoth Hotel Oasis, the largest hotel in the resort.

Larsen reached for the mike of the VHF radio. All three boats had been monitoring channel 16. "There it is," he told the others. "Home for the next two months."

"Roger that. You want to tell them we're coming in?" Larsen's radio crackled. It was Stanton on the *Tempest*.

"Yeah." Larsen told him. He switched his radio to channel 79, the one the marina usually monitored. "Puerto Aventuras Marina, Puerto Aventuras Marina, the *Predator*," he called into the mike.

"Marina back," came the response. "How's it going, Dan?" Larsen recognized the dockmaster.

"It's going great," Larsen said. "I've got the *Tempest* and the *Slammer* right behind me."

"Roger that. I'll send some dock boys down to help you tie up. Same slips as last year, all right?"

"You got it," Larsen told him. "See you in a few minutes."

He almost hung up the mike but then he said, "You get that, Terry?"

"Yeah." He'd been listening.

"Me too." Masters this time.

The three boats headed for the marina entrance. Excited to finally be there, Larsen pushed the throttles up near their limit and smiled as the *Predator* broke thirty knots.

The resort at Puerto Aventuras was not just a marina, but a self-contained community. In addition to the three hotels and several large condominiums, there were general stores, bars, restaurants, even a nine-hole golf course. A wide range of recreational facilities was available, including tennis, two dive shops, and a small health spa run by a girl from Newport Beach, California, who dated the mate from the *Slammer*.

Ten years earlier, the resort didn't even exist. A young group of entrepreneurs, however, had watched the rapid growth of Cancun and seized the opportunity to acquire the property and build a resort in the heart of the Maya Caribbean. Almost entirely man-made, the resort was built around an F-shaped marina, blasted out of the limestone before any water had been let in. The inlet to the marina or "cut" as it was called was not blasted through until most of the construction was complete. The majority of the architecture was of a Spanish style, with concrete and stucco buildings topped by red-clay, tile roofs.

In the marina itself, the docking was Mediterranean style, with the front of the boat moored to a single anchored buoy and the stern of the vessel backed up to the concrete wall of the dock. In this manner, the boats sat side-by-side all the way around the marina There was dockage for sixty or seventy vessels. Extremely well protected from rough seas, the marina at Puerto Aventuras was the perfect base for the spring billfish season. The only negative aspect of the marina was the entrance. Narrow and quite shallow in places, the "cut" was bordered on each side by huge rock jetties, designed to protect the marina, but in reality, only making it more dangerous to pass through the inlet in rough seas and high wind conditions.

Standing behind the *Predator* and looking down the dock towards the cut, Dan Larsen could see that there were only a few boats in the marina. It was early in the season, but he knew that within a week or two, the side of the marina where he was docked would be full. Commonly referred to as Park Avenue, the main leg of the marina always filled up first. Its close proximity to the marina entrance as well as easy access to the marina center and its shops and restaurants made it the place to be docked. At night, during the height of the season, Park Avenue took on the look of a small carnival, the powerful quartz spreader lights mounted on the boats lighting up the dock and the menagerie of colorful tents lining it. Tourists and locals strolled the docks, gazing in awe at the incredible display of wealth represented by the expensive yachts tied up there.

Immediately behind the dock were several condo buildings, most of them three stories tall, each consisting of one or two-bedroom apartments. During the fishing season, the apartments were usually filled with people from the boats: usually owners and their guests and at other times, the crews. Larsen and Kurt stayed in a two-bedroom condo behind the *Predator*, and they stored most of their supplies there. Irv, the owner of the *Predator*, also believed that the less time the crew spent living on the boat, the better shape it would stay in. Larsen knew he was right and since he wasn't the one forking out almost three thousand dollars a month, he didn't argue.

Larsen glanced at his watch. Four-thirty. Almost happy hour. He'd spent most of the day working on the boat, changing the oil and filters, unloading supplies and taking them to the condo. Kurt had already assembled the barbecue grill and was busy setting up the little sun-shade tent. No less than five Mexican dock boys insisted on helping, turning the simple task into an engineering nightmare. But you had to have your tent. All the boats had them right behind their slips, not only to block the scorching rays of the sun, but to sort of say, "this little area is our territory".

A bit further down the dock, Terry Stanton was still putting together his own grill. On his ass, hunched over. He'd been at it for over an hour and Larsen could see he was having a hell of a time. He went to help.

"What's up, Cappy?" Larsen asked. "You need a hand?"

"No, I'll get it dude," Stanton said, just as a nut fell out of his hand and promptly rolled off the dock and into the water like it was on a mission. As Stanton hung his head in disbelief, Larsen stifled a laugh.

Frustrated, he stopped what he was doing and took off his glasses. Wiping the sweat off his face with his shoulder, he began cleaning the lenses with his t-shirt. He looked up at Larsen, squinting although he was in the shade.

"Man, I'm half-blind without these things. Cost me an arm and a leg, too. Prescription." He dug in the little plastic bag for another nut.

"You all right, man?" Larsen asked. "You look like your dog just died or something."

"Yeah. I'm just worried about my kid. She's been kinda sick lately and we're not sure what's wrong with her. Doctor bills are eatin' me up."

Larsen knew his daughter well. Cute little girl, about six. Loved the water.

"That's a bummer, man. I'm sorry to hear that." Larsen knew she was Stanton's only child. Half his whole world. The other half was his wife, a waitress at the Sailfish Marina on Singer Island. "Well, don't worry, man, I'm sure she'll be all right. You gonna be flying them down?"

"I don't think so, Dan." Clearly depresssed about it. "Can't afford it. Besides, if Jessica's sick, this is the last place I want her to be."

"I hear you. But if you need to borrow some money, man, just let me know," he offered, even though he knew Stanton had too much pride to accept.

"Yeah, thanks man. I'm supposed to have a couple of charters this year. Supposed to be pretty big tippers. I sure hope so."

"So how about a little practice, then?" Larsen suggested. "You want to do a little fun-fishing tomorrow. You know, just the guys?"

"I don't know, dude." Stanton looked towards the marina entrance.

"Come on, Terry. Now's the time to do it. With no boats here, they're probably snappin'!"

"Yeah, I know. But what about the cut?" Stanton asked. "Every time I come in here when it's rough, I'm shakin' like a leaf." Twice the last season he had almost put the *Tempest* on the rocks, and he figured he had only one more strike before he was out. It didn't help matters that the old *Tempest* was a twenty-five-year-old fifty-three foot Hatteras with a top speed of eighteen knots. Downsea.

"Don't sweat it," Larsen told him. "We'll take my rig. That way I can show you boys how it's done," he said with a wink. He could see that Stanton had just about finished with the grill. "Come on. Let's go get a cold beer."

Stanton got to his feet. "What about all these?" As usual, he had a handful of extra nuts and bolts.

"See if they float," Larsen suggested.

Stanton laughed and threw the parts into the water.

Washington D.C., Capitol Hill   38°52.34"N   77°02.01"W
March 12, 1996 1013 EDT

Bob Constance stood in front of the man's desk and tried the best he could to tune him out. From the size of the vein popping out on the side of the ranting man's forehead, Constance was sure his crimson mug would either explode or burst into flames at any moment. Only hours before, Constance had been summoned to Washington to the office of Thomas Jensen, chairman of the Mexican-American Affairs Senate Subcommitee. He was right in the middle of a serious ass-chewing regarding the DEA's recent raid in Juarez, and Jensen was the one selected to provide it. Fucking politician, Constance thought. He knew their kind well. They were wolves in sheep's clothing and he'd been dealing with them for years. Hair slicked back, thousand dollar suits, five hundred dollar shoes. Long on promises and short on integrity, they gave civilians a bad name. Always pissing and moaning about the way other agencies did things, but never getting off their own asses and putting them on the line once in a while.

Constance had spent plenty of years in the field, and they hadn't been easy. He'd been wounded and had the scars to prove it. The deep creases in his face and forehead were scars in their own right, permanent reminders of years of hard work, heartache and bureaucratic bullshit. Now, standing before a man whom he didn't even know, he felt like a third grader, head bowed before the principal, begging forgiveness and awaiting punishment. And that was starting to piss him off.

"You can't just go charging in there with a team of commandos every time you goddamn feel like it!" Jensen screamed, leaning forward over his desk, his face just inches from Constance. Stale breath, but perfect teeth. "We have rules, treaties..."

"The hell with the goddamn rules! My agents were fired upon while conducting an operation. They were protecting themselves!" Trying hard to control his own anger, Constance clenched his fists and stared down at Jensen. At six-four, Constance was intimidating.

"But your agents went in there completely unescorted," Jensen whined. "They killed five men and were going to just sneak out if it weren't for their being caught with their pants down by the *Federales*. Sounds like the work of assassins to me. People want answers!"

Constance fought off the urge to just grab Jensen's neck and snap it. "Do you live in the fucking dark, Jensen?" Constance could feel his composure slipping away. "Do you have any idea what it's like to try and coordinate with the Mexican authorities? Every time we go in there to make an arrest on one of the big guys, we come up with zilch—*nada*! They don't want us to take them down. The traffickers are fucking heroes. The people write songs about them! And the authorities—they could give a shit. They're all on the take! You of all people should know that. It makes me fucking sick!" He was breathing heavily.

"Yeah, yeah, I know that Bob. Calm down," he said in a condescending tone, further infuriating Constance. "I know all about the corruption," he lied. "That still doesn't give you the right to break the law."

"Look Jensen," Constance said, purposely using the chairman's surname to show his displeasure, "like I told you, I didn't even know about the operation until it was well underway. Even had I wanted to, I had no means of canceling it. The office in El Paso received a tip that Carrillo would be at the warehouse. Carrillo! This man is personally responsible for smuggling more cocaine into the U.S. than anyone in history. He makes Pablo Escobar and the rest of the Colombians look like fucking Boy Scouts!

"The head of the El Paso office assured me that there was no time to coordinate with Mexican law-enforcement. We took a gamble." He stared hard at Jensen, trying to regain his composure.

"And lost," Jensen said.

"And lost. That's right," Constance repeated, his level of anger building once more. "But did anyone tell you what happened to the cocaine stashed in that warehouse? What about the smugglers that shot two of our agents? You didn't hear what happened to them, did you?" He was shouting again. "That's because all the coke disappeared. The report on the raid estimates the quantity in that warehouse at several tons. Neither the local police nor the *Federales* have any record of a drug seizure or arrests made in the vicinity of that warehouse or all of Juarez, for that matter! Now you tell me. You think there's a problem with my men?"

Jensen could see he was fighting a losing battle and began to fidget in his puffy-leather chair. "It's obvious we have problems, Bob," Jensen said, trying to weasel his way back to controlling the conversation—as a true diplomat surely would. He leaned back and smoothed his hair. "Mexico is in a sad state right now. The economy is in shambles. The peso is worth less than half what it was worth two years ago. Several of the states are experiencing peasant or guerilla uprisings as we speak. And NAFTA...

NAFTA only appears to have had the opposite effect than what we wanted. Right now, Mexico needs our help. I've spent years traveling to Mexico. I remember how it used to be. It's a beautiful country. All they need is a little more support from us, a little more aid..."

Suddenly, it became crystal clear to Constance why he was there. This little talk was all about money. Constance knew all about the Foreign Assistance Act. Every year, the President was required to identify the major drug producing and drug transiting countries and determine whether they have fully cooperated with the U.S. or taken adequate steps on their own to curb the narcotics traffic. If the country receives positive "certification", they are eligible for foreign aid packages that the current administration seemed so willing to dole out. It was obvious to Constance that Mexico was failing miserably. Although he didn't know Jensen personally, he had heard that he had his sights set on the ambassadorship to Mexico. He'd also heard that Senator Jensen had friends in high places. Constance knew the stepping stones: Ambassador, Governor, President.

Looking around the room, Constance could see the evidence of the typical politician. Huge mahogany desk, big chair, framed diplomas and plaques of achievement on the wall, even a fucking mirror. Looking at the framed photos on Jensen's desk, he saw one of the Senator and the President, arms around each other on what looked like the eighteenth hole at Pebble Creek. Another showed Jensen and an attractive young girl. Too young to be his wife. This guy doesn't give a damn about Mexico, Constance thought. All this brown-noser is concerned with is furthering his own ass-kissing diplomatic career, and looking good while doing it. Constance looked down at his own tired suit and tried to smooth the wrinkles. More scars that would never go away.

"So what is it you want from me?" Constance asked. "You want me to say 'We're sorry, we won't do it again'? Because that's not going to solve anything, Jensen. You keep handing these people money, the more corrupt they're going to get. Try cutting off the bastards' funds for a while, and we'll see what happens then."

"But the local governments are trying," Jensen whined again. "President Zedillo has promised to fight the traffickers and deal with corrupt

Mexican officials. They've already expanded the role of the military. More and more narcotics checkpoints are popping up every day. Just ask anyone who's been down there lately. But they lack funds. With more aid, they can do a better job."

Constance grabbed his forehead in disbelief. Was the man really that dumb? "Don't you understand?" he pleaded. "You can't trust Zedillo! You can't trust anyone! Money corrupts. Pure and simple. Look at Salinas! He was the goddamn President!" Carlos Salinas had led Mexico from 1988 to 1994. His brother, Raul Gortari, had been indicted for murder and accepting payoffs from the Cali cartel. Millions of dollars had been found in his secret Swiss bank accounts, and there were many who felt that the former Mexican president was just as guilty. "Until we cut off the cash and they deal with the corruption, nothing is going to change. And as long as the corruption exists, the only chance we have at catching these bastards and stopping the flow of cocaine, not to mention other dangerous drugs, is to go in there and take them out ourselves. And I hope to hell someone else realizes that!"

Jensen gave him a startled look. "What do you mean by that?"

But Constance didn't answer. Hoping he had thoroughly pissed the Senator off, he turned, opened the door, and stormed out.

4

Marina Puerto Aventuras
March 13, 1996

At six-thirty in the morning, hardly a soul was on the dock in Puerto Aventuras. Awake since five, Kurt Landau wandered down the path from the condo where he and Larsen stayed and headed for the *Predator*. Dressed in nothing but a pair of worn cut-offs and his sandals, Kurt crossed to the boat and went inside to zap himself a cup of coffee in the microwave.

Coffee in hand, Kurt went back outside to begin the task at hand, the rigging of the baits for the day's fishing. Preferring to get the baits and tackle ready early, Kurt was often awake to watch the sunrise. Looking to the east, the horizon was bathed in a soft orange-pink, with just a scattering of cumulous clouds. A fresh breeze came out of the southeast, and a moderate chop had begun to build on the blue-green surface of the water. Perfect for sailfishing, he thought. He reached into the cockpit freezer and removed three packs of ballyoo, twelve baits to a pack. Three dozen pre-rigged baits was usually enough to get started and he could always rig more as the day wore on. Fishing with live bait in Mexico was illegal, and almost all the boats used slow-trolled ballyhoo in their quest for billfish. The ballyhoo was an odd-looking fish, similar to a sardine, but with a long needle-like lower jaw that helped it catch its own food. They were available in all sizes, but small fish between six and ten inches were preferred by most captains and mates.

Slicing open the packs of bait, Kurt dumped them in a bucket of salt water to thaw. He then went and got the rods from inside the bridge and positioned them in the "rocket launcher", the rod holder mounted just above the fighting chair in the center of the cockpit. He and Larsen usually fished six rods at a time, using four TLD30 Shimano conventional reels and two Penn Baitmaster spinners.

Looking down the dock, Kurt noticed that Matt Kirchner, the mate from the *Slammer*, was also up early.

"And another season begins," Kurt shouted over to him.

Kirchner headed his way and took a seat on a large bait cooler.

He hung his head and tried to come alive by rubbing his eyes and then squeezing his temples to relieve the pressure.

"Rough one, huh?" Kurt asked.

"Yeah, but not as bad as the other night," Kirchner said. A wave of nausea swept over him and he took a deep breath. "I'm gettin' too old for this, man." At twenty-six, he was a couple of years younger than Kurt, but lately he'd been sporting a scruffy black goatee that made him look older. He always wore a t-shirt with the sleeves cut off—the poor man's tank-top—and his fishing shorts had enough bloodstains to make any butcher proud. He was experienced and like Kurt, he took his fishing seriously.

"You gotta learn to pace yourself," Kurt told him.

"You're one to talk," Kirchner snapped back.

"Hey, what can I say? I rebound quickly." He reached into his bucket and with a small bait knife, sliced open the packages of ballyhoo. "Besides, you feel that wind?" He held his hand up. "Southeast, man. They're gonna be chewin'. Wouldn't miss it for the world."

"Yeah, I hear ya. But sometimes I wonder how long it's going to last," Kirchner said. He watched Kurt poke the eyeballs out of the baits with an aluminum hunting arrow, took another deep breath, "sometimes I wonder if I'm doing the right thing..."

"Shit. A college boy like you?" Kurt looked up at his friend. "You're smart enough to make your own decisions." Kurt knew that Kirchner was one of the few mates with a degree. He'd studied marine biology at Florida State and his knowledge of fish and their behavior made him one of the best mates around. "Your parents hassling you or something?" Poke, poke, and a few more eyeballs were gone.

"Yeah, kind of. See, my father doesn't really care what I do," Kirchner explained. "His father was a fisherman too, commercial, up in Stuart: Kingfish. The only reason my father quit was to take care of us. Couldn't make enough money fishing, so he went to college and became an engineer. Now my mother wants me to get a real job. Says I've had enough fun. Maybe she's right."

Finished poking, Kurt began squeezing the shit out of the baits by running his finger down their bellies. "Maybe she is right," Kurt agreed. "But you can have that real world bullshit. I'll take what I've got any day. Workin' outside, fresh air, gettin' paid to fish... Think about it! Most people pay to do it. They dream of catching a sailfish, a marlin. We get paid to do it! It's fuckin' unbelievable!"

Kirchner had to admit, it was a very convincing argument, but there was another thing that bothered him. "You gonna do this your whole life?" he asked Kurt.

"Who knows? Who knows what might happen to me later today? Or tomorrow?" He got up and went to grab his hooks. "I live every day as it comes, man. You should, too. We only live once, man. Make the best of it. And don't listen to any of that other crap."

Down the dock, a tall, lanky boy came out of the *Tempest* and stepped onto the wooden covering-board of the gunwale. He gave a look in their direction, and went and sat on a stump behind the boat.

"What's up with that dude?" Kirchner asked.

"Stanton's new mate. Johnny. He was with us the other night in Cancun. Johnny Flynn or something like that."

"Oh, yeah. Looks like a geek," Kirchner observed. Flynn's t-shirt was about three sizes too big, a tent that hung down past his knees. Looked brand new. He was pale and his hair was buzzed short like a kid whose father had caught him smoking.

"He's cool," Kurt told him. "Just shy. Terry told me he's had a pretty rough life."

"Where's he from?"

"Riviera Beach." Across the water from Singer Island. The wrong side of the tracks.

"I've seen him before, somewhere," Kirchner said.

"Probably pumpin' gas at that Exxon on Blue Heron. Terry told me that's the only job he's ever had."

"That sucks."

"Yeah. Terry said he raised his whole family by himself. Two younger sisters and a little brother."

"What about his folks?" Kirchner asked.

Flynn got up onto the dock, looked their way again, and then began throwing pebbles into the water.

"Mother's a drunk. Or stoned, or both," Kurt said. "His father took off like ten years ago. Just left the whole family one morning and never came back."

"Wow. That sucks. Looks like he probably gets picked on a lot."

"Yeah. Terry says he's a good guy. Good worker, too," Kurt added.

"Hey, you've got to start somewhere, man." Kirchner stood up. "Let's invite him over."

Kurt agreed. "Hey you," he shouted. "John." He motioned with his hand. "Come on over here."

Flynn looked over and approached with a sheepish smile.

"Have a seat," Kurt told him, and he sat next to Kirchner on the cooler.

"Thanks," Flynn said. A little nervous, voice on the high side. "I'm John. I was with you guys the other night, but I forget your names."

Kurt and Kirchner introduced themselves and shook his hand.

"Watch closely and maybe you, too, can learn from the master," Kirchner said. They were ready to rig.

"Well, if that's the case, then I better show you," Kurt told him. He grabbed a bait out of the bucket and holding it upside down, stuck a hook through the ballyhoo's gill and watched as the pre-sharpened point poked out of its belly, just beneath the head. It was well known that bill-fish will try and eat another fish headfirst and by rigging the bait in this way, one's chances of hooking up were much better. He took the small piece of copper wire, wrapped it around the back of the gills, across the ballyhoo's head, and ran it twice through the eyes, closing the gills. Then he poked the thin wire up through the top part of the small fish's mouth and wrapped it around the beak of the lower jaw until the wire was used up and the mouth was thereby closed. Finished with one bait, Kurt held it up for Kirchner's inspection.

61

"That's worthy," Kirchner told him. "Here. Let me do one." Together the mates finished rigging the rest of the baits in the bucket. After screwing up the first two, Flynn finally got the hang of it. They placed the rigged baits side-by-side in a large cooler of ice, with the cooler stationed behind the fighting chair for easy access.

By eight o'clock Larsen and the other two captains had arrived, slightly hung-over, but ready to fish. As always, Larsen disappeared into the engine room to check the oil and water level of the engines. Unlike most of the other sportfishing yachts, the engine room of the *Predator* was huge. Standing in the middle of the room, Larsen was dwarfed by the massive Detroit Diesel 16V92 DDEC engines that lined each side. Each of the engine's sixteen, ninety-two cubic inch cylinders worked together in producing nearly fifteen hundred horsepower per engine, for a combined total of almost three thousand. To say that they were powerful was an understatement.

An on-board computer that kept track of every component of the engines' operation, from temperatures and pressures to engine rpms and fuel consumption, controlled each engine. A series of digital senders fed continuous performance updates from the engines to the computer and all readouts were displayed on screens on the instrument console inside the flybridge as well as the control station at the rear of the bridge. Larsen took great pride in having an engine room that was immaculately clean, and he and Kurt spent many hours with cleaners, degreasers, rags and Windex trying to keep it that way. Almost the whole engine room, as well as the motors themselves, was painted with white Awlgrip, a glossy marine finish that pinpointed the location of even the tiniest oil leak.

Seeing that the oil and water levels were fine, Larsen started the Onan generator, which would provide twenty continuous kilowatts of 110-volt power to the boat while they were underway.

Back in the cockpit, Larsen told Kurt it was okay to switch the power over to the generator and disconnect the shore cord, which delivered power to the vessel while docked. Then he went up the ladder and disappearing into the flybridge, he fired up the two giant diesel motors. Twin clouds of thick black smoke enveloped the cockpit but quickly dissipated. Emerging from the flybridge, Larsen gave the thumbs-up sign to the men below, who quickly got busy undoing the stern and side spring lines. As Kurt made his way up the side towards the bowline, Larsen climbed the tower legs to the upper control station, from where it was easier to dock or leave the slip. Now able to see the bow as well as the stern, Larsen slowly put the clutches in gear and eased the huge sportfisher from its slip. Putting the port engine in forward and the starboard in reverse, he spun the *Predator* ninety degrees and slowly idled towards the cut.

With several successive blasts of spray, the *Predator* thundered out of the cut and headed for deeper water. Turning the monster craft towards the south, Larsen headed towards the point just offshore of a large radio tower, situated along the narrow roadway just three miles from P.A. His eyes scanned the water for any signs of telltale activity: birds diving, schools of bait breaking the surface or changes in the surface of the water, such as upwellings of current or changes in color. Bait tended to congregate around such areas and where there was bait, there was sure to be billfish. The southeasterly flow of the wind had stirred the water up fairly well and not seeing anything unusual, Larsen glanced at the Furuno full-color bottom machine and watched for the point where the ocean's floor dropped off in a steep wall. The bottom machine's transducer, mounted underneath the boat, sent Larsen a two-dimensional picture of everything below, highlighting in different colors any large objects, including schools of bait.

Rob Masters opened the door slowly and being careful not to lose his balance in the choppy sea, slid inside the flybridge.

"Good a place as any, huh?" he asked Larsen, the two men staring together at the bottom machine, which indicated a depth of 138 feet. Suddenly the depth increased to 278 as the drop-off appeared on the screen.

Larsen brought the throttles back to about five knots, a good speed to begin trolling. "Yeah, we'll start out by working back and forth across the edge for a while. The water looks pretty good here. Those guys ready down there?"

"Pretty much. I think we're suffering from too much talent. Probably won't catch shit," Masters said, smiling. Heading outside, the two men began to lower the outriggers, long chrome arms that kept the fishing lines spread out and away from the boat as well as each other.

"Man, I love fishing here. Think we're far enough from shore?" Larsen asked sarcastically. The shoreline was only about a mile away, and this was one of the reasons Puerto Aventuras was such a great place to fish. The trolling was done so close to shore that it was possible to watch boats fight fish from the beach.

Down in the pit, Kurt and the others were busy putting out the lines. The baits in the cooler were attached to a five-foot piece of 60-pound-test Ande monofilament leader, and then connected by a snap swivel to a twenty-foot piece of 60-pound Ande leader, known as the wind-on. When the fish approached the boat, the mate could grab the wind-on, and by wrapping his hands once around it, begin a hand-over-hand motion, pulling the fish close enough to release it. The wind-on itself was attached to the remainder of the reel's spool, which was filled with 30-pound-test monofilament line. The spinning reels used for the flat lines directly behind the boat were filled with 20-pound test.

After letting the long line out about fifty yards, Kurt grabbed the line and ran it through the outrigger clip, which he then sent up to the end of the outrigger by means of a heavy-test monofilament halyard. The line ran straight through the clip, not twisted, and in this way the distance of the bait from the boat could be adjusted without popping the line out of the clip. Flynn and Kirchner helped put out the other long and short lines and Kurt got busy putting out the flat lines, the spinning rods which were fished through a clip attached to the transom, dragging the baits about twenty yards directly behind the boat. Within a few minutes, all the baits were in place. Kurt looked up at Larsen and Masters who were standing at the rear of the bridge, watching the baits for signs of activity.

"How's that look?" he shouted up at the bridge.

"Left long can go back a little," Larsen replied, seeing that it was in a little too close. "Pull down the rigger clips a little. The baits are jumping around too much."

Kurt did as he was told and the problem was solved.

Sitting with their backs against the rear bulkhead, Kurt and the other men stared out at the baits, prepared to leap into action at the first sign of a bite. One could never be sure when a bite might come and Kurt was surprised that he didn't have high blood pressure as a result of all the waiting and anxiety. Any time a line popped out of the clip, or a splash was spotted behind one of the baits, a blast of adrenaline shot into his bloodstream, whether it was a false alarm or not. All day long little bursts of energy increased his pulse and gradually wore off. He wondered if it was good for his heart.

"Hey! Let the teasers back a little bit," Kurt shouted up to the bridge. The teasers, one for each side of the boat, were hookless lures trolled behind the boat to attract billfish. They created a great deal of turbulence, or "smoke", and were more easily seen by the fish swimming below. When a billfish appeared chasing the teaser, the captain would pull the teaser in by hand, or reel, mounted on the bridge. As the fish followed the teaser the mate would then toss out a "pitch bait", presenting the baited hook to the fish, which would usually fade off the teaser, pile on the bait and eat it. On the left side, Larsen liked to pull a chain of rubber squids, with a large blue and white "hawaiian eye" at the end—a nylon skirt pulled in front of a hookless, foot-long "horse" ballyhoo. On the right he used a large purple white and blue "chugger" lure.

Larsen pulled the teasers in a few feet and resumed watching the baits, trolling back and forth across the "edge" or drop-off below. Taking the *Predator* in as shallow as ninety feet, he would slowly make a turn and head back out to four or five hundred. This method of trolling back and forth in a series of giant, wide S-turns had proven to be very effective in raising billfish in the local waters. With one hand on the steering wheel and one holding on to the tower leg, Larsen swept his eyes back and forth, scanning the baits as they dragged through the water. He looked for any sudden change, a shadow, a splash, a break in the pattern of the waves. His peripheral vision was excellent and he often caught movement out of the corners of his eyes as fish struck the baits. From his vantage point high above the water, Larsen was usually able to spot the fish before Kurt could and, hopefully, before they attacked the bait and popped the line out of the "pin", the part of the outrigger clip holding the line.

"What the fuck, over?" Masters said, sitting down on the small padded bench and opening the refrigerator to grab a coke. He looked at his watch. "We've been trolling for almost an hour. Water looks good...I can't believe we haven't had a bite."

"Really. This sucks." Larsen leaned over and peered around the side towards the bow, to make sure they weren't about to crash into anything. The water was a deep blue and very clear—usually great for sailfishing. He wondered why it was so slow. Turning the boat slowy back out to sea, he braced himself tightly as a large swell rocked the boat violently, once to the left and then back to the right. He heard laughing from down in the pit and hoped that the others weren't losing interest.

"Don't fall asleep..." Larsen began to shout but quickly cut himself off when he spotted a large black shadow following behind one of the baits. "There he is! Right long! Looks like a sail," he screamed and immediately Kurt appeared down in the pit and grabbed the correct rod out of the rocket launcher. He pushed the drag lever down, and put the reel in free spool just as the fish grabbed the bait. Having trolled for years, Kurt knew how the sailfish usually ate. First they came up and swatted it with their bill, thinking the bait was alive and trying to stun it. Then they swam off with it, turning it around and eating the bait headfirst. With his thumb on the spool, Kurt watched as the line popped out of the pin. He pointed the rod tip at the fish, let him have it for a couple of seconds, then pushed the drag lever up to the strike position. Cranking the handle a few times to ensure that the line was tight, he reared back on the rod to set the hook. A smile came across his face as the rod tip bent over.

"Got him on!" he cried, just as the water exploded one hundred yards off the right hand side and a sailfish burst from the depths, thrashing violently in a frantic attempt to dislodge the hook and set itself free.

"Pretty work," Larsen told him and immediately put the boat into a turn, in hopes of a multiple hook-up and bringing the *Predator* around towards the hooked-up fish, which jumped a few more times and then submerged. "Dump the two left rods," he shouted into the pit. Putting the outside reels in free-spool while going into a turn caused the bait to sink, and it was often snatched up by another fish lurking in the depths well behind the boat. He watched as Kirchner and Flynn each followed his instructions. The line flew off the reels.

"That's good," Larsen said and Kirchner put the reels back in gear.

Seconds later, the line closest to Flynn popped out of the rigger. He locked up his reel by pushing the drag lever up, but when he lifted the rod to set the hook, nothing happened.

"You gotta feed him, John", coaching the young mate while keeping his eye on Kurt's fish. Flynn frantically put the reel in free-spool again, but whatever had been eating his bait was gone. After reeling in the line, he found that all that was left of the bait was a head.

Matt Kirchner suddenly let out a whoop. "Got him on right here," he alerted everyone, turning and smiling up at Larsen and Masters, the rod in his hands bent over. Raising his fist in the air, he high-fived Kurt and moved to the opposite side of the transom and faced his fish, which was peeling off line in that direction. Terry Stanton slipped fighting belts onto the two men and they began to wind furiously.

"Clear those other lines," Larsen shouted. He reeled in the port teaser while Masters did the same on the starboard side. Then, bringing the throttles all the way back, he put the clutches first into the neutral position and then quickly into reverse. After a slight delay, the DDEC electronic controls assured that the rpms were low enough to make the shift into reverse and the *Predator* slowly began to move backwards. "All right, we'll take Kurt's first, he yelled into the pit, seeing that Kurt's fish was closer. He slowly backed the boat towards the first sailfish while Kurt cranked the handle of the reel like a madman. "How are you doin' down there, Matt?" Larsen asked. He leaned over to see that the other mate's reel wasn't being stripped of line by the second fish. Kirchner assured him that he still had plenty. Known as "backing down" on a billfish while in reverse wasn't the most sporty method, but it was fast and effective. The men in the cockpit cheered as each wave slammed into the transom, sending up a wall of water that completely soaked them.

Seeing the double knot that signaled the beginning of the wind-on approaching the rod tip, Kurt stepped back as John Flynn reached out and took a few wraps on the line. Pulling the sailfish in slowly, he waited until he saw the swivel, then reached out for the hook. But before he could get to it, Kurt leaned over with a small bait knife and cut the leader just below the swivel. Swimming away slowly with the huge dorsal fin on its back fully extended, the billed hunter disappeared into the deep-blue darkness below.

"You left the hook in!" Flynn cried.

"Damn right I did!" Kurt said. "You don't want to fuck around with a lively fish. He'll stick that hook in you before you know it," he explained. "It rusts out in a couple of days anyway."

After backing down on Kirchner's fish in the same manner, Kurt took the final wraps on the leader and released it. Every billfish caught in Puerto Aventuras was released, and with sixty or seventy boats fishing the local waters during the season, the number of sails and marlin set free added up quickly.

The men in the cockpit put the baits out once more, and Larsen continued to troll in the same area. Inshore, a blue and white helicopter flew down the coast.

"That's the third one I've seen today," Masters said. "I wonder what they're looking for."

"They're looking for drugs, man, what else." Larsen had seen the choppers plenty of times before, but never with such regularity. "Those guys are like the Mexican DEA. They fly along the coast looking for the shit floating or for boats picking it up. Most of the time a plane or boat drops it offshore. Then a *panga* picks it up, takes it to land, and they move it up the coast. Next stop, U.S. of A. There's definitely a lot of that going on. You've seen the checkpoints, right?"

"Yeah, but it doesn't really seem like those guys are checking too hard. Who's going to hide hundreds of pounds of blow in their glove compartment?" Masters laughed. He'd been through the local checkpoints several times in the last two seasons. Manned by the Mexican Army, the checkpoints were set up along the highway between Belize and Cancun and usually consisted of four or five bored-looking soldiers, many of whom appeared to be in their teens. Most of the time they just asked where you were going and waved the vehicle through, and occasionally they asked to see what was in the glove compartment. They almost never looked in the trunk.

"Have you ever thought how easy it would be for us to smuggle a shit-load of coke back to the U.S. from here?" Masters asked Larsen.

"Yeah, I have. Have you ever thought what it would be like if you got caught?"

Masters disregarded the question. "How many times have you made the trip from Cancun to Key West?" he continued.

Larsen thought about it for a second. "Six or seven, I guess."

"And how many times has your boat been checked? How many times have you been boarded? Never, Right?" Masters looked at Larsen, a gleam in his eye. "Shit, we could smuggle anything in there. Illegal aliens, coke, heroin..."

Larsen knew he was right. Officials had come on the boat in Key West before, but none had ever looked around. He'd never been boarded by the Coast Guard and only knew one or two captains who had. It was no secret to anyone that the U.S. Coast Guard and Customs Service were severely underfunded and understaffed. They simply didn't have the time, money, or manpower to search every boat coming into Key West. The DEA was more concerned with vessels coming into Miami from the Bahamas and other parts of the Caribbean.

Masters had made a good point and Larsen's brain urged him to consider it further. He stored the thought for later use, and the two men didn't discuss it again.

Over the next several hours, Larsen and the others managed to catch four more sails, a wahoo, and a blackfin tuna. While fun fishing was always good practice, Larsen wasn't completely focused on the task at hand. He kept thinking about his conversation with Masters: how easy it would be to smuggle drugs into Key West on their boats. He wasn't sure how much coke he could hide, but he was sure it was enough to get a smuggler's attention.

Bringing the baits in and heading for home, the wheels in Larsen's brain were turning continuously as he began to formulate a plan. And inshore, the blue and white helicopter flew back up the coast. They were watching. That was for sure.

It was already getting dark as Larsen headed south down the beach towards the Papaya Republic, a popular bar and restaurant that he had been going to every time he was in Mexico. Walking barefoot at the water's edge, a tiny swell lapped at his ankles as he stared out at the calm waters of the bay. The day's earlier wind had completely dropped out.

During the last season, Larsen had met a waiter at the Papaya Republic who seemed to be well connected to the local drug scene. He had been very surprised at the amount of cocaine that was being done within the resort and it hadn't taken him long to find out the source. A little poking around and a few well-placed twenties had led him to Carlos, a chubby, dark-skinned Mayan with a wispy mustache and medium-length, straight black hair.

An unremarkable man who dressed like a local peasant when he wasn't working, Carlos kept a low profile in the restaurant and around the resort as well. When Larsen first met him, it was hard to believe that he was the head of the largest coke operation south of Cancun. Smuggling or dealing, Carlos had his hands in all of it. He had offered several times to get Larsen any amount of cocaine he wished, but Larsen had always politely declined. Larsen had decided to keep his valuable contact on ice and he vowed to burn the fat little scumbag, some day, and stop his sucking the life out of people.

Sitting alone on a piece of property that was not owned by the resort, the Papaya Republic had been around for years, back when Puerto Aventuras was nothing more than undeveloped jungle. The building itself was a mammoth thatch *palapa*, its walls, ceilings, and floors built from nothing but palm wood and bamboo. Even if the food wasn't that great, the place certainly had character. Completely open to the air, the bamboo tables and chairs were covered with fake leopard-skin tablecloths, adding to the jungle-like atmosphere. Larsen walked into the place and quickly surveyed its occupants. A couple speaking German sat holding hands in the corner and a waiter was preparing the tables for the dinner crowd. Besides that, the place was deserted and that was good.

The restaurant's star attraction was a trio of spider monkeys, three females leashed to their own little *palapa*, located just a few feet from the porch of the restaurant. They'd been there for years, at least as long as Larsen had been coming there. Making his way over to their little haven,

70

Larsen was saddened to see that their leashes had been shortened considerably. Usually lively and energetic, all three appeared listless and uninterested, their lonely eyes gazing at Larsen as if asking for help. Disheartened, he went back to the bar to look for Carlos.

"What's the story on the monkeys?" he asked the young bartender, who looked at him as if he'd spoken in Latin. Larsen pointed at the monkeys and used sign language to show that the leashes were very short.

"They bite some people," he answered in broken English. The bartender bared his silver-rimmed teeth and worked his jaw back and forth just above his hand.

He ordered up a Dos Equis beer and asked the bartender if Carlos was around. The young man said that he was in the back, and sliding Larsen a slightly chilled beer, he went off to fetch him. Taking a sip, Larsen pondered the lack of cold beer in Mexico in general, suddenly realizing why so many of the locals drank it over ice. Spotting Carlos emerging from the back room, Larsen waved to him and took a seat at one of the small tables on the side porch, away from the other diners. In the center of the table, the flame from a small candle struggled for its life. Carlos joined him and the two men made small talk for several minutes. Carlos looked about the same, more a bored waiter than a drug dealer. He wore the standard Papaya staff uniform, and it was obvious he'd put on at least twenty pounds. His brown button-down shirt was tight and a dirty, white undershirt showed through the gaps between the buttons. The black slacks threatened to burst in several places. It was no wonder they called him *El Gordo*—the fat man. Larsen noticed that Carlos was sporting a huge gold diamond studded hoop in his left ear. Business must be good.

And Carlos was the first to get down to it. "So, how can I help you, Captain Dan?" He lit a Marlboro Light and exhaled slowly, blowing several tiny smoke rings up towards the ceiling. The smokes were American-made, smoother than their Mexican counterpart. Only the good stuff for *El Gordo*.

Larsen explained to him how none of the sportfishing boats were ever checked when they came back into the states.

"Look, Carlos, I know they're dropping the coke right offshore."

"How do you know this?" Carlos looked alarmed. Like it was a big secret.

"I'm not blind, Carlos. Listen to me." He looked around and leaned across the table. "If I were to pick it up in my boat, I could hide a large quantity and sneak it into the States. A large quantity."

"What is large quantity?" Carlos was interested now. He had started to sweat and his round face glistened in the candlelight.

"Probably several hundred pounds," Larsen told him. "We can hide it under beds, in the bilges. They'd never find it..."

"Kilos!" Nearly shouting. "How many kilos?" Carlos demanded.

"I don't know for sure. Two, three hundred maybe."

"That much!" He was excited, but then his face changed. He suddenly looked worried. "Could cost *mucho dinero*. Where you get the *dinero* to pay for it?"

"I dont want to buy it, I just want to move it," he explained. Larsen watched Carlos closely. He had learned long ago how much people gave away with their expressions. But Carlos had put on his poker face.

He seemed to ponder this last proposition and ran his hand across his forehead and on down to the back of his head before answering. "Ah, you want someone to pay you for that."

"That's right."

"And do you want to be paid in *dinero* or in product?" the smuggler asked.

"I prefer cash. I don't have the connections to distribute the stuff."

Again Carlos remained silent. A waiter appeared and brought Larsen a fresh beer. Carlos leaned forward across the table. "Maybe," he said in a hushed tone. "Maybe I can help you. You wait. I contact you." And with that, he struggled his fat ass up from the table and disappeared.

5

The Mansion in Vera Cruz
March 14, 1996 0213 Local Time

Lost in the dream, Carrillo moaned softly as his body twitched in the darkness. He was on the outside patio of the fine restaurant Ochoa Bali Hai in Mexico City. Seated around the rectangular marble tables, Carrillo, his wife, and two children were in the middle of dinner. Across from them sat Manuel Miranda Urrutia and his family. Miranda—"the engineer"—responsible for coordinating Carrillo's intricate transportation network along the entire Southwest border. And Ramon was there. Ramon Salazar Salazar, Miranda's up and coming *traficante* apprentice. Smiling and laughing and carrying on as always. It was a rare occurrence for the men to be dining in public, but Carrillo's bodyguards had swept the place before they had entered and, for the moment, they were safe.

Carrillo looked over and smiled at his wife, Lucia. God, how he loved her! Lucia, with her dark brown eyes and long, silky black hair. Such a beautiful woman. And Eduardo, five, playing with her hair while Anna Claudia, just four, made faces at him and giggled. They were fine children. Had to spend more time with them. Had to get away from it all, away from the violence, the greed, the death and destruction. They would go to the sea, and tell the tourists about the fish and the whales, to a place where they would be safe, where the desert collides with the ocean.

And then Eduardo and Anna Claudia were grasping his arms, his neck, pulling and giggling. "Play with us! Play with us!" they begged him. Play their little game, something innocent, unlike the games played for life and death in Carrillo's world, the world of the *traficante*. And he shooed them away, much to their dismay.

But first a toast. Yes, a toast! "To the most important things in our lives," he proclaimed. "To our families! We must never forget that." And he was proud. Happy. Safe.

And then his world became dark. There was shouting. Slamming car doors. All heads turned to the parking lot. The raised glasses and cheerful proposals drifted away. The staccato of automatic gunfire erupted in the night. The peaceful evening was shattered. The smiles on the faces of the diners turned to masks of fear and several armed men charged into the restaurant. And then screaming. Horrible, piercing screaming.

There was flying glass and the acrid smell of gunpowder filled the air as the intruders sprayed the restaurant with gunfire, their AK-47s held at hip level.

It couldn't be happening! His family! Where was his family? And then he was on the floor, held by the strong arms of one of his bodyguards. "Lucia! Lucia!" he screamed, yet he could hear nothing. "The children..." And the automatic weapons continued their song of death.

And then bang, silence. An eerie silence, the silence of death. It floated on the breeze throughout the room. A silence so thick he felt he could touch it.

And then the crunch of boots on broken glass. Coming closer. Closer. They stopped above him. To kill him. Please, no...

Carrillo raised his head. Trembling, a frightened animal. And there they were. Oh God, no!

Lying in a heap just a few feet away, the bloody, bullet-riddled bodies of his wife and children lay with their eyes open, their mouths contorted in silent screams. Frozen in fear. Asking why? Why?

And Carrillo's tormented mind asked the same. Why? Who? Who would slaughter innocent women and children? And the glass crunched again. The smoking barrel of an automatic assault rifle appeared in front of his eyes. Nudged his cheek. Burned the skin. Don't look, his mind screamed. But he had to.

And there, standing above him with an evil, twisted smile was the face of Paco Herrera. Carrillo opened his mouth to scream. But the only thing that came out was silence.

Carrillo awoke from the nightmare. Fear lodged in his throat as he struggled to convince himself it wasn't real. With his heart racing and hyper-ventilating, he saw that Lucia lay next to him sleeping peacefully.

For Carrillo, the dreams always started the same; the restaurant Bali Hai, the gunfire, the assassins. But at the end of each nightmare, the faces of the assassins would change. At first he had seen the faces of other cartel leaders: Quintero, Gallardo, Abrego, but more recently, the face behind the automatic belonged to Paco, his own right-hand man. Carrillo's mind was trying to tell him something.

It had been almost three years since the assassination attempt at the Bali Hai. In August 1993 the Mexican navy seized more than nine tons of cocaine off the coast of Mazatlan. Carrillo's organization was acting as distributor of the cocaine for Colombia's Cali cartel. The seizure was almost certainly made possible by an informant among Carrillo's ranks and amounted to a twenty-million-dollar loss for the Colombians. It was not long after the seizure that the attempted assassination occurred, certainly a payback for the Colombians' loss. When the assassins entered the restaurant, it had been Paco Herrera who flipped over the table and shoved Carrillo to the floor. Then Herrera returned fire as he ran to another table, flipping it and providing a shield for Carrillo's wife and children. In the ensuing gun battle, Miranda and one of Carrillo's bodyguards were killed. Herrera killed two of the Colombian hitmen, but more importantly, he proved how he would react in such a situation. Carrillo immediately promoted him to lieutenant.

Leaving the bedroom to check on Eduardo and Anna Claudia, Carrillo tiptoed down the hall. He could see the outlines of two of his bodyguards as they patrolled the front of the mansion. Another man sat watching the video monitors at the security desk. With Herrera off to the Yucatan for almost a week, Carrillo was beginning to feel unsure of the mansion's security features. He could never be sure whether a traitor existed among his men, an informant who might lead a team of assassins right to him. And why had Herrera been popping up in his nightmares as the assassin? Paco had always shown complete loyalty. His penchant for violence worried Carrillo, but he knew that Paco's killer instinct not only kept them both alive, but deterred treason within the ranks of the cartel.

Looking in on his children, Carrillo wondered if it might be time to get out. As he stared at their peaceful little forms, he knew that he had all he wanted; two beautiful children, a loving wife, more money than he could possibly spend. He'd worked his way from the fields to the top of the most powerful cartel in the country. Respected by some and feared by others, the "Lord of the Skies" had stayed alive through it all. But like other men, the effect of power for Carrillo was intoxicating. The more he had, the more he wanted, never thinking he had enough, like the street drunk who continues to partake until he can walk no further. For the leaders of many of the cartels, the quest for more and more power eventually resulted in death—death being the only thing that would satisfy their hunger. Carrillo wasn't ready to turn the reins over to Paco and be put out to pasture. The entire Yucatan Peninsula was ready to be taken and Carrillo would not rest until he conquered the area, expanding his kingdom, driven by a hunger that would not be satisfied as long as he lived.

Returning to his bedroom, Carrillo lay awake and stared at the ceiling as his mind worked overtime. The Colombians were pressuring him to move larger quantities all the time. By developing a network within the Yucatan, perhaps they could receive the loads deep in the jungle, storing them until they could be moved to the coast, where the product could then be shipped by boat to various parts of the Northern Gulf states and Florida. With the power and financial backing of the Juarez cartel behind him, Herrera would have no problem acquiring the necessary contacts and means of transportation to open a new corridor to the U.S.. But could he trust him?

Drifting off to sleep, Carrillo prayed that the nightmares would not return. Stay in or get out? It was tearing him apart.

Marina Puerto Aventuras
March 14, 1996 2113 Local Time

Larsen slid into the battered taxi and ordered the driver in broken Spanish to take him to Playa del Carmen. He found that keeping his fluency in the language a secret often proved beneficial while traveling, knocking off the idle banter that usually spewed out of the driver's mouth in his quest for a bigger tip. It also allowed him to eavesdrop on conversations between Mexicans who thought he was just like the other tourists, too lazy to learn the language, preferring to put an "o" at the end of every word, butchering the syntax and making asses out of themselves.

Carlos had gotten a message to Larsen, who had sneaked away from the docks and was now headed for the Blue Parrot, a bar on the beach in Playa del Carmen, ten miles north of Puerto Aventuras. Apparently Carlos had set up a meeting for ten o'clock that evening. Who Larsen would be meeting he was not sure. "Blue Parrot: ten o'clock," was all he had been told. At least the ball seemed to be rolling in the right direction.

Leaving the resort, the taxi slowly rumbled across the last hundred yards of the driveway, a section of inlaid stones and boulders that basically functioned as one long speed bump.

Somehow still in one piece, the driver pulled the taxi onto the narrow highway, nothing more than a semi-paved dirt track, that ran from Belize in the south all the way to Cancun in the north. Known among the fishermen as the "highway of death", the road was traveled by vehicles of all types, from bicycles to eighteen-wheelers. Accidents were certainly not unusual, and to come upon the scene of an overturned car, truck or bus was common. More than once Larsen had closed his eyes at the sight of dead bodies strewn across the narrow lanes or shoulders, the steam and dust of a head-on collision just moments earlier still hanging suspended in the air. The Mexican equivalent of Interstate 95 on the East Coast of the U.S., the roadway that served the Yucatan peninsula was the most dangerous Larsen had ever seen.

Heading north, Larsen looked around the taxi's interior as the driver babbled on in Spanish about some of the local tourist attractions. Three-inch Jesus on the cracked vinyl dash. Rosary hanging from the rearview. You had to pray to someone to stay alive on these roads. Pointing towards the radio, Larsen spoke the single word for music, hoping the radio worked and the annoying little driver would shut up. There was no such luck tonight.

Within a few minutes, the soft, orange lights of the traffic cones signaled their approach to the military checkpoint where young Mexican soldiers were supposedly checking vehicles for drugs. Larsen could see that they had set up a couple of sandbag machine-gun emplacements, complete with thatched roofs. To Larsen it looked like they were selling lemonade, most of the soldiers appearing to be in their teens. Under a garage off to the side was a Humvee, an American army vehicle, that certainly came as part of the latest aid package. The soldiers appeared extremely bored with their duties, waving on some vehicles and stopping to chat with others with an air of indifference that clearly showed they were not very serious about their job. Larsen knew it was all a big show: a show designed to make it look like the Mexican government was doing something to combat the drug problem, and therefore continue to receive foreign aid. A joke to Larsen, the military checkpoints tended to scare the living shit out of American tourists. Larsen rolled down his window as the taxi coasted to a stop in front of a soldier waving them over with a flashlight. Seeing yet another *gringo*, the soldier said nothing and motioned for them to proceed.

Making the right-hand turn onto the main street of Playa, Larsen could see that the town was busy, the locals walking up and down the sidewalks and gathered in small groups all the way from the highway to the beach, where the taxi was forced to turn left. The abundance of stray dogs, the smells of local food stands, and the presence of various military and law enforcement officials gave Playa the feel of a third-world country, a feeling that could no longer be found in the tourist-filled streets of Cancun.

Directing the driver towards the Blue Parrot, Larsen cursed silently as the road turned to dirt and a veritable minefield of potholes shook the cab. The driver mumbled something in Spanish about an amusement park, but Larsen feigned a lack of understanding and told the driver to make the next right turn down the short hill into the parking lot of the Parrot. Parting with a fifty-peso note, Larsen paid the driver and walked off towards the beach and the bar.

A favorite among locals and tourists alike, the Blue Parrot was a huge, thatch *palapa* situated no more than one hundred feet from the water's edge and, instead of bar stools, the long rectangular bar was surrounded by swings. The varnished wooden swings were built for one or two people and hung on thick double-strand ropes from the rounded beams supporting the pointed thatch roof. The floor was nothing but sand and the patrons were often seen swinging back and forth as they consumed lethal amounts of beer and tequila, only to find themselves sprawled in the deep sand moments later.

The bar was crowded and the only available slot was between a couple of American jock types. Their drunken bellowing and backward-turned baseball caps set them apart from the rest of the crowd, which Larsen could see was made up mostly of locals and Europeans. He waved at one of the barmaids and ordered a Dos Equis. Scanning the crowd, he saw no sign of Carlos, but noticed that as long as he kept his mouth shut, he fit right in. With his long hair and buttoned down shirt, he looked like a half dozen other guys scattered around the bar. Many appeared to be German and he heard a smattering of Dutch and Italian spoken as well.

His observations were interrupted by one of the jocks, who had decided it was time to speak up and protect the valuable space between himself and his severely intoxicated buddy.

"Where ya from, surfer boy?" he slurred, his bloodshot eyes struggling to focus.

"Florida, East Coast," Larsen replied. The jock immediately launched into a drunken tirade about the University of Florida's football team, the Gators. The barmaid showed up with his beer and sucking down a third of it, Larsen searched the crowd for someone he knew, a means of escape from the two Neanderthals flanking him.

"I said what are ya doin' here?" Larsen tried to ignore the second jock, who he was sure must have gone over three hundred pounds. When he spoke, small flecks of white spittle flew onto his tight, blue t-shirt. His breath smelled like a mixture of beer, dead fish and stale cigars.

"Fishing." Larsen's one word answer was followed by the jock letting loose with an intense description of Lake Okeechobee's large-mouth bass fishing. Ashamed to be from the same state as the two wasted losers, Larsen excused himself to use the restroom.

Returning to the bar, Larsen spotted an empty swing at the end closest to the water and quickly made his way to it. Ordering another beer, he looked around the bar and then glanced at his watch. Ten-twenty. A couple slid into the space next to him and he turned to look at one of the most attractive girls he'd ever seen in Mexico. Incredible green eyes looked deep into Larsen's own. Not contacts. Eyes that were searching for something. Larsen's heart fluttered with excitement as she smiled; her thick pouty lips revealed near perfect teeth, unlike most of the locals. Her brown hair was bleached by the sun. Her rust-colored vest revealed a set of firm breasts, barely covered by a thin black crop-top. Larsen smiled back at her as his eyes took in the rest of her body, not surprised to see that she also had a great set of legs and just about everything else. Searching his mind for a good one-liner to open the conversation, Larsen looked past the girl to see what kind of guy she was hanging out with.

The man leaned forward, their eyes met, and Larsen stared straight into the face of Paco Herrera.

"Hello Captain Dan," Paco said, as if they'd already met. Larsen suddenly knew that Carlos would probably not be showing up. "I am a friend of Carlos. He told me you would be here. My name is Paco and this is my friend Teresa." Paco looked around slowly to see if anyone was paying attention to them, but they were lost in their own conversations.

"A shot of tequila and another beer for my friend," Paco shouted at the barmaid. Nothing for Teresa. Maybe she didn't drink. Or maybe he was just plain rude.

"Where are you from?" Larsen asked. His eyes locked with Teresa's.

"Teresa and I are from Mexico City, but we've been living in Cancun, doing some business. We come down here often, though. It's quieter and we like that." His English was nearly perfect. "What about you?"

"Florida. Palm Beach Gardens, a little town near West Palm Beach. It's on the east coast."

"Yes, I know it," Paco told him. "I've spent some time in Miami and Fort Lauderdale."

I'll bet you have, Larsen thought. Sizing Herrera up the whole time they spoke, Larsen had instantly noticed the silk shirt, the expensive boots. Herrera's open shirt revealed several thick, gold chains and a huge gold turtle medallion with diamonds for eyes. Typical high profile smuggler. Cocky. Arrogant. Such desirable qualities. And the woman. They always had the beautiful woman.

"Carlos tells me you are down here fishing," Paco said. "It is pretty good this time of year, am I correct?"

"Yeah, that's right. We spend about two or three months in Puerto Aventuras every spring. We're mainly after billfish—sailfish, blue marlin, and white marlin, but we also catch a lot of tuna and *dorado*." Larsen wondered when Paco would get to the point. Surely Carlos must have told him about their conversation at the Papaya.

Paco leaned forward, glancing around the bar. "Carlos also told me you might be fishing for something else."

And there it was. "Yes. Maybe. I'm not sure what Carlos told you, but he said that he might be able to help me. Then I received a message telling me to come here. I thought he might be here," Larsen said.

"Carlos said that you were interested in transporting some, how shall we call it," Paco paused. "Some artifacts. In exchange for payment, of course." He grinned at Larsen like a mischievous child and Larsen had the feeling that it was all going quite well so far. This guy may not be the top dog, but maybe he could lead the agent to him.

Paco grabbed his drink, a small glass of straight tequila, and suggested that the three of them move to an empty table, closer to the beach. Looking across the water, the lights of Cozumel were visible on the horizon. A light, ocean breeze blew in from the east and kept the evening temperature quite pleasant.

"Have you ever done anything like this before?" Paco asked.

"No, but I've thought about it a lot and I think this is the time to do it," Larsen replied.

"Can you handle five hundred kilos?" Paco asked.

And Larsen knew that Carlos had told Paco Herrera everything.

"I don't know. Maybe," Larsen told him. "It's a big boat."

"I'd like to see it."

"I'd like to show it to you."

"When?"

"How about tomorrow? Nine o'clock."

"We'll be there." No hesitation. Obviously he knew where it was.

"Do you guys dive?" Larsen asked. He knew it would give them a chance to get out of the marina, and he'd been looking forward to a dive on the wall in Cozumel.

"Yes, we do." Paco reached out and squeezed Teresa's hand. It looked like she tried to pull away, but Larsen couldn't be sure.

"Well, then. We can continue our discussion tomorrow. On the boat." Larsen was itchy to get back to the marina. He stood up, draining what was left of his beer.

"Yes. That would be fine with us," Paco said. They got up to leave and the three of them headed down the beach towards the taxi stand.

"Why don't you come join us for another drink? We're renting a house here in Playacar. A villa, actually. Not too big."

Larsen knew all about the Playacar resort. Huge homes. Palaces. Nothing under a hundred grand. Most around half a million. "No thanks, Paco. Although I am tempted."

"Well, come on, then."

"Nope, not if I'm diving tomorrow."

"Ah, a safety-conscious man. I like that."

Larsen made no comment and a few minutes later, they reached the taxis. "Until tomorrow..." Larsen said, opening the door of the first available taxi

"Nine o'clock," Paco assured him, and he and Teresa jumped into their own.

As they drove off, Larsen felt good... Alive... And concern for his own personal safety was the last thing on his mind.

Marina Puerto Aventuras
The Following Day

"You're shittin' me!" Kurt said. He'd been handing Larsen scuba tanks, from the dock to the boat, and what Larsen had just told him had stopped him dead in his tracks. "And how long did you say you've been doing this?"

"Almost eight years," Larsen said. "C'mon. Hand me another."

He took the tank from Kurt, and laid it on its side on a piece of carpet in the cockpit. Only seven o'clock and he could tell it was going to be a scorcher. No wind. He wiped the sweat off his face with the shoulder of his t-shirt and looked up at his mate. "Hard to believe, isn't it?"

"Fuckin' right it is! Now let me get this straight. You work undercover for the DEA and sometimes on the side for the CIA? It sounds like a fuckin' movie!" Kurt stared at Larsen as if for the first time. "I knew it," he said. Pointed his finger at Larsen. "I knew there was something special about you, the way you're so smart about different things. Secret phone calls, disappearing all the time and all that other spy-type shit."

"Yeah, well, now you know. Hand me another tank." Larsen reached up. Fucking things were heavy, close to sixty pounds. "My main job is with a special task force for the DEA in West Palm," he explained. "We trade a lot of information with a certain office of the CIA up in Virginia. Sometimes my guys in Florida sort of loan me out, which is what's happening right now. Anyway, the whole thing is completely undercover. You're the only person I've ever told."

"Wow, man. This is some heavy shit," Kurt said. "What made a guy like you ever want to join the DEA?"

Larsen took a sip of his coffee and looked up and down the dock. Still pretty empty. "I had a little sister once," he said. Quietly, like he didn't want anyone to know.

"What do you mean had?"

"She died." Just saying the words made him hurt inside. His throat swelled with emotion.

"I'm sorry," Kurt said. "I never knew. What happened?"

"She OD'd on coke. She was only seventeen." Larsen didn't feel the

83

need to go into any more detail. There was an awkward moment of silence between the two men.

"I'm really sorry to hear, that," Kurt repeated. "I guess I can't blame you for what you do. I just never had any idea. Sometimes I dream about losing my parents, or my brother. I don't know if I could deal with that, you know?"

"Yeah, well don't sweat it, man. It was a long time ago. You get over it," Larsen lied. Kurt handed him the last two tanks and he laid them next to the others on the deck. "Anyway, here's the deal. This guy I met last night, I guess he's well connected around here. Into the drug scene, I mean." He told Kurt about the conversation he'd had with Paco Herrera the night before. Told him about the plan.

"Let's say we do this. Where are you gonna hide all the stuff? And how are we gonna do it when Irv is around?" Kurt was always looking for a reason things could go wrong. Which was good.

"I don't know. I haven't figured all that stuff out yet. But I will. First let's see what this Paco guy has to say."

"Well, what happens if somebody finds out what's going on? What if we get caught?" Kurt asked.

"We're not going to get caught."

"That's easy for you to say. Your ass is covered. What about me?"

Larsen was prepared for the question. "Don't worry," he told his mate. "I'm going to talk to my people and make sure everything's cool. They'll grant you immunity or something like that."

"Can I get that in writing?" Kurt asked. The funny thing was, he was serious.

"Don't count on it. Listen to me," he told Kurt sternly, "These drug dealers are killers. They play for keeps. If they find out we're trying to set them up, we could both wind up dead." Larsen hoped it was sinking in. "I'm not trying to scare you, dude, I'm just being honest."

Kurt sat quietly for a moment. "What about the money?" he finally asked.

"What money?"

"The money they're going to pay you for doing this," he said. Like he knew how it always worked. "What's in it for me? If I'm putting my ass

84

in the fire, I sure as hell want to be paid for it."

"I don't blame you!" Larsen said. "But to tell you the truth, I'm really not sure how they're going to work it. The money, I mean. The CIA is going to be footing the bill for this one. They pay better than the DEA anyway. I'll get you some money. Don't worry about it."

"A lot of money," Kurt demanded.

"More money than you'll know what to do with."

"Oh, I'll know what to do with it. Don't you worry about that."

"So you'll do it," Larsen said. Telling, not really asking.

Kurt adjusted his visor and extended his hand. "I hope your little plan works, Cappy. Count me in." Already thinking of all the new tackle he was going to buy, once he got home.

"Holy shit," Kurt mumbled.

"Told ya," Larsen reminded him as the two men watched Paco and Teresa walking slowly down the dock towards the *Predator*. Larsen glanced at his watch and saw that it was ten-fifteen. Not bad, he thought. Only a little over an hour late. Both men tried not to be obvious as they stared at Teresa. Dressed in a fluorescent-orange thong bikini, she wore some sort of silk sarong wrapped around her waist, leaving little to the imagination. The see-through yellow fabric rippled slowly as she walked, parting in front with each step, revealing a set of sleek, golden legs. Her breasts strained against a tiny, triangular top, more exposed than not. To top it all off, she wore a set of silver, high-heeled sandals that were more at home in a disco than on the dock. All heads turned as she approached the *Predator*, clinging to Paco's arm more for balance on the jagged coral surface than for protection or a display of affection. A couple of the local boys whistled loudly, their shrill catcalls not unnoticed by Paco. His shit-eating grin said it all.

"Nice suit," Kurt said sarcastically, referring to the tiny black, speedo-style swimsuit Paco was wearing. Paco's lean, well-muscled body glistened with a sheen of perspiration and sweat ran down the sides of his face. "He probably just did a big fat line," Kurt mumbled softly. "That's why he's so skinny."

"Now, now. Let's be nice," Larsen scolded. "*Buenos dias amigos!*" he said, extending his hand to help Teresa cross from the dock to the stern of the boat.

"I'm sorry we're late," Paco said, hopping on and handing his small beach-bag to Kurt. "We were a little busy this morning. We had a hard time getting out of the bed." He winked at Kurt and introduced himself. Teresa blushed and remained silent.

Larsen had the generator running before they got there, so they wouldn't waste time with idle chitchat. He hated small talk, maybe because that was what he heard all day when he was fishing with his owner. Kurt had already laid out all the equipment, so they were pretty much ready to go.

"It's a hot one today, so let's get the show on the road," Larsen said, placing his guests' bags inside the salon door. He motioned for Kurt to begin getting the dock lines and headed for the bridge. "C'mon," he said, and motioned with his hand for Paco to follow. Once inside the bridge, he fired up the engines and checked the most important gauges.

"This is an incredible machine," Paco said as he looked around the inside of the flybridge and walked over to the huge control panel.

"Thanks. I'll be right back. It's easier for me to drive from up top when we're going out." He walked outside and scrambled up to the tower. Checking to see that everything was set down below, he slowly eased her out of the slip.

Once clear of the cut, Larsen returned to the bridge. Paco still looked amazed. "Where are we going to dive?" he asked.

"Well, the water is flat calm today. How about Cozumel."

"That sounds great. How long will it take to get there?"

"About forty-five minutes," Larsen said. He'd already made the trip several times and he knew it was only about eighteen miles. If they cruised at just over twenty knots, they would definitely make it in less than an hour.

"What do all these things do?" Paco had been on some big yachts before, but had never paid much attention to how they were operated and what all the electronics were used for.

"Well, for starters, this is the GPS, the Global Positioning System."

Larsen walked over and pointed at a small rectangular box that was mounted in the face of the horizontal part of the control panel. He punched the keypad and the machine displayed the current position of the *Predator* in both latitude and longitude. "This tells us where we are at all times and is used for navigation. A series of satellites orbiting the earth send and receive information that they process and use to determine the position of any vessel. Airplanes have them too. All I need to do is punch in the latitude and longitude of any place and the GPS will tell me how far away it is and what heading I should take to get there. It's like a little computer. It also tells us how fast we are going, so it can compute how long it will take for us to get somewhere. The important thing is: if you give me the coordinates of a certain spot, I can get this boat within about a hundred yards of that spot. So if you want to drop something out of an airplane, as long as I know the exact coordinates of the drop, I can be right there. You see how it can be very useful?" He looked at Paco to see his reaction. The smuggler smiled and nodded his head slowly. He looked deep in thought.

Larsen reached into a drawer underneath a small couch behind him and pulled out his little black datebook which contained the coordinates of some of the best dives in Cozumel. He punched the coordinates into the keypad and within seconds the information he needed appeared.

"See? Exactly fifteen point two miles to go. Forty-three minutes to the beautiful reef at Palancar."

"How deep is that dive?" Paco asked. "Teresa sometimes gets nervous about the deep ones."

"It starts about seventy, but it gets real good after a hundred feet. You and I can dive there first and then we'll slide up to the north a little where it's shallower. Kurt and Teresa can dive there and you and I can discuss a little more business."

Larsen assumed that Paco had no problems with diving deep. Anyone involved in the nasty business of smuggling coke was sure to have big balls, he thought. And if he didn't, Larsen knew that it was a good way to gain the upper hand in their little machismo contest that he was sure had already begun. He'd seen the way Paco had been eyeballing him since they met and was used to smugglers sizing him up, always a little suspicious at first. Larsen was the master of making them feel at ease, however, and many of them now sat in jail as a result.

"This one here is called the plotter, or chart navigator," Larsen said, continuing with his explanation of the various electronics. He pressed the power button, and a small monitor the size of a personal computer sprang to life, displaying a multi-color map of the local area. "This little cursor is us," he said, and pointed at a tiny image of a boat, headed along a blue line towards the southern coast of Cozumel. "This machine tells you most of the same things as the GPS, but puts it in a visual perspective. The chart nav and the GPS are both tied in with the autopilot, so the boat can practically drive itself."

Larsen described to Paco how the autopilot worked and explained how all the machines relied heavily upon the compass, which was actually the most important navigational aid on board. He pointed out all the digital readouts and their corresponding manual gauges.

"This is a cellular phone, no?" Paco asked. "What is this?" He pointed at a rectangular-shaped handset, mounted next to the radios.

"Yeah, that's right. That's the cellular and this one is the AT&T sea phone. It's tied in with the single-side-band radio. Sometimes when we're at sea, we're too far out of range and the cellular doesn't work. The sea phone allows us to get in touch with the AT&T high seas operator directly and the call is scrambled, so no one hears it. Otherwise we can get in touch with any of the monitoring stations and they will connect us with the operator, but everyone can hear you."

"Why do you have two of the same radios?" Paco asked.

"Actually, they're different," Larsen explained. "The VHF is for close distances and this one is called the single-side-band. It's for transmitting and receiving over a much broader range. It can reach thousands of miles."

"What's this?" Paco pointed at a small black device mounted directly underneath the radios. It displayed four tiny numbers in black against a white background and it looked like the numbers could easily be changed by hand. A little red light glowed just to the left of the numerical display.

"This is the ringer," Larsen explained. "Every boat that has one is assigned a four-digit number. It's tied in with the single-side-band. I put in the number of the boat I want to call and with the single-side-band set on a certain frequency, I just press this button and the radio sends a transmission to the other boat and his little ringer makes a sound. It sounds more like an alarm than a ring. When someone rings me, my alarm sounds and the number of the boat calling is displayed up here." He pointed to the blank, dark area above the four numbers. What he didn't tell him, however, was about the special crystal which Macki had given him and he had installed in the single-side-band, enabling the two men to contact each other on an ultra-high frequency with a secure, scrambled communications link.

Pointing out the obvious functions of the radar, Larsen concluded their little electronics lesson. With the coast of Cozumel visible in the distance, the two men sat back for a moment and they cruised in silence.

"Let me go check on Teresa," Paco said, breaking the ice.

"Go ahead. Can you tell Kurt that we're gonna be there soon? He needs to get everything ready."

"Sure." Paco went out the door and disappeared down the ladder.

The *Predator* continued on its course, headed for Palancar reef, driven only by the autopilot. Larsen gazed out the windshield, watching for other craft. He hoped he had piqued Paco's interest with his description of the boat's electronics and their abilities. The GPS had seemed to interest him the most and Larsen was not surprised. With the assistance of a GPS, Paco's contacts could drop a load almost on top of them, and the ability to pick it up and be out of the area without a lot of time spent searching for it was crucial. Larsen was certain Paco now understood this and wondered how long it would take for Paco to arrange a drop.

There had to be other players involved. Whoever was running the show would never keep as high a profile as Paco, and it was no secret that most of the cartel leaders rarely showed their faces in public. It was simply too dangerous, not only because of a fear of law enforcement officials, but because there were always enemies within their entire federation, jealous of the power and willing to take out anyone or anything in their struggle to get it for themselves. No, Paco was not the one calling the shots. But who was and where was he?

Larsen watched as the GPS slowly counted down the distance to the waypoint. When they reached the spot, he noticed a few other small boats in the area. The southern reefs of Cozumel were considered by many to be some of the best dive sites in the world and, during the spring, were often crowded. Easing back the throttles, he put the engines in neutral and went outside the bridge to activate the rear helm station. Looking into the water from above, he could easily see the bottom. The depth finder had shown eighty feet and he was sure the visibility was twice that. Larsen made his way down the ladder and stepped over a pile of equipment to give Kurt a hand.

"Did Paco tell you the plan?" Larsen asked.

"Yeah. He said you guys were going to dive here first." He gave Larsen a wink and smiled devilishly. Stay alone on the boat with Teresa? No problem. "Then we'll go up north where it's a little more shallow and Teresa and I will dive up there."

Paco slid over next to her on the gunwale's covering board and put his arm around her. "Is that all right with you?" he asked, leaning over to kiss her on the cheek.

"That's fine," she said with indifference, and stared directly into Larsen's eyes. He was sure he had seen her trying to pull away from Paco's grasp, as if she feared him.

Seeing that Paco had already put on his wetsuit, Larsen slipped into his own neoprene, plain black shorty. Not being a slave to fashion, he had no need for the fluorescent, multi-colored wetsuits that seemed to be quite popular among many divers. He knew that the bright, red legs of Paco's suit would quickly appear washed-out and brown as they plunged into the depths and the visible spectrum of light was lost. He saw that Kurt had already attached the BCDs, the buoyancy control devices, similar to a backpack and used for controlling buoyancy while descending, during the dive, and while ascending to the surface. Each regulator aboard the *Predator* was equipped with a Dacor dive computer and two separate air hoses and mouthpieces, one the diver's main air source and the second, the octopus, used in the event another diver ran out of air and needed an emergency supply. The computer itself displayed digitally the divers depth, the duration of the dive and the amount of air remaining. It also calculated the amount of nitrogen in the diver's system and alerted the diver to any necessary safety or decompression stops. At depth, the amount of nitrogen in the bloodstream increases as a result of breathing compressed air. If a diver attempts to surface too quickly, without a decompression stop to exhale and bleed off the excess nitrogen, it dissolves out of solution and tiny bubbles form in the tissues and joints of the body in a painful and possibly deadly condition known as "the bends". Turning the knob that turns on the air, Larsen saw he had 3250 psi. Paco did the same with his tank and informed Larsen that he had 3300. Both men put on their weight belts and Kurt lifted up Paco's tank, helping him slip into his BCD. Larsen bent over his, and slipping his arms through the straps, lifted it up and over his head, sliding it down his back and into place. He checked the location of the various hoses and tightened his shoulder straps. Making sure that everything was all right with Paco's gear, the two men put on their fins and masks.

"Go on up and take us in to about seventy feet," Larsen told Kurt. "And slide back south a little. The current is movin' pretty good." Kurt maneuvered the boat as he was told and put the engines in neutral once more. Larsen walked to the stern and opened the tuna door, originally designed for bringing big fish into the boat, but very useful while diving.

"All right, Paco. We'll start getting ready to come up when we have about 1000 psi left. Make sure you have enough in case we need to decompress." He looked at Kurt and said, "Just follow the bubbles, man. We'll probably drift pretty far." Kurt gave him the thumbs up sign. "Go ahead," Larsen told Paco. The smuggler made a giant step into the water. When he surfaced, he gave Larsen the O.K. sign. Larsen turned to Teresa. Jesus Christ she was gorgeous! "*Adios, Senorita,*" he said and jamming the mouthpiece of his regulator into his mouth, plunged headfirst into the deep.

6

CIA Headquarters
March 15, 1996 1046 EDT

"Pardon my French, but fuck that self-serving asshole." John Macki looked up into the face of Bob Constance, Administrator of the DEA. Constance had made the trip to Langley and had just told Macki about his meeting with Jensen. Towering above Macki, who sat with his chair tilted back and his hands folded in his lap, the man was clearly distressed.

"I just wanted to let you know that he'll probably be sticking his nose into any operation geared towards taking down Carrillo," Constance said. "And you know why."

"Oh, I know why," Macki told him. "It's no secret he's got his eye on the ambassadorship. And that damn subcommittee he's got going is designed to make everything just hunky-dory for our friends across the border. They're up for certification soon and the way things are going, they're not going to get one more cent. What do they owe us now, seven billion or something like that?" He motioned for the big man to sit. With reluctance, Constance settled his stocky frame into a large wooden chair near the windows. Macki took a sip of coffee. Hot and black, just the way he liked it. A throwback from his Navy days, he'd been drinking it like that ever since.

"I'm just pissed off at the whole situation," Constance said. "This guy Jensen has no idea what it's like to deal with the authorities down there. It's like pissing in the wind."

"I can imagine how frustrating it can be, Bob." Macki looked at his old friend and felt sorry for him. The two men had worked together several times in the last decade and Macki's office was a valuable asset to the DEA. They exchanged information constantly. Together the two men had worked on some of the biggest cases in the history of both the CIA and DEA, from the takedown of the Medellin and Cali cartels to the break-up of some of the largest money-laundering rings in the Bahamas and Panama. Macki knew that Constance had a lot to be proud of. But the man who sat in the chair across the room looked tired and burned out. Years of fighting against the cartels had seemed to accomplish nothing. Good men and women that both men had known had died in vain. Things were no better now than they were fifteen years ago.

"How long have you been after this bastard Carrillo—six, seven years?" Macki questioned, not expecting an answer. "I've been asked to see what I can do, Bob, and believe me, I'm not going to let some pathetic politician get in my way in his pitiful quest for promotion. Sometimes secrecy seems to be the only way. I want you to work with me on this one but it must be kept under tight wraps. The fewer who know anything about it, the better. Otherwise, like you said, we'll be pissing in the wind. You got me?"

"Loud and clear, Mr. Macki. But let me tell you John, we don't have a metric shitload of information on this guy, but we do have a little—so if you need anything, don't hesitate to ask."

"Well, then let me ask you this. Where do you think Carrillo is right now?"

"He's gone underground. Every time we get close to him or there is a significant seizure, he disappears. Only this time, we haven't seen a large number of executions or assassinations, whatever you want to call them. It's possible he's left the Juarez area entirely. Lord knows what happened to the blow that was in that warehouse. But if it wasn't his, and belonged to the Colombians as usual, he's probably scared shitless right now. You remember what happened in ninety-three, right? The attempted assassination at Bali Hai in Mexico City?"

"Yeah, that was when the Colombians fucked up, right?" Macki remembered that the Colombians had killed a couple of other big players, but missed Carrillo.

"That's right. Two of Carrillo's guests, Ramon Salazar and Manuel Miranda made a run for it. Miranda was killed, Salazar was wounded. Supposedly the hitmen didn't even have a decent picture of Carrillo and figured one of the guys running was him. I'm telling you, the guy keeps a low profile. He's like a ghost. There one minute, gone the next. Rumor also has it that one of Carrillo's bodyguards fought off the Colombians single-handedly and Carrillo promoted him to lieutenant. Somebody is playing a major role in this operation and maybe it's this guy."

"Well let me tell you what we've got, Bob." Macki had noticed that Constance was now perched forward on his chair and was happy to see that he appeared more alert and enthused. "Customs in Fort Lauderdale seized a couple hundred pounds of stuff coming in on a container out of Puerto Morelos, which is about twenty-five miles south of Cancun. When we traced it, it led us to one Manuel Salcido. And guess who he had ties with."

"The Juarez cartel"

"Right"

"So why don't you pick him up?" Constance asked. "A little question-ing never hurt anybody."

"Because old Manuel is dead. In any case, I think Carrillo and his Juarez cartel are going to move back to the East. There's room for a Yucatan cartel. You boys and the FBI and the Justice Department and everybody else who's over there have done such a good job at shutting down the Southwest border, we're going to see a shift back to the water routes and the Southeast."

"I don't know about doing such a good job along the border, but it makes sense to me." Constance stood up and stared out the window. A light drizzle had begun to fall.

Continuing to stare out the window, he said, "Let's say you're right. What's the next step?"

"Are you familiar with a guy named Dan Larsen?" Macki watched Constance closely for a reaction. While being sure that Larsen's activities were well known within the DEA, he wasn't sure how much Constance knew about the work Larsen and Macki had done together.

"Let's see," Constance said, stroking his chin in deep thought.

"Larsen. Isn't he one of our guys, the one who was responsible for that big seizure in Walker's Cay in the Bahamas a couple of years back?"

"That's him."

"I've met the guy, but to be honest with you, I don't know much about him. I do remember that it seemed he had a pretty good cover. Long-haired guy, about thirty, right?"

"Yeah," Macki replied. "Drives a sportfishing yacht for some rich cat who lives in New Jersey. The boat sits just outside of Palm Beach all year. Larsen is one of the best undercover agents you've got, Bob. Real smart, quick thinker. I've worked with him on and off for six years now. Poor bastard found his younger sister dead of a cocaine overdose and joined DEA immediately. Believe me, he's driven." Macki understood the driving force behind the undercover agent because it was very similar to his own: revenge, one of the most powerful of human emotions. "Anyway, Larsen is fishing for a couple of months out of a marina fifty miles south of Cancun. Goes down there every year. He's already done a bit of poking around into the local scene, but this time, I've got him on something a little more serious. We've got a direct, secure communications link with his boat down there and I expect to hear from him any time. If anybody can find out what's going on down there and be discreet while doing it, it's Dan."

"Well, we're not giving up on our end either. I've got a whole slew of agents in El Paso who are chomping at the bit. They're not about to stop looking for Carrillo and they want nothing more than to see him six feet under. So like I said before, if you need any help, I'm here for you. But I warn you, John, if the political pussies in Washington find out you've got some kind of secret mission going on down there, they'll be all over you." Constance approached Macki's desk, extending his hand and preparing to leave. "One more thing, Mr. Macki. If you do find Carrillo, what then?"

"I'm not sure, Bob. But we will find him and when we do, we'll figure something out. I'll keep in touch." Macki rose from his chair, shook Constance's hand, and watched as his large frame ambled out the door.

Macki sat down in his chair once more and leaned back. He tried the coffee. It was cold: cold like Carrillo's trail. But he knew it wasn't a question if they would find Carrillo. It was when. And when they did, the former naval officer already knew what they had to do.

Immediately upon hitting the water, Larsen began kicking towards the ocean floor awaiting him in the darkness of the deep water below. Downward and deeper he went, occasionally pinching his nostrils and blowing, equalizing the air spaces within his ears and sinuses as the force of pressure on his body increased. Larsen concentrated on slowing his breathing as he approached the bottom, the huge formations of coral and rock looming up below him.

Checking his depth on the computer display, he saw that he was at ninety-six feet. He pressed the button of the inflator hose for his BCD a few quick times in succession, stopping when he felt himself begin to rise. Then, depressing the BCD's release valve, he let off just enough air so that he neither sank nor floated, but achieved neutral buoyancy. Hanging suspended like an astronaut in zero gravity, he looked up towards the surface and watched as Paco slowly dropped feet-first towards the bottom, as if jumping from a cliff in slow motion. Settling onto the bottom beside him, Paco added enough air to his BCD to achieve neutral buoyancy and then made a circle with his thumb and forefinger and signaled Larsen that everything was all right.

Knowing that it was safer to perform the deepest part of the dive first, Larsen led the way as the two men swam into deeper water, gliding silently just above the bottom as it gradually sloped downward and out of sight. At 125 feet, Larsen held them up and they peered over the edge of a jagged coral outcropping into the total darkness below. With only the sound of their own breathing, each inhalation followed by an explosive release of bubbles, the two men looked over the wall, wondering what lurked in the unknown abyss that seemed to dare them to come closer. But both men had heard the stories of divers being swept over the wall, others just swimming into the inky blackness never to be seen again. They went no further.

Paco looked over at Larsen and made a circling motion around the side of his head. Too much nitrogen in the bloodstream. Always happened down deep. Like laughing gas, a good day at the dentist, but 125 feet down. It made you lightheaded, euphoric. They called it nitrogen narcosis. Feeling slightly buzzed himself, Larsen turned away from the wall and began to swim upward towards a huge structure of coral, a giant wall of its own covered in sponges and other plant life. Giant, purple sea fans swayed gently in the invisible currents and huge brown-orange tubular sponges stuck out from the sides of the reef like the pipes of a church organ. Damselfish of all sizes, shapes and colors darted in and out of their hiding places, defending their turf with the ferocity of even the largest predators of the undersea world.

Hearing Paco screaming underwater to get his attention, Larsen turned to see that a large black grouper—probably better than fifty pounds—had approached from the side of the structure and was showing curiosity about the two intruders of the deep. Used to seeing divers, most of the big groupers were very tame and came around in hopes of scoring a tasty meal. Larsen watched as the grouper hovered inches from the smuggler's mask, its pectoral fins slowly waving back and forth. Paco reached out to touch the great fish, hesitantly and unsure of himself, and just when he brushed his side, the grouper flapped his wide tail and darted away.

Checking his depth, Larsen saw that they were just over 100 feet. He used sign language to see if Paco felt all right. He did, and the two men continued up towards a series of underwater passageways that Larsen had dived many times before. Winding through the interior of the reef, the tunnels were always filled with different fish and other deep-sea critters that used them as a hiding place from the larger members of their species who wished to eat them. Spotting one of the openings, Larsen swam over towards it, stopped, reached out, and grabbed Paco's dive computer and saw that he had twelve hundred pounds of air left. With fifteen hundred pounds himself, both men had plenty of air to negotiate the entire passageway, and even decompress if they had to. Motioning for Paco to go first, Larsen waited as the smuggler flicked on his dive light and slowly glided by, his fins stirring up the sand as he squeezed through the narrow opening and disappeared. When the sand had settled, Larsen turned on his own light and followed. He knew that it was important to stick together at all times, but especially in a tunnel or cave. With the light, the fish were exposed in full color, even at 100 feet. He trained the beam of his light on a queen angelfish, its blue, yellow and orange markings lit up like a neon sign. Continuing up the winding, jagged path through the inside of the reef, Larsen thought that it seemed narrower than he had remembered. He spied a small cave off to his right and swam over to investigate. Unable to squeeze his whole body through the opening, he stuck just his head and arm through the hole. Playing the beam of the light left and right, he spotted a pair of spiny lobsters. Backed against the wall of the small, coral room, they waved their feelers back and forth in defiance, submarine insects using their antennae to pinpoint the location of an unknown opponent. Knowing that the southern reefs of Cozumel are part of a marine sanctuary and that it is illegal to take lobsters anyway, he pushed on the bottom to back himself out of the hole. But above him something gave way.

After the third attempt to slide out of the hole, Larsen realized he was stuck. A blast of adrenaline entered his already nitrogen-saturated bloodstream and he immediately felt sick. His heart thundered in his chest, his own pulse throbbing in his ears, and he began to hyperventilate.

"Calm down, dammit," he screamed to himself and tried to be still and catch his breath. Underwater, panic was a killer. Large amounts of nitrogen in the blood often disrupted the process of rational thought and losing one's cool only made matters worse. Concentrating on breathing deeply, Larsen tried to calmly assess the situation. The top part of his regulator had obviously become stuck in the rock that had broken off from the top of the hole. He was wedged in tight. He wiggled his body back and forth slowly in an attempt to dislodge his equipment, but it was no use. With his free hand, he unlatched the buckles in the front of his BCD and attempted to slide out of it, again without success. The tank on his back and the small size of the hole kept him effectively pinned in place, and he felt the sense of dread returning. Struggling to fight off the panic, Larsen fumbled behind him with his free hand, searching for the extra mouthpiece of his octopus. Surely Paco will realize something is wrong. Larsen depressed the button on the mouthpiece, sending a huge cloud of bubbles up the naturally formed shaft. More sickening adrenaline shot into his system when he suddenly realized that his air supply would only run out much more quickly this way. An attempt to check the amount of remaining air on his computer failed, and he realized any type of struggling was burning more and more. It was now a race against time and, if he lost, he was a dead man.

But Larsen refused to give up. He began to breath shallowly, waiting for each breath to become a little more difficult, when he would be sucking harder and harder on the mouthpiece, until no more air remained and his world would slowly fade to black: all the time thinking. There had to be something he could do. His life didn't flash in front of his eyes. Instead, he felt a great sense of sadness, a feeling that somehow he had been ripped off, thwarted in his attempt to punish the wrongdoers and gain revenge on those who had total disregard for the lives of others. The cartel would carry on.

Suddenly Larsen felt a tugging on his legs and for a moment he thought it might be some nitrogen-induced hallucination, one last desperate attempt by his tortured mind to fool him into succumbing to this watery death. But then he felt the hands on the top of his tank, pulling and shoving, and then finally he was free. He looked wild-eyed at Paco, grabbed him by the shoulders and shook him, silently thanking him for saving his life. The display on Larsen's computer showed two hundred pounds left and he jerked his thumb up towards the surface. Paco acknowledged this and the two men headed back the way they came into the passageway, ironically heading deeper in a desperate attempt to make it to the surface alive.

Popping out of the opening with Larsen now in the lead, Paco followed closely as they headed towards the surface, careful not to rise any faster than their own bubbles. The alarm on Larsen's computer warned him of a necessary decompression stop for eight minutes at fifteen feet. Eight long minutes that he did not have.

He reached out and tugged on Paco's leg, and showed him the decompression information on his computer's display. He pointed to the fact that he only had one hundred pounds of air. Paco held up three fingers to indicate that he had three hundred, and held up his spare octopus.

Larsen nodded and at fifteen feet both men stopped. Larsen wanted to take tiny breaths from his tank, but he knew that most of the excess nitrogen responsible for causing the bends was released from the body during exhalation and holding his breath longer than normal would only put him in greater danger. As the air in his tank slowly ran out, each breath became harder and harder to draw. He was sucking his life out of an empty tank. And then it was gone.

Pulling his finger across his throat, Larsen reached out and took the octopus from Paco's tank. He knew that with two men breathing from the one tank, the small amount of air Paco had left would soon disappear. Glancing at Paco's computer, he saw that the smuggler had no need to decompress and could head for the surface whenever necessary. Suddenly the panic returned as Larsen felt the familiar change in available airflow. He motioned for the smuggler to head for the surface, but Paco stayed close, their eyes wide and locked in a strange sort of mutual fear. Larsen couldn't figure out why Paco wouldn't go up, when he wasn't the one in danger. Sucking the tank dry, Larsen pulled Paco's mouthpiece from the smuggler's mouth and removed the octopus from his own. He watched as Paco was forced to head for the surface. Then, using the inflator hose for his BCD, Larsen sucked one last breath out of the device and headed slowly for the surface, exhaling a tiny stream of bubbles as he prepared to become bent.

Larsen broke the surface and sucked in huge gulps of air.
"What happened?" Kurt screamed down from the bridge. Paco had surfaced first and shouted to him that there was something wrong, but in his excitement Kurt was unable to understand.

"Get the oxygen bottle quick! I might be bent!" Larsen swam to the open tuna door and held onto the transom as Kurt bolted inside the boat. Larsen took off his weight belt and threw it onto the deck. After slipping out of his BCD, he handed his floating equipment to Paco and kicked hard, pulling himself onto the deck of the cockpit. He lay there motionless, taking deep breaths and waiting for the pain to begin, a gradual aching that he heard began in the joints and increased until the victim was hunched over and twisted like a human pretzel.

Kurt returned in less than thirty seconds with the small, portable oxygen bottle, which Larsen kept on board for just such an emergency. Slipping the mask over his face, Larsen sucked the pure oxygen deep into his lungs, letting it seep into his nitrogen-rich blood. Kurt brought the dive equipment into the boat and then helped Paco slide into the cockpit. Teresa stood by silently, her arms wrapped around her body, trembling slightly as she tried to understand what had happened.

"He was stuck in a hole much deeper than I," Paco explained. "After a while I saw he wasn't right behind me. I went back and freed him. By then he didn't have much air. On the way up, his computer said he needed to decompress for eight minutes. I think we stopped for about four. I tried to share my air with him, but then mine was gone, too. I hope he will not get the bends." He looked at Kurt and the mate saw an honest look of concern on his face.

"Maybe he won't get bent," Kurt said. "These dive computers have a safety margin built into them. If he only came up four minutes early, he'll probably be all right."

"I hope you're right," Teresa said. She reached out and stroked Larsen's head, smoothing his wet, salty hair.

Larsen turned towards Paco and took the oxygen mask away from his face. "You saved my life, man. I owe you."

"Don't worry about it, *amigo*. I know you would do the same for me."

"I don't really feel like diving any more," Teresa said softly.

Kurt hid his disappointment well. "Neither do I," he lied.

"Sorry, buddy," Larsen told his mate. "You want to just head us towards home? I'll be up in a minute." With some effort, he got to his feet and closed the tuna door as Kurt went up the ladder to the bridge and pointed the boat towards the marina.

7

Poughkeepsie, New York   41°42.05"N 73°51.37"W
March 18, 1996 1414 EDT

Kym Jensen stood in front of the full-length mirror and carefully scru-
tinized the fit of her new fluorescent-yellow bikini. She twirled slowly
around, glancing over her shoulder, her long brown hair flying loose,
finally coming to rest just above the small of her back. Her long tanned
legs seemed to go on forever and, with her bright brown eyes and perfect
smile, it was not hard to believe that she had once considered a career in
modeling. In fact, so many people had compared her to Elle McPherson,
she had become sick of it and was happy she had decided to continue her
education rather than become an object, a piece of meat, for men to stare
at and other women to envy.

Working on her masters degree in psychology at Vassar, she was looking forward to her upcoming trip to Cancun. The winters in upstate New
York seemed endless, and the last couple of months had been nothing
but gray days and brutal cold.

"How's this look?" she asked her roommate, Sharon Hatch, who lay
on her side at the corner of Kym's bed. Hatch was majoring in political
science at Vassar and spent a little too much time in front of the television during the winter, snacking on pizza and twinkies. At five-two and
about thirty pounds overweight, she could only dream about having a
body like Kym's. What she lacked in looks, she more than made up for in

smarts. The valedictorian of her graduating class in high school, she was destined to graduate from Vassar with honors. She watched with envy as Kym spun around in front of her, tugging on the thin straps which seemed custom designed for her hips.

"Come on, Kym. You look great in anything. I can't believe how tan you are. How many times did you go to that salon?"

"Only four or five. You think it looks real?" she asked Sharon, tugging at the small top and trying to adjust it over her medium-sized breasts.

"Sure it does. Besides, who's gonna know? I won't tell. I just wish I were going with you." Sharon got off the bed and walked over and put her arm around Kym, standing on her tiptoes to do it. Both women looked into the mirror.

"I wish you were too," Kym said sincerely. She knew that Sharon was putting herself through school and had to work during spring break. Kym was lucky. Her father was Thomas Jensen, the Senator, and he had helped Kym financially during both her undergraduate and graduate work and she was able to concentrate more on her studies than on some lame part-time job.

Sharon went over to the window and looked out at the bleak, late-winter landscape. Most of the trees were bare, mere shadows of their former selves, giant oaks and maples that now stood naked without their leaves. Cars on the street cruised by slowly in a mixture of slush and mud, their tires noisily spinning through the mess, the sound gradually diminishing as they headed down the block. "I think the high today is supposed to be forty," Sharon said wearily. "I can't wait for spring to get here."

Kym crossed over to join her roommate at the window. "Look at that. That's why I can't wait to get out of here. I wish it was for more than ten days."

"Did you tell your Dad you're going to Mexico?" Sharon asked.

"Yeah, I did. He wasn't too thrilled about the idea. He thinks it's too dangerous down there. Something about guerilla uprisings or peasant revolts. I thought most of that was happening somewhere else. Isn't it?"

"Don't you watch the news?" Sharon asked. "It's getting pretty bad down there. Some of the problems are in the Mexican states on the West

Coast, but the Zapatistas are a rebel group operating down in Chiapas, which really isn't that far from Cancun. Maybe your father is right."

"He's always right. That's why we don't get along."

Sharon grabbed Kym gently by the arm. "Listen, Kym, your father has been going to Mexico for years. He's chairman of the damn subcommittee for Mexican-American relations. You told me yourself that he wants to be the next Ambassador. If he told you not to go down there, I'm sure he has a damn good reason. Things are messed up everywhere in Mexico right now. It's a politically explosive situation. Your father is just concerned. He cares about you and so do I."

"Oh, I know you do, Sharon. But my father never seemed to care until my mom died. Now he sticks his nose into everything I do." When Kym's mother had died of a heart attack six years earlier, her parents had already been separated. For years her mother had fought a battle with alcohol and in the end, it was too much for her father to bear. Kym had sided with her mother and had just begun school at Vassar when she died. An only child, Kym was forced to spend time with her father in Washington when school was not in session and, although she relied on her father for financial support, the relationship was strained.

"And he's always setting me up with the lamest guys," Kym continued. "Like Kevin for example. I can't believe I stayed with him for so long." Kevin McCarthy, the son of another prominent Senator, had been introduced to Kym at a Washington social function. She liked to refer to them as "ass-kissing festivals".

"What did you see in that guy anyway?"

"I honestly don't know," Kym admitted. "At first he seemed interesting, you know? The whole Washington thing was kind of exciting. We did a lot of cool stuff, met a bunch of interesting people..."

"So what happened?"

"Well, after about a year he started to seem—I don't know, boring is the word, I guess. He was more concerned with what was going on in the Washington political circles than with the rest of the world. Me included."

"And then you met that boat captain guy."

"Yeah, and you already know what happened."

"It was love at first sight," Sharon said.

"Right again. It just happened. At the time, it seemed so right. I guess I was looking for something more..." She drifted away for a moment, remembering. Her first sailfish. Diving in the warm Caribbean Sea. And the sex. That was the best part.

"How did Kevin find out?" Sharon's question brought her back to reality.

"I don't know. He said he could tell. Said I was different. Said I was cold."

"I'm sure you were."

"I hurt him, Sharon. I hate doing that. I hurt him badly. He said he would change. Promised to treat me better, but by then it was too late."

"So why did you stay with him?"

"I felt sorry for Kevin. He really didn't do anything wrong. Maybe it was me."

"So is it over for good this time?"

"Yeah."

"Good. He treated you like shit, anyway. And you're going to see the other guy again, aren't you?" Sharon asked, smiling.

"Who?"

"The boat captain guy!" Still smiling.

Kym could feel herself blushing. "I'll take the fifth."

"I'll bet you will, girlfriend. But listen to me," Sharon warned. "Be careful. He may seem like a great guy, but you hardly know him."

"I know," Kym said. "But this time I'm really going to find out what he's all about." She winked at her good friend. "Let me ask you one more thing." She turned to face Sharon and squeezing her breasts together, asked, "Do you think my tits are too small?"

"You know what they say, honey. More than a mouthful is a waste."

The Mansion in Vera Cruz
March 20, 1996 1815 Local Time

It was late afternoon and the sun had just dipped down behind the rear wall of the mansion. Carrillo sat alone at the round marble table alongside the swimming pool. Herrera had called from the airport and the cartel leader awaited his arrival with great anticipation. Dressed in a light brown button-down shirt with khaki slacks and his favorite blue blazer, Carrillo struggled to effect an air of power, of superiority. But even his snappy clothes couldn't hide the fact that he was a tired man. Dark, half-moon shaped bags hung beneath his eyes and his shoulders slumped with fatigue. The creases around the corners of his mouth and across his lower forehead now appeared more pronounced, changing from thin lines into deep rifts. His usually well styled, jet-black hair was unruly and streaked with gray, a fact that even he found impossible to believe.

The sound of a vehicle's engine was followed by the slamming of a car door. Carrillo rose from the ornamental white deck chair as Paco came around the corner, a carry-on travel bag slung over his shoulder. As usual, Paco was dressed to make a statement—snakeskin boots, black jeans and a maroon long-sleeved silk shirt. His shirt was half open to show off his myriad gold chains. Carrillo wondered what possessed his lieutenant to keep such a high profile and, feeling suddenly ancient, decided it must be Paco's age. He'd met plenty of traffickers who lived their lives in the same way but most of them were now in jail, or dead. He was concerned for Paco and felt almost a sense of fatherly love for the man. Together the two of them had come through some tough times and Carrillo had seized every opportunity to teach the young man something about their trade, particularly when it came to staying alive. Paco was a quick learner and had proven to Carrillo that he could take care of himself.

The two men embraced and kissed each other first on one cheek and then the other.

"Jesus, man, you look like shit." Paco held Carrillo by the shoulders and cocked his head to one side and looked into the cartel leaders weary eyes. "Are you all right?"

"I'm fine, Paco, fine," he lied. "I haven't been sleeping well. The dreams have returned." Carrillo had told Paco about the nightmares, but always left out the part where the identity of his family's murderer was revealed. "Tell me about the trip," he said, quickly changing the subject. "How are things going over there?"

"Everything has been going just as we expected, Amado. I've been poking around Cancun, and down the coast, too. That's where things are really happening."

"What have you found? Are there any major operations?"

"From what I can tell, no. I've seen most of the people you told me to, and they seem eager to help us. Most of the local players are small time. They're more concerned with moving small quantities into Cancun and making fast money. And when I mention your name, I can see the fear in their eyes. I am sure we'll have no problems setting up something big."

"What about moving the product to the states?" Carrillo asked. "We need to know where, how much..."

"I'm getting to that," Herrera told him. He held up his finger. "I've met a man."

"You've met a man," Carrillo echoed. Like it was something special.

"An American boat captain," Herrera explained. "A big boat. The kind they use to catch marlin. But fancy—more like a house. Expensive, too," he added. "Two million dollars."

"And?" Carrillo tapped his fingers on the table, waiting to hear more.

"He's interested in moving a large quantity. He'll be the middleman. He'll move it, we pay him."

"Cash or product?"

"Cash."

Carrillo was silent, but Herrera was used to it. He knew his boss was thinking. "If we can drop it in a certain area," Herrera continued, "he can pick it up. His boat has all the latest electronics. The GPS, he called it..."

"Yes, I know it well."

"He can pick up a load and hide it on his boat."

"How much are we talking about?" Carrillo asked, more interested by the moment.

"He said he could easily conceal between four and five hundred kilograms. He showed me the inside of the boat. I've seen the bilges. The front bilge is huge, and he said it's always dry. He could probably fit most of it in that space alone."

"Where he hides it is not important to me. Four or five hundred kilos is child's play. The Colombians are expecting me to move tons of product. If they're going to risk sending a plane over there, it better be worth their while."

"I understand that, boss. But my thinking was that first we could do a drop as a trial run. If it is successful, I'm sure this captain would be able to persuade some of his buddies to join in. Of course, I won't tell him that until the time comes."

"I don't know, Paco. We're lucky the Colombians have not sent a death squad to take us all out. While you were gone, our brothers in Juarez managed to get most of our coke back. Without killing a lot of people, I might add. It turned out that the local *Federales* had taken it, not the DEA. That's why there was nothing about it in the papers. Anyway, with a few threats made to the right people, we got it back, and it's being moved as we speak. It just goes to show, you don't have to kill people all the time. Remember that." He hoped Paco didn't interpret the decision as a sign of weakness. "Now I'm getting off the track. Where does this guy want to take it and what makes him so sure he won't be caught bringing it into the states?"

"He told me they clear out of a marina called Hacienda del Mar in Cancun sometime towards the end of May. Key West in Florida is only three hundred and fifty miles from there. He says it takes about sixteen hours. In five years, he's never been checked. They clear customs and immigration in Key West at a marina called Oceanside. It's not real busy and doesn't have many facilities, just fuel. When he gets there, he clears customs and immigration by telephone!"

"And you believe that?" Carrillo could not.

"He even showed me the sticker on his boat that allows him to do it that way."

"It only takes one time to get caught, Paco. That area around Key West is a zoo of law enforcement authorities, especially when it comes to drugs. Why do you think the Colombians gave up on that area?"

Paco could feel his plan falling apart, and he knew he'd have to do something to get Carrillo interested. "The captain told me that he could even arrange some sort of diversion, like a boat sinking, on the other side of Key West. He said he could pay off the guy at Oceanside and that he could clear early in the morning before it gets light."

"Now you said that this isn't even his own boat?" Carrillo's question was filled with skepticism.

"No. He drives it for some rich guy who lives in New Jersey. So the whole thing would have to happen when the owners weren't there."

Carrillo grasped his chin in deep thought. "Why would he want to do something like this?"

"He told me he's tired of working for someone else and this would be his chance to get enough money to buy his own boat."

"The plan sounds risky and complicated enough," Carrillo explained, "but let's not forget that you know nothing about this guy."

"He seems to me like he can be trusted," Paco said.

"Seems! Seems? You know better than that," Carrillo snapped. "Trust no one, Paco!"

And Paco knew he was right. Carlos, the waiter from the Papaya Republic, had assured him that Larsen could be trusted, but what did he know? He was nothing but a peon, a minor player and, more dangerously, a user. Carlos had seen Larsen every spring for three or four years, but that didn't mean shit. Paco had heard the stories about undercover operations where the Americans used informants and agents who had been in place for years. Could Larsen possibly be some kind of agent and the whole thing a set-up? Something in Herrera's mind screamed at him to consider that possibility.

And there was something else that bothered him. He saw the way Larsen looked at Teresa. No problem there. Teresa was an attractive woman. But it was the way that Teresa looked at Larsen that alarmed him. He'd warned her about that kind of behavior and didn't want to have to show his displeasure again...

"Paco!" Carrillo barked. Herrera hadn't even heard him talking.

"If we go through with this, you'll have to go wherever it is he's from and check him out."

"I can do that," Paco assured him. "Does that mean you might consider it?"

"I am considering it Paco, and let me tell you why. Remember that group of *pasadores* you put together, the poll runners, back in '94? That was your idea." *Pasadores* were smugglers who used vehicles with hidden compartments to move cocaine across the border throughout the Southwest. Paco had assembled a special group who simply drove their vehicles up to the checkpoint at the El Paso border and if motioned into the lane for a search, they mashed the accelerator and sped across into the U.S. Some were caught but, before the authorities broke up the ring, more than 250 poll runners moved almost ten tons of cocaine for Carrillo's organization.

"Yes, it was my idea, and I'm glad you have not forgotten it." Paco reached out and smacked Carrillo a few times on the shoulder. "I only want what's best for us and the organization. This can work and is only the beginning. It may be risky but that's the name of the game. I'm always looking for fresh ideas."

Carrillo sat back in his chair, and brought his hands up, rubbing his eyes and face. He exhaled loudly through his nose. "I know that, Paco. That's why you are my right arm. I will get in touch with our people in Colombia and see what they can do. In the meantime, find out how much money this guy wants and for God's sake, don't offer to pay him anything until he delivers the coke. Find some time to go to Florida and check him out. I know I'm a bit paranoid lately, but that doesn't mean they're not out to get us, right?"

Paco agreed and the two men sat in silence and watched as the setting sun behind them bathed the sky, first in orange, then in pink and within ten minutes it began to get dark. Paco rose from the table and getting up from his chair, stretched his body, trying to work out the kinks from the long flight from Cancun. "Don't worry, boss, everything will work out."

Carrillo did not answer. He was fast asleep.

8

Marina Puerto Aventuras
March 22, 1996

It was almost three o'clock and the rip was already crowded when the *Predator* cleared the cut. During the previous week, fishing boats from around the east coast of the U.S. and other states along the Gulf had descended upon Puerto Aventuras. The marina was nearing capacity and the fishing "season" was in full swing. Larsen and Kurt had spent the morning and the better part of the afternoon waiting at the dock for the arrival of Irv and Michele Mendel, the owners of the *Predator*. Kurt had been impatient and aggravated, but Larsen reminded him that the best bite had come in the afternoon and just before dark for the last week. When Irv and his wife had finally arrived, they were in a good mood. Larsen had seen them coming down the dock and had immediately started the generator and prepared to leave the slip. Irv was serious about his fishing, and he had no problems getting out on the water right away. That had been just fifteen minutes before and Irv was already on his second vodka and soda when Larsen looked down and spied Irv attempting to climb the ladder to the bridge—drink in hand.

Larsen grinned in amusement as his short, stocky boss slowly ascended the ladder, using only one hand and struggling to hold on as the boat rocked back and forth in the light chop. Half way up the ladder, his progress had all but stopped. Somewhere in his late fifties, Irv Mendel possessed all the agility of a blind man. His round, fleshy cheeks and large nose were flushed with effort when he finally realized there was a better way. Sticking the large, red plastic cup between his teeth, he laboriously made his way to the top of the ladder and took a spot next to Larsen, grabbing the railing at the rear of the bridge for balance.

"Whew!" he gasped. "Not in shape like I used to be." Larsen smiled at him, wondering if he ever was. "How ya doin' Danny my man? Good to see ya! I tell ya, I love it here. Too much stress at home. This is where it's at. This place is fuckin' beautiful." Irv spoke like a machine gun, the words coming out rapid-fire, yet intermittent, as he struggled to catch his breath.

"Yeah. Good to see you too buddy. How was the flight?"

"Piece a cake, my man. But let me tell ya, that fuckin' bitch is crazy." Larsen knew he was referring to his wife, but he also knew Irv was kidding. Irv and Michele were always giving each other a hard time, but it was just in fun. Married for thirty-five years, they were inseparable. "She's gonna drive me mad!" he continued, "I'm not shittin' ya. How much to throw her overboard?"

"Don't you worry about her, Irv. She's fine right where she is." Larsen had seen that Michele was in deep conversation with Kurt, sitting on the covering board of the gunwale, glass of wine in one hand, cigarette in the other.

"Yeah, fuck her," Irv said. "Chicks in the cockpit. Only men on the bridge." They both laughed.

To say that Irv Mendel was a piece of work was an understatement. The man simply did not operate on anything but full speed, and it was no surprise that his blood pressure was a little high. Like most of the owners of the monster fishing yachts, Irv was a self-made man. He'd been in the shoe business since he was young, and had just taken his company public to the tune of twenty million dollars. He oversaw almost every aspect of the operation, from the purchase of raw materials and the manufacture of the shoes in factories in Hong Kong and China, to the actual wholesale of the finished product in the U.S.. Larsen could understand if Irv found it a little difficult to calm down. As far as owners went, Larsen knew he had one of the best. Whatever the boat needed, it got, and for the most part, Irv stayed out of the way. Unlike some of the other owners, who knew just enough to be dangerous, Irv left the operation and maintenance of the *Predator* to Larsen and Kurt. All Irv asked was that the boat be in working order and immaculately clean whenever he and his wife and guests were in town, and Larsen knew that he was not asking too much. He and Kurt were well paid and the Mendels treated them both like family, rather than employees. So what if the man wants to run the washer, dryer and dishwasher with nothing in them. It was Irv's boat. He'd certainly heard worse stories about other owners.

"Where are we gonna start?" Irv asked. He'd set his drink down and was now slathering his body with sunblock; something made by Hawaiian Tropic called Ozone. The sun was high in the sky and although the hardtop above their heads provided a little shade, the reflection off the water could burn even the toughest skin. Larsen pointed out a few white spots on Irv's face where his boss had missed.

"I'm not sure yet." Larsen had the *Predator* pointed towards the South and he could easily see at least fifteen boats spread out through the next few miles, working back and forth across the edge. A few boats were working further offshore in the deep, and from their faster trolling speed, he guessed they were hunting for blue marlin. They cruised along at close to eight knots, staying far enough offshore so they wouldn't disrupt the trolling of the rest of the fleet. Off in the distance, Larsen could barely make out the outline of the *Tempest*, Terry Stanton's 58 Monterey. He reached inside the door of the bridge and grabbed the mike of the VHF radio.

"You on there, Terry?" he asked and released the button and waited for the response.

"Yeah, Dan. Go to the other one," Stanton replied. Larsen walked to the instrument console and switched the channel from 80 to 102. Most of the boats' radios only went as far as 88, but Larsen had learned from another captain a couple of years before that a specific button in the back of certain units could be pushed, and the unit would be set up to handle additional channels up to 110. Not everyone had that capability, but Larsen knew that he and Stanton, as well as Masters, had identical VHF units and they had all decided that 102 would be "the other one". He smiled as he envisioned all the other captains on the rip frantically searching for the secret channel.

"You there, man?" Stanton's voice was weak, but audible.

"Yeah, man," Larsen came back. "What are you doin' for 'em?"

"Right now we're four for about eight or nine. Catch a double header this morning, then got covered up about an hour ago and catch two out of that. Missed a couple more a few minutes ago. I wouldn't say it's been red hot, but it hasn't been too bad." Whenever the captains discussed the days catch, they always began with the number of sails. It always amazed Larsen that most captains liked to say "catch" rather than "caught" and to him it just made them sound ignorant about the proper use of the English language. He wondered if any of the other captains felt the same way. He was pleased to hear that Stanton had been "covered up", which meant that as many sailfish had come up behind the boat as they had lines in the water. Catching two out of the five or six fish that hit the baits at one time wasn't that bad. More than three sails hooked up at one time usually resulted in a Chinese fire drill and, during the pandemonium, it was usually inevitable that some got away.

"How's the water look where you are?" Larsen asked.

"This morning it was awesome. The pretty water was pushed way in, almost to the beach. There was a nice color change and I worked that for a while. That's when I had my first double."

"How deep was that bite?"

"Right on the edge, about 140, I think. Then, right before lunch, the dirty water moved in and we didn't catch anything for a while. I found a nice rip a couple of hours ago and that's where we got covered up. That bite was in about 200 feet." For many of the captains, the secret to having a good day in the last couple of years was to find the "clean" water, deep blue and clear. Apparently the sailfish found it easier to see the bait in the clear stuff, and most of the multiple hook-ups occurred there. But on some days, there was no clean water to be found and numerous fish were still caught. The debate between clean versus dirty water raged on.

"Where are you going to set out?" Stanton asked.

"Just down the road here a bit, Terry. I've got Irv and Michele here and they don't want to stay out too late."

"Oh yeah? Tell them I said hello. I'll see you when you get in. We're gonna pick it up here in a minute. Good Luck!"

"All right, man. Thanks for the check." He switched the radio back to 80.

Off in the distance, Larsen could see several white buildings—the houses and hotels that made up the small town of Akumal. Ten miles south of P.A., it seemed like a pretty good place to put out the lines. A blue and white helicopter flew by, heading south along the coast, no more than a hundred feet above the water.

"That guy is pretty low," Irv said.

"Yeah," Larsen said softly, lost in his thoughts. He wondered how far out on the horizon the chopper could see. Both he and Paco had agreed that any drop would most likely be made in the dark, but they hadn't decided where or when. "Probably looking for the evil Mexican drug smugglers," he said nonchalantly.

"I hope you guys aren't stupid enough to get involved with that shit." Irv looked his way and Larsen suddenly felt a little guilty. He made a mental note to check with Macki and make sure there was no way the *Predator* could be seized if anything went wrong with his plan.

"Don't worry, Irv. We're smarter than that."

Down in the pit, Kurt was listening impatiently as Michele Mendel ranted on about her terrible morning. Apparently Irv had been rushing her and they were already half way to Miami when she realized she didn't have the plane tickets and they were forced to return to their house in Boca Raton.

"He gave me shit all the way to Cancun," she whined. "We still got to the airport twenty minutes before the flight left."

"Twenty minutes?" Kurt tried to appear interested. "You're supposed to get there two hours before the flight leaves." He went to the tackle center just to the right of the salon door and pulled out a handful of vari-colored nylon skirts.

"Whatever! We're here, aren't we?" She took a sip of her wine and then a drag off her cigarette. Exhaling, she said, "That man is going to give himself a heart attack."

Kurt did not respond, but instead went over to his bait box, opened it, and slipped the skirts down the leaders of several pre-rigged ballyhoo. Nothing wrong with a little color, he thought, especially if the sails weren't eating aggressively, which he'd heard from one of the other mates. He closed the lid and hopped up on top of the engine room hatch, his short but strong legs dangling over the edge, nervously working back and forth. He wanted to fish so badly he could taste it.

Leaning back against the rear bulkhead, he smiled over at Michele, wondering what made the lady tick. Also in her fifties, Kurt could tell that Michele Mendel had once been a very attractive woman. With her straw-colored, kinky blond hair and huge chest, Michele exuded a sort of sensuality that many men found hard to resist. Certainly not shy, she was a master in the art of flirtation, and Kurt had often wondered whether there was something more to her casual touches and seemingly innocent smiles and kisses. In fact, Kurt and Larsen had even discussed her intentions and Larsen had convinced him that it was just the mother in her coming out. Her two sons were now grown and through Kurt and his captain, Michele could continue to live what she said were some of the happiest times of her life.

Feeling the boat slow down, Kurt sprang from his perch and immediately began getting the baits out. Within minutes he had six lines in the water: two long, two short, and two flat lines run off the stern. He leaned against the back of the rocket launcher and scanned the water behind the boat for signs of activity.

"Hey man, you want to turn on that watermaker?" Larsen shouted from above.

Kurt had no need to answer and opened the door to the salon.

"You need anything while I'm in there, Michele?" he asked. "Get ready, because it never fails. As soon as I go inside, we'll get a bite."

"No thanks, honey. I'm fine. If anything happens, I'll handle it."

"Sure you will," Kurt muttered under his breath as he disappeared inside the boat. Once in the pump room, situated alongside the crews quarters on the starboard side, Kurt pressed the button to turn on the Sea Recovery Systems watermaker. The system used the process of reverse osmosis as it forced raw seawater through a series of membranes and filters, all under intense pressure, removing not only all the salt but virtually everything, minerals included. Cranking the pressure dial up to 900 psi, Kurt watched as the float meter rose on the gallons per hour gauge, finally stopping at 40 gph. Satisfied that the system was functioning properly, he returned to the cockpit.

He checked the outriggers and saw that all the lines were still in place. Then he walked over to the port side and leaned over to make sure that the discharge valve for the watermaker was flowing properly. It was then that he saw them.

"Got some birds working up ahead, Dan," he shouted. He watched as several small black and white birds dipped towards the water, then circled around, then dipped again. He didn't have to look up to know that Larsen had seen them, and he was filled with a rush of adrenaline and anticipation as the large craft turned slightly offshore.

Two minutes later, a shout from above. "Here they come, Kurt. Dolphin! Gaffers—all of them." Kurt looked off the side and towards the baits and saw the onslaught approaching, tiny little wakes parting the water as the school of fish screamed towards the baits. 'Green hornets' he liked to call them—the Mexicans called them *dorado* and the Hawaiians knew them as *mahimahi*. Considered to be the fastest growing fish in the sea, Kurt knew that all they did was swim and eat. All four outrigger clips popped almost simultaneously, the corresponding rods suddenly bending severely as the fish dolphin sucked down the baits, hooking themselves. Kurt ran to one of the long lines as two more sped towards the flat lines, their pectoral fins stuck out like wings, electric blue with excitement.

"Get a belt on!" he screamed at Michele and he yelled for Irv to hurry up and join them. Irv made his way down the ladder as Larsen reeled in the teasers.

Putting the boat in neutral, he also came down into the pit and joined the others, picking up a rod. With six large fish dolphin on the lines and only four anglers, two of the rods remained in their holders. Kurt quickly worked his fish to the back of the boat and sticking his rod into an empty holder along the port side, he grabbed the gaff from under the gunwale. Grabbing the leader with his bare hands, he carefully pulled it alongside, skillfully stroking the green and yellow eating machine right through the head.

"Pretty work" Larsen said and used his free hand to open the fish box as Kurt stuffed the fish inside and deftly worked the large hook out of its head. "That guy will go thirty pounds easy," Larsen commented and held down the lid as the dolphin attempted to thrash his way out.

"I can't do it," Michele whined. "My arm is tired." Kurt looked at Larsen and rolled his eyes back in his head.

"That's our dinner out there! Shut up and reel, bitch." Irv's teasing caused them all to laugh.

During the course of the next fifteen minutes, Kurt managed to put Michele's, Irv's and Larsen's fish into the box. One of the other two fish was lost at the back of the boat and the sixth dolphin pulled the hook.

Larsen returned to the bridge and Kurt headed inside for a couple of ten-pound bags of ice as Irv and Michele caught their breath.

"All right, now we've got dinner. Let's go get some billfish."

Larsen knew that catching sails and marlin was Irv's favorite and his suggestion from the bridge was met with approval by his boss, who headed inside for yet another drink.

Kurt returned to the cockpit and proceeded to dump the ice on top of half-dead fish, whose colors were now fading rapidly. Closing the lid once more, he instantly got busy getting the lines back out and, being one of the best in his profession, he had a fresh spread of baits set out within five minutes. By now the sun was blazing and wrapping a moist chamois around his head and face, he attempted to protect himself from its scorching rays. The heat had proved too much for Michele and she had gone upstairs into the cool, air-conditioned flybridge. Irv came out with his new drink and headed up the ladder, cup in mouth, to join her.

Larsen had steered the *Predator* back towards shore and they now began the familiar pattern of zigzagging back and forth across the edge, working in—as shallow as eighty feet—and then back out as deep as eight hundred.

The sound of distant rotor blades drew Kurt's attention and he watched as the tiny speck down the coast flew closer and when it was even with the boat, he saw that it was the chopper with the familiar blue and white markings. Larsen had told him that the men in the chopper were like the Mexican DEA, and his thoughts immediately shifted to the plan Larsen and whoever it was he was working for had cooked up. He had a brief vision of the chopper circling the *Predator*, guns blazing as they attempted to pick up a load of cocaine from the water, but he quickly pushed the fantasy from his head. Kurt knew that Larsen would do everything he could to keep them out of danger and he had assured Kurt that as part of the CIA sanctioned plot, he would be free from prosecution if anything went wrong. Whether or not that was true, he did not know, but Larsen was not just his captain, he was his friend, and Kurt trusted him. But while Larsen could protect him from the long arm of the law, Kurt had second thoughts about their safety when it came to the smuggler who called himself Paco. He'd disliked the character right off the bat, his instincts telling him that the man was trouble. The smuggler's eyes reminded him of a snake, and when he'd pointed this out to Larsen, the captain had told him to try and put his prejudices aside.

Focusing on the baits, Kurt wondered when and if they would get a billfish strike. Catching marlin was his favorite and he had hooked and released more than any other mate on the dock. The other mates often came to Kurt for advice on the hook-up, especially when they had whiffed a few earlier in the day. Kurt knew that the secret was all in the length of the dropback. If the fish was hungry, they usually just piled on the bait, practically hooking themselves. But if he wasn't, which was often the case, you had to tease the fish up, making him want the bait. When he finally did grab it, you gave him a little bit of line, or dropback, allowing the fish to turn off and begin eating the bait before locking up the reel and hooking him. Aggressive "eaters" were given a short dropback and vice versa. With years of experience under his belt, Kurt had become a true master of the art.

A cry from the bridge nearly scared him half to death. "There he is! Left short!" Larsen had a much better angle and, as usual, he had spotted the fish first. "It's a white marlin," he added.

Kurt's heart instantly kicked into high gear. He grabbed the left short rod from its holder and was just putting the reel in free-spool when the line snapped out of the clip. Giving the fish almost no dropback, he lowered the rod, and locked up the reel as he waited for the line to come tight. He reared back on the rod, which bent slightly for a moment, then sprang back straight. "Shit!" he shouted in frustration, knowing he had missed the fish.

"Reel it back up!" Larsen yelled from the bridge. Irv and Michele had heard the commotion and were standing against the railing at the back of the bridge.

Kurt wound the bait back into the center of the spread, holding the rod high above his head to make what was left of the bait skip across the surface of the water.

"Here he comes again. He's on ya, Kurt! He's all lit up!" The excitement in the captain's voice was evident and Kurt knew it was all up to him. "Feed him this time," Larsen warned.

Kurt could hardly see the bait, but there was no mistaking the bill that rose above the surface of the water as the marlin pounced on the bait once more. This time, he left the reel in free-spool for several seconds, giving the fish a much longer dropback before locking up the reel and attempting to set the hook.

With incredible strength, the white marlin launched itself from the water, hooked solidly, and began a magnificent aerial display of jumps and tailwalking as it made its way along the starboard side of the boat in an arc that stretched nearly one hundred yards. Known as one of the most spectacular billfish to fight, the white marlin was a favorite of almost any serious saltwater angler.

Kurt nearly lost his balance as Larsen threw the boat into gear and headed forward in an attempt to circle around on the fish. "Jesus! Take it easy," he yelled and Larsen mumbled an apology from the bridge. Winding furiously, Kurt tried to keep the slack out of the line as the *Predator* closed on the spot where the fish had recently submerged. When the boat finally slowed, Irv awkwardly made his way down the ladder. Kurt slipped a belt on him and handed him the rod, just as the marlin took off again in the opposite direction, with a series of leaps known as "greyhounding". Kurt immediately cleared the other rods as Larsen wound in the teasers from the bridge.

The *Predator* took off in reverse as Larsen slammed her in gear and pushed the throttles forward, the twin diesels rumbling with torque, shaking the cockpit floor.

"You better reel, Irv," Kurt told his boss, noticing a little slack in the line.

"I am, my man, I am. Tell ya what, let's get my fuckin' wife down here and let her crank for a while! It's what she does best." Irv laughed at his own joke as Kurt slipped on his gloves, preparing to wire the fish. Within five minutes Kurt had pulled the exhausted marlin alongside.

"You see the rounded dorsal and pectoral fins, Irv?" He held the fish by its bill as Irv leaned over to see what he was talking about. "That's how you know it's a white. A blue marlin has pointy ones." He leaned over and cut the leader and the two men watched as the marlin lazily swam away.

By the time the sun had set, the *Predator* and its crew managed to release three more sails. As Kurt brought in the last of the rods, he couldn't help but think how the fishing they were doing was the same as the plan Larsen had for entrapping Paco and if possible, Carrillo. Tease them up and present them the bait, then drop it back a bit before locking up the reel and bringing in their catch. Kurt hoped that they were as successful in implementing Larsen's plan as they were on the water. But approaching the cut, Kurt couldn't help but think there was one big difference. Fish were stupid and easily fooled. Kurt had the gut feeling that Paco was not.

Up in the tuna tower, Larsen looked behind him and saw that he was first in a procession of four or five boats that were heading into the cut. Easing back the throttles as he passed the jetties, he watched as the *Predator* came off a plane, its curling wake spreading ever wider until it smashed against the rocks that lined each side of the narrow cut. Giggles from down near the rocks drew his attention and he looked down to see several young Mayan boys watching the huge vessel pass. From his perspective high in the tower, Larsen had an incredible view of the entire Park Avenue section of the dock. Nearly all the boats had turned on their quartz lights, their bright halogens shining on the tents below. The entire dock was busy with activity as the crews worked on the cleaning of the day's catch and hand trucks made their way up and down the dock in an effort to replenish what seemed like a never-ending supply of Dos Equis, Sol, and Corona beer. The owners and their guests hid beneath their tents, sipping cocktails, and chattering on about anything and everything as the local wash-boys attacked the sportfishers, errant spray from their hoses flying in all directions.

It was a scenario that was repeated nightly, and Larsen smiled as he made the turn towards his slip, idling slowly past the other multi-million-dollar machines, lined up side-by-side, rigger-to-rigger, like giant fiberglass and steel insects. With a great feeling of pride, he spun around, worked the controls from behind and carefully docked what was certainly one of the nicest boats in the marina.

Looking down from his perch, Larsen watched as Kurt made his way up the side towards the bow and tied off the line, which he had clipped onto the mooring buoy. Irv reached out and grabbed one of the stern lines from a dock-boy, but made no attempt to tie it off on the cleat, due to the fact that he had a drink in one hand.

"C'mon! Let's get her tied off down there," Larsen shouted and he breathed a sigh of relief as Kurt reappeared and secured the stern.

As Kurt went up the side to put on the starboard spring line, Larsen made his way down from the tower, disappeared into the flybridge and shut down the engines.

A small crowd of curious onlookers gathered behind the *Predator* as Kurt began tossing the stiff lifeless bodies of the fish dolphin onto the dock.

Making his way down to the pit, Larsen reached under the gunwale and unscrewed the large chrome cap for the shore power. He mashed the "out" button and squatted on his haunches, waiting impatiently as the thick yellow electrical cord slowly snaked its way out. From the corner of his eye he saw Terry Stanton coming his way.

"How'd ya end up?" Stanton asked, reaching for the end of the shore cord, which he shoved into the 50 amp outlet in the small electrical box mounted on the dock.

"Three for five on the sails and one white."

"Not bad, not bad. We went in right after I saw you. Randy caught twenty six."

"No shit," Larsen said, feigning disbelief. "They must be doing something right." The boys from North Carolina had shown up the previous week and had already been reporting incredible numbers of sailfish releases.

"He said they were fishing all the way down. Past Tulum." The ruins of the ancient Mayan city were another thirty miles south of Puerto Aventuras, perched right on a coastal cliff.

"That's too fuckin' far down for me," Larsen told the other captain. He could understand why the boats from North Carolina caught so many sails. They left early in the morning, just after dawn, and didn't return until dark. They traveled way down to the south and intercepted the northward-moving sails before the rest of the fleet. The crews also had a great deal of experience trolling for billfish, fishing out of marinas in Cape Hatteras and Oregon Inlet almost three hundred days a year.

Much to Larsen's dismay, the fishing season in Puerto Aventuras had become a numbers game—who caught the most, how many shots they had—and Larsen refused to play it. To him, the camaraderie and enjoyment of the fishing was more important. Quality, not quantity, was what he looked for and showing his boss and his guests a good time was his number one priority. But now, his secret life was threatening his usual behavior. He hadn't heard from Paco in at least a week and he wondered when the smuggler would contact him again.

Terry Stanton had been saying something to him and he hadn't heard a word he said.

"What's that?" Larsen asked.

"I said, we're going to have a big dock party tomorrow night.

"I'm going to cook up a shitload of chicken and ribs and fajitas and stuff like that. Maybe you can get Michele to make a big salad or something. Everybody's going to pitch in."

"Yeah, no problem, Terry..." Larsen said, but he had other things on his mind. He headed inside to switch over from the generator to shore power, wondering when he would again make the switch from captain to DEA agent.

9

Miami, Florida 25°43.62"N 80°23.42"W
March 22, 1996 1113 EDT

Paco Herrera stepped through the sliding glass doors at Miami International Airport and searched for the small shuttle bus that would take him to his rental car, somewhere outside the terminal. Within seconds the humidity had pasted his ridiculously expensive shirt to his upper body; he cursed the oppressive heat and rolled up the sleeves. He didn't have to wait long, as the National minivan approached from a short distance down the covered passageway. After hopping on, he shoved his small carry-on into the rack and passed the rental agreement to the driver. Within ten minutes, he was dropped right next to his mid-sized four-door, a burgundy Nissan Altima. After checking with the guard at the gate, he headed east towards Interstate 95.

Once on the highway, he tilted his seat back, found a rock-and-roll station on the stereo, and slid into the left-hand passing lane, ignoring the carpool lane restrictions as he headed for Palm Beach. A feeling of resentment grew within him as he whizzed by numerous BMWs, Jaguars and Porsches, their occupants chattering into cellular phones, indifferent to their surroundings as they sped towards their multi-million dollar homes.

Ever since he was a young boy, Paco could not comprehend how his own people could have so little and the Americans, just across the border, could have so much. Growing up near a small town in the state of

Durango, he discovered the importance of providing for his family when his father was killed in a drunken bar-room brawl. Paco was thirteen. His father had refused to join the ranks of his drug-smuggling brothers and, as a result, the family was forced to scrounge a meager existence from the small farm his father had toiled upon for as long as he could remember. His relatives had taken pity on the family and put Paco to work in the opium fields, where he first remembered seeing Amado Carrillo Fuentes. Every week, Paco would bring home to his family ten times as much money as the farm would produce. Through his relatives he gradually learned the drug smuggling trade. They told him stories of the rich Americans across the border and made him understand that, as long as they continued to buy the drugs, the Mexicans would continue to supply them and, finally, his people and his family would be much better off.

To Paco killing came naturally. When he was sixteen, he returned home one day to find his sister being raped by the local *Federale comandante*. Paco felt no remorse as he promptly blew the man's brains all over their tiny little kitchen. His uncles and peers within the organization treated him like a hero and, by his late teens, he was regaled as an experienced assassin, killing not only out of revenge but out of necessity. When it came to providing for and protecting his family, no one would stand in his way.

In his early twenties, the lure of bigger and better deals took him to Juarez and it was there that he took up with Carrillo. The cartel leader had remembered Paco as a boy, during his own rise to power. He had even heard of the young man's prowess as an assassin within the Herrera organization and, always on the lookout for decent bodyguards, Carrillo had taken the young assassin in. That had been almost seven years earlier.

Paco realized that almost an hour and a half had passed and he must be nearing his destination. Passing the exits for West Palm Beach, he finally spotted the sign for Blue Heron Boulevard. Getting off on the ramp, he headed east towards the beach and the Buccaneer Marina. The directions the woman on the phone had given him were perfect so far and he meant to thank her when he arrived. He crossed the huge bridge over the Intracoastal Waterway onto Singer Island and made his next right searching for the Buccaneer Marina, which he found less than a mile ahead.

The valet insisted on parking the car and Paco slipped the teenager five American dollars as he made his way towards the docks. When he got there he saw that only four or five of the twenty slips were filled and the dock itself was deserted. He remembered that Larsen had told him most of the boats went to the Bahamas or other points South for the spring. He noticed another marina next door and walked along the seawall to a black, wrought iron fence with a locked gate, spiked at the top. Looking around him, he saw no one watching and he skillfully mounted the gate, carefully swinging one leg and then the other across the top and onto the other side before hopping off to the ground.

The sign told him he was now in the Sailfish Marina and he continued walking along the seawall until he came to a small building, which, he discovered, was for charter reservations. He opened the door and ducked inside.

"Hi! Can I help you?" A young girl smiled up at him from behind the counter.

"Yes. I'm looking for the *Predator*."

"They're usually docked at the Buccaneer, next door. I'm pretty sure they're in Mexico right now."

"Yes, I went next door but there was no one around. I was hoping to speak to the captain. What's his name, again?" Paco stared towards the ceiling and snapped his fingers, as if trying to remember.

"Dan Larsen," she said.

"Yes, that's it. I was interested in chartering his boat. It's a 65 Hatteras, right?"

"Yeah, but I think it's private. I mean, I don't think they charter, but I'm not sure."

"Oh, that's too bad. Let me ask you. Are they docked in the marina there most of the year?"

"Let me think. I know they go to the Bahamas for a while in the summer, but besides there and Mexico, I think they spend the rest of the year here. Dan usually takes like a month off every summer to go windsurfing, too."

"A month off, yes? That must be nice. To have such a great job and take a vacation, also..." He made a mental note of it. His eyes focused on her nametag. "Ronnie. Such a beautiful name."

"Oh, I'm sorry. My name is Rhonda Greenberg. Ronnie for short.

"I'm in charge of the reservations for charter and the rooms here at the Sailfish."

"Nice to meet you. My name is Sergio Ruiz," Paco lied.

A slender woman entered the office. She was attractive in a way, and Paco's eyes swept her body in an instant. Her hair was a mess. The bags that hung beneath her eyes stole the beauty away from them. Something was bothering her, and she was having trouble hiding it. Their eyes met and her hands dropped to her apron, covering it in shame.

"Hi Sheila," Ronnie said, "This is Mister Ruiz. He was looking for Dan Larsen."

"Hello. I'm Sheila Stanton," the woman said, shaking Paco's hand. My husband and Dan are good friends. They're in the same marina down in Mexico. Maybe I can get a message to him for you."

"Oh, no, that's quite all right. I'll catch up with him when he gets back. Thanks for the offer." He turned back towards the counter. "And thank you for the information Ronnie." He turned to go. "Nice meeting you Sheila," he said with a wink as he went out the door and headed for his car back at the Buccaneer.

Walking towards the car, he was still not sure about Dan Larsen. During the rest of his trip back to Cancun, a tiny seed of suspicion planted in the corner of his mind continued to grow.

Marina Puerto Aventuras
March 23, 1996 2102 Local Time

It was a beautiful night and the dock party was in full swing. A soft breeze wafted in from the east, gently stirring the silk flags of the boats in the marina. The sky was an ocean of stars, floating on the waves of the heavens with the passage of time, their brilliance eclipsed by nothing but the full moon, which rose ever higher as it changed from a pale yellow to a bolder white.

A large crowd had gathered behind the *Tempest*, the partygoers swarming around the huge coolers packed to the brim with beer and ice. Three seperate barbecue grills cooked up a variety of fish, chicken and beef, the flames noisily searing the fillets, breasts and steaks, as a tantalizing aroma filled the evening air. The din of many different conversations was only slightly diminished by the thumping beat of the boats' powerful sound systems, competing for attention in a mixture of rock, country and reggae.

Dan Larsen stood under the *Tempest*'s tent and stuffed another banana and a handful of ice into the blender before pressing the "whip" button. The mixture of ice, fruit and Bacardi rum spun violently and he wondered for a moment if the glass container might crack. A minute later, the snap of the last chunks of ice subsided and, removing the lid, he began pouring another round of daiquiris. He'd spent the last fifteen minutes chatting with Terry Stanton about the past few days' fishing. Stanton, who seemed to have a never-ending supply of energy when it came to dock parties, was busy tending the grills and had suggested that some of the best fishing was yet to come. Down the dock, Kurt was engaged in a furious discussion over the merits of dead versus live bait.

"It's still not as good as it was three and four years ago," Larsen said.
"Yeah, I remember." Stanton flipped all the chicken breasts to their opposite side. "We used to get forty bites a day. Now we're lucky if we get ten or fifteen."

Larsen went over to the cooler and grabbed an ice-cold bottle of Dos Equis, popping the top off with a butane lighter. "Our luck is bound to change," he said, lifting the green bottle to his lips.
"Looks like yours just did. Look what's coming down the dock."
Larsen's heart felt as if it skipped a beat when he saw Teresa approaching. Her full lips parted in a smile as she spotted him and it took him a moment to realize she was alone.
"Well, look who's here," Larsen said, taking her hand and kissing her on both cheeks. "Where's Paco?"
"Who cares?" she replied. "I haven't seen him in almost a week. He told me he had business to take care of."

"You look great, as usual." Once again, her wild hair flowed freely, and she had added just a touch of mascara to highlight her eyes. She wore a faded blue cotton shirt, the long sleeves rolled up to her elbows and knotted in the front, just high enough to expose her firm stomach. A quick glance at her chest told Larsen that she was braless and when he looked down he saw a pair of jeans so tight, he wondered how she even got into them.

"Are you going to offer me a drink?" she asked with a devilish look and, after finding out what she wanted, Larsen went to mix her a rum and coke. He was stopped several times along the way, each time explaining who Teresa was, describing her as "just a friend". The other captains and mates stared at her with desire, jealous of their captain friend, and most of them telling him so.

When he returned Teresa was deep in conversation with Stanton who was carefully stacking the chicken breasts on a large metal tray.

"She wants to know if this is a special occasion or if everyone drinks this much all the time," Stanton told him.

"This is a special party but there's always a lot of drinking." For almost all the owners and their guests the fishing in Mexico was a vacation. They didn't have to wake up and go to work, so many of them drank nightly, often to excess. While Larsen and most of the other captains were careful in their consumption, it wasn't uncommon to see plenty of hung-over faces each morning.

A loud uproar drew their attention to a group of men stationed around a long plank which they had placed on top of the pylons behind one of the boats. Larsen could see that the men had a bottle of tequila, which they were pouring into a shot glass and mixing with just a splash of Sprite or Mountain Dew soda. After covering the top, they would bang the shot glass hard on the plank and proceed to down the resulting foamy mixture, known as a "slammer". When the tequila bottles were empty, they were hung from the leafless branches of a nearby tree, a testament to the evening's intoxication.

"Hey Larsen," one of the drunken men called and, before they headed off to eat, both Larsen and Teresa succumbed to the peer pressure and did three slammers each.

After they'd eaten, Larsen noticed that the drinking had resumed full strength. Seeing that Irv and Michele were totally absorbed in conversation underneath the *Predator*'s tent, Larsen went aboard and grabbed a bottle of white wine. Slyly concealing it from his owners as he stepped off the boat he returned to Teresa and, taking her soft hand in his own, they slipped quietly away from the party. Leading her through the darkness he headed for the beach, ignoring her pleas to admit where it was they were headed.

"You'll see," he told her, having learned from experience that all women loved a little mystery. "Watch the rocks." He gripped her hand tightly and she responded by putting her arm around his waist as he led her to the water's edge at the north part of the beach.

"It's beautiful," Teresa said. The surface of the water in the bay was nearly slick calm and the incredibly bright light of the full moon danced across it.

"It sure is." Larsen looked up at the moon and then pointed out their shadows in the sand, tall and thin, stretched like alien beings in the moonlight. Teresa laughed and began a series of wild gestures with her arms and legs, giggling like a young girl as her shadow mimicked her actions, the proportions of her arms and legs grossly distorted.

"Come on." She grabbed his hand once more and tried to pull him farther down the beach.

"Hold on a second." Reaching into his pocket, Larsen pulled out a Swiss Army knife and carefully flicked open the pig-tailed corkscrew. Using the sharp point at the end, he removed the foil before twisting the screw in to its hilt and removing the cork. "I'm sorry, I couldn't get any glasses."

"Who needs glasses?" Teresa reached for the bottle and took three or four gulps of the fruity, intoxicating liquid before passing the bottle. "Are you trying to get me drunk so that you can take advantage of me?" She came closer, her face mere inches from his own and, as she looked at him with those teasing green eyes, he fought off the urge to take her right then and there.

"Nope, I just want to find out a little bit more about you." They walked arm in arm down the beach, passing the bottle back and forth.

"What do you want to know?" she asked.

"Well, I don't want to ruin the moment, but what's up with you and Paco?"

"I was waiting for you to ask that. Paco and I have a strange relationship. When I met him a few years ago, I had just come to Cancun to look for work. I am originally from Mexico—Mexico City that is. Growing up, my family had very little. My father was a drunk and my mother died when I was quite young. I learned English in school, but when I finished, I could not afford to go to the university. My brothers and sisters—I have two of each—they needed my help. So I thought it best to take a job, but I had no qualifications. One of my friends suggested modeling. In Mexico City there is too much competition, so I came to Cancun. I was able to find some modeling work, but all the men who give this work, they want something in return, if you can understand. When I met Paco, he was different. He took me to nice restaurants and bought me nice things. He told me I didn't have to work: that he would take care of me. I did not see him all the time, I think he was living in Juarez."

When Larsen heard that, he stopped her. He had to play it very carefully now. "What do you think about what he does?"

"I know what he does. I don't really like it, but as Paco says, it doesn't concern me. Besides, what else can I do? I still have no qualifications."

"Where is he now?" Larsen asked. His heart began to beat with excitement. He was close. The conversation was more than he could ask for.

"I'm not sure. I haven't seen him in a week. He took his bag so I'm sure he flew somewhere. I think he was going to see about whatever the two of you have going. He doesn't often tell me where he's going. He just goes."

Larsen didn't want her to be suspicious, so he decided to back off with the questions about Paco's whereabouts. "Do you love him?"

"I'm not sure," she replied. "I thought I did, but now I'm not so sure. Paco is a very jealous man. Sometimes too jealous." She hesitated. "How can I say this...sometimes he is so jealous, he shows me how unhappy he is."

"He hits you?"

Teresa remained silent and Larsen studied her closely in the moonlight. Her silence had answered his question and he suddenly felt a deep need to protect her, this fragile creature who was slowly drawing him closer into something that would best be left alone. It was none of his business, he told himself. He had no time for other peoples' troubles. If there was some way he could help, he certainly would. But there was too much at stake to allow himself this kind of distraction. He passed her the wine and she drank once more. "I don't imagine he would be too happy if he knew you were here."

"No. But he doesn't know." Teresa set the bottle on the ground and moved towards him, her warm body sliding into his own, her head coming to rest on Larsen's chest. Wrapping her arms around him, she looked up into his eyes, a look that portrayed both desire and a plea for help. Larsen met her lips with his own. He could feel her breath becoming heavy, and a low moan escaped Teresa's lips. His hands gently caressed her breasts through the soft fabric of her shirt and his mouth wandered to her neck, which he began covering in short yet aggressive kisses. Teresa's hands slowly worked their way down his chest. In an attempt to control himself, he pulled away slightly.

"This is dangerous."

"Yes, but you are a dangerous man. I can see this in what you do." She moved to him again, her lips hungrily searching out his own.

"Hold on," Larsen cautioned her. "I want you to meet somebody." He pulled away from her grasp, grabbed the bottle of wine, then took her by the hand and led her south along the beach. Beneath the bright moonlight, the huge *palapa* of the Papaya Republic could easily be seen in the distance. They walked on.

Breaking the silence, Teresa suddenly spoke with a question of her own. "What about you, Dan? Are you married?"

"Nope. Never have been."

"Why not?"

"I guess I just haven't found the right girl." Larsen once had a girlfriend, but since joining the DEA, he had been single. Between the boat and his secret life, he was completely absorbed by his work, and found little time for a steady girl. Lonely sometimes, it was certainly easier not to have to explain where he sometimes disappeared to and what he did when he was gone.

"Nobody special?" Teresa asked.

"Well, there was a girl. Last year at about this time. It turned out that she was cheating on her boyfriend. He wasn't treating her very well and when she left me here, she went back to him. It's funny how women do that. The guy treats them like dirt, yet they keep going back for more. I just don't understand it."

"I'm not surprised she was attracted to you." She squeezed his hand tightly. "Where is she now?"

"I'm not sure. We sort of lost contact with each other." Larsen's memory of Kym was a painful one and he tried to put thoughts of her out of his mind.

They reached the sandy trail that led through the palms to the Papaya Republic. The lights were off and the restaurant was closed. He guided Teresa around the side of the porch and towards the monkeys' tiny *palapa*.

"Where are we going?" Teresa whispered.

"To meet my friends." Teresa watched as Larsen released her hand and carefully stepped over the thin rope that kept people from getting too close to the monkeys.

Suddenly the still of the night was shattered by the sounds of the monkeys' chattering, and a small figure swung down from its platform underneath the miniature *palapa*. Scampering across the ground, the monkey made its way to Larsen and climbed up his legs into his arms.

"Amazing. Even in the dark, they know you."

"Of course they do. I've known them for years. This is Pony. She's the youngest." Larsen stood still as the other two monkeys made their way to the ground. "That little one there is Nikki and the bigger one is Chango."

Teresa went to step over the rope.

"Be careful," he warned. "See the sign?"

Due to the moonlight Teresa was just able to read the small hand-painted sign which hung from a post underneath the *palapa*.

"*Los changos muerden*—the monkeys bite," she whispered.

"Yes, but they only seem to bite women. All three monkeys are females. Must be a jealousy thing." He carefully removed Pony's long, thin arms from around his neck and set her on the ground. Then, fishing in his pocket, he pulled out the Swiss army knife once more, and flipped open the largest blade.

"What are you doing?" Teresa cried.

"Something I've wanted to do for a long time." He reached for Pony's leash and sliced it in half. "I'm setting them free." He made his way over to the other two monkeys and cut their restraints as well. "Go! Run!" he urged and smiled with satisfaction as the three of them scurried off into the heavy underbrush.

When he turned, Teresa had her hand over her mouth, a look of astonishment on her face. He could hear her giggling as they tore back down the path to the beach, leaving the empty wine bottle behind.

Halfway back to the marina Teresa pulled up to catch her breath. Flushed from excitement as well as exertion, she gazed over at the man who had suddenly made her feel more alive than she had in a long time. The moonlight reflected off Larsen's white-gold hair and the strong features of his face were clearly visible in the night.

"I can't believe you did that," she told him.

"It's something that needed to be done for a long time. Tied to a short string is no way for an animal to live. Only someone who is an unfeeling monster himself would treat those poor monkeys that way." Larsen stripped off his shirt. A sheen of perspiration covered his entire upper body and was clearly visible in the soft moonlight.

"I'm very hot now," she said, removing her shirt as well.

"Yes, you are." Larsen took her in his arms and she knew she must have him this night and at that moment. As her mouth found his, a tremendous feeling of lust spread through her body. She felt his hands float down to her chest, gently massaging her breasts, his long thin fingers expertly pinching the nipples, now taut with excitement. With her own hands she undid her belt, prying the tight jeans off her hips and sliding them down her long legs to the ground. Their hungry mouths never parted as Larsen slipped his hands under the waistband of her black lace panties, gliding over the smooth round curves of her rear as they, too, fell to the sand. Breaking the kiss, Teresa squealed like a young girl as Larsen removed his shorts, and together they ran into the dark waters of the sea. Momentarily sinking beneath the surface, Teresa burst from the waist-deep water, flinging her head back, her long hair trailing a stream of water as it flipped past her face. Larsen emerged from the water next to her and again they fell into a long embrace. She could feel his hardness pressing against her.

How long it had been since she felt this way! For Teresa it felt like her first time all over again as Larsen's strong arms scooped her up, carried her to shore and lay her gently on top of her clothes. The excitement and

fear of being discovered fueled her passion. Feeling her legs gently parted, she closed her eyes as Larsen entered her and began to make love to
her in a way she knew she would never forget.

Playa del Carmen   20°37.32"N 87°04.75"W
Later that night

It was nearly four o'clock by the time the taxi dropped Teresa off at the
villa. The house was still dark, which meant that Paco had not yet returned
from wherever it was he had gone. After the incredible session on the
beach, Larsen had taken Teresa to his condo and there had continued their
lovemaking for what seemed like hours. Afterwards, Larsen had fallen
asleep and she had reluctantly slipped out. She knew it was not just the
wine that had made her so horny, but something about the man himself.

A warm feeling of contentment flowed through her body as she used
the key to get inside. She wondered when she would be able to see the
captain again and was already thinking of some way to sneak away from
Paco as she reached for the light on the small glass table in the living
room. The room was very dark and her eyes had not yet adjusted when a
voice from the corner startled her so severely, she could barely breathe.

"So, the whore has returned," the voice said with an evil edge, and
another lamp turned on and lit up the familiar yet frightening face of
Paco Herrera. Teresa immediately noticed the bloodshot eyes, the half-
empty bottle of tequila on the small table next to Paco's chair.

Teresa's heart felt as if it were about to explode out of her chest and
all her wonderful feelings changed to one of nausea as she made her way
across the room. "So, you're back," she stated, her voice cracking with
nerves.

"You're damn right I'm fuggin' back. Where the fugga' you been,
whore? It's four in the morning." The words were slurred and she could
smell the stench of stale alcohol on his breath. She wondered why he was
speaking to her in English.

"I was down in Puerto Aventuras." She decided that mixing the truth with the lies would be best. "I was bored and lonely, so I went down there. They were having a party on the dock. After, we went to the disco. It was fun, Paco. I didn't know when you were coming home. You never tell me anything!" She was pleading now, but inside she knew it wouldn't do any good.

"So you thought you'd go hang out with your new American friends," he said, mocking her. He got up from his chair and smacked her hard across the face, nearly knocking her down. In an instant he had her by the hair, yanking her head back. Teresa screamed and the smuggler struck her again. "You don't fool me, bitch. I see the way you look at him! Did you fuck him? Did you fuck your sweet little captain?" He was shaking her, banging her head against the wall. His eyes were wild like an animal. "Because if you did and I find out, I promise you, I will fucking kill him."

"It was only a party. We were all dancing..." And then she was crying, all thoughts of the earlier part of the evening erased from her mind as she stared at the madman, fearing for her life.

"Don't lie to me!" he screamed and threw her to the unforgiving tile floor. Teresa curled herself into a ball, sobbing uncontrollably as Paco pounced on top of her, straddling her and tearing her shirt open.

"Stop," she whimpered, but in his rage, Paco was deaf.

"You were lonely? I'll take care of that, you whoring bitch."

She could feel him tearing at the waistband of her jeans, and when she tried to push his hands away, he smashed her in the mouth. The warm, sweet taste of her own blood filled her mouth as she struggled to remain conscious. "I own you, bitch. You are mine..." She was fading out.

"Please, please," she begged as he began to enter her. Violate her. Her body shook and she cried silently, the tears streaming down her face as she attempted to shut down the terror. But it had just begun.

10

Playa del Carmen
March 26, 1996 2204 Local Time

Three days after Teresa had paid him the surprise visit, Larsen received a message from Carlos. Blue Parrot. Tomorrow. Ten. Nothing more.

Now, sitting on a swing and sipping an unusually cold Dos Equis, Larsen scanned the crowd. The place had already begun to fill up.

He had not heard from Teresa or Paco since the night of the dock party, but after hearing what she had said that night, Larsen was convinced that Paco was the key, the conduit that would lead the agent and his superiors to Carrillo. The anticipation of getting on with his plan was killing him and he noticed that his palms were sweating. The air was thick with humidity.

Not even the slightest breeze drifted in off the sea. Wondering if he looked out of place drinking alone, he'd just ordered another beer when a hand grabbed him on the shoulder. The sudden touch startled him and he spun rapidly, his heart pounding with adrenaline as he stared into the face of Paco Herrera.

Paco held up his hands in mock self-defense, a grin of confidence spreading across his face as he spoke. "Are we a little nervous tonight, Captain?"

"Jesus Christ, Paco. You shouldn't sneak up on people like that." He struggled to appear calm, smiling and slapping the smuggler on the shoulder—old friends greeting each other. "Nice message. I didn't know what to expect."

Paco slid in next to him and leaned on the bar. "A little suspense is good for the heart, no? How do you say it—keeps you on your toes?" The smuggler chuckled softly, a sinister laugh that made Larsen want to take him by the throat.

"So! Teresa tells me she had quite a time the other night." He looked Larsen straight in the eye and the agent returned the stare. "I think maybe she had too much of a good time," Paco added. Larsen sensed the smuggler was testing him and wondered if Teresa had told Paco something. Or maybe everything.

"What do you mean?" Larsen asked.

"I mean, the next day, she was so hung-over, she couldn't even get out of bed. You need to take it easy on my girl." Larsen decided to let that one slide by. "Anyway, I have good news and bad news," Paco told him. "First, the good. My business partners like your idea. They are prepared to move ahead with it. Maybe it can be the start of a long, prosperous relationship. For both my organization and yourself."

Paco signalled the bartender, a short chunky Mayan with the standard, wimpy mustache. He ordered a shot of tequila and the two men remained silent, scanning the crowd, which once again was predominately European. No one seemed to be paying much attention to them and Larsen understood how the obvious could be the best form of discretion. Clandestine meetings often took place in public, conversations and appearances simply blending in with those around them. The bartender returned with Paco's tequila, which the smuggler downed without salt or lime.

"The bad news," Paco continued, "is that we cannot pay you until our product is safe in the hands of our people on U.S. soil."

"That doesn't seem fair," Larsen bluffed. Whether or not he was paid in advance was immaterial to him, as all the money that changed hands would be seized as evidence. "How do I know you won't screw me once the stuff is in Key West?"

"Because I am a man of honor. I give you my word."

Larsen almost choked on his beer. Man of honor. Please.

"So how much?" Larsen asked him.

"How much what?"

"How much per pound? For me to move it."

"Two thousand dollars per kilo." Paco waited a moment for Larsen to do the math. "The first shipment will be five hundred kilos."

"What do you mean, first shipment?" Larsen tried to keep his voice low.

"If we are successful, perhaps we can do it again."

"I don't think so." And Larsen meant it. "Where do you want to make the drop?"

"Away from the marina. Somewhere between Akumal and Tulum. I don't have the exact coordinates yet. There's an air corridor that passes right through there."

"When are we going to do it?" Larsen asked.

"You tell me. Sometime next week. When it gets dark. Get a message to Carlos. It must say nothing but a day of the week. I will make sure we can set it up. Get back to you with the coordinates."

"I still need some money up front," Larsen insisted, just to make it look good.

"I'll ask again, but I can't guarantee it."

"Then I don't know, Paco. I'll have to think about it."

"There is no time to think!" Paco struggled to keep his voice down, the sense of urgency obvious. "Our contacts are prepared to deliver the product immediately."

Larsen looked around the bar and noticed two men across from them staring. Their eyes quickly looked away. They hadn't been there just moments before. Turning back towards Paco, he watched them out of the corner of his eye as they once again turned to stare.

"Don't look up," Larsen warned. "Two men—across from us. One tall and thin, the other much shorter. Both have mustaches. Street clothes. They're watching us. Order another tequila and look, but don't really look, you know what I mean?"

Larsen laughed loudly at nothing as Paco did as he was told. He pretended to count his money and spoke softly to Larsen as the two unknown men again looked away.

"Yes, I see them now."

"Recognize them?"

"No, but I have seen their type. Undercover narcotics officers. Mexico is filled with them. They may be checking the whole bar. There are a lot of drugs being bought and sold here."

"I think it's about time we left," Larsen said.

"Yes." He downed the shot of tequila and glanced over at the two men once more. "They certainly don't fit in."

"I don't think we should leave together."

"No," Paco said. "You leave first. Head down the beach towards the pier. I will wait a minute, then leave by the entrance and take the road. If they stop you, tell them you just met me. I'll meet you in half an hour at Senor Frog's next to the ferry. If you're not there, I'll contact you soon at the marina. Now go!"

Larsen stood up, drained his beer and shaking Paco's hand, headed off towards the beach into the darkness. He did not look back.

Once into the soft powdery sand of the beach Larsen removed his sandals and, carrying them in his hand, made his way towards the pier, shifting directions and hopping occasionally in an effort to thwart any pursuers who may have been following his tracks. Dim lights from some of the beachfront restaurants and small hotels created shadows across the beach and he nearly stumbled several times on couples sprawled in the sand. He moved to the water's edge and ran nearly two hundred yards. The small waves filled his footprints and washed away his tracks.

He stopped to catch his breath in the darkest stretch of beach, ducking behind the trunk of a giant coconut palm. He stood in the darkness for nearly five minutes and was convinced he had not been followed when the sounds of heavy breathing approached. Feeling the vibrations through the sand, he stood absolutely still as the short man from the bar ran by in the darkness, panting from exertion. Larsen's eyes had long ago adjusted to the dark, and he could easily see the pistol in his hand.

Larsen stepped out from behind the tree and continued down the beach in a series of short sprints, darting from palm to palm. Where the hell did he go?

He wasn't sure if he should keep heading for the pier or slip up a side street to Fifth Avenue, the shop-filled pedestrian walkway which ran parallel to the beach just one block up.

Suddenly, he felt more than heard someone coming up behind him and spun around just as the tall thin man from the bar appeared out of the darkness. His facial features were concealed in the night but his intent was perfectly clear. He swung his arm down from above the butt of a pistol aimed at Dan's head.

Larsen stepped aside as his own hand shot up, warding off the blow. He seized the man's arm, twisting it brutally in an unnatural direction. The distinct sound of tearing tendons and popping cartilage could easily be heard. Then a scream and the two men fell to the sand.

The man pounced on top of Larsen, clawing at his face with his uninjured arm, kicking wildly as he desperately searched for his pistol, which lay in the sand a few feet away. Spotting it, the man began scampering across the sand, his good arm outstretched, the other dragging loosely alongside his body, no longer connected securely to his shoulder.

Before Larsen could reach him, his opponent grabbed the pistol, a large automatic. Spinning to his right, Larsen had just seen the flash when the shot assaulted his ears. Pain tore through his side as the high velocity projectile ripped through his left shoulder. Before the man could fire again, Larsen flung sand into his eyes and a second shot shattered the tranquil beach. This one went wild.

Nothing mattered to the agent now, nothing but the need to preserve his life and Larsen was instantly on top of the man. Knocking the gun away once more, he began beating the man savagely in the face. The fire in his arm burned and spread as he delivered blow after blow, the warm sticky blood spraying in the darkness, the sound of flesh colliding with flesh, the feel of teeth cutting his knuckles as they were bashed from their roots by the force of his blows. Larsen was pure animal now, a man possessed and with no control over his actions. Later he would be unable to remember much of the beating. As he reared back to finish off his assailant, a flash of bright white light filled his head. Recovering slightly from the blow, Larsen squinted in the darkness and was able to make out the silhouette of the shorter man who had originally pursued him down the beach. A second blow nearly knocked him unconscious as the short one hit him again with a blunt, waterlogged piece of wood.

"Kill him!" the thin man hissed from the darkness where he lay in the sand.

"No. We must first find out who this *gringo* is and what he is doing here. He will tell us what we need to know. Then we will kill him." The short man grabbed Larsen by the hair and jerked the agent's head upright. "Isn't that right, *gringo*?

"When we are through with you, you will wish you had never come here. Then you will die like the dog you are." He spit the words out and Larsen barely heard them as he struggled to maintain consciousness. Kneeling in the sand, he gazed up at his attackers through blurred eyes, his mouth dry and filled with sand, his tongue thick. He could smell the men, their perspiration foul and ammonia-like, their heavy breathing competed with his own. In his delirium, he watched as the thin man slowly got to his feet and, retrieving his gun, staggered over to him. He slapped the short man's hand away from Larsen's hair and placed the cold, steel barrel of the automatic pistol against the agent's forehead.

"Who are you?" he demanded. "Have you anything to say before your miserable life on this earth comes to an end?" Although the man's Spanish was quite rapid, Larsen understood the gist of what he had said but preferred to keep it a secret.

"Fuck you," he managed. As he had expected, his interrogator pistol-whipped him in the face and the brief flash of light slowly faded as he slipped into the dark void of unconsciousness.

Paco was almost halfway to Senor Frog's when he saw the skinnier of the two men who had been watching them at the bar. As he had expected, one man had followed him and the other had taken off down the beach after Larsen. Were they definitely narcotics agents? Why hadn't they simply picked him up right then? Did they even know who he was?

All sorts of questions floated through the smuggler's mind as he watched the man from inside the dimly lit cafe on Fifth Avenue. Trying unsuccessfully to blend in with the other tourists, it was painfully obvious that this man was searching for someone, his eyes darting left and right down the crowded cobblestone walkway. Suddenly the man made a hard left and disappeared down one of the short side streets that led to the beach.

Paco emerged from the café and made his way down the same deserted street, moving through the shadows with the stealth of a cat, stopping occasionally and all the time searching for and pursuing the man who hunted for Paco himself. Nearly five minutes had gone by when he heard the shot from the beach and, running through the alley behind a beachfront hotel, he made his way to the seawall, where he crouched and remained concealed in the shadow of the three-story building. His heart beat heavily and he was filled with indecision as his ears strained the night for a telltale sign of activity along the water, any indication of Larsen's or their pursuers' whereabouts.

A second shot exploded in the dark just below his position and Paco scampered on all fours behind the waist-high seawall until he could hear the sounds of a struggle emanating from the sand just beyond. Still under cover of darkness, he peered over the wall and could barely make out the silhouettes of two figures in the sand, less than twenty meters away. He recognized Larsen, crouched on top of the same man who had been chasing him along Fifth Avenue just a few minutes before. He smiled with satisfaction as he watched the captain relentlessly pounding his adversary. The sounds of the beating excited him, the violence intoxicating as the adrenaline coursed through his veins, wishing it was he delivering the punishment and pain.

Just as Paco was about to hop over the wall and join the captain, the short man from the bar appeared out of the darkness and smacked Larsen on the head with what appeared to be a piece of timber that must have washed up on the beach. Paco winced as if he himself had felt the blow and wondered if he should attempt to help the American who was obviously dazed and out of it. All his earlier excitement had turned to a feeling of contempt for the two unknown men as Larsen was again struck in the head. How easy it would be to surprise and finish them! He cursed himself for being unarmed. In horror, Paco watched as the thin man retrieved his weapon. His face was a bloody mess, covered with sand that also stuck to his bloodstained shirt. He approached Larsen with wild eyes and placed the barrel of what Paco could see was a huge automatic against the captain's forehead. Paco refused to watch what he was sure would be Larsen's execution and focused on the faces of the two Mexicans, burning them into his memory.

But instead of killing Larsen, the thin one struck the captain in the face with the butt of the gun, knocking him out and he collapsed in the sand. Paco stayed absolutely motionless as the two men dragged Larsen by his arms, down the beach until all three of them disappeared into the darkness.

Paco had seen enough. It was time to get the hell out of there. Melting into the shadows, he went back towards Fifth Avenue and the main road.

It was like waking up in a strange bed and not knowing whose place you were in. Except there was no bed, just a cold stone floor. Larsen slowly opened his swollen eyes and was instantly greeted by an excruciating pain that pounded through his head. He lay motionless, his face pressed against the wet floor, the smell of urine and feces wafting across the floor and into his nostrils. His stomach convulsed and he retched, the pounding in his head increasing with each heave, nothing but bile rising in his throat to mix with the taste of stale blood that filled his parched mouth.

He rose to a sitting position, his back against the bare concrete walls of what was obviously a holding cell. Fingering the deep blood encrusted gash above his left eye, he stuck his finger in his mouth and probed the inside. All of his teeth were still there. His shoulder ached and remembering the shot, he peeled back his shirt and examined what turned out to be a deep flesh wound that had not penetrated the muscle or bone. The bleeding had stopped.

Glancing around the eight by ten foot cell, he saw he was sharing it with four other men, most of whom appeared to be drunks, their shirts stained with dirt and vomit. Paco was nowhere to be seen. He had the sudden urge to relieve himself and spotted an old iron bucket, the flaking white paint spattered with dried puke and shit. His stomach rolled once more and he staggered to the corner of the cell and urinated on the floor, the smell of which told him was common practice. All of the men were either sleeping or in such a state of complete inebriation that none seemed to notice or give a damn.

What had happened? The previous night was still a blur, but bit by bit he began putting the pieces together as he slumped back to the floor, his back dragging down the slimy bare wall. He remembered the beginning of the confrontation with the thin man on the beach, but he had never made it to Senor Frog's. What the hell had happened to Paco? And where was he now? He had to get out of here, had to get back to the marina. What would he say had happened?

Getting to his feet once more, he made his way over to the heavy iron door and peered through the bars. There was no one in sight.

"Hey!" he tried to yell but instead it came out as a hoarse, raspy sound. He was desperate for a drink, anything to wet his parched lips and throat. Swallowing, he tried again, a bit louder this time. The sound of a metal chair sliding back came from around the corner down the hall. A heavy-set Mexican, in a faded blue uniform, finally appeared. His hair was clipped short in a military cut and he wore a battered black nightstick slipped through a loop in the belt which strained to contain the guard's thick flabby belly. He approached the cell and stared at Larsen with lifeless, uncaring eyes.

"Please. I need some water," Larsen told him. The guard returned a stare of total incomprehension. "*Agua. Por favor,*"

Larsen repeated in Spanish this time and the guard said nothing and walked away. "*Por favor!*" he gasped again as the guard rounded the corner.

Larsen could hear a muted conversation taking place around the corner and he remained standing, his hands grasping the cool steel bars that fronted the small cubicle.

A few minutes later, the guard returned and opened the cell door, remaining silent as he led Larsen down the dimly lit hallway and into another larger room. The walls were also bare, covered with a pale green paint, peeling in several places. A lone fluorescent bulb hung from the ceiling above a plain metal fold-up table, flickering occasionally and casting a dim white light across the empty room. The guard motioned him to sit on one of the four metal chairs and left the room closing the heavy steel door behind him.

The waiting had begun. Larsen knew all about the Mexicans' little psychological games, wait for this and wait for that, and then the payoff for whatever it was you really wanted, which in Larsen's case was his freedom. It didn't surprise him that Mexico's economy was completely fucked up, wasting time with mountains of unnecessary paperwork to achieve anything. Anything could be had immediately if the payoff or bribe was big enough and he knew damned well that the judicial system worked the same way. His mind began working wondering where and how he could get the funds to bail him out of this mess. Had the whole operation been jeopardized? He would definitely need to contact Macki. Perhaps he could deliver the necessary funds through a diplomatic channel if necessary and his cover would remain intact as the entire operation continued as planned. His mind had begun to clear and function as it should. He would continue to deny everything and plead innocence or ignorance as the situation warranted.

Ten minutes later the door swung open and Larsen turned to face the short man from the Blue Parrot. He was dressed in a black t-shirt with black pants and he wore a sidearm on his left hip, which looked to Larsen like a standard issue Colt 45. The short man's body looked solid, his biceps straining against the material of the short sleeves and his barrel chest appeared thick with muscle. He set a small pitcher of water and a solitary dirty glass on the table in front of Larsen.

The agent didn't like the appearance of the cloudy water but, dying of thirst, he poured a glass, rinsed his mouth and spit it out on the floor.

The Mexican scowled at him for several moments, then finally spoke. "*Habla espanol?*"

"No," Larsen replied. "*Solo un poco*. Only a little."

"Then English it will be," His words were crisp and precise. "Your name." A demand, not a question.

"My name is Dan Larsen. I am an American citizen who is being unlawfully detained. I demand to see an American lawyer."

His interrogator laughed. "An American lawyer will serve you no purpose here. This is my country. You dared commit a crime under our laws and will be punished likewise."

Larsen knew damn well that American lawyers had no jurisdiction in Mexico. "I have committed no crime."

"You assaulted an officer of the *Federales Judiciale Policia Antidroga.*"

The name did not ring a bell with him but Larsen realized the men were with some type of anti-narcotics outfit. "I was acting in self defense. I was walking down the beach when a man—who I assume is your friend—snuck up behind me and tried to hit me with his gun. I fought back and then he shot me! I was trying to save my life when I guess it was you who came up and knocked me out. Am I to assume that you are also an officer of whatever it was you said?" He was doing a good job at looking innocent, but he wasn't sure if it was working.

"I am the local *comandante* of the FJPA here in Playa. Right now you are in the town jail. The other man, one of my best officers, says that he only wanted to question you when you began to beat him."

"That's bullshit!"

"He is now in the hospital. He says you were trying to kill him. From the looks of him, I think you almost did. He wanted to kill you, you know. You are lucky I didn't let him. But I have many questions for you, Mr. Larsen."

"What kind of questions?"

"What are you doing here in Mexico?"

"I'm captain of a sportfishing vessel in Puerto Aventuras. We come here every year at this time for two or three months." He explained to the man a little bit about the sportfishing lifestyle, but it wasn't long before the *comandante* cut him off.

"What business do you have with the man you were with last night?"

Larsen had to play this one carefully. "I have no business with Paco. I just met him last week. We went diving once and I haven't seen him since. When I went to the bar last night, he happened to be there. We were having a few drinks and I told him I was heading down to Senor Frog's. Thanks to you two, I never made it. He's probably wondering what happened to me last night."

"As we are wondering what happened to him. Perhaps you can tell us." The *comandante* stared at Larsen.

"I don't know what happened to him. He said he had to speak with someone and then he would meet me at Senor Frog's. That's all. When I said good-bye to him at the Parrot, that was the last I saw of him."

"Let me tell you something about this man. We have had our eyes on him for two weeks now. His name is Paco Herrera Tejeda." He watched Larsen closely for signs of a reaction as he spoke. "He is a drug smuggler of the highest sort. He has strong ties to many cartels along the western border of Mexico and the Southwest border of the U.S., most recently the Juarez cartel which operates along the border with El Paso, Texas."

Larsen's heart nearly burst from his chest upon hearing the revelation. Paco was connected to the Juarez cartel and most likely still connected to Carrillo! The *comandante* continued. "He is considered one of the most dangerous and feared assassins in all of Mexico. He makes deals for the cartels with bullets or money; *plomo o plata* is how we say it. Our men have been tracking him since he first passed through the airport in Cancun nearly a month ago. We cannot let the cartels move into our area. There is already a big drug problem here. Corruption is on the rise and we are trying to stop it before it explodes in our face. Can you blame us for being suspicious?"

Larsen's situation seemed to be improving by the minute. He had to be careful what he said so he wouldn't screw it up.

"No, I don't blame you," Larsen began. "But how was I to know who this man is? Like I told you, I have only met him a couple of times and we went diving once. He seemed like a nice guy."

"The devil wears many faces, Mr. Larsen."

"If he's such a bad guy, why don't you just arrest him?"

"It is not that easy. Arresting this man usually turns out to be deadly. The retaliations and executions that follow a cartel arrest are a strong deterrent. Others have tried and have paid with their lives. We have wives, families..."

"Well what am I supposed to do? What if he contacts me again?

"And what if he wants to know what happened to me last night and asks about my arm or my eye?" Larsen pointed out his wounds.

"Tell him you were robbed and beaten. There are many *bandidos* around here. I'm sure he'll believe it. Paco Herrera is an extremely dangerous man. I suggest you avoid him in the future. Stick to your fishing and return to the United States. For now I will release you. There is a clinic down the street, one block in from the main road. I will let them know you are coming and they will tend to your wounds." The *comandante* got up and prepared to leave.

"What should I do if Paco doesn't believe my story?" Larsen asked, continuing to profess his innocence.

"Don't worry Mister Larsen. We will be watching Paco Herrera.

"He will turn up very soon. You see, we know his type. He is a perfect example of the most despicable breed of *traficante*. Very high profile. He loves to be seen, flaunting his cash, power and women. In the end, that will be his downfall."

"So you'll know it if he contacts me because you'll be watching him," the agent said, pretending now to be afraid of Paco.

"Yes, we will, Mr. Larsen." The *comandante* stopped at the door, turned back and stared intensely into Larsen's swollen, bloodshot eyes. "Because we will also be watching you."

11

CIA Headquarters
March 27, 1996 1155 EDT

Deep beneath the ground in a part of the sub-cellar communications complex of the CIA, two men wearing headphones sat hunched over their desks. The walls were white and bare, except for one side that was completely filled with electronic equipment. The temperature was slightly cool creating the need for long-sleeved shirts. The two were not only multi-lingual specialists in international radio traffic, but were also experienced cryptographers and, for days, had been monitoring the region of the Northwest Caribbean. The men were part of a group of six which worked around the clock, four hours on and eight off. It was nearly noon and close to the end of their tour.

The younger of the two, who appeared to be in his mid-thirties, reared back on his swivel chair and caught the attention of his colleague, a gray-haired man who seemed bored to tears.

"Might have something here," he said.

"Origin?" the older man asked

"Yucatan Peninsula. No, closer to Cozumel. Transmitting on alpha band 1251. Nothing very complex. Barely coded."

"Better notify the Big Mac."

The man who had intercepted the transmission went to the small black intercom located on a desk in the corner of the room.

Within a minute John Macki, Director of the ONII stormed into the room. The specialist pointed to a headset with a microphone and began pushing buttons and turning dials.

"I need this scrambled both ways; transmitting and receiving," Macki told him.

"Say no more." The specialist punched another button. He smiled at Macki, who was obviously excited. "Done deal."

The two specialists went back to their headphones and there was no need for Macki to seek privacy.

"That you Danny? Talk to me boy!"

"Just checkin' in chief. Everything's going *muy bueno* down here."

Macki smiled at the sound of Larsen's voice. The signal was amazingly clear. "Well, we haven't heard from you in a while. I was getting nervous. What's the latest? I've got all kinds of people breathing down my neck."

"It's definitely our boy," Larsen replied. "Paco, I mean. Definitely tied in with Carrillo, I'm sure of it now." He explained to Macki what he had learned from Teresa and recounted the episode on the beach in Playa and the following morning at the jail.

"You're probably right," Macki told him. "We fired Herrera's name into the computer. He's a known assassin within the Juarez cartel, but we have no intel on him calling the shots for any major deals. Could be he's been promoted. But listen to me, Dan. If you get thrown in jail, man, there's no way I can get you out. That would blow the whole operation. If the wrong people get wind of what's going on, we're in big trouble, my friend."

"Isn't there any way you can call off these FJPA guys?" Larsen asked.

"Same answer, Dan. Negative. This whole operation was begun black and has to remain black. The key here lies in secrecy. There's only a handful back here who know anything, and, believe me, they're as high up as the clouds. We pull this one off and it'll change the parameters within which we can operate forever."

"Well can you send me a little help? Maybe one guy? We can keep an eye on Paco and probably get an idea where Carrillo is. This girl Teresa—his girlfriend—she's not sure where Paco goes when he's not here, but she's pretty sure he's flying somewhere."

"Yeah, sure," Macki told him. "We're still not getting much intelligence on this end. It's like Carrillo has just vanished. The Administrator himself has offered me any help we might need. I'll get a guy down to you. That's a good idea."

"So for now you want me to continue with everything as planned?"

"You mean go ahead with the drop? Yeah." Macki told him. "It'll buy us a little time to find out where Carrillo is hiding and then we'll wrap this whole thing up."

"It looks like they're ready to make the drop some time next week. You want me to let you know when so you can get a bird up there to take some pictures?" Larsen was always thinking and that was one of the reasons Macki enjoyed working with him.

"No, that won't be necessary, Dan. All we need to do is find out where Carrillo is and we'll take it from there. Let's not forget who the big fish is."

"Well, what about Paco?" Larsen asked, clearly alarmed.

"Don't worry, Dan. We'll nail him too. Contact me again when your help arrives. I'll send him ASAP."

"One more thing, Admiral. When you send the guy, make sure he's wearing a Guy Harvey t-shirt."

"You got it."

Macki took off the headset and leaned back in the swivel chair.

They were getting close now, he could feel it. But the closer they got, the more dangerous it would become for Larsen. He didn't like the idea of putting the agent in harm's way, but it was part of the job. The Director of the Agency had been leaning on him for results and now he would have something to give him. From the way the Director had been acting, he was sure he was taking his own heat from the President himself.

Getting out of the chair, he waved to and thanked the two specialists. They nodded but did not remove their headphones. He wanted to tell them they could relax for a while, but decided against it. As he left the room, he could only think of one thing. What in hell was a Guy Harvey t-shirt?

Marina Puerto Aventuras
That Same Day 1605 Local Time

Larsen was getting damn tired of people asking him what had happened to his eye, and he was glad they couldn't even see the bandage where the bullet had dug a path through his left shoulder. Most of them seemed startled at the possibility of being mugged in Playa, and so far, the lie had been working well.

Most of the fleet was out on the rip and Larsen had spent the better part of the day trying to figure out where he could stash 500 kilos of cocaine. Macki had given him the green light to go ahead with the drop and now the important thing was to find Paco. He had just decided to go to the Papaya Republic and see if Carlos knew anything when he looked out the salon window and saw Matt Kirchner—the mate from the *Slammer*—wandering down the dock. Larsen was just putting on his sandals when Kirchner leapt into the *Predator*'s cockpit and came inside the boat. The mate removed his sunglasses and Larsen saw that he had already acquired the "racoon look", the skin beneath the glasses a white mask which stretched from ear to ear due to its lack of sun. He wore a *Predator* t-shirt that Larsen had given him and he saw that Kirchner had whacked the sleeves off.

"You seen my captain, man? Holy shit! What happened to your eye?"

Larsen wasn't sure which of the mate's questions to answer, so he went with the standard story about the eye first; Kirchner seemed to buy it, and he stopped for a moment to think if he had seen his good friend Rob Masters. "Nope, but I've been inside the boat all day," he told Kirchner. "Why? Is he lost?"

"I don't know. He talked to the boss this morning, and when he came back, he looked really upset. Not his regular happy self at all."

"When was the last time you saw him?" Larsen asked.

"At about two o'clock. I asked him where he was going and all he said was 'to the bar'. I thought he was only kidding." The mate's voice sounded nervous and Larsen wondered if there was really a cause for concern.

"I'll tell you what, Matt. I'm headed towards the Papaya to talk to a guy anyway, so if I see him, I'll tell him you're worried."

"No, don't do that. Just check and see if he's all right. He was really depressed."

"Will do." They went back outside. Kirchner headed back towards the *Slammer* at the end of Park Avenue while Larsen crossed the dock and took the path which led between the condos and out to the beach.

Due to the fact that he needed to speak to Carlos, Larsen actually hoped that Masters would not be at the restaurant. But that was not the only reason. He knew that the Papaya was one of his friend's favorite places, and if he had actually gone to get wasted, he was sure that was where it would be. Near the booze. And the coke. And that scared Larsen.

Several minutes later he had reached the small pathway at the south end of the beach and as he headed between the palms towards the giant *palapa*, his fear was confirmed. There, at the table closest to the beach, Rob Masters sat drinking a *caipirina*. The restaurant's famous house drink, it was a blend of rums, limes, and sugar—served in a goblet the size of a fish bowl. One was enough to make most people feel pretty good and more than three could be dangerous. From the looks of him, Larsen knew that he must have had five or six already. He looked at his watch. Four-thirty. The big man had probably been drinking for almost two and one half hours.

Larsen approached the table. Masters looked up and with what appeared to be great effort, he spoke.

"*Hola, amigo. Como esta usted?*" Masters said, his words slurred.

Larsen felt pity for his friend. He almost never used Spanish; perhaps the few words were all he knew.

"What are you doing?" Larsen felt like he was admonishing a small child.

"Gettin' fucked up! What's it look like I'm doing?" He took another sip of his drink and looked up at Larsen with eyes that floated freely in his head, without focus.

"Why?" Larsen demanded.

"Harold sold the fuckin' boat," Masters said.

"No way." Larsen was shocked.

"Right out from under me. The new owners are takin' over right after we get back to Palm Beach." He looked as if he was about to cry, and

Larsen knew why. It was every captain's nightmare. Just when you felt you had a secure job, the owners would sell the boat and you'd most likely be out on your ass. He'd often worried about it himself and he wasn't sure what to say.

"What about the new owners?"

"They've already got their own captain."

"Shit." Larsen had met Harold Emery, the owner of the *Slammer*, and had immediately disliked him. He'd come across his kind before. As president of a huge corporation that imported automobiles into the U.S., Harold Emery had plenty of money. He was a loud, obnoxious asshole who was only concerned with his own good time and not the welfare of his crew.

"I've driven that fuckin' boat for seven years. Across the fuckin' world!" Masters pounded his huge fist on the table.

"Take it easy, man. You're causing a scene."

"But what am I gonna do?" Masters whined.

"Don't sweat it, Rob. You're a good captain. You'll get another boat..."

"Yeah, but it won't be the *Slammer*."

Larsen knew it was true. The *Slammer* was one of the most famous sportfishers in the world. The 61 Buddy Davis was the original, a prototype so praised that it was used as the blank for the mold that would produce several others with the exact same hull. The *Slammer* had fished the waters of the entire East Coast of the U.S., the Bahamas and all the way down the chain of islands to Saint Thomas, Puerto Rico and Venezuela. Several world records had been caught aboard the boat and it had a fifteen-thousand-dollar audio-visual system that had documented all of them. Marlin. Tuna. Wahoo. The *Slammer* raised the fish, no doubt about it.

The two men sat in silence as they gazed out towards the rip. It was a typical Caribbean day, a strong yet balmy breeze coming in from the Southeast, the turquoise water choppy but not rough. A handful of sportfishers trolled the edge out in front of the resort; a cloud of black smoke erupted behind one of them as the vessel slowly began moving in reverse, backing down on a fish.

"You see that?" Masters' words snapped the men out of their reverie. "That's what it's all about. Fishing is my life man. There's somethin' about teasing up that monster of the deep, making him think he can have what you've got, you know?" His eyes lost focus and Larsen knew he was far away somewhere, watching a fish come up. "Then bam!" he suddenly shouted. "The cold steel hooks him solid and the fight begins. It's all a big game, man."

"I know," Larsen told him. "That's why I do it. That's why we all do it."

"I'll tell you what I need, Dan. I need my own boat. Then I wouldn't have to listen to any of these assholes. I'd take that bitch to Australia. Catch some big fish."

"Yeah," Larsen agreed, but he was hardly listening. A movement out of the corner of his eye had drawn his attention to the inside of the restaurant, cloaked in shadows as the sun moved into the western half of the sky. Larsen squinted, just barely making out the form of Carlos, who nodded towards the rear of the restaurant.

"I gotta take a leak," the agent told Masters, who was busily sucking the last inch of intoxicating liquid from the giant glass. He rose from the table.

"You gonna have a fuckin' drink with me or what?" Masters managed.

"Just get me a beer." Larsen made his way around to the side of the restaurant, past the empty monkey *palapa* and towards the bathrooms. He relieved himself, flushed the toilet and turned to find Carlos standing just outside the door. The waiter appeared nervous; his eyes darted left and right, and he smoked his Marlboro Light with trembling fingers.

"Tell me," Larsen ordered. "Have you heard from him?"

"Yes. He told me to contact you, but not at the boat. He thinks you are being watched. Go to the ruins of Tulum in two days time. Do not take the main entrance. Go past it and take the road to the beach. Enter the ruins at exactly five-thirty. Once inside, he will contact you. If it rains or you cannot make it for some reason, contact me here."

"Is that it?" Larsen asked. Carlos was waiting for something, but he was ill at ease, the usual smirk replaced by a mask of concern.

"I think for you there is much danger, Captain Dan. And because you are in danger, so am I. I am not sure how long I can continue to help you." He looked around again, and stubbed his cigarette out on the wooden floor and immediately lit another. "What can you do for me?"

It suddenly dawned on him what it was Carlos wanted and Larsen fished an American fifty out of his wallet. "Will this guarantee your help for a while?" He held it out towards the nervous man.

"*Si. Muchas gracias.*" He snatched the bill and hurried away.

Returning to the table, Larsen found Masters with one of the short Mayan waiters in a headlock. The young boy thrashed and squealed while his co-workers giggled.

"C'mon big fellow, let's hit the road." Larsen asked for and paid the check.

"What about that drink?" Masters whined. He'd yet to order another round since Larsen had gone to speak to Carlos.

"We already drank it," the agent lied. "Let's go. If you're going to be looking for another job, you need to keep up a professional image." He wrapped his arm around his drunken friend's shoulder and guided the man towards the beach.

The two men headed back towards the marina, once again in silence. Masters looked down at the sand, struggling to maintain his balance. Larsen stared out at the horizon where the Caribbean Sea disappeared as it met the sky.

"You're not on the shit, are you?" Larsen asked. He was always suspicious. A couple of years earlier, during a brief but painful battle with alcohol, Masters had begun to dabble in cocaine. Not a lot, but a couple of lines here, a half gram there. When Larsen had found out, he had been furious.

Masters stopped walking. "I'm not on the shit. Why do you even ask me that?"

"Because I remember what happened before. First the booze, then the blow."

"I can handle it now. The booze, I mean."

"Yeah, well I hope so. Don't forget what happened to my sister."

"I won't. That's what helped get me off the shit the last time."

"Then make sure you stay off it." Larsen put his hand on Masters' shoulder. "I don't mean to hassle you, man. I'm just looking out for you."

"Yeah, I know. But let me ask you something," Masters said, his words still slightly slurred. He closed one eye to focus on Larsen. "Don't you ever get tired of being perfect?"

Larsen did not answer; he knew he was far from perfect. And his thoughts were consumed by images of many different things. Airplanes. Boats. Ruins.

Cancun
March 28, 1996 1542 Local Time

The immigration officer at the Cancun International Airport glanced at the photo on the passport that lay open before him, and compared it with the tall, well-built tourist that stood before him; he looked like the Marlboro Man—without the hat.

"Please remove your glasses," the officer told the man sternly.

The tourist did as he was told and the officer looked into the same set of eyes that appeared on the document before him. Deep blue, they had a quality; piercing and intense; unlike those of most of the Americans, they were the eyes of a man who had seen a lot, perhaps too much.

"Your destination here in Mexico? Cancun or elsewhere?"

The man answered in a nasal, almost Southern drawl that the officer had heard often. "Right here in Cancun. The Sierra Radisson in the hotel zone."

"And how long will you be with us?"

"Two weeks is all. Two weeks of rest and relaxation. Plan on doin' a little fishin' while I'm here. Gonna catch me a grand slam. You see?" The man pointed to his t-shirt, a Guy Harvey Original. Harvey, a marine artist from Jamaica, was famous for his life-like paintings of billfish, and t-shirts bearing his artwork could be found in almost every marina in the world. "That's right! A blue marlin, a white marlin and a sailfish." He pointed out each type of fish on his shirt as he spoke. "Yep, gonna do it in one day, too!"

The immigration officer had heard enough. He flipped to the back pages of the obnoxious tourist's passport, banged the date of entry with his rubber stamp, inserted the thirty-day tourist visa, and handed it back. The officer said nothing—didn't even look at the tourist again—and focused on the next passenger in line.

Moving on to the baggage claim, the man grabbed a large, khaki-colored duffle bag and made his way towards customs. He informed the short, thick-waisted woman that he had nothing to declare and after examining his customs declaration, she sent him over to what looked like a street light that stood only head high.

"Please press the button," she instructed him. He did so and was rewarded with a green light. She waved him through and hoisting his duffle over his shoulder, he headed out into the hot, humid Cancun air.

"That's efficient," he muttered to himself. He was sure that Cancun's security measures were probably just as big a joke. It certainly wouldn't surprise him. Nothing about the Mexicans ever surprised Wes Gates.

Standing in the hot sun, he quickly grabbed a taxi and, appalled at paying such a high price for such a short distance, he forked over the eighty dollars that would get him to the marina at Puerto Aventuras. So much for Mexico being the land of the bargain. Welcome to the land of "screw the tourist". But at least he was there; he still couldn't believe it.

The "fuck-up in Juarez"—as the infamous blown attempt to catch Carrillo at the warehouse had been billed—had nearly cost him his job and the last few weeks had been nothing but a living hell of reprimands and frustration. Absolutely no new leads had developed in the search for Carrillo and the dedicated agent had been filled with hollow-belly feelings of impotence. It had been only two days since he was summoned to DEA headquarters in Virginia. He had expected the worst, possibly a termination of his career as a special agent for the DEA. And when he had been directed to the office of Constance, the Administrator himself, he had been almost sure of it.

When he reached Constance's office, the Administrator had company. A middle-aged man, white shirt, no sleeves, red tie. CIA written all over him.

"I see you're a veteran of the Gulf War," the man began. Constance had Gates' personal file on his desk and the man was slowly flipping through it. The agent was sure it wasn't the first time. "Recon for a Special Forces unit, is that right?"

"That's right," Gates had answered. His unit had been devastatingly effective at penetrating behind Iraqi lines and gathering intelligence regarding troop strengths and armaments of the Republican Guard.

"You were wounded." Not really a question, but the man stared straight into Gates eyes.

"Yes, sir." Gates told him.

"Eight members of your unit were killed."

"That's right." It was all in the file! What in hell was this guy getting at? He shot Constance a quizzical look.

"We're looking for a special man for a special mission," the man told him. "I believe you may be the one."

Then they hit him with it. A covert operation in the Yucatan area had discovered what could possibly be a direct link to Amado Carrillo Fuentes and his help was needed in establishing the exact whereabouts of the cartel leader. Constance assured him that the operation was of such a sensitive nature that its discovery and exposure could have devastating ramifications within the DEA, the CIA and as far as the Presidency itself. They told Gates everything about the operation, from the existence of Paco Herrera to Larsen's cover as a sportfishing captain. They said they were giving Gates a chance to redeem himself. As if what had happened in Juarez was all his fault.

All that had gone down just two days earlier. Now, whizzing along in the taxi headed for the marina, Gates stared out the window. Paco Herrera was here! That meant Carrillo could not be far. And Gates would find him. The pieces to the puzzle were all there; he just had to let them fall into place. The agent closed his eyes and attempted to relax. It was difficult; the road was extremely narrow, the potential for disaster obvious. But as they sped southward, he felt confident. Confident that the plan they had laid out would work, because it had the one element that all the other operations aimed at taking down Carrillo had lacked: Secrecy.

Washington, D.C.
That Same Day

Senator Thomas Jensen leaned back, put one leg across the other, and watched the man seated across from him with amusement. Ambassador to Mexico Marcus LeGrone had been trying for at least ten minutes to get the attention of the twenty-something waiter, who was clearly in the weeds. They were seated in a small outdoor café not far from the capitol building, a trendy Italian eatery that had recently become the place to pull off what had come to be known as the "power lunch."

Jensen took a look around to see what kind of players had been attracted today to the white iron chairs and red and white tablecloths. A couple of congressmen sat at the table next to them and, a few tables away, another Senator sat with an attractive young girl who giggled at everything he said. Lunch time fling? Or secretary, it was hard to tell. A few news types were gathered near the entrance and the rest of the crowd was made up of interns and other political wannabes. No tourists.

LeGrone finally reached out and tugged on the back of the waiter's apron. "Young man," he said sternly.

The waiter spun in anger. "What is it?" he snapped. He had what appeared to be a tiny silver barbell stuffed through his left eyebrow. Snow white hair that looked like it was bleached. Didn't even look Italian.

"Do you know who I am?" LeGrone stared up at him, indignant.

"No." Not lying a bit. "Should I?"

"I'm Ambassador Marcus LeGrone. Ambassador to Mexico." As if everyone knew that.

"Yeah? And I'm Tom Cruise having a bad hair day." A couple at a table nearby laughed at his spontaneity. "Wait your turn," he ordered.

LeGrone was flabbergasted. He turned to Jensen. "Did you hear that insolent little bastard?"

"I heard him," Jensen said. "One of our future world leaders," he added. But the waiter's response wasn't surprising. To Jensen, LeGrone looked like a worn-out, old soldier who'd found his way into politics. Always whining and bitching, like the country owed him something. Washington was full of the type, and Jensen knew LeGrone had never been a soldier.

Jensen spotted a waitress headed their way. "Could we get a couple of drinks, please?" he asked.

"Sure," she said. No problem. Big smile. "What would you like?"

LeGrone ordered a diet coke. What a pansy, Jensen thought. He ordered a double Dewars, straight up. Scotch. A man's drink. A powerful man.

Jensen knew that for him, Ambassador would not be enough. But if the President were to sit down in here, they sure as hell would know who he was. Jensen sat up straight. Tightened his tie. Smoothed his hair back. It was time for discussion.

"Have you spoken with Zedillo?" he asked LeGrone.

"Yes." After the episode with the DEA in Juarez, LeGrone was one of the first people the Mexican president had called. "He's pissed off, and he should be," LeGrone said.

"What did he say?"

"Said he wants more money."

"More money?" Jensen found it hard to believe. "We just gave him several billion dollars, for Chrissakes!"

"He lost it in the stock market," LeGrone said with a straight face.

"Be serious, Marcus."

"I'm not bullshitting." He paused to let that sink in. "But we'll discuss that later. Zedillo thinks now would be the perfect time to ask for more foreign aid. While the DEA has seen that we have egg on our face. Otherwise he's going to make a big stink."

"What's he need the money for?" Jensen asked. Like there was one reason.

"He's got a goddamn rebellion going on down there. Where the hell have you been, Tom? It's not just in Chiapas anymore. It's spreading, you know."

"I don't even want to know," Jensen told him.

The waitress brought their drinks. Jensen took a sip. Smiled as it burned its way down to his stomach.

"Well, he wants it," LeGrone went on. "And we need to get it. Can we lean on Constance? He's got the President's ear. What kind of dirt do we have on him?" The question surprised Jensen. He thought LeGrone had dirt on everyone. "Maybe we can make a deal. Give Zedillo what he wants if he gives up Carrillo."

"It won't be that easy," Jensen said.

"Why not?"

"The whole matter with Carrillo has been turned over to the CIA," Jensen explained.

"The spooks?"

"That's right, Marcus. It's all very hush-hush."

"Always is with those bastards. What section?"

"The ONII," Jensen said. "The drug intelligence people."

"Those are the guys who finally took down the Colombians," LeGrone remembered. It hadn't been public information, but both LeGrone and Jensen had gotten the inside scoop.

"Same people. Very effective," Jensen added. "We'll need to move fast if we want to cut a deal with Zedillo."

"Who's in charge?"

"Same guy," Jensen told him. "Name's John Macki. The President's golden boy of narcointelligence."

"Doesn't ring a bell. What do we know about him?" LeGrone asked.

"Started out in the Navy. He was an intelligence officer aboard the Nimitz in the early eighties."

"The first nuclear carrier," LeGrone pointed out.

"Thats the one. Anyway, they were on a training mission off Florida one night when a jet crashed on the deck. EA-6B. A Prowler."

"What happened?"

"Nobody knows for sure. The Landing Signal Officer said the Prowler was coming in too high and drifting left. Told the pilot to abort."

"Which he obviously didn't," LeGrone said.

"No. He skidded onto the deck, missed the final arresting cable and wham, slammed broadside into a six-pack of F-14 Tomcats."

"Not good."

"Quite the understatement," Jensen said. "Fourteen killed, dozens injured. The total damage was more than 150 million."

"So how's Macki fit in?" LeGrone asked.

"Autopsies on the dead marines, the crew of the Prowler, showed traces of cocaine and marijuana. Mandatory drug testing was ordered for the rest of the Nimitz's crew."

"I can see where this is leading," LeGrone said. "What did they find?"

"Eleven percent of the ships crew tested positive for either coke or pot."

"Wow."

"Wow is right," Jensen said. "And suddenly all the senior officers' careers are stopped dead in their tracks, Macki included. Most of them resigned within six months. End of story."

"And from that time on, Macki's got a hard-on for dope smugglers," LeGrone said.

"Exactly." Jensen was amazed. Sometimes LeGrone was more astute than he appeared.

"So what are his plans for Carrillo?" LeGrone asked.

"I don't know," Jensen said. He signalled the waitress to bring the check, and looked back at LeGrone. "But I'm going to find out."

Marina Puerto Aventuras
That Same Day

Larsen knew it was him from the moment he saw him coming down the dock. The large, imposing figure of the man in the Guy Harvey t-shirt moved with a walk that had purpose, a definite destination. His head turned from side to side as he surveyed his surroundings and the fat canvas duffle slung over his shoulder was a dead give-away. Larsen could tell a military man when he saw one; he had worked with several. The man's body looked strong and tight. No sign of the flabby beer gut that many fishing enthusiasts displayed prominently. The hair was dark, thick and wavy; not a trace of gray. The appearance of a five o'clock shadow of a beard gave the man a rugged look, a man not afraid to get his hands dirty. The kind of help Larsen had been hoping for and the timing was perfect.

Larsen had been rinsing the deck of the cockpit when he'd spotted him. He put down the hose and grabbed the chamois mop, beginning to dry the deck as the stranger approached the transom of the *Predator*. He looked up just as the man spoke.

"I'm looking for Dan Larsen." There was no sign of a Southern accent; in fact, Larsen had trouble detecting any accent at all.

"You're lookin' right at him."

"Some friends of yours sent me. Wes Gates." He leaned towards the cockpit and shook Larsen's hand, the grip firm, nearly crushing.

"Let's go inside," Larsen said and nodded towards the inside of the boat. "Leave your bags here in the pit and I'll tell you where you can get a place to stay." Gates boarded and the two men disappeared into the salon.

Once inside, Gates removed his shades. "Nice cover! What do you have to do to get one of these rides?"

"Just be in the right place at the right time, I guess. Somebody's got to drive these things. Might as well be me. What about you? You don't really look like a fisherman, although I do like the shirt."

"I'm out of the office in El Paso. Been there for almost five years. Before that I was in the army—Special Forces, recon mostly."

The statement did not surprise Larsen. It was obvious Gates had been carefully selected. "Were you involved in the raid in Juarez?"

"Team leader," Gates replied. "Still trying to live that one down."

"I can imagine. You want a drink or something?"

"I'll take a beer if you've got one. It's been a long day."

Larsen went to the small fridge in the galley and came back with two cans of Coors Light. "This is all we've got right now. Bottles tend to break when we're out fishing."

"Thanks."

"So I guess I should start at the beginning."

Half an hour later, the two men had exchanged enough information that each felt he had a better grip on the situation. Gates told Larsen stories about Carrillo that only intensified the agent's desire to take him down and Larsen's own descriptions of Paco Herrera made Gates sure their energy was being focused in the proper direction.

"Oh, I'm sure it's the same man," Gates said. "He's been Carrillo's lieutenant, chief assassin and right arm for about three years. He does all the dirty work and Carrillo gets all the credit. Now he shows up here and Carrillo has fallen off the face of the earth. I'll bet Herrera's probably getting ready to make his move, maybe even start his own cartel. All he needs are his own connections to the Colombians and he's in business. But right now Carrillo is the one who holds those cards—that's why Paco disappears now and then. He must be operating with Carrillo, but the question is—where?"

"Can't you just follow him the next time he goes to meet with Carrillo?"

"Sure. But its not going to be easy. The PJFA, the guys you told me about from the beach—they'll be watching. They had some people in Juarez, and, believe me, they're not very nice. But they're smart. They know what can happen when you arrest members of the cartel. Instead, they identify their targets and make sure they just "disappear". They shoot first and that's it. Screw the questions. Very effective." He paused and finished the rest of his beer, crushing the can.

"Before Herrera, there was another man named Cruz. He was always showing off, flashing cash and all that bullshit. One day he vanished. The PJFA claimed responsibility and vowed that Cruz was just the first of many smugglers who would go down. But Carrillo was more powerful and better connected than they thought."

"What happened?"

"He found out who and where they were and had virtually every member of the PJFA executed. The people of Juarez and the local law enforcement agencies were petrified. You see, no one wants to be even remotely connected to any attempt at bringing Carrillo to justice. That's why we're up against a fucking wall. To take him ourselves is the only way."

"But if Carrillo had all the members of the PJFA executed, then who are the guys here, in Playa?"

"Obviously some that got out of Juarez and ended up here. My guess is that they'll follow Herrera and when the time is right, they'll make their problem go away."

"I'm supposed to meet him tomorrow," Larsen said.

"Herrera?"

"Yeah. At the ruins in Tulum. You been there?"

"No."

"It's down the coast about thirty miles. I'm supposed to be there at five-thirty."

"That'll work. It'll give me some time to scope the place out."

"Then you can follow him." Larsen liked the plan already.

"Exactly," Gates said. "And he'll never even know I'm there."

"We'll need to rent you a car. You got any more clothes like that?" Larsen pointed at the Guy Harvey t-shirt.

"Yeah."

"They're perfect. Real touristy."

"Whatever you say," Gates told him. "You know this place better than I do. What about tonight? I need a place to stay."

"There's a little hotel up near the marina center. I'll show you where it is."

"One more thing." Gates got up to leave. "They said you'd have a piece for me."

"Right." Larsen went down the stairs for a moment and returned with a 9-millimeter Berretta and a box of shells. He handed both to Gates. "Clip's full."

Although not his favorite, Gates was familiar with the weapon. He drew back the cocking mechanism and let it snap back into place, chambering a round. "Thanks, man. I feel better already."

12

Tulum 20°12.35"N 87°21.02"W
March 29, 1996 1745 Local Time

To some, the ruins of the ancient city of Tulum hold a mystical quality; to others it is nothing but a pile of rocks. But one cannot deny that
on that very spot, high above the emerald and turquoise waters of the
Caribbean, there once existed an extraordinary race of people, a race that
built their city in the form of a fortress, which in the end was proved vulnerable.

Larsen stood facing the sea, trying to imagine the city as it once was,
the buildings immense and ornamental, alive with activity. He'd been to
the ruins several times before and, each time, he had discovered something new about the place and the people who once thrived within the
walls. On this day, however, he had not come for a history lesson.

He had entered the ruins at exactly the time specified, and had wandered up to the nearest overlook of the sea. It had taken him no more
than fifteen minutes. Still no sign of Paco. He made his way down the
slope towards a large group of tourists gathered at the base of one of the
larger buildings. The rocks had been worn smooth by the feet of countless others who had gone before and, nearly falling twice, he wound up at
what he remembered was the Temple of Priests. A Mexican tour-guide
was rattling on in broken English to a group of Asians who seemed more

concerned with preserving their memories in the family photo album than learning about the monument that stood before them. Larsen watched as they scurried around like ants, snapping away from all angles with an incredible arsenal of cameras, the whole time yammering in what he assumed was Japanese. If a crowd was what Paco was waiting for, it was the perfect opportunity to make contact. Gates was also somewhere on the property, and although he hadn't seen him, Larsen guessed he wasn't too far away.

Turning away from the sea, Larsen shielded his eyes from the late afternoon sun. He stared down into the shallow valley below, back towards the way he had entered the ruins. Small groups of tourists marched slowly towards the break in the rear wall, the stone passageway which was the only entrance or exit. The site would be closing soon, and still no sign of Paco. The Asians moved on towards another small temple in the lower part of the site.

A hushed voice from immediately behind his ear was eerily familiar. He turned slowly, knowing whom he would find.

"How's your head?" Paco asked, grinning. He had done it again. Silently, like a snake.

"You fucking bastard," Larsen accused, his voice a harsh whisper. "You were there!"

"Yes. I wanted to help you, but I was unarmed. You were doing well until the second man arrived. Tell me what happened. Walk this way."

Paco led them higher up the path, towards the highest ruin in the site. There was no need to make up a story. Paco had been there, seen everything. Larsen told him of the jail and what the man from the PJFA had said. He watched Paco's reaction and wondered if the truth would make Paco trust him even more. Did he trust him so far?

"The *comandante* said he would be watching you. And me," Larsen added.

"This is true. They are here already. The same two. They came into the ruins right after you. You must learn to pay attention. Yes, Captain Dan. You have much to learn." Paco's words were startling, and condescending. He was toying with Larsen again. Like it was a game.

"How long have you been here?"

"Almost an hour. I came by boat. I've been watching you from up there since you entered." He pointed to the ruin that they were headed for. "I'm sure they have seen us together. Right now they are down below. Soon they will come."

Where in hell was Gates? Would he realize what was happening? Larsen looked around as the two men reached the base of the ruin. For Gates. Or the men from the PJFA. But there was no one.

The dirt pathway turned to stone and they made their way up two tiers of the intricate, hand-carved foundation until they reached the single room at the top. Pausing to catch their breath, they ducked down and entered through the single, north-facing doorway. With his back to the wall, Paco sat down below a tiny window that faced west and the other ruins below.

"Do you see them?" The smuggler appeared calm, almost bored.

Larsen walked to the window, hunched over in the tiny Mayan room, and peered out. The property was deserted, the last of the sightseers filing out the exit. The setting sun had already stretched its fire across the sky, the red ball sinking below the trees of the jungle as the valley was plunged into shadow. It would soon be dark. "Not yet."

Paco leaned forward and removed a huge knife from behind his back. The blade was wide and sharp, slightly upturned at the end, nearly six inches in length. "Do you know how to use this?" he asked, looking Larsen directly in the eye. "Don't be afraid to tell me if you don't."

"Not really." Larsen had been through some training in hand to hand combat, but had never used a blade on another man.

"Then take this." A black, silenced automatic had somehow appeared in the smuggler's hand and he handed it to Larsen.

He couldn't figure out where Paco had hidden it, but he reminded himself that he was dealing with an experienced killer. He ran his hand over his face and took a deep breath, exhaling loudly.

"I guess there's no way out of this one," he told the smuggler, who was studying and stroking the shiny blade.

"Don't worry, *amigo*. We've got the high ground. Unfortunately, that didn't help the Mayans." He giggled sadistically. Just a game.

Larsen returned to the window. Down below, in the darkness, he could just make out two figures sneaking up the narrow, winding trail. They moved in short spurts, running a short distance and then stopping, crouching. He could see they were armed and headed his way. He turned to the smuggler. "They're coming."

Gates was on his third coke of the afternoon when Larsen entered the ruins. As planned, the agent from El Paso had traveled to Tulum ahead of Larsen and had come through the main tourist entrance off the highway, taking the small shuttle bus to a spot outside the walls. The tiny cafe he had chosen was perfect. Nestled between two of the open-air shops jammed with Mexican curios, the small metal table at which he sat was well concealed in the shadows, less than thirty yards from the stone passageway that led to the site. Just another tourist seeking respite from the scorching rays of the Yucatan sun, Gates had been waiting nearly forty-five minutes when Larsen wandered down the narrow road that came in from the south. He watched as the undercover agent purchased a ticket and headed up the steps, disappearing through the narrow break in the wall.

Draining the last of his luke-warm cola, Gates waited several minutes, anticipating what he hoped would be the arrival of Paco Herrera. But fearing the smuggler may have already been inside, he got up and crossed the dusty street to the base of the steps. Surveying the faces of the people in the immediate vicinity once more, he spotted no one out of the ordinary and marched up and into the ruins.

Once inside the compound, the former reconnaissance expert scanned his surroundings, seeking out positions of advantage or disadvantage. Years of experience pinpointed areas of possible danger spread throughout the eight acres of the ancient city. Within two minutes he had spotted Larsen on a small rise overlooking the water. He was still alone. Scanning the higher ground, his gaze fixed upon the Castle, the highest and most remarkable of the sixty restored temples. A thin yellow rope was strung across the bottom of the stairway, forbidding entrance to the temple above. The sun was nearly down. The former Special Forces soldier slid between the ruins, moving from shadow to shadow as he headed for the higher temples, stopping only to keep his eye on Larsen.

He was nearly at the top of the temple nearest the Castle when he paused behind a wall to catch his breath. Movement atop the Castle caught his eye and his pulse quickened as the figure of Herrera appeared from behind the ocean side of the giant stone temple. Even in the dim light, there was no mistaking the smuggler; the thin yet strong body, the long hair pulled back in a ponytail. Gates watched as Herrera carefully monkeyed his way down the side of the temple, hanging and hopping from level to level, completely unnoticed by anyone except himself. It was too dark to tell whether the smuggler was armed. Holding his position, Gates removed the Berretta from his waistband, checking the function of the firing mechanism once more. The weapon felt good in his hand and he had the sudden urge to use it. He trained it on Herrera as the smuggler made his way down towards Larsen, who had moved into the lower part of the valley and stood alone near one of the smaller temples. In his mind, he pulled the trigger and watched the smugglers head explode just as he reached the other agent. But that was not the plan. He was only to follow Herrera when he left the ruins; a confrontation was out of the question. Reluctantly, he shoved the pistol back in his waistband. Herrera and Larsen turned and were now coming towards him. But why? The site was closing soon and was nearly empty. How would the two men get out? They were getting closer, and Gates melted into the dark shadows once more.

"Wait for them to enter, and then we will take them," Paco told him, and Larsen took his position across from the smuggler on the opposite side of the opening in the temple wall.

"They will come together, I am sure of it. Be ready." The smuggler crouched down, barely visible in the darkness of the tiny room. What little light there was reflected in his eyes. They were wide open now, and wild with excitement.

The crunch of small stones underneath barely moving feet came from outside the opening and Larsen took a deep breath, holding it as he prepared for the two-man assault which he was certain would come at any second.

There was a brief flurry of scuffling feet and, as expected, the two men from the PJFA charged through the stone doorway, silenced automatic pistols drawn. Paco fell upon the *comandante* and plunged the blade into the man's tough belly, twisting and thrusting upward as he sliced through the vital organs. The *comandante*'s eyes were bulging with horror and disbelief. As he died, his silenced automatic spit twice, the shots wild. Splintered fragments of rock flew in all directions as the smell of burnt stone and gunpowder filled the air, mixing with the aroma of fresh blood and the stench of internal organs.

The thin man from the beach hit the floor with a grunt and rolled, raising his weapon to fire, just as Larsen pounced on his chest, knocking the man's pistol to the side as his own came crashing down on the Mexican's head. The man cried in pain as the Larsen raised his weapon and brought it down again and again. The skull of the man gave way and his thrashing ceased.

Larsen shoved off him and dropped the silenced weapon, as if it were hot. His chest heaved, the shock of what he had just done gradually affecting his body; he was suddenly nauseated.

"Good job," Paco said from across the room. "I knew you had it in you, it was only a matter of time."

"Fuck you, Paco. I didn't know there would be any killing!"

"What do you think this is, the play of children? Would you rather we sit here and let them kill us? Because, believe me, my friend, that is what they were going to do." Paco was staring at Larsen like a maniac, breathing heavily and wiping the blood from his blade on the leg of his pants. Larsen searched the floor until he found the gun Paco had given him. The butt was wet with blood and in disgust, he held out the weapon to the smuggler.

"Here, take this."

"Keep it," Paco said. "Learn to use it properly. It's a gun, not a hammer." He laughed like a madman.

A groan came from the floor; the thin one was still alive! Larsen felt a glimmer of hope. Perhaps he was not a murderer.

"What are you waiting for?" Paco demanded. "Finish him!"

Larsen sat silently, still huffing, his mind a mess of conflicting emotion. The man had been prepared to kill him, and could not be allowed to live if the operation was to succeed. Yet he could not bring himself to end the man's life, a man like himself who wanted nothing than to rid the world of trash like Paco Herrera. Indecision kept him motionless.

Before he could react, Paco leapt from his spot on the floor, grasped the dying man and pulled his head back. Larsen watched in horror as the smuggler drew his knife swiftly across the man's throat, the skin of his exposed neck parting like butter beneath the razor-sharp blade. The legs quivered, and became still. The smell of urine and blood floated on the air. Paco turned to face Larsen. "There is no time for weakness! You must learn that if you are to survive in this business." The words were horrifying, yet true.

"Jesus Christ, Paco! Now we're really in trouble," Larsen said.

"No. Now we are out of trouble," Paco told him. "These two were in the way, an obstacle which had to be removed. Now we can carry on. Let's get out of here. We have much to discuss."

"What about the bodies?" Larsen asked.

"We'll leave them here. This part of the temple is closed to the public. They won't be found for days. By then we will be long gone." Paco grabbed the dead men's guns and pointed to the door. "Now go!"

Gates stood in the darkness and squinted across at the entrance to the room at the top of the Castle. He'd seen Larsen and Herrera enter the small stone room only to be followed minutes later by two men, both armed. Nearly ten minutes had passed, yet he had heard no shots. He breathed a sigh of relief as he recognized the forms of Larsen and Herrera exiting the room and he remained completely still as the two men made their way down the outer tiers of the temple, slipped through a break in the cliff, and disappeared. He descended from his hiding spot and made his way to a bluff which overlooked the water below. Lying on his belly, he peered over the edge and watched as the two men approached a small wooden *lancha*, a popular type of Mexican fishing boat. Larsen leapt in first and after pushing the craft off the beach and out to sea, Herrera climbed aboard, made his way to the stern and pull started the small outboard motor. They sped off towards the south and within a few moments were completely out of his sight.

Gates pressed his sturdy frame from the ground and surveyed the general area from where he sat crouched in the darkness. The two armed men had not re-emerged from the room in the temple across the way. It was not hard for him to guess their fate as he made his way down from the higher ground to the valley below. He reached the exit; the heavy, wrought iron gate was closed and locked. He went back and finding its

174

lowest spot, hoisted himself up on top of the extensive rear wall. He ran south along it until he came to a tree, jumped out onto it, and climbed down to the ground.

The small *lancha* glided silently towards the beach, just another fishing boat returning with its daily catch. Paco had killed the motor moments before and the craft rode the incoming swell with just enough momentum to take the bow up and onto the sand.

Since leaving the ruins, Paco had steered the small craft less than a mile, careful in the darkness to avoid the small sections of reef that paralleled the shore. It had taken Larsen a few minutes to recover from the shock of what they had done, but he had listened intently as Paco gave him instructions on when and where he should locate himself for the upcoming drop. They were preparing to go ahead with it now that the two men from the PJFA were out of the picture.

"Now get out of here," Paco whispered softly. "Follow the dirt track to the road above. This place is a campground called Las Palapas at San Francisco. From what you told me, your car should be right up there." He pointed towards the tree line that ran along the bluff above the beach. There was a small open-air restaurant off to the right, with an old lighthouse towering just behind it. Both were deserted, and dark.

"When will we meet again?" Larsen asked.

"After the drop. I'll contact you. You're sure there are no problems?"

"No problems," he told the smuggler and dropped to the sand. He stripped off his bloodstained shirt and threw it into the boat. "Do something with this," he said and headed off into the darkness, disappearing within the maze of palms and small bamboo *cabanas*.

Within minutes Larsen had made his way to the road, and his eyes searched the surrounding blackness as he approached his rental car. Seeing no one, he unlocked it and slipped behind the wheel. The small engine had just sprung into life when a slight tapping at the passenger window nearly paralyzed him. Reaching under his seat, he grabbed his pistol and was prepared to fire when he recognized the face of Gates staring back at him, the corner of his mouth turned up in a friendly smile.

"Jesus Christ, man," Larsen told the other agent as he leaned over and opened the door. "You're not gonna live a long time sneaking around like that."

"I beg to differ, my friend. Sneaking around is what I do best. It keeps me alive." Gates used the shoulder of his shirt to wipe the sweat and grime from his face. He explained to Larsen where he had parked his car and the two men headed back towards the highway and the main entrance.

Larsen described to him what had happened in the room at the top of the temple, including the fact that he and Paco had left the bodies behind.

"He killed them. Just like that," Larsen said.

"All in a day's work for an assassin."

"What's going to happen when somebody finds the bodies? Within a few days, they're going to start to smell."

"Hard to say," Gates replied. "Chances are, they didn't tell a lot of people about it, if taking out Herrera is really what they planned to do. What did he say about the drop?"

"They're ready to go through with it. This Wednesday at eight o'clock sharp. It works for me. Paco gave me the coordinates. Looks like somewhere between Akumal and here, about ten miles offshore. I'll have to look at the charts to make sure." They reached the highway. Larsen made a right and headed north towards the main entrance to the ruins.

"You'd better get in touch with your man back in the states," Gates warned. "Once the drop is made, the stakes are raised another notch. You don't want to be facing a smuggling charge if something goes wrong."

Or a murder charge, Larsen thought. He knew all about the Mexican code of Napoleonic law. Guilty until proven innocent. The agent from El Paso was right. After the drop, the stakes would be raised even higher. But with the murder of the two men from the PJFA, he had already reached the point of no return.

The two men rode in silence, heading north on the highway of death. After several minutes, they arrived at the vast, deserted parking lot at the main entrance to the ruins. Gate's vehicle, a small Japanese rental sedan, sat alone in the dark. Larsen turned in and they swung up next to it. He killed the headlights.

"Tomorrow I'll move to Playa del Carmen," Gates told him. "Now that I've seen Herrera again, I'll find him and track his every move. When and if he goes to see Carrillo, I'll be there. He'll go, I'm sure of it. After the drop is made, he'll report in."

"I think you're right, Larsen said. "And once we find out where Carrillo is, our job is done."

"Let's hope so. I'll be in touch." Gates got out and jumped into his own car. He started the engine and roared away in a cloud of dust, leaving his headlights off until he reached the paved road.

Larsen sat in the vehicle and watched as Gates' taillights grew smaller, then winked out of sight. How easy it would be if they could just find out where Carrillo was, and that could be the end of it. In the back of his mind, he knew that would not be the end of it. What had happened between him and Paco had now escalated into a personal vendetta, an overwhelming need for revenge.

As he pulled onto the highway, Larsen wondered how far he would have to go. The smuggler had crossed the line. The agent had seen the madness. And now he was part of it.

13

Aboard the *Predator*
April 3, 1996 2026 Local Time

Eight and a half miles from shore and just over six miles south of the town of Akumal, the *Predator* wallowed in the swells. Inside the bridge, Larsen and Kurt anxiously awaited the aircraft that was supposed to drop over one thousand pounds of high-grade Colombian cocaine within a few hundred yards of their boat.

The water was deep and the current strong; the last reading had measured sixteen hundred feet before the bottom machine went blank. A strong breeze had sprung up out of the northeast, and from the size of the swells and blowing spray, Larsen estimated its speed at twenty-five knots. The seas were getting ugly and as both men stared out at the brewing storm, they knew it was not a night for boating.

"You sure this is the right spot?" Kurt asked. The mate had been reluctant to come at first, but after Larsen had reminded him of the windfall of profits that awaited them, he quickly changed his mind. And he knew Larsen couldn't handle it alone. They were still a team.

"We're exactly where we need to be," Larsen replied. "Twenty, nineteen point four six North and eighty-seven point two three degrees West."

Upon leaving the marina three hours before, they'd trolled to the south and two sailfish and three *dorado* later, they'd arrived at the precise spot Paco had written down for him. Thirty minutes had passed and there had been no sign of activity in the air or on the water. The rest of the fishing fleet had headed in an hour earlier, just before dark. The other captains had seen or sensed the foul weather, and were now safe inside the marina at Puerto Aventuras. Larsen envied them. He walked over to the instrument console and glanced at the bright green display of the radar. The occasional sweep of the radar's hand indicated a wide band of showers just south of the island of Cozumel, and they were definitely heading his way. A gust of wind howled eerily through the outriggers and the two men looked at each other like frightened children.

Kurt was the first to break the silence. "What time is it?"

Larsen glanced at his watch. "Eight-thirty." The plane was already half an hour late. Had they missed it? Larsen had the urge to turn on the spotlight and sweep the surrounding area, but he decided against it, fearing it might give away their presence. He looked towards shore; there was nothing.

"How long are we gonna wait?" Kurt asked.

"As long as we have to," Larsen replied. "Whoever is making the drop probably ran into this same piece of weather. They'll show. Besides, what's your hurry? You got a hot date or something?" He was willing to try anything to ease the tension.

"No. I just want to get this over with. I swear, this shit gives me the creeps." Kurt was pacing back and forth and Larsen suggested that he go outside.

"Leave the door open," Larsen told him. He needed to hear if the plane was approaching. The low resonating rumble of the diesels was loud, and after he moved the boat into the exact position according to the GPS, he shut the motors down. Now all was deathly quiet, except for the shrieking of the wind and slap of waves against the hull. He had just decided that he would wait only another thirty minutes when a shout from below caused him to bolt to the doorway.

"Here he comes. Listen!" Kurt cried. There was no mistaking the faint drone of aircraft engines, and they were getting louder. Larsen ran to the console and flashed not only the running lights, but the spotlight as well.

He continued flashing as the aircraft drew nearer, and its dark form suddenly took shape as the huge steel bird descended and loomed towards them, just barely visible in the darkness.

"Jesus Christ!" Kurt yelled. Larsen ran to the doorway as the plane flew past, its four turboprop engines roaring as it buzzed by less than a hundred feet above the water. Both men watched in awe as the military-type cargo plane disgorged its payload, which looked like multiple bales of hay, strung together as they fell from the sky and tumbled across the surface of the water less than fifty yards away. Larsen's eyes followed the craft through the dark sky. Within seconds it was gone.

"All right, let's go!" Larsen shouted to Kurt down below. "Open up that tuna door!" He went outside and activated the rear control station, and cranked up the engines. He motored over to the load, which bobbed atop the surface of the choppy black water. After backing down on it just as he would a fish, he put the engines in neutral and ran down to give his mate a hand.

Kurt had already grabbed the rope with the gaff and was attempting to hoist the first of what appeared to be ten bundles into the cockpit. Larsen got on his hands and knees to help. Although smaller than he would have thought, the bundles were quite heavy; he was surprised they didn't sink. The *Predator* was rocking violently in the heavy seas and getting the bundles in the boat was an absolute bitch. Several times, they would pull a bundle in, only to have it jerked back out again by the next passing swell. They began tying the rope to the rear cleat each time and the problem was solved. Twenty minutes later, the load was aboard. Both men lay on the cockpit floor, exhausted.

Kurt got to his feet and stared down at the load. "I wonder how much all this is worth!" A huge swell passed by and he nearly lost his footing. He grabbed the leg of the ladder for balance.

"We're looking at millions right now," Larsen told him. "There's supposed to be more than a thousand pounds here. Enough to put us away for a long time if we're caught. C'mon, let's get this stuff inside."

After rinsing the bundles with fresh water, they cut them apart, dried them with a chamois and carried the ten bundles, one by one, into the forward stateroom. Larsen removed the hatch in the floor that allowed access to the forward bilge. Much to their surprise, all ten bundles fit neatly inside the large, dry compartment.

"Shit, man. That was easy," Kurt said. "Maybe we should get some more." Larsen glared at the mate in disbelief. "Relax, Dan. I'm only kidding."

"Yeah, well, we're not out of the woods yet." Larsen replaced the hatch and got to his feet.

"What do you mean?" Kurt asked nervously. He followed his captain towards the rear of the boat. Larsen opened the door and they stepped into the pit. At the foot of the ladder, he hesitated and looked back at Kurt.

"We still have to deal with the cut."

By the time they reached the marina, the seas were horrendous. Larsen hit one of the wiper switches and peered out into the inky blackness. The ocean was moving all around him, the giant sportfisher tossed back and forth like a small dinghy. But it wasn't until he turned on the powerful spotlight and trained its beam on the cut that the seriousness of their situation became clear.

What he saw made him feel sick to his stomach. Waves of ten to twelve feet were relentlessly assaulting the inlet, rushing in off the angry sea before pitching forward in a thundering explosion of spray and foam that could easily be heard above the moaning sounds of the wind. He walked on unsteady legs to the rear door of the flybridge and stepped outside to summon Kurt to the bridge. Blowing spray stung his face as the driving wind blew the tops off the whitecaps at close to twenty-five knots. It was time to make a decision, but he did not want to make it alone. He leaned over the wet, salty railing, gripping it tightly as he searched for Kurt in the darkness of the cockpit below. It was empty. Cold fear flowed through his veins as he shouted desperately for his mate, whom he feared may have gone overboard.

"Yeah man, somehow I'm still here," came the faint response from down below and a feeling of relief washed over him as Kurt suddenly appeared, his shirt and shorts completely soaked. The mate scrambled up the ladder and both men entered the bridge. The interior was dark, lit only by the dim lights of the gauges and the eerie red filters that covered the lenses of the tiny quartz lights above the console.

Larsen again swept the narrow beam of the spotlight back and forth across the cut. He turned to Kurt. "What do you think?"

The mate was quiet for a moment, then finally replied, "It doesn't get much worse."

"Thanks for the support."

"You think this wind is going to last?" Kurt asked.

"I don't know. Take a look at this." Both men focused on the radar and watched as the hand swept by twice, illuminating a huge patch of green, which clearly showed rain heading their way. "It's fuckin' nasty right now and it's not even raining yet. At least I can still see."

"It's all out of control out there," Kurt said. "No organization to the swells."

"I know," Larsen said. The despair and tension in his voice were obvious. He knew better than to expect any sort of sets or pattern from a wind-generated swell. The proper way to negotiate the cut in a heavy sea was to get on the back of the last wave of a set, and ride it in at planing speed as the wave broke in the mouth of the inlet. But on this night, that was not to be. All the waves were huge, and were rolling in without a lull, and there was no chance to sneak between the jetties safely.

"Hey. Shine the spotlight on the south jetty," Kurt said. He'd spotted some movement in the dim fluorescent wash of the range markers, tall vertical lights used for navigating the inlet in the dark.

"Shit," Larsen said. "Looks like we've got an audience." The figures of several people could be seen gathering along the rocks. "Just waiting for us to crash. Goddamn sickos. Like a bunch of vultures."

Suddenly the VHF radio cackled to life.

"*Predator*, Marina Puerto Aventuras."

"Goddamn it, I knew I should have turned that fuckin' thing off." Larsen reached for the mike.

"Go ahead, marina. *Predator* back." Larsen's voice sounded tired and angry.

"Yeah, Dan, what are your plans?" The dockmaster had driven his beat-up little fourwheeler to the end of the dock, and was now looking at the *Predator*'s lights and speaking with Larsen on his hand-held VHF radio. Each transmission was weak and mixed with static.

"Actually, we had a little trouble and had to come back from down south on one engine," Larsen lied. "But I just got it fixed. This storm seems like it's going to get worse, so I'm just sitting out here checking it out for a minute and then I'm going to bring her in."

"I don't think that's a good idea, Dan. The cut looks really mean from here."

Larsen knew the dockmaster was right. He couldn't afford to let a boat crash and possibly sink in the middle of the inlet. No other boats would be able to enter or leave the marina. He remembered a story about a thirty-foot Sea Ray that had gone down in the middle of the cut the last time it happened. It had taken a week before they figured out how to remove the wreck.

The dockmaster's voice came from the radio once more. "Why don't you go and sit in Cozumel for the night? The direction this wind is blowing, you'll be in the lee of the island and it will be flat calm over there. That's where everybody thought you were."

Kurt looked at Larsen as if it might be a possibility but the captain shook his head. The *Predator* was not well known in that marina, and a boat coming in that late, in the dark, might arouse suspicion.

Larsen keyed the mike. "I don't think my boat can take the pounding. We already got beat to shit out here. Plus, it seems like it might get worse, so I just want to hurry up and get in." It seemed to Larsen like a reasonable argument, but he wondered if the dockmaster would go for it. Only a crazy captain or reckless fool would attempt to enter the cut under such conditions. Larsen was neither, but he had no choice. For a moment he had a vision of the *Predator* veering out of control, smashing into the rocks—metal, fiberglass and cocaine flying everywhere—but he snapped himself out of it. He had no time for such fantasies.

Larsen was just reaching for the radio when the dockmaster came back with the words he was afraid he might hear. "I'm sorry, Dan, but I just can't let you do it. Don't try to come in. It's too dangerous."

Larsen keyed the mike several times in succession while he spoke a series of garbled nonsense, then shut the radio off. "I think he said bring her on in," he said to Kurt with a wink. It was an old pilot's trick. His loyal mate agreed.

Putting the boat in gear, Larsen took the *Predator* in a giant circle, out to sea and then back in. His eyes focused on the vertical lights of the range markers, and when one was immediately above the other, he knew that was a direct line through the deepest part of the inlet. The swells behind them gradually pushed the vessel towards the treacherous cut.

"Keep the spotlight on the edge of the north jetty," he told Kurt. "And cross your fingers." He looked over at his mate in the dark and saw his own nervousness reflected in the younger man's eyes.

"You can do it, man," Kurt said.

Putting both the port and starboard engines in gear, Larsen gradually pushed the throttles forward. With a dull, throaty roar, the thirteen hundred horsepower engines propelled the *Predator* towards the mouth of the inlet. Slowly at first, but once on a plane, she picked up speed and headed towards the point of no return at twenty-five knots.

Once in the impact zone of the waves, Larsen tightened his white-knuckled grip on the wheel and held his breath. He could feel the power of the swells tugging on the keel and he fought desperately to maintain control as the *Predator* suddenly veered sharply to port.

Kurt swung the spotlight to the left and aimed it at the rocks of the south jetty, illuminating the figures that scrambled for cover like crabs.

Pulling the starboard throttle back, Larsen grasped the port throttle and pushed it forward to the stops. The engine screamed to twenty-four hundred rpms, yet the *Predator* continued tracking left.

"Shit! Shit! Shit!" Larsen cried and both he and Kurt braced themselves for the impending impact. Larsen refused to give up and spun the wheel violently to the right. Somehow the keel and rudders caught once more and the sixty-ton vessel lurched to the right, into the safety of the middle of the inlet.

Whistles and shouts erupted from the rocks of the south jetty. Larsen exhaled loudly and ran his hand across his face and forehead; it came away covered with sweat. "I'm glad that's over," he told Kurt.

"You and me both. For a second there I thought we were going to buy it."

"Yeah, me too. Remember, if anybody asks, we had transmission trouble on the starboard motor."

"All right. What now?"

"Just tie this pig up and head for the bar," Larsen replied. "I can use a stiff one after all that."

"Me too." Kurt left the bridge and Larsen watched him disappear down the ladder. He thought about the bond that now existed between them. Besides Kurt, there were few people in the world who had any idea how fucked up his life really was. He was glad to have at least one person around who might understand, if his mate even did.

14

Vera Cruz
April 4, 1996 1916 Local Time

Something moved across his leg and Gates lay still, waiting several moments before turning his head to the side and looking over his right shoulder. As he had feared, a black scorpion nearly five inches long probed the denim of his faded jeans, claws raised in defiance against the foreign substance, armored tail curled upward and ready to sting. With a lightning reaction, Gates swung his arm out and back, his hammer of a fist coming down dead on target.

Raising the heavy binoculars to his eyes once more, he resumed his reconnaissance of the outside wall of the compound. Besides the two heavily armed guards posted at what appeared to be the only entrance, he had seen no one since he had taken up the position nearly thirty-minutes before.

Concealed beneath a small clump of bushes less than a hundred yards from the compound's west wall, Gates could see the top of what was obviously a residence of immense proportions. Adrenaline flowed through his veins and he had the old familiar feeling, a feeling he always got when he'd discovered the target, and was able to observe it without detection. The razor wire atop the gigantic wall, the armed sentries—all were dead giveaways that Carrillo was inside.

Tracking Paco to the compound was easy. With the aid of a few crisp American twenties and the right questions, he found Herrera and his attractive female friend dining at an open-air restaurant called La Choza, conveniently situated on Fifth Avenue, the main drag in Playa. Paco Herrera seemed to have no qualms about dining out in public; he seemed very much at ease, laughing and carrying on with the waiters, and he seemed to know everyone. To Gates, Herrera's audacity was amusing. He wondered if the smuggler would realize his mistakes when he was taken down.

From La Choza, Gates simply followed Herrera in a taxi to the villa in Playacar and when the smuggler headed for the airport in Cancun, the day after the drop, the agent from El Paso was ready. He watched from a safe distance as Herrera purchased a ticket to Vera Cruz, and a few minutes later, both hunter and quarry boarded the same flight.

Arriving at the airport in Vera Cruz, Herrera jumped in a taxi and Gates hailed another to follow. Everything was going well as they headed into the hills and towards the water, but the skinny bearded driver suddenly became very nervous when Herrera's taxi made the turn onto the narrow winding dirt road which led to the compound.

"*Mucho peligro,*" the driver said, pointing towards the top of the hill where the compound sat high above the water.

"*Si.*" Gates agreed. He knew it was dangerous. But forty dollars convinced the man to take him most of the way and he dropped the agent off in a heavily wooded turn, and forgot he had ever seen him.

It took Gates nearly an hour to reach his current position, but he wanted to be closer. He'd been watching the two armed sentries for some time now and was certain his approach had gone unnoticed. Both men were smoking and talking, not even watching the area below them. The agent looked up and behind him. The bright orange fireball of the sun was blinding. Now was the time to move. He slung his duffle over his shoulder and crept forward on his hands and knees...

Inside the compound Paco sat alone at the same marble table at which he had last spoken with Carrillo in person. He had not been invited inside the mansion itself and, as he sat in the shadow of the building itself, he felt as if he were an outsider of sorts, an intruder.

The drop had gone off without a hitch, except for the bad weather Larsen had experienced and his hair-raising entrance into the marina. With the five hundred kilos of cocaine stashed safely aboard the vessel, Paco was anxious to see what the cartel leader expected him to do next.

The weather was perfect once again; a light breeze from the east, not a cloud in the sky, warm in the sun and slightly cooler in the shade. The sliding glass door behind the pool slid open, and Paco gazed upon the cartel leader in disbelief as Carrillo stepped into the late-afternoon air. The man was an absolute chameleon. Since he'd last seen him, Carrillo looked ten years younger. His hair was well groomed and there seemed to be less gray. His eyes were bright and full of life. He wore his favorite navy-blue blazer, and approached Paco with the gait of a terminally ill patient who had suddenly been given a new lease on life. He smiled at Paco and took a seat, studying him before speaking.

"You look well. I assume there were no problems with the drop."

"Nothing major," Paco replied. "The seas were a bit rough, but there is not much we can do about that. The load is secure."

"Any opposition from the local authorities?" Carrillo asked.

"There was some. It was taken care of." Paco told him about the two men from the PJFA and their subsequent demise.

"Do you expect any further resistance?"

"No."

Carrillo yelled at one of his bodyguards who marched back and forth in front of the mansion and told the man to bring him a bottle of tequila. The man returned within moments with a dark brown bottle and two small glasses. Paco noticed there was no label. Carrillo poured each a glass and the two men sipped the golden liquid. Fine tequila was meant to be enjoyed, not bolted down as the Americans did.

"We have a small problem," Carrillo continued. "As I expected, the Colombians are pressuring me to move larger loads. They think five hundred kilos is not worth the risk. Perhaps they are right. In any case, they are threatening to do business elsewhere, with the other cartels."

"We cannot allow that." Paco knew that Carrillo's ties to the Colombians were vital; they gave the Juarez cartel its power, an advantage, an edge.

"No, of course we can't," Carrillo refilled the glasses. "Perhaps we need to return to Juarez. Since we've left, there has been a void, a space to be filled. The other cartels are fighting amongst themselves to take our place. They assume we are out of the picture. We must prove to them, and the Colombians, that they are wrong."

Paco immediately realized the reason for his boss's return to his former self. It was the struggle for power that drove Carrillo, the desire to be number one. He had lost it and now he wanted it back.

Since they had left Juarez, Paco had felt what it was like to have power and to call the shots. Like cocaine itself, power was intoxicating and addictive. Paco had tasted it and now he wanted more.

"It has been only two months, boss," Paco began. "Nothing has changed in Juarez. You must not forget why we came here. The heat is on along the border. That's why we need new routes. You said it yourself. You must think about your wife, your family." And for a moment he saw it in Carrillo's eyes. It was only a brief flicker, but it was there. He watched the cartel leader closely as Carillo closed his eyes and rubbed his forehead in indecision. "Listen to me!" he continued. "Using the boats is just the beginning. We can make more drops, bigger loads. The American boats will be returning to the states in less than a month. Until we can fully develop our network, we must take advantage of this opportunity." He was pleading now and Carrillo eyed him with suspicion.

"And how do you know you can trust these people? You always seem to forget that, Paco. We are running a business here. The loyalty of our employees is of the utmost importance and we both know what happens when we don't have it! You won't even know the people you will have working for you."

"Have I ever failed you so far?"

"No."

"Well then, let me prove to you that I can develop this network. I will personally accompany these loads to the U.S. and guarantee their safe delivery. The Colombians will be happy and you and your family will be safe. Let the other cartels fight over Juarez and the Southwest border. We will expand and develop our operation in the Yucatan until we start moving huge quantities again. As long as we have the Colombians, we have the power."

Carrillo stared across the table at Herrera. Paco sensed that something troubled the man and wondered what it was. The cartel leader reached for his glass and tilted it to his lips, finishing what was left in it. "Alright, Paco. I'll arrange another drop. One thousand kilos this time. You let me know when and where. And you'd better be careful or I'll be looking for another lieutenant." Paco wasn't really sure what he meant and didn't want to ask. The cartel leader got up from the table and headed around the edge of the pool towards the sliding glass door. One of the bodyguards opened it from the inside. "One more thing," he added, turning to Paco. "Don't forget that 'I' have the power, not 'we'." Before Paco could answer, he disappeared inside the mansion.

The Magellan 5000L portable GPS was an amazingly compact and lightweight instrument. While lacking some of the features of the larger permanent models found on most ocean going vessels, it could quickly and accurately determine a latitude and longitude position and, at the moment, that was all Gates needed.

The agent had made it to within twenty yards of the compound's seemingly impenetrable wall, and once again took refuge in a small stand of dry thick bushes.

He had kept the two sentries at the gate in view, and they were now so close he could smell the smoke from their cigarettes and the stink of their unclean bodies.

The air on the back side of the wall was almost still; every movement the former recon expert made had to be precise, its silence crucial.

Very carefully, he removed the miniature GPS unit from his duffle and flicked the short, plastic antenna to the side. He mashed the button on the tiny keyboard labeled "position" and before his exact location was displayed, a tiny peep emitted from the unit. His heart felt as if it had stopped cold. Although no louder than the beep of a digital watch, it might as well have been the blasting screech of an air horn. The two sentries leapt to their feet, unslinging their weapons. They frantically scanned the area from which the foreign and certainly electronic sound had come.

Both men shielded their eyes from the setting sun. While one remained near the gate, the other slowly approached Gates position, his AK-47 leveled and ready. While the sentry could surely see almost nothing, Gates could make out the man's physical attributes perfectly; he was skinny and frail looking, no match for the agent from El Paso. The sentry's curiosity drew him yet closer, close enough for Gates to see the mixture of fear and indecision in his eyes. Gates reached into his duffle and slowly withdrew his blade. The sentry stopped, and cocked his head to one side, straining the air for the faintest sound. Gates heart thundered in his chest, the rush from adrenaline pulsing through his ears. Crouched behind the bush, he was wound tight, defensive yet aggressive; ready to strike.

But then the blaring of a vehicle's horn came from inside the compound. Its piercing wail was sporadic, yet incessant, the operator of the vehicle in a hurry and most likely annoyed. The sentry in front of Gates was startled and spun where he stood, motionless as he stared at the gate in alarm. Gates was tempted to take him right then, one hand over the mouth, the other drawn swiftly across the jugular. But in that brief moment of hesitation, the sentry made up his own mind and sprinted off towards his partner, who was opening the heavy, wrought iron doors of the gate, the only break in the never ending thick stone wall.

Gates seized the moment of distraction and made his way back down the hill, not stopping until he was once again more than a hundred yards from the wall. He crawled on his stomach, dragging his duffle alongside and wound up at the edge of the drive, where he stopped to regain his breath. Within seconds, the sound of the vehicle's engine approached. Gates looked up as a dark-green Suburban rumbled past in a swirling cloud of dust. In the last flickering rays of the sun, the outlines of a driver and passenger were clear. He didn't recognize the man behind the wheel, but there was no mistaking the other. It was Paco Herrera.

Carrillo was right behind that wall, he could feel it. And there was no doubt the cartel leader had a security system that would be hard to beat. Like Larsen, there was no way Gates could do it all by himself. But he had accomplished what he had set out to do, and that was to find Carrillo. He removed the GPS unit from his duffle and made sure he had saved the location, and memorized it. There would be one more raid, of that he was certain. And he would do everything within his power to make sure he was there.

Marina Puerto Aventuras
April 8, 1996 2023 Local Time

Nestled in the far corner of the marina, at the end of the canal closest the cut, the Latitude 20 sports bar was one of the most popular hangouts for the fishermen and their guests. Along with a never-ending supply of beer and hard liquor, the quaint open-air *palapa* offered a satellite television system that could pick up almost any sporting event at any time.

On this night however, the place was deserted except for Larsen and Paco and a few locals. A light drizzle had been falling for hours, a mere nuisance when compared to the front which had blown through earlier in the afternoon. The torrential rains and gale-force winds had knocked out all the power to the entire resort, which remained cloaked in an eerie darkness. Small table candles provided the only light in the damp and quiet bar and the two men spoke in hushed voices at the small white plastic table set off in one corner.

"You're kidding me," Larsen said. "Please tell me this is just a joke." Paco had just told him that there would be at least one more drop. Paco was dressed once again in his full *traficante* regalia, the long-sleeved silk shirt spread open to display the yoke of gold chains, and another set of outrageous boots, clearly made out of some type of reptile skin. Larsen couldn't be sure in the dim glow of the candles, but he thought they might be python.

Paco sipped from his glass of tequila slowly, then tilted his head back and killed it, bringing the shot glass down on the table with a bang. He looked Larsen squarely in the eye. "No. I am not joking," he whispered, his tone menacing. "I think you would call it dead serious."

"You never told me there would be more than one drop," Larsen whispered back. "That was never part of the deal. I don't have the storage for any more!" He glanced around to see if anyone was paying attention, and was relieved when it was clear that they weren't.

"Then you will have to find someone else. I know it isn't part of our original plan, but my suppliers say they need to move at least one thousand more kilos."

"A thousand more kilos? That's a metric ton!" Larsen couldn't believe it. That was twice the amount of the first drop, and the *Predator* was already full. It would require at least two more boats. He had to find some way out of it. "Why don't you just tell your suppliers to fuck off? You've already got enough to make millions. Do you realize the risk of another drop?"

The young *traficante* spoke slowly and calmly. "Of course I realize the risk. Believe me, I would love to tell the suppliers to back off. But these are powerful people. They are pressuring us to move more product. If we don't, they will find someone who will. And we cannot afford to lose this contact!"

Paco's mind was made up, that much was obvious. Larsen knew that if he refused to go through with another drop, Paco would find someone else and the whole operation would be put at risk. Gates had been certain he had tracked down Carrillo, but they needed time to be sure and develop a plan for his capture. "If there has to be another drop, then when?"

"Soon. Within a week," Paco told him.

"And what about the money?"

"Same as before. Half when we are ready to leave here, and the other half when the product is safe in the hands of our people in the states."

"What do you mean 'we'?"

"I mean that when it is time to go to Key West, I will be going with you," Paco said, as if he couldn't believe Larsen would have thought anything different. "Do you expect me to just let you sail off with my money and my product?"

"No, I guess not." It would actually be easier to take the smuggler down on American soil and Larsen didn't argue the point. When the time came, he really didn't want to let the murdering bastard out of his sight.

"All right then. Set it up." Paco got up from the table and prepared to leave. "Here's for the drinks." He laid a hundred peso note on the table.

"What a guy," Larsen said. "Let me tell you something, Paco. Finding someone who's willing to pick up another drop might not be that easy. I want to make sure it's someone we can trust."

"You'll find someone. As for the trust, leave that to me. Once the drop is secure, I will see that we maintain that trust. It is what I do best."

Larsen watched as the killer swaggered off into the darkness, the click of his heels on the concrete slowly fading away. I will see that we maintain that trust. He wondered what Paco had meant.

Ten minutes later, Larsen was on the bridge of the *Predator* trying to contact Macki. It was nearly nine o'clock in Puerto Aventuras, making it almost ten in Virginia and, as he had expected, Macki could not be found at the CIA headquarters in Langley. He left a message. Another thirty minutes passed and the ringer for the single-side-band radio went off.

Larsen had been sitting in the dark, lost in deep thought. He reached for the mike. "This is the *Predator*, go ahead."

"Yeah, how do you read me, Dan?" Macki's voice was slightly tinny, yet amazingly clear. It was late and there was less traffic and no interference.

"Read you five by five. All secure on this end."

"Got some good news, Dan. Gates is here and with the information he gave us, we're going to get a photo recon bird up and see what we can find out. He says the place in Vera Cruz looks like it was built to stop a fuckin' army. We'll see about that."

"Yeah, that's what he told me. But get this, John. I just met with Paco Herrera and he wants to make another drop. A thousand kilos this time." Larsen waited for Macki's response.

"Jesus, can your boat handle that much?"

"Definitely not. I'm about maxed out after that first drop. Paco wants me to bring somebody else in on it."

"Absolutely out of the question," Macki said. "I had a hard enough time convincing the Administrator to let your mate in on it. We can't go granting immunity to every Tom, Dick, and Harry you want to turn into a smuggler. Can't you stall or put him off somehow?"

The question had come to Larsen as no surprise. "I've been trying to think of some way to do that. Paco says they want to make the drop within a week."

"Shit, Dan, it'll take us at least a day or two to get any satellite photos back for analysis. And then we still need to come up with a way to get that bastard Carrillo out of there. Assuming he is there."

"And without the Mexicans knowing it," Larsen added.

"That's right. They're definitely not going to be in on this one."

Larsen waited to see if Macki had anything else to say, but the radio was silent. He keyed the mike. "So what do you want me to do?"

"Just hang in there, captain. Stall if you can. We're working as fast as possible on this end. If you have to, enlist somebody else, and we'll deal with the immunity thing later. But remember, Dan. These people aren't playing around, and your average sportfishing crew isn't trained for this sort of thing."

"Alright, John. But get a move on, will you? I'm about ready to get the hell out of here. Check me as soon as you know something. *Predator* out."

Larsen replaced the mike and turned to face the dock. Most of the spreader lights were off, and a light rain was still falling. The dock was deserted. He left the bridge and made his way down the ladder to the pit, not bothered by the rain. It was a welcome change, a chance for him to relax, to think. Think about who would be willing to make a pickup of two thousand pounds of high-grade cocaine, enough to put a person behind bars for the rest of his life, enough to take the lives of thousands of innocent people. Who had the balls? Who had the greed?

15

State Department Washington D.C.
April 10, 1996

It was only eight o'clock in the morning when Secretary of State Vance Johnson opened the door to the conference room located across the hall from his office. A tall man, Johnson had a thick mop of white hair and a hook nose; it always seemed slightly red, due to the stress of the job or a little too much alcohol, or probably both. Always impeccably dressed in his signature charcoal suits, he carried himself with an air of superiority that was often misconstrued as anger. On this day, however, it was clear that he was an unhappy man. Seated at one end of the mahogany table, in the electronically swept room, were two men; U.S. Ambassador to Mexico, Marcus LeGrone and Senator Thomas Jensen, Chairman of the Mexican-American Affairs Subcommittee. As Johnson entered, both men got to their feet.

"Sit, sit gentlemen," he commanded. "I don't think you're going to like what you're about to hear. I've just gotten off the phone with the President and he has just spoken with the Director of Central Intelligence. It appears that a certain faction of the Zapatista rebels, a cell so to speak, has moved from Chiapas to Cancun. Were you aware of this?"

LeGrone was first to speak. "We have heard rumors, and we are working with the Mexican authorities to substantiate them."

"Rumors?" Johnson looked at the Ambassador with contempt. LeGrone was a skinny man, his hair worn in a half-inch, military crew cut, ironic for a man who despised authority.

His unnaturally pointy ears stuck out as if his mother had been a sugar bowl, and his thin, upturned and sharp nose gave credence to his nickname "the weasel". Johnson knew that the man would do anything and everything to improve his despicable reputation. LeGrone was quick to shift the blame when it came to covering his own ass. "What have you heard, Tom?" He shifted his angry gaze upon Jensen, whose own reputation was no better. Together, the men were two peas in a pod.

"Well, we know that there have been increased troop movements between the southern and western states and Cancun. As far as rebel activity is concerned, all we've heard is that the level of activity in Chiapas has dropped off."

"Doesn't that signal anything to you?" Johnson snapped. "The Mexicans know goddamn well what's going on, but for some fucking reason they've been trying to keep it quiet. Thank God some of our own people have infiltrated this cell and what they've found is a well armed band of pissed-off farmers preparing to mount what looks like a major rebel offensive!"

Both LeGrone and Johnson looked at the Secretary in shock. Both had heard the rumors, but neither had wanted to believe them. Mexico had enough problems. The economy was struggling to hold itself together amidst a domestic revolt. In a country that appeared to be going down the tubes, Cancun was its last saving grace. And now a rebel offensive...

"And what type of action are we preparing to take?" questioned the Ambassador.

"I'll tell you what!" the Secretary began curtly. "The President is this close to issuing a tourist advisory." He held up his thumb and forefinger, less than an inch apart.

"He can't do that!" Jensen cried. "That would be economic homicide. The tourist industry in Cancun is worth three billion dollars a year. Most of it comes from the U.S. We deny them the tourist dollars and their economy is finished!"

"I understand that, Tom, but what you don't understand is that the President has got his back up against a wall. What is happening is the rebels finally smartened up. What a brilliant plan! They move into Cancun and threaten to disrupt one of the biggest tourist destinations in the world. And, believe me, once the first shot is fired, tourism from everywhere, not just the U.S., is going to drop through the floor! Right now, they're just posturing. They don't want a war. They know how important the tourist dollars are. But they want to be heard. The Mexican government has forced their hand." To Johnson it was obvious what was going on and he couldn't believe he needed to lecture the man.

"We need to keep this quiet," LeGrone said. The weasel was at work. "If the press gets hold of this, it'll be just as destructive as an actual advisory. Who knows about this?"

"No one yet. The President, the DCI and the three of us. But we cannot afford to waste time. You need to get with Zedillo as soon as possible." Johnson was certain the Mexican president knew what was going on. "Tell him we're getting ready to issue the advisory and that he'd better get back to the fucking bargaining table."

"And if he refuses?" LeGrone asked.

"Then we'll start with the tourist advisory. After that, we'll begin pulling our people out. Including you, Marcus."

"Are you serious?" the Ambassador asked, his face a mask of disbelief.

"Goddamn right I am! The Mexicans might not give a shit about their own people, but I'm not going to just sit here when American lives are at risk." Johnson shifted his gaze to Jensen.

The Senator had remained relatively quiet and appeared to be lost in thought. Johnson banged his hand on the desk.

"Tom!" he shouted, snapping Jensen out of his reverie. "What's the latest on this Carrillo fellow? The President wants to know."

Jensen looked perplexed, as if he were wondering what the Secretary was talking about. Then it registered. "Oh. They're working on it."

Johnson repeated the words in disgust. "They're working on it. That's great, Tom. That's what I'll tell him." He turned to leave and spoke to the Ambassador. "Get in touch with Zedillo and then let me know what he says."

LeGrone and Jensen got to their feet and prepared to follow the Secretary out the door. "What do you want us to do in the meantime?" Jensen asked.

"Try doing your fucking jobs, for christsakes," Johnson barked. "Both of you."

Poughkeepsie, New York
Later That Evening

It was late when Kym Jensen walked into her tiny apartment and grabbed the remote for the television. The image of David Letterman filled the screen and she could tell the talk-show host was just finishing his opening monologue. That meant it was still before midnight and she might even be able to get a decent night's sleep. She'd been up late all week, cramming for an upcoming exam in a class called Abnormal Psychology and Aberrant Behavior. Most of the class focused on serial murderers and, though fascinating, the core material was a little spooky and she often had trouble falling asleep. The Late Show went to a commercial break and it was then that she noticed the blinking red light on her answering machine.

Unlike most of her friends, who used a service called voice mail, Kym preferred the good old-fashioned, record-your-own, cassette mechanism. Due to her popularity on campus, she was on the receiving end of hundreds of calls for dates. Together, she and Sharon would sit in the small apartment and screen the calls, laughing hysterically at the voices and ill-fated attempts by her many male suitors. She replayed her messages and was surprised when one of the first was from her father. He had called early, and his voice sounded concerned. The message had said to call him at whatever the time.

She punched the numbers into the phone's handset and he answered on the first ring.
"Hi Dad, what's wrong?"
"Hi, honey. What makes you think something is wrong? I was thinking about you and wanted to see how you were doing." Jensen was a master of mixing lies with the truth.

"Well, I'm doing just fine. Studying a lot, getting ready to go on Spring Break. I can't wait, it's only a couple more weeks."

"How's Kevin?" he asked. And that was strange. He hadn't asked about him in weeks.

She paused briefly before answering. "We're not dating anymore."

"What? Why not?"

"He just wasn't my type," Kym told her father. She didn't feel the need to tell him the whole story. It was none of his business.

"I think you're making a mistake," Jensen said. "Kevin has a bright career ahead of him."

Kym was quick to seize the opportunity. "You of all people should know what happens when someone gets too caught up in their career." She knew the words were cutting and painful, but he deserved it.

The other end of the line was silent for several moments before Jensen spoke again, changing the subject. "Have you given any thought to coming here to stay with me during your vacation?"

"I already told you, Dad, I'm going to Cancun."

"And I already told you," he said, the anger in his voice rising. "It's dangerous down there right now. There's a lot of rebel activity."

"I know, but my roommate Sharon says it's all happening somewhere else. Is that true?"

"Well, yes," he said hesitantly. "But there are signs that it's spreading."

She felt as if he were holding something back. He was on that subcommittee, so maybe he knew things other people didn't. "Is there something you're trying to tell me?" she asked.

"Only that I would like to see you come here or go someplace else. I thought it might be a good chance for us to spend some time together."

"Well, I'd love to, Dad." She lied, not wanting to hurt his feelings. "But I already have my tickets, and a lot of my friends are going. My heart's set on it."

"You're not going to see that boat captain guy, are you? Wouldn't you rather be with someone who has a future, someone who can offer you some security?"

"My personal life and what I want is my business, Dad, not yours." She regretted ever telling her father about the captain. But after she had met him, she felt alive and excited, and wanted to share it. She knew her father pictured boat captains and fishermen as old salts in a yellow slicker with a corncob pipe. He didn't understand the sportfishing, and that most of the jobs paid quite well.

"I'm sorry, honey," Jensen began. "I know your life is your own. I just want what's best for you. I miss you and worry about you. Please believe that. Do me a favor. Think about what I said."

"I will, Dad. Thanks for calling. I'll talk to you soon."

She hung up the phone and laughed to herself. Oh yes, she'd think about what he said. Think about it while she was sitting on the beach in Puerto Aventuras, sipping a frozen margarita with Dan Larsen.

Marina Puerto Aventuras
April 10, 1996 1134 Local Time

Dan Larsen had known Terry Stanton for nearly ten years. And in that time, the captain of the *Tempest* had turned out to be one of the most valuable friends the agent would ever have. From his very first days in Florida, Stanton had taken Larsen under his wing, teaching him the ins and outs of the sportfishing world, always putting in a good word for him in Larsen's quest to upgrade from mate to captain. Unlike Larsen, Stanton had been born into the world of fishing; it was his life, his livelihood, and he had long ago realized the advantages of becoming an expert in all aspects of it. Whether it was trolling for blues or bottom fishing for grouper, Stanton had done it all, fresh water or salt, and he was more than happy to share his knowledge.

His private life, on the other hand, was another matter. With both his father and older brother in federal prison on smuggling charges, the man spoke little about his family and youth, keeping it to himself in what Larsen had come to realize was a sense of profound shame. Only through his own research was Larsen able to find out about his friend's tragic secret and, out of respect, the agent had never mentioned it. Several times, he had heard Stanton tell others who had asked about his parents and siblings that they were dead. Larsen guessed that, to Stanton, they probably were.

When Stanton stepped aboard the *Predator* and opened the salon door, he looked at Larsen and did not speak. It was obvious to the agent that something was wrong. Behind his clear, metal-framed glasses, Stanton's eyes were red and puffy; he'd been crying.

"Someone died," Larsen said somberly, attempting to guess what was wrong, and inwardly hoping he was wrong.

"No," Terry said softly. "It's Jessica. She's real sick." Stanton could barely get the words out. His eyes filled to the brim and his lower lip was quivering.

"Don't worry, man, kids are always sick. She'll get better." Larsen had known that Stanton's little girl had been ill, but he thought she had gotten over it. Stanton's daughter and wife were all his friend seemed to live for, but it seemed like the man was over-reacting.

"No, she won't," Stanton told him. "She's not going to get better, she's going to get worse. The tests came back and she's got some sort of disease. It's like leukemia. I can't even pronounce the fuckin' name of it." A tear rolled out of his right eye, dragging behind it a small stream that ran down his face and into the corner of his mouth. With a watery sniff, he wiped it away.

Larsen's heart sank; a lump formed in his throat and he thought he might cry himself. He had watched the spunky little six-year old grow up and hadn't missed one birthday party. They were very close and Larsen felt a great sense of pride when she referred to him as "Uncle Dan." With great difficulty, he struggled for the right words to say. "Leukemia is curable," he offered. "I'm sure whatever she has is also."

"Yeah, if you're a millionaire," Terry said. "They said that what she has is almost always fatal. The only chance is a bone-marrow transplant. Hundreds of thousands of dollars that I don't have." Another tear rolled out.

"What about insurance?" Larsen asked.

"I missed a couple month's payments and my coverage expired," Stanton said weakly and began to sob.

"Take it easy, man. We'll figure it out." Larsen took a seat at the table and stared out the salon window. There sat millions upon millions of dollars worth of boats and a little girl needed money to survive. The inside of the boat was quiet, except for the low hum of the air conditioner compressor in the pump room below. Neither man spoke. Larsen was lost in thought and Stanton's presence was only given away by the occasional sniffle.

The sound of rotor blades thwacking the air approached and just as quickly faded as the unseen craft flew south along the beach. Something set off an alarm in Larsen's brain and suddenly it was all crystal clear. He hesitated for a moment, but he knew it had to be done. Turning to Stanton, he spoke.

"I know where we can get the money..."

Down in the engine room of the *Slammer*, Rob Masters stared at Larsen in disbelief. He'd been busy changing the oil on his 61 Buddy Davis when Larsen had suddenly made his way down the two-step ladder. "Did you just ask me if I wanted to make almost a million dollars smuggling cocaine?"

"That's right," Larsen told him, smiling.

"I think you've been breathing a little too much diesel," Masters said, laughing as he wiped the thick, black oil from his hands and where some tiny drops had splashed his face.

"I've already got over a thousand pounds on my boat."

Masters smile quickly faded. "Oh my god, you're serious."

"Dead serious." Larsen told him of the plan, but like he had explained it to Stanton, he left out the part about his involvement with the DEA and that the whole operation was secretly sponsored by the CIA.

"I thought you'd been acting a little weird lately," Masters said.

"Now you know why."

"You crazy motherfucker... Let me guess. You picked it up that night it was really rough and came in late."

"You're brilliant."

"This is heavy shit. And you say Stanton is gonna be in on this next one? That sucks about his kid."

"Yeah. He's trying to figure out a way to tell his mate. What about Matt?" Larsen knew that Kirchner, like Masters, was not a complete stranger to drug use. College was often a testing ground, and he couldn't blame him.

"He's kind of a wild man. He'd probably do it just for the thrill of it. That and the money, of course."

The two men spent the next few minutes discussing what they would do with the money. As Larsen had expected, Masters tried to think of things that could go wrong, ways that they could get caught. But in the end, his greed had prevailed. Masters wanted his own boat. Without taking such a risk, he would never get it. And if they were all in on it, somehow it seemed less dangerous, less illegal.

Now all Larsen had to do was figure out a way to get these men their money, uphold his end of the deal. He would keep the fiscal aspects of the operation a secret from his superiors, just as the entire operation was a secret from the public. They were all putting their lives on the line, and they deserved as much.

"So when is all this going down?" Masters asked.

"Soon. Whenever we can all coordinate it." Larsen turned to go back on deck. "So I can count you in?"

Masters flashed him the thumbs up sign. "Hundred percent, man."

16

Aboard the *Slammer*
April 13, 1996 0915 Local Time

The huge frigate bird floated on the morning sea breeze with no detectable pattern. Its flight was smooth and effortless. Interrupted by only the occasional flap of its wings, it soared above the deep blue waters of the Caribbean with only one thing in mind. Food. Also known as the man-o-war bird, the great winged creature was not only a predator, but a thief as well. Lacking the protective oils of other types of waterfowl, the frigate was forced to snatch fish from the surface of the water or straight from the claws of its competitors. With a wing span of six feet or more and an incredibly long, forked tail, the intimidating feathered hunter was easily recognized. On this day, it did not go unnoticed.

"Got a frigate up ahead," Kirchner cried up to Masters, who was busy watching the baits from the bridge of the *Slammer*.

"Yeah, I've been watching him for a while now," the big captain replied. "He's not on anything yet, but he's lookin'." Even with his sunglasses, it was necessary for Masters to squint as he followed the bird's flight path up and down the coast, in and out from the shore. A few early morning clouds had since burned off and it looked like the beginning of another near-perfect day. Without much wind, the sea was relatively calm and since leaving the cut almost an hour earlier, Masters had been working the 61 Davis back and forth along a prominent color change that he spotted in just over a thousand feet of water. It was a little deep for sail-fish action, but he didn't care; today he was after the big guy, the king of the billfish—the elusive blue marlin.

It had been less than three days since Larsen had told him of his plan to pick up and smuggle a load of over two thousand pounds of cocaine. He still couldn't believe he was going to do it. When he had first mentioned the idea to Larsen a month earlier, he hadn't been serious; it was theoretical, a joke, a crazy idea. But when Larsen had taken him aboard the *Predator* and shown him the bundles from the first drop, it became a startling reality. He felt oddly responsible, and he hoped his good friend knew what he was doing. Masters looked down at Larsen, who was down in the pit, joking and laughing with Kirchner. As if he had sensed the other captain's gaze, he looked up and smiled, the expression of his true feelings invisible behind the blue lenses of his shades.

The drop was to take place at dusk, just after the sunset. Masters had estimated that to be about seven-thirty. It was hard to believe they were fishing, but what Larsen had said was right. They needed to carry on as they always did, to act normal. To fish.

Larsen had shown him the coordinates of the drop point; they were the same as the first drop, somewhere south and east of Akumal. He wasn't worried about finding the right spot because he knew the GPS would put him right on it. Stanton in the *Tempest* would also be there, and the load would be split evenly, five hundred kilos per boat. Share the risk, and share the money. If they got caught, they would share the blame. Perhaps they would even share a jail cell. He tried not to think such negative thoughts.

Larsen had assured him his plan would go off without a hitch, and Masters hoped he was right. What he couldn't understand was his friend's motivation. He knew Larsen was well paid and had one of the better jobs in the business. Why would he risk it? And what about his sister dying and all that stuff? Larsen had been furious when Masters had gotten into the blow scene just a couple of years earlier. Was all that bullshit?

Whatever it was, it had been good for him. He'd gotten off the dead-ly, addictive white shit and had gotten on with his life, focusing on remaining one of the best and most respected sportfish captains around.

Larsen had kept Masters' drug use a secret between them, and there was no question the entire episode had brought them closer together, strengthening the bond between them.

Being a sportfish captain was no easy job, and it wasn't surprising when a captain stepped off the path into the quagmire of drugs or drink. The days were long and hard, the nights long and lonely. Foreign lands were filled with foreign peoples and foreign languages. If not for the camaraderie of the captains and their crews, Masters doubted if he would be able to take it. Always on the road and sometimes not returning home for months, there was little time for a wife or family. But still Masters pressed on, saving his money for a day when he would have both. And with the latest developments that he considered dangerous and insane, he was willing to risk it all, with the chance he could soon begin the life he had always dreamt of. A life where he made the choices, and his own livelihood didn't rely on the whims of another.

Offshore, and high overhead, the frigate bird stopped its aimless wandering on the rising thermal and began to circle. The change in its flight caught Master's attention; his keen eye was trained to spot changes, whether above or upon the water. Seconds later, the great bird tucked in its wings and fell from the sky like a stone, hurtling towards the water at blistering speed. It swooped just above the surface, but when it came up, its claws were empty. It rose slightly higher, floated momentarily, then swooped again with the same result. Masters pushed the throttles ahead another thousand rpms and steered the *Slammer* toward the spot in the water the frigate was intent on. From behind his sunglasses, his eyes scanned the spread of baits for signs of activity. The prop wash billowed just off the stern, swirling clouds of bubbles, momentarily obscuring the flat lines before rising to the surface and dissipating.

Down in the pit, Kirchner and Larsen had become silent, their eyes also focused on the baits. They had felt the increase in speed and had also seen the bird, which now soared almost directly above. The three men waited for something to happen; the tension was electric.

"Left long!" Masters cried as the line popped out of the rigger with a snap. Kirchner was immediately on the rod and put the reel in free spool as the line floated to the water yet hardly came tight. The skirtless bally-hoo continued to skip across the surface of the water; there was no sign of a fish. They waited nearly a minute and when nothing happened, Kirchner pulled the clip down, snapped the line back in place, and ran it back up the rigger.

"What was it?" Kirchner asked. Both he and Larsen looked up towards the bridge for an answer, as if Masters always had one.

"I don't know. I didn't see shit." He was just about to tell Kirchner to check the same bait when a shadow appeared beneath and slightly behind the left teaser. Masters was momentarily speechless as he watched the shadow take shape, rising from the deep and displaying its incredible size. Like a submarine breaking the surface, the huge dorsal fin was the first thing to rise from the sea. Then the body and tail came up, slicing the water and pushing it aside with its great strength. "Blue Marlin!" was all Masters could gasp.

There was no need to call out the left rigger; both Kirchner and Larsen had already seen it. "Get the pitch bait," Masters shouted once he had found his voice, but Kirchner was way ahead of him. The mate had already grabbed the Penn 50TW and was busy dropping back a naked horse ballyhoo, rigged with a Mustad 10/0 stainless steel hook.

Masters pulled the teaser in by hand, the hungry blue chasing the hook-less lure with unabated fury. The pectoral fins stuck out straight to its sides, wider than a man's shoulders, and all three men watched as the fish "lit up", its fins and stripes changing from a dark to an almost electric blue.

Kirchner dropped the bait back until it was almost even with the teas-er. He watched in disbelief as the huge marlin swam past the bait, its left eye as big as a saucer, and clearly focused on the purple, white and blue plastic of the teaser. He was shocked when Masters continued to pull the teaser in further, but he knew that Masters was doing the right thing. If the fish was able to get a hold of the teaser, he would eat it and swim off; unfortunately, it had happened before. When the teaser suddenly left the water, the marlin faded off and disappeared.

"Put the fuckin' teaser back in the water!" Kirchner screamed. Masters did and instantly the fish was back on it. The scenario was repeated for a minute or so as they tried to tempt the great fish with the bait. Finally, the big blue spotted the ballyhoo, veered sharply to it's left, and piled on it with a huge splash, swimming off into the depths.

"Feed him good," Masters warned, and Kirchner obliged by free-spool-ing the reel for at least ten seconds. All three of them held their breath as Kirchner pushed up the drag lever, took a few cranks on the reel and reared back to set the hook. The rod slowly bent over, and went so far that they were all afraid it might crack in half. But at the same time the reel erupted with an incredibly loud grinding noise as the marlin took off, peel-ing off drag, the tension of the line singing as it reeled off the spool at an incredible rate. Kirchner waited a moment, then raised his right fist in the air, supporting the rod with his thick, left arm. As Larsen got busy clear-ing the other rods, Kirchner let loose with a victorious shout. "Fish on!"

Aboard the _Tempest_
That Same Time

High above the water in the tower of his Monterey, Captain Terry Stanton was watching a bird of his own. Like a scavenger, it also flew without a particular destination, searching and hunting. But unlike the frigate, its body was steel, its wings were rotors and it sailed across the sky by means of a powerful turbine engine. Stanton watched the blue and white chopper as it flew down the coast, thwacking the air in a manner that was anything but silent. He'd seen the steel bird before and he knew its purpose, and the sight of it now made his stomach nervous.

When Larsen had first approached him with his plan to help him get some money, Stanton had been in shock. At the time, he'd still not recov-ered from the initial news of Jessica's illness, and had he not been emo-tionally stressed, he would have considered his friend's offer preposterous. When he'd first heard the word "smuggle", such terrible thoughts had rushed into his mind! His father and brother had both chosen that route and now would spend the rest of their lives paying for a gamble that they had lost. They had taken the easy road to riches and like the pot of gold at the end of the rainbow, their rewards had never materialized. From them he had learned, learned about taking such incredible and dangerous risks. For years he had avoided drugs and those who sold or used them. But now his little girl, his own flesh and blood, his angel Jessica was in trouble. He needed to come up with a huge sum of money and, while he searched, her precious life hung in the balance. Even if he could borrow the money, they would be in debt for the rest of their lives. He couldn't let Jessica grow up that way. It wasn't her fault! He had missed the insurance payments and had no one to blame but himself. Only he could make it right and give her the chance to grow up as she deserved. He couldn't be a coward! And so, when Larsen had propositioned him, he had not refused. Had not then, and would not now.

As the chopper disappeared down the coast, Stanton removed his special prescription shades. He looked down into the pit at his mate John Flynn, who was busy changing the left short bait. Squinting from the sun as well as the fact that he was nearly blind without them, he wiped the salt from the lenses of the glasses with the front of his shirt.

"Hey John. Come on up here for a minute." The skinny mate closed his bait box and came up the ladder.

"What's up?" So young. So innocent. And Stanton was going to corrupt him.

"I just want you to know that if you don't want to do it, that's all right. Don't do it just to fit in with the rest of us, you know?"

"That's not it at all, Terry. You don't understand. All my life, I've lived in the shadows. No money. No car...I used to sit on the bridge going over to Singer Island. Watch the guys with the boats get all the chicks. I promised myself that one day I'd be one of those guys. Now I'm light years ahead of that. I'm finally getting the chance to be somebody, you know, do something exciting. I've got to do this."

"You realize if we're caught, we'll go to jail for a long time."

"That's a chance I'm willing to take, Terry. My decision." His expression was serious.

Stanton could see that Flynn was growing up fast. He wasn't a kid anymore, and they were all responsible. God help him.

Aboard the *Slammer*

Less than thirty seconds after its initial run, the giant blue surfaced, shaking its head back and forth in a combination of fury and distress. From his position on the bridge, it was clear to Masters that the fish was gut-hooked, the bait and steel point lodged deep in the marlin's stomach. With each shake of its head, the pink hues of bloody water flew in all directions.

"Reel! Reel! Reel!" Masters screamed as he threw the *Slammer* into reverse, pushing a wall of water as the responsive Carolina hull headed for the fish, engines roaring. Down in the pit, Larsen had taken a seat in the fighting chair and was winding like a machine.

Leaning against the rear covering board of the transom, Kirchner watched the line as well as the fish, shouting out the necessary changes in direction and speed as they hastened towards the struggling finned giant. He'd already slipped on the heavy leather gloves, and his razor-sharp bait knife was clenched between his teeth as he prepared to make the release.

With less than twenty yards to go, the marlin took off again, and thrashing its huge tail, charged across the top of the water, twisting and turning its body violently as it raced along the starboard side. Kirchner immediately ran to the rear of the chair, grunting as he muscled the heavy mahogany and chrome contraption into its proper direction, facing the fish. Both men howled at the awesome spectacle, and once again the line peeled off the reel at an alarming rate.

Before Masters could react, the marlin had gone clear past the bow and appeared to have no intentions of stopping. He shifted gears into forward and in a classic maneuver, swung the *Slammer* completely around as the line came tight, pulling the fish back to the south and into the current. Thick black smoke poured from the exhaust as diesel flooded into the screaming engines. Within a minute, the fish stopped its run. The spool of the reel stayed motionless and Larsen began to crank. But off it went again and the two men looked at each other with a mixture of understanding and alarm.

"There he goes," Kirchner said softly. He stood up straight and sighed. There was nothing they could do as the amount of remaining line gradually decreased.

"Bastard," Larsen muttered. "He's takin' us deep."

Fifteen minutes later, the fish finally stopped. Kirchner looked up at the bridge. "How deep?"

"Eleven hundred," Masters replied.

"Goddamn..." Kirchner said.

"It's gonna be a long fight," Larsen added from the chair.

"Yep. But we've got all day. All we have to do is get him in by dark. If he lives that long and the sharks don't get him first." Masters knew they had all been thinking it, and he hadn't wanted to say it. But he also felt for the fish, a sense of sadness and respect that told him they had to get him up as soon as possible.

An hour later, they were getting close. All three men had taken turns winding, and Kirchner was in the chair when the heavy mono leader came into view. Larsen snatched the gloves and had them on in less than a second. He grabbed the heavy nylon wind-on leader and began to pull the great fish to the surface, alternately taking wraps with each hand, his body straining against the dead weight of the fish. His face reddened and his arms were on fire as the blue finally broke the surface, dragging lazily on its side. The once bright blues were now dark brown, almost black, and the eyes of the exhausted creature were cloudy. All three of the men had expected it, but they were still filled with remorse.

With one hand, Larsen removed his glasses, opened the tuna door and flopped onto his belly, pulling the fish closer and grabbing the big blue by the bill. "Go ahead," he grunted to Masters. The captain put the *Slammer* in gear and they began dragging the fish, forcing water through its mouth and gills in a desperate attempt to revive it. Five minutes passed with no change in the condition of the fish.

"It's no use, Dan," Masters called down from the bridge.

"Yeah man. Give it up. He's had it," Kirchner added. He put the rod in the holder on the chair and disconnected the swivel from the leader.

"Might as well pull him in." Masters said dejectedly.

"No fucking way!" Larsen screamed. He turned to look at Kirchner with eyes filled with fury. His teeth were bared and when he spoke, bits of white spit flew out with the words. "We're not going to be the first ones to lay a blue on the P.A. dock! Just keep going."

"Hey, man, shit happens. It's better than feeding him to the sharks." What Kirchner said was logical, but Larsen wasn't listening. He continued to drag the blue, and his tired arms felt no pain as his mind drifted to a time years before.

His sister lay in his arms, and he was trying desperately to revive her. Her skin had lost its natural color and was a ghostly white, her lips a pale green. He'd promised to protect her! How could he have let her die?

"Hey, he's coming back. He's coming back!" Kirchner's screams snapped Larsen out of it and he felt the boat increase speed.

Both men saw the colors change as the marlin came back to life. His arms begged for relief, and the pain came flooding back. When he could stand it no longer, he let go. The fish slowly swept its wide tail once, and then again, and slid back to the deep.

"Yeah! Yeah!" Kirchner cried, raising his hands to high-five Larsen as he got to his feet, exhausted. "You did it!" His exuberation faded immediately when he looked into Larsen's eyes. They were filled with tears.

"Wow, man, it's just a fish," the mate told him.

"I know," Larsen managed, taking a deep breath, his eyes glistening. He walked away, wiping his eyes. "I know."

Aboard the *Tempest*

At exactly seven o'clock, Stanton eased back the throttles of the *Tempest* as the GPS alarm sounded. They had reached the exact coordinates of the expected drop. As if tired, the sleek sportfishing yacht came off a plane, its diesel engines groaning as the rpms ticked down. When the craft's forward momentum had ceased, Stanton put the engines in neutral, and scanned the surrounding area for other vessels. There were none. The wallowing exhaust of the idling diesels was distracting, and with one hand, Stanton hit both black rubber "stop" buttons, killing the engines.

The sudden silence was intense. The bright orange orb of the sun, which had beat down mercilessly upon Stanton and Flynn all day, had, only minutes before, slipped below the western horizon, and the purple sky was on its way to black. The surface of the sea mirrored the sky above and the dark waters were empty as far as the naked eye could see. Bobbing and rocking only slightly in the nearly calm water, there was no question they were alone.

Looking for companionship or perhaps a partner in crime, Stanton walked to the rear of the bridge, grasped the waist-high chrome railing, and leaned over the edge. The pit was almost dark, but he could just barely make out the figure of his mate, seated on top of the tackle center with his legs crossed and his back up against the smooth, varnished teak of the rear bulkhead.

"Hey," Stanton called softly. "You all right down there?"

Flynn slid down from his perch and looked up at his captain. His answer was barely audible. "Yeah. Is this the spot?"

"Yep. GPS says it is. I think we're a little early."

"What?"

"I said I think we're a little early." Stanton's second utterance wasn't much louder.

"Why are we whispering?" Flynn asked quietly.

"I don't know," Stanton said, still not raising his voice. "It all just seems so—so sneaky." He cleared his throat and resumed his conversation in a normal voice. "I guess nobody's gonna hear us."

"Where's Larsen and Masters?"

"Not sure," Stanton replied. He hadn't heard anything more from the *Slammer* since Masters had reported releasing a large blue earlier that morning. "They'll be here soon."

"He told you dusk, right?" Before Stanton could respond, Flynn pointed out the obvious. "Well, its definitely dusk. I call this pretty damn dark."

Stanton looked in all directions again. The only visible light was a faint glow to the west, just above the water. He guessed that was Akumal.

Reaching for the radio, he raised the squelch to be sure the unit was functioning properly. The obnoxious static sound told him it was. The unit was set to the secret channel, but all day he had heard nothing on it. They're just running a little late. Both men remained silent for several minutes, watching as the stars became brighter and the background of the evening sky turned to black.

Both Stanton and Flynn heard the sound simultaneously. It was faint at first, but unquestionably the familiar drone of twin diesels and they were getting louder. Five minutes later the ghostly outline of the *Slammer* appeared out of the darkness as Masters steered the other vessel broadside, and for a moment, Stanton was afraid they might collide. But with great expertise, Masters threw his boat in reverse, and the sportfisher stopped less than twenty feet away, the surge of its wake rocking the *Tempest*.

Holding the rail for balance, Stanton waited for Masters to shut down his engines before shouting over at the other captain.

"Better late than never!"

"Seven-thirty on the nose," Masters cried. "We were busy catching the white as part of our slam." The pride was evident in his deep voice and Stanton was jealous. He and Flynn had also managed to catch a white marlin and several sails, but no blue.

Whether it was skill or luck he was not sure, but to Stanton it seemed that Masters always had just the right amount of both.

"Pretty work, man," Stanton shouted at him, but quickly changed the subject. "You think these guys are gonna show?"

Another voice came from the bridge of the *Slammer*. Stanton hadn't even seen him, but Larsen was right beside Masters. "They'll show. They're going to wait until its good and dark," the captain of the *Predator* said. His voice was loud, confident.

"Why'd you tell me dusk?" Stanton asked.

"I wanted to make sure you weren't late."

"Jesus, Dan, don't you ever take anything seriously?" Stanton couldn't believe how he could be so nonchalant about what they were going to do.

"Of course I do Terry. I'm taking this very seriously. But you need to relax so you don't fuck it up. Just get half the load on your boat and forget about it. The rest will be gravy."

"Alright, man. I'll try," Stanton said. He knew he would never be able to relax. There was too much at stake.

A few minutes later, the drone of distant aircraft engines could be heard. Stanton's heart lurched in his chest and his pulse quickened as the moment of truth approached.

"Here they come," Masters shouted at Stanton. "Fire it up."

The twin diesels rumbled to life and Stanton stared into the sky, searching for the plane. Taking a deep breath, he grasped the throttles with sweaty palms. Against his better judgement, he prepared to do the unthinkable.

17

Marina Puerto Aventuras
Later That Night

The *Slammer* and the *Tempest* had returned to the marina together, the two vessels rumbling into their respective slips as if returning from just another successful outing on the rip. The grand slam caught by the *Slammer* was much celebrated by those on the dock, but the true catch of both vessels was unknown to all but the three captains and their crew.

Now they were seated at a wobbly marble table at the Café Olé restaurant, another open-air joint in the marina center. The six men raised their shot glasses for a toast. Larsen spoke, once again the leader.

"To a good day," he began. "And one that will never be forgotten as long as we live." His words rang true, but for reasons unknown to the other diners. The men clinked the glasses together, and in unison, they each bolted down an ounce and a half of tequila.

As it burned its way down their throats and into their stomachs, they celebrated the creation of a bond—they were all in it together now—partners in crime. The load had arrived just like the first, fast and right on target. The two boats had split it evenly, half a metric ton each, and the cocaine had been carefully stowed in the forward bilges of each vessel. The *Slammer*, being a Carolina hull, narrow and more flared, was forced to stash several of the bulky brown packages in a space under the bed in the master stateroom on the port side. To Masters, it seemed like it had all happened days ago, but in reality, it was just over an hour. He looked at his watch.

It was five minutes to nine. He was fidgety.

"So now all we have to do is sit tight for two weeks," he said.

"No we don't," Larsen countered. "We carry on just like we always do. Fish, dive, party—everything the same. Then we go back to Florida—just like we always do." The agent looked at each of the other men as he spoke, to be sure they understood the importance of acting normal. "The hardest part is over," he added, "it's gonna be smooth sailing from here on out."

"Motoring," Kirchner corrected.

"Yeah, sorry. Motoring," Larsen said and all of them laughed.

It was forced, edged in nervousness, but he couldn't blame them. All the men were risking a lot, and not only for their own reasons, but because he had asked them to. Should anything go wrong, it would be Larsen who would ultimately be held responsible, and no one knew that better than himself. But nothing would go wrong. Think positive, he told himself.

Stanton signaled the waiter for another round of shots.

"You go, boy!" Kurt shouted. They all knew that the quiet captain rarely drank, but they also understood why this night was an exception. Stanton seemed to have the most at stake, with his little girl's life depending on the success of their new "mission".

The evening air was again thick and itchy. There wasn't much of a breeze and the mosquitoes were vicious. The little bastards had been pestering Larsen's ankles since they first sat down and he bent down below the table to be sure the green coil of supposed repellent was still burning. As he had feared, the coil had gone out. He borrowed a lighter from one of the waiters and bent over to relight it. When he sat up again, he froze. Masters had gone pale, a look in his eyes of pure terror at whatever he had just seen. The agent turned to see a jeep full of *Federales* cruise by the restaurant, their piercing stares menacing. He quickly counted six, no, eight men and they were all in uniform and heavily armed with automatic rifles and sidearms.

Masters leapt to his feet while the others just stared hypnotically. In a flash, Larsen's arm shot out and grabbed Masters, pulling the big man back to his seat. His grip was strong, perhaps too much so. Masters turned to face him, his expression a mixture of fear and anger.

"What the hell are you doing?" Masters demanded.

"Sit the fuck down!" Larsen whispered sternly through clenched teeth. The other men stared at him, unsure what to do. None made a move. The restaurant had begun to buzz, the other diners also alarmed at the presence of the armed law enforcement officers. Larsen spoke slowly and confidently. "Listen to me. Are you trying to fucking blow it already?" His tone was stern. "Just relax and we'll see what's going on."

As they watched, six of the eight men made their way down the first part of the main dock, the part they called Park Avenue. The wallow of diesel motors was heard and a 31 Bertram, one of the local charter boats, appeared out of the darkness and pulled up to the dock in an empty spot, side-to.

Mesmerized, the men at the table watched in silence as the six *Federales* boarded the boat. One of the *Federales* shouted a command to the two men who had remained with the jeep, but Larsen couldn't make it out. The Bertram motored away from the dock and idled away in the darkness, heading for the cut.

Larsen turned to face his friends. "See? They definitely don't know what's going on."

"Don't know exactly what's going on," Stanton said, his voice high-pitched and clearly filled with fear. "But it's obvious they know something."

Larsen saw that he needed to restore their composure immediately. They couldn't fall apart at the first sign of trouble. "Yes, that's obvious," he said calmly. "But let's not all freak out. They might be looking for the drop, but they must not know that it's already come. Everybody relax until we find out what's happening." He looked at the others and they returned his stare. "Everything will be fine. Trust me."

One of the Mexican wash-boys was pedaling by on a dilapidated beach cruiser. Larsen recognized him as Pancho, a young guy from Tabasco who washed boats during the season to help support his family back home. He'd been around the marina for the last three seasons and in that time, the agent had watched him change from a boy to a man.

"Hey *Flocko*." Larsen called the boy by his nickname, which in Spanish meant "skinny". "*Que pasa con las Federales?*"

Pancho pulled his bike up to the table and grinned as he delivered the news. "They are looking for cocaine," he told the men as nonchalantly as if he had said they were going night fishing. "A large delivery is expected tonight. They hope to find it before the *traficantes.*"

Nearly half an hour passed and the six men were having a hell of a time acting normal. Three more rounds of drinks had arrived and while Larsen and Stanton switched to beer, the mates and Masters had continued with the shots of tequila. The three younger men were clearly showing the effects of the alcohol, but Masters was still sober and jumpy.

"Stop fucking looking over there, goddammit!" It was the third time Larsen had to tell them. Out of the corner of his eye, he could see the two men in the jeep staring, discussing, and talking on the radio. Unfortunately, they were just out of earshot. It was then that he decided it was time to go. He signaled the waiter for the check and they all got up to leave.

Following Larsen's instructions, Stanton and the three mates headed for the sports bar a bit further along the water in the marina center. Their laughter and carrying on were genuine; the alcohol had calmed their nerves.

Masters, on the other hand, was another story. The man simply would not or could not settle down. The sight of the *Federales* had completely freaked him out.

"You need to fuckin' relax, man," Larsen told him. It was more an order than a suggestion.

"I can't. I swear I'm trying, but I just can't. I know we're gonna get caught." Masters voice was nervous and whiny.

They were headed towards the boats on Park Avenue, a path that would take them directly past the two men in the jeep. Larsen was calm and focused.

Act natural. Paranoia is the killer.

Just before they reached the jeep, Larsen slung his arm lazily across Masters' muscular shoulders. As they reached the jeep, he called out to the *Federales*.

"*Buenas noches, amigos!*" Larsen purposely slurred his words. Just another intoxicated fisherman.

They continued to walk. Larsen steered Masters down the ramp and along the dock, expecting a whistle or shout. It never came. When they had rounded the corner, he heaved a sigh of relief. The dock was deserted.

"Listen to me, goddammit!" He spun Masters around, gripping his arm tightly. "You've got to get with it or we are going to get caught. You should see how guilty you look."

"I can't help it! Maybe we're not all as cool as you, Dan. Maybe this whole thing was a bad idea. I'm sorry I ever brought it up."

Somehow his good friend blamed himself for the situation they were all now in. "It's not your fault, man. All you did was suggest what I had already been thinking. I'm the one who acted on it. I'm the one who asked for your help. Maybe it was a mistake, but now we're all in it and we've got to see it through to the end. We're in it now," Larsen repeated, "and believe me, these dudes play for keeps. I've seen it."

Masters brooded silently for a moment before speaking. "That's what scares me. I know these guys don't give a shit about our lives when it comes down to the big score. But what scares me even more is the idea of spending the rest of my life rotting in some Mexican shithole in Chetumal." It was well known that foreigners charged with crimes wound up in the prison near the Belize-Mexico border. The conditions were appalling. Trials? Convictions? Forget it! In Mexico it was guilty until proven innocent.

"Yeah, well, don't worry about all that. It's not gonna happen."

"What do we do when the *Federales* come back with nothing and want to search our boats?"

"They can't. Our boats fly the United States flag. Each one of these boats is a little piece of the U.S.." Finally, they approached the *Predator*.

"They're not allowed to get on our boats. It would create an international incident."

"Fuckin' right it would!" Masters fired back. "And that would be the end of us." He laughed a little and Larsen was glad to see that he was settling down a bit.

"Like I said, it's not gonna happen. Two more weeks, man. Fourteen days of fishing and partying. Then it's home free and hello new life!"

"For me it's going to seem like two years," Masters told him. "Two long years."

"A small price to pay for what lies ahead, my friend. Hang in there, man, we'll be fine." The agent smacked his buddy on the shoulder. "Now go get some rest. Tomorrow's another day." Larsen turned and jumped down into the cockpit of the *Predator*. He watched as his friend ambled down the dock, broad shoulders slumped.

"Hey!" the agent called out. "Trust me."

Masters stopped and turned to look at him. He said nothing, and simply turned and kept walking.

Masters bounded onto the teak deck of the *Slammer* with a thud. With Kirchner off at the sports bar and no guests or owners aboard, he was alone. He flicked off the spreader lights and the *Slammer* was plunged into darkness. Feeling his way through the dark into the galley, he opened the freezer door and soft white light spilled across his massive frame and the galley floor. Grabbing a handful of ice cubes, he spun around and stuck them in a red plastic cup he found next to the sink. Then, leaving the freezer door open just a crack, he made his way carefully across the salon to the bar, where he poured himself half a glass of rum. He found half a bottle of coke and was annoyed when it turned out to be flat. Adding just a splash, he stirred the mixture with his thick index finger before taking several big gulps. The cool liquid warmed his throat as it slid into his belly. Taking a deep breath, he shrugged his shoulders and moved his neck from side to side. God he was tight!

Must relax, he told himself and trudged down the stairs to the forward stateroom. Placing his drink on the night-table, he lay down on the mattress and closed his eyes. He felt himself floating and smiled to himself as the alcohol took effect and the tension began to slip away.

Maybe Larsen was right. No one could possibly know what they had aboard and within two weeks it would all be over. If Larsen was right...But what if he wasn't? He could feel the anxiety and tension creeping back, clawing at the back of his neck like a parasite. How could Larsen be so calm, so sure? Did he have a get out of jail free card? What was his motivation?

Two weeks. He could make it. They would all make it. Or would they?

As if in a trance, the big man made his way to the master stateroom and turned on the tiny halogen lights. After locking the narrow door, he lifted the mattress and removed the panel underneath. Bracing the mattress with his shoulders, he removed several cases of Miller Lite and exposed the huge plastic-wrapped bundle. Digging a small pocketknife out of his shorts, he carefully sliced open one end of the package. Peeling back the plastic, he found several individually wrapped smaller packages. He sliced one open and then he felt it. The urge. He'd felt it before. It was powerful.

He dug in the blade, turned it sideways slowly, and carefully removed it, balancing the precious substance on the edge. It was chunky and more crystal than powder. Holding the blade over his open palm, he moved both hands closer to him, bending over to meet his demon halfway. His hand trembled slightly as he snorted the cocaine first up the left nostril, and then cleared the blade with his right. He tilted his head back and inhaled deeply. There it was. The old familiar burn, more pleasure than pain, like an old friend coming back into his life.

His body seemed to come alive as he felt the drug begin to snake its way through his bloodstream. His confidence was flooding back, the dam burst, a waterfall of pleasure he did not want to stop. He could do it. They could all do it.

He leaned over and dipped again with the blade.

The room was huge and white, like a cafeteria filled with little cubicles; the air was cool, dry and antiseptic. Throughout the room, men sat hunched before their machines, their hands moving, the images before them changing.

"Incredible." John Macki's statement regarding the image now displayed on the computer screen before him was a gross understatement. "The new technology these birds use never ceases to amaze me."

"Listen to me, spook-man, I tell you, you ain't seen nothin' yet." Alan Hastings, Senior Satellite Imaging Analyst, looked up at Macki and smiled. Through his thick, coke-bottle glasses his eyes appeared huge— magnified and full of intelligence. "Look at this." With Macki leaning over Hastings shoulder, the two men peered intently at the screen as the satellite photo and digital image analyst zoomed in on an overhead view of what Macki hoped was Carrillo's compound on the shore of the western Gulf.

"Jesus," Macki remarked. The digital photograph looked more like it had been taken ten feet above the compound, not ten miles. The entire layout of the compound could be seen and what Macki guessed were people dotted certain areas of the property. The huge wall and the mansion's front border with the sea were obvious. "Can you get any closer?"

"Sure." Hastings short, fat fingers flew across the keyboard of the computer as one hand occasionally slid the mouse across the pad, one finger clicking intermittently. His hands only complemented his portly figure and it was amazing that he managed to squeeze himself into the narrow, metal chair. With his thin, wispy red hair and his pink, clown-like ears, the man resembled a pig with glasses.

Hastings zoomed in on a small dot—closer and closer—until the image finally took form; it was a man. He was dark-haired and wore dark clothes, and was armed with some sort of automatic weapon; probably an AK-47.

"Let's see if he needs a shave," Hastings said, giggling like an excited child. The image of the man zoomed yet closer.

"Amazing," Macki whispered. He watched in awe as the man's features came into view.

"Recognize him?" Hastings asked.

"No."

"Looks like one bad dude." A scar was visible on the man's cheek. Hastings clicked back to the earlier image, moved the mouse to another human-like dot near the swimming pool and zoomed in once more. The image of a woman slowly evolved on the screen. She was not unattractive. Dark hair. Spanish features. He zoomed closer.

"Nice tits," Macki said. He didn't recognize her. "Try another one. Close to this one."

Hastings began the process once more. "You mind telling me who we're looking for, Mr. Bond?"

"You know that's classified, Al."

"Then I'll guess. Don't tell me if I'm right. I'll know. The expression on your face always gives it away, John. You know, you really should pursue another career. You make a terrible spy." He looked at Macki and winked.

"All right, smart guy. Give it your best shot."

"Well from the location," Hastings began, "I'd say we're looking for a politician on the lam, drug kingpin, or rebel leader. And based on what I know of your occupation, I would guess we're looking behind door number two." He began to zoom in on the next figure.

"You know where we're looking."

"It's my job," Hastings said, lowering his voice.

"How?"

Hastings pointed to the information transposed on the lower left-hand corner of the screen. It had the date, time to the fraction of a second, latitude and longitude coordinates, and a bunch of other numbers designating which satellite and other miscellaneous information. "You forget, my good man, I'm a highly trained, although sometimes unappreciated individual. I can look into your bedroom and tell you what color underwear your current lover is wearing. Which, knowing you, she probably isn't!" Hastings began laughing, his face reddening, his eyes once again pig-like.

"Al. Be serious. Please." Macki waited impatiently while the analyst composed himself. "How did you know so quickly where the coordinates were?"

"Are you kidding me? State has had me analyzing troop movements throughout Mexico for the last month. Rumor has it, there may be another rebel offensive, peasant uprising—you know, something like that—in the works. From what I've seen, John, I'd say your little hacienda here is somewhere on the Western Gulf. With the cliffs, the water and everything... His voice trailed off. I'd say, north of Vera Cruz. Jalapa maybe?"

"Close." Macki watched as the next person zoomed into view. It was a man, also with dark hair and Spanish features. Thick mustache. Rugged face. Macki had seen the eyes before. Cold. Hard. The clothes were neat, and they looked expensive. The figure wore a sportcoat...

"That's him." Macki and Hastings spun in alarm. The voice had come from Wes Gates, who had silently slipped into the cubicle. Macki had known he was coming, but he couldn't wait. Hastings was a busy man.

"Jesus, Wes, didn't they teach you to knock?"

"Actually, no they didn't. And had I wanted it, you'd both be dead right now." He introduced himself to Hastings and made it a point not to crush his hand. The analyst just stared at him, obviously intimidated. Gates was dressed in casual attire, and had no badge or credentials attached to his person.

"How did you get in here?" Hastings squeaked.

"Don't ask." Gates pointed to the screen. "Nice work. That's him. That's Carrillo." He looked at Macki without speaking, silently asking if he were free to talk.

"Go ahead, Wes. Al and I go way back. I guess I've got the authority to let him in on this one. We need information and we need it fast. How do you know that's Carrillo?"

"Because I've spent the last two and a half years trying to nail the bastard. I've seen every photo of the man that exists. There's only a few. That's him. Look at the eyes."

Gates looked around the cubicle. "Mind if I sit?" He wheeled over an empty swivel chair. "Can I see the overview of the entire compound?"

Hastings leapt into action and after saving Carrillo's digitized face, he brought up the first image Macki had seen. "Wow." It was all the agent could say at the moment.

Over the next few hours, the three men studied the satellite images like scientists with a microscope. Not being computer wizards, Gates and Macki were forced to let Hastings in on their observations as well as their hypotheses. He was helpful, and added valuable insight as the two formulated a plan.

"Then it's obvious the water is the only way," Macki said.

"Absolutely," Gates agreed. "With the guys on the back wall and that double-A-gun in the center—not to mention all those bastards roaming around inside—it's the only way."

And both men knew what that meant. SEALs.

The Mansion in Vera Cruz
April 16, 1996 0213 Local Time

The room was dark, but not pitch black, and as Carrillo lay on his back and stared up at the ceiling, he swore the walls were closing in on him. His mind was a tangled mess of complications and possibilities. What should be his next move? When he was in Juarez, things were too dangerous and he had to leave, to be somewhere else. Now that he was, he felt the need to go back. The new routes could never hope to be as successful or profitable as those already established along the Southwest border. Every day he stayed in the mansion he felt himself growing softer, weaker. And every day he stayed out of Juarez, the other cartels grew stronger, more powerful. And the fear had begun to control him once more. Even behind the walls of his fortress, he no longer felt safe. They were coming for him, he could feel it. Who was coming, he did not know, but he always relied on his instincts; they never told lies.

Outside, the surface of the pool swirled in the evening breeze. The underwater lights cast a myriad of shadows that danced across the ceiling of Carillo's bedroom, drifting in time with the ripples that slapped against the side of the pool. Carrillo turned his head to the side and focused on the red numbers of the digital clock. It was after two. Next to him in the bed, Lucia lay on her side, facing away from him. He'd barely touched her in weeks and he inwardly cursed himself—his behavior recently had become cowardly, unmanly. Her hair spilled around her head, mussed about on the pillow, and in the dark, he could barely make out her angelic face as she dozed. How he loved her! He yearned to reach out and touch her. But why? To seek protection? To share his feelings of inadequacy? He remained still.

Suddenly a large shadow moved across the ceiling. Carrillo's breath seized in his chest as his heart pounded into high gear, the sickening feeling of dread pumping throughout his body. For a moment he was paralyzed— then he broke free of his terror and grabbed his pistol from the drawer of the night-table. He leapt from the bed and made his way to the left side of the picture window, hiding behind the bunched up verticals. Outside and below, the figure of an armed man moved along the edge of the pool. The man stopped and looked up towards the window. The cartel leader's breathing stopped again as his knees went weak. His pulse pounded in his ears as the man drew on a cigarette, the tiny orange glow barely lighting up his features. Carrillo recognized the thick mustache, the bushy eyebrows. A wave of relief washed over him. It was one of his sentries making the rounds. The man continued on, the barrel of his automatic weapon sweeping back and forth, probing the darkness, searching out an enemy.

Making his way back to the bed, Carrillo replaced the gun and slipped beneath the covers. Once again he focused on the ceiling as he struggled to bring his labored breathing under control. He felt old and ashamed of himself. After a few minutes his eyelids grew heavy and he began to drift off...

Just then a hand grabbed his arm and he nearly jumped from the bed.
"Mother of God, Amado, what's the matter?" Lucia asked, nearly as frightened herself. She whispered so as not to wake the children.

"I'm sorry. I can't sleep." He turned towards her and grasped her hand, caressing it lightly. He remained silent for a moment. "I can't live like this."

"You're right, Amado. But it's not just you. We can't live like this. How long have we been married, ten years?"

"Almost eleven." She had stuck by him for over ten years and he had never forgotten an anniversary.

"And for all that time, I have been a good wife. Not once have I questioned your behavior—never told you what you should or shouldn't do."

It was true. She'd never stuck her nose in his business; she obviously knew who he was, what he did. But throughout the years Lucia had remained silent. At times he confided in her, but she was careful to not say too much, as was he. She was devoted and faithful, while his behavior outside the marriage was anything but commendable. She had been with him during his climb to power and had given him two beautiful children whom he loved more than anything in this world. But things had changed and she knew it.

"Things are different now, Amado." Her voice was stronger now, yet full of emotion, both stern and fragile at the same time. "I feel like I hardly know you. You're distant and quiet. Sometimes I wonder if you still love me."

Her words struck Carrillo's heart like daggers. He stared at his wife in the darkness and could see she was crying. He reached out and wiped away the tears that were immediately replaced by more. "Of course I love you," he told her. He wrapped his arms around her and held her tight, but she pulled away.

"And your children, Amado. You don't even play with them anymore. These are the best years of their lives and you've got them living in this—this prison." She was losing control now, the tears a steady flood as she began to sob, her body shaking slightly.

He wanted to reach for her but was afraid he would be rejected.

"You're right, Lucia. I'm so sorry. Please forgive me. I know I've been neglecting all of you. We'll get out of here. We'll go back to Juarez."

"No!" she screamed. "Don't you see? We can't live like this. Our children need to grow up normally. We're not living, we're hiding! I can't stand it: wondering if you're going to come home at night or if I'll have to come to identify your body at the morgue! Do you think I've forgotten the Bali Hai? What about your dream, Amado? Our dream! To live a normal life by the sea and watch our children grow up to have children of their own, who lead decent respectable lives. I can't live like this anymore," she hissed. "I won't."

Lucia was right. He had to get out. They had to get out. But when? How?

A shadow passed across the ceiling but he was not alarmed. He'd made up his mind.

"All right, we'll get out. The whole thing. We have plenty of money. We'll move to another country or something."

"When?" Lucia whined softly.

"Soon," he told her. Because they were coming. "Soon."

18

Marina Puerto Aventuras   Aboard the *Slammer*
April 16, 1996 0706 Local Time

Rob Masters' head was exploding. As he drifted out of what had been a short and fitful period of sleep, an incessant thumping was coming from just outside the boat, right next to his head.

"Jesus Christ. Hold on a fuckin' second!" he growled, and sat up in bed. More pain. He looked around the room and saw several grim reminders of the previous night's behavior. A full glass of warm rum and coke sat on the nightstand, its ice long ago melted. Beside it lay his pocketknife, the blade still out, a thin coating of white crystals stuck to its sharp, chrome tip. He couldn't even find his clothes.

And then it all came rushing back to him. Flying high on the cocaine, he had tried to drink himself to sleep, without much success. He vaguely remembered the sky getting lighter at about five o'clock and a quick look at his watch told him that only two hours had passed since then. The knocking began again, and he could hear muffled voices from just outside the bow. "Yeah, yeah, I'm coming," he barked, and clad only in his boxers, he ambled through the salon and out the door.

The early morning sun stabbed into his eyes, and he winced in pain. His mouth was dry as sandpaper, and raising his hand to shield his eyes, he peered around the side of the bulkhead and up towards the bow.

"Well, well. If it isn't Sleeping Beauty. Rise and shine, captain!" Dan Larsen's cheerful voice called back from a smiling face that had obviously had a decent night's sleep. Larsen was seated in the middle of a tattered rubber dinghy and behind him sat none other than Paco Herrera, who stared out from behind a pair of extremely dark, wrap-around shades. "C'mon, man, we've got a busy day." Larsen said. "Let's get rolling!"

"I feel like shit, man." The big captain's usually strong, deep voice was weak and whiny, nearly pleading. "I need to get some more sleep."

"You look like shit," his friend fired back. "But you'll get over it. Where's Matt?"

"I assume he's inside sleeping, which is where I should be right now." He honestly wasn't sure if his mate was in there or not; he'd heard something in the salon at about three, but hadn't opened the door to check.

"Well, wake him up. We've got some important shit to talk about." Larsen shot Masters a look that told him not to argue.

With a sigh, Masters turned towards the cockpit. "Jesus Christ," he said in disgust. "Give us a minute and we'll be right there." He stormed into the boat, slamming the door behind him.

Down below, Masters flung open the door to the crews quarters, and was met by a blast of stale air. It reeked of booze. He chuckled at the figure on the bed, wrapped so tightly in a blanket that he resembled a cocoon. Grabbing what he assumed was Kirchner's shoulder, he shook the still form.

"Wake up," he ordered. "We're goin' for a ride." He continued shaking him until he was met with a long, agonized moan.

"Where?" Kirchner asked.

"With Larsen and some other guy. I'm not sure where we're going."

"Can't you go? I just want to stay here and die." Kirchner and the others had gotten into the tequila a little bit too heavily.

"Yeah, me too. But Dan seemed pretty serious. C'mon, get up." He grabbed the blanket and began pulling it off.

"Alright, alright," Kirchner groaned, and sat up and swung his legs over the side of the bunk. He looked at Masters through bleary eyes that were mere slits. "I need Advil."

"I hear you, brother. There's some in the galley."

231

Ducking into the head, Masters looked in the mirror. Pretty bad, but he'd seen worse. He brushed his teeth and slurped some water directly from the faucet. Then he went back into the stateroom and got dressed. No time for a shower.

Before he knew it, he was back in the head, reaching behind the small mirror of the medicine cabinet and retrieving the small paper bundle he had carefully stashed there a couple of hours earlier. His hands shook in anticipation as he opened the packet and tapped out a long fat line. He fished a bill out of his wallet, rolled it up and proceeded to snort half the coke up each nostril. Then he wet his fingers, and sticking one up each nostril, sniffed three times. The back of his throat began to go numb. Tilting his head back, he searched his nose for any telltale signs. There were none. Confident, he headed for the door. Things were going to be just fine.

Twenty minutes later, the four men were cramped into the inflatable, with Masters and Larsen in the middle and Kirchner hunkered down in the front, trying without success to stay dry. Since leaving the marina, they had been on a predominately easterly heading. The light chop was just big enough to take an occasional wave over the bow, and the water which lay on top of the rotting wooden floorboard was a least a couple of inches deep. Paco remained silent, simply staring ahead at the horizon, obviously searching for something. The old, air-cooled outboard motor wailed in protest, its throttle pegged, yet they were barely making ten knots. The numerous patches dotting the dinghy's aged rubber hull didn't do much for Larsen's sense of security and he noticed there were no life preservers. At this point, he realized, they could probably still swim to shore—if the critters didn't get them first.

Just then Paco spotted something and swung the little boat towards the southeast. It only took Larsen a moment before he also spotted it. A small speck on the horizon, another vessel.

"Where the hell are we going?" Masters asked Larsen, shouting to be heard over the annoying little outboard. Larsen only shook his head and shrugged. He didn't know.

Fifteen minutes more and they had reached the other vessel. They were wet, and covered with salt. Kirchner scrambled up and tied them off to the rear cleat of what was one of the ugliest and most ungodly-looking fishing boats they had ever seen. Larsen assumed it must have been some sort of long-liner: a boat that trailed miles of line with thousands of hooks in an attempt to catch whatever it could. To Masters it looked more like a tug, stripped of its rubber push-rail. Kirchner had never seen anything like it. The vessel was short, no more than thirty feet and at least half that wide. The deck was open and rusty; whatever was not covered with rust or peeling paint seemed to be stained and splattered with blood. The pilothouse extended above-decks and was a makeshift mess of old plywood, sheet metal and fiberglass. At the helm was an old-fashioned wooden wheel. What lurked beneath in the cabin was unknown.

"Go on, get aboard," Paco ordered, and Kirchner hesitantly pulled them closer and scrambled over the side. He leaned over and held the dinghy while the others climbed aboard. Once on the deck, the stench was overpowering; a mixture of blood and fish, guts and ammonia. Larsen searched for its source. Several five-gallon oil buckets lined one side, filled to the brim with what looked like fish, blood and chunks of meat and internal organs. He didn't want to think where it was from.

Just then, Paco stomped hard on the deck. The door to the tiny cabin opened abruptly and a nasty looking character armed with an AK-47 climbed out from down below. He was tall and thin like many of the Mexicans, with hollow black eyes that looked like they had seen their fair share of death. The skin of his face was creased and pockmarked, and a nasty scar, from a wound which was obviously not well tended to, ran from his left eye to the corner of his mouth. The last bit was covered by a thick, black mustache. He wore a dirty, faded military uniform that was stained top to bottom with dried blood. He looked like he smelled, and when he came closer, it was obvious he did. He stared at Larsen and his friends through eyes that were vacant and expressionless, but did not acknowledge them.

"Meet Raul," Paco said. The smuggler nodded at the buckets and the silent man made his way to the side of the boat and began dumping them overboard.

The Americans looked at each other, bewildered. It was Masters who first spoke. He looked at Paco. "Would you mind telling us what the hell's going on?"

"We need to talk about last night," Paco said.

"Yes, we do." Larsen's tone was serious. "I assume the *Federales* found nothing."

"No, they didn't," Paco said, squinting. "But they knew something. We were almost sold out. It's obvious there is a traitor among us."

Larsen was quick to defend his friends. "You don't believe any of us would be so stupid!"

"No. I believe I have determined who has betrayed us. Betrayed me, you, the cartel. No one betrays the cartel." Paco looked at the deck for several moments before raising his head and looking each of the three Americans directly in the eye. Then he whispered softly, almost hissing. "No one."

"Who do you think did it?" Masters asked.

"You will see in a moment. Soon we will have a full confession, I assure you."

There was a splash from over the side where the armed man had been pouring the buckets. He stepped back abruptly and mumbled something in Spanish to Paco. Larsen caught the word "*tiburon*"—shark.

"What in hell are you doing?" the agent asked. "Chumming for sharks?" All four men made their way to the side of the boat and stared down into the water. Paco smiled as the first dark shadows appeared below the surface, circling first, then darting in to snatch a piece of meat.

"Yes, that is exactly what we are doing. And it appears we have been successful." There were now half a dozen sharks tearing up the ever-growing chum slick and they began snapping at the surface as Raul continued dumping the buckets. "Tell me, good captain," he asked Larsen. "What kind of sharks are they?"

"They look like blacktips, and maybe a couple of bull sharks. Can't tell for sure."

A shark three times the size of the others glided into view, rose up and snatched a huge chunk of bloody meat that was floating on the surface. Its greedy mouth opened wide as it did so, revealing a spectacular array

234

of razor-sharp teeth which seemed to point in all different directions. All the men backed away from the rail.

"That one was a mako," Kirchner said. "Big one, probably close to four hundred."

"A man-eater," Paco said.

"Maybe," Kirchner agreed. "If he's really pissed off."

Paco caught Raul's attention and nodded towards the cabin. Raul made his way over to the small door and climbed belowdecks. There was some commotion from down below and suddenly another man appeared in the doorway.

Raul shoved the man from behind and he went sprawling face first on the bloody steel deck. Raul followed him out and kicked him savagely in the ribs. The man cried out and attempted to protect himself, curling into the fetal position. He was fat, and his flesh billowed out to the sides.

"Get up, pig," Paco ordered, but the man remained still.

Raul poked him in the side with his AK-47 and grabbed him by his hair, jerking him to his knees. The prisoner looked up. It was obvious he had already been severely beaten. His face was a bloody mess, one eye swollen shut, the other barely open, the flesh around it scraped raw. His lips were bleeding and he was missing several teeth.

"Here is your traitor. Betraying pig!" Paco spit on the man, and turned to Larsen. "Recognize him?"

Larsen looked at him closely. He seemed vaguely familiar. The beaten man spoke, his voice weak. "Cap-ee-tan," he gasped, and nearly fell over. Raul jerked him upright.

"My God!" Larsen cried, suddenly recognizing him. "Carlos?"

"*Sí. Sí.*" The waiter from the Papaya Republic could barely hold his head up.

"Why?" the agent asked. "Why?"

"Mother of God, I swear to you. It was not me," he managed, his lower lip trembling.

"Liar!" Paco screamed and smashed him in the face, knocking Carlos to the deck once more.

"Stop it!" Larsen yelled, and went to help him.

Paco slammed into the agent, knocking him onto his ass and into the side of the boat where he quickly sprang to his feet, turning to face the smuggler. "You motherfucker. How can you be so sure he did it? Did he confess?" He spit out his words while his two friends looked on in confusion.

"No, but he will," Paco said.

"I forgot. With you guys it's guilty until proven innocent, just like your whole fuckin' shitty country."

"That's right, *gringo*. So you just stay out of my way. Consider this a warning."

Larsen just stared at him. "Motherfucker," he said again under his breath.

Paco pretended not to hear, looked at Raul and nodded towards the side of the boat. Without hesitation, Raul dragged Carlos on his side to the gunwale, latched onto the whimpering man, and somehow hoisted him up and over the side. Larsen and his friends dared not move; they could only look on in horror.

Carlos was screaming in Spanish, a terrifying babble that was borderline incoherent. The man was begging for his life.

In an instant, Carlos' hands appeared on the side of the railing as the doomed man tried desperately to climb back into the boat. Weeping and muttering something about sharks, his gnarled hands gripped the railing like claws.

There was no need for Paco to speak. Raul raised his automatic and brought the hard steel barrel crashing down, again and again, on Carlos's shattered knuckles. The sound of bones crunching was sickening; it was more than Masters could bear. Overcome with rage, he rushed the armed man, determined to stop the torture. His attempt was short-lived. Raul swung the barrel swiftly, and caught Masters square in the gut. The move had been unexpected; it knocked the wind out of the big man and he crumpled to the deck, clutching his stomach and gasping for air. Shocked, Kirchner could only stare in disbelief.

Raul turned to the railing once more. Raising his weapon above his shoulder, he brought it down butt-first, bashing Carlos in the face. The blow knocked him back in the water, yet he was still conscious—and still screaming.

Paco leaned over the rail. "Confess, you lying pig," he demanded.

Larsen and Kirchner ran to the rail and watched in horror as the frenzied, ravening sharks moved in and began ripping chunks of flesh from Carlos' arms and legs. The water had turned into a boiling cauldron of red froth. Time and time again, the dying man's head was sucked beneath the carnage on the surface, only to pop up moments later, wailing in agony.

Masters had struggled to his feet and made it to the railing just in time to see the huge mako glide in slowly. As if in slow motion, the voracious eating-machine opened its vise-like jaws and closed them around Carlos' left arm. With one shake of its wide, pointed head, it rolled its eyes back and tore it off, just below the shoulder.

Masters and Kirchner vomited on the deck.
Larsen tried to force the scene out of his mind, but he knew it was useless. It would be etched in a dark corner somewhere in the back of his brain.

With a long drawn-out moan, Carlos reached towards the agent in a last desperate plea for help.
"For Christ's sake, Paco, kill the man!"
"You want to join him?" the smuggler sneered, not waiting for or even expecting an answer. "Then shut your fucking mouth."

Paco reached for Raul's rifle and brought it up to his shoulder, taking aim on Carlos' battered face. "You Americans are all spineless," he gloated. "It's obvious you don't have the stomach for this business." He motioned towards Larsen's friends, who sat slumped and weary against the transom. He turned back to fire, but before he could, the big mako swept in one last time, grabbed Carlos by the midriff, and plunged into the swirling, blood-filled deep.

Paco turned to Larsen and smiled. "Sometimes nature takes care of the dirtywork."

"You sick bastard," Larsen told him.

"Fucking murderer." It was Masters. He'd gotten to his feet and glared at Paco with accusing eyes.

"Murderer? No," Paco said. "Judge, yes. Jury, perhaps." He was looking at both men now. "But definitely executioner. How do you say it? The punishment fit the crime? It is the only way to send a message to such low-lying scum. There is no room within the organization for such treason. Maybe you have all learned something today."

Paco turned to Raul. "Get us underway." Raul moved to the pilot-house, cranked up the single-screw diesel and headed northwest towards the marina. Thirty minutes later the red roofs of the resort at Puerto Aventuras could be seen in the distance. Raul stopped the boat and Paco and the three Americans boarded the rubber dinghy. The four men watched as Raul headed south. The rest of their trip to the marina was made in total silence. The gruesome scene played itself out again and again in Larsen's mind. But there was one thing that bothered him more than anything else—the fact that throughout the whole ordeal, Carlos had not confessed.

Darkness had descended upon the marina and Larsen sat alone in the salon of the *Predator*, surfing the four available channels that were piped down to the boats from the marina office. Kurt had yet to return from Boca Paila, a small fishing resort located about seventy miles down the coast. It was famous for its incredible bonefishing. He'd gone by car with Terry Stanton and John Flynn. They'd left before sunrise and Larsen was glad that his mate and friends had not witnessed the ugliness that had transpired that morning offshore. It was obvious that Masters and Kirchner had been deeply disturbed, but neither man had said anything yet. Larsen was more than ready to tell Paco how he felt about the atrocity, but the smuggler had simply dropped them off, told him he'd be in touch, and motored back out the cut—destination unknown.

A knock on the door interrupted his thoughts. Larsen yelled for whoever it was to come in, and when the door swung open, he wasn't suprised to see Rob Masters.

"Have a seat," he told him. The agent studied the other captain's features; he looked worried, and was nervous and fidgety.

Masters took a deep breath, exhaled loudly, and got right to the point.

"I want out." His expression was grim, determined. "Matt too," he added.

"Whoa, hold on there a second, buddy. What do you mean you want out?"

"Just what I said. I don't want to be a part of this. Matt feels the same way." The big captain was gnawing at his fingernails.

"Are you fuckin' crazy? Don't you think it's a little late for that?" Larsen raised his voice.

"Jesus Christ, keep it down," Masters whispered.

Larsen continued, his voice more calm and controlled. "He got to you, didn't he?" The agent had been prepared for this.

"You're goddamn right he did! It wasn't supposed to be like this! You made it sound like a piece of cake. I'm a big boy, Dan, but I don't need to see shit like that!" Masters was so worked up, he was shaking. "Don't try to tell me it didn't bother you!"

"Calm the fuck down," Larsen snapped. "Of course it bothered me. How do you think I feel? Carlos may have been innocent! But that doesn't mean we can just quit. It doesn't work like that. We're in, man. And we're in for the long haul. I told you last night, it's only two more weeks."

"And I told you, that'll seem like two years! No way, pal. I want out. I want that shit off my boat."

"Are you kidding me? That would defeat the whole purpose, put the whole fuckin' plan at risk."

"Then I'll go out there and dump it in the goddamn ocean."

"Don't be stupid! Do you know what would happen to you then?"

"Of course I do! You signed my death warrant, Dan. You signed all of ours when you got us into this mess."

The agent looked at Masters in silence. It was true. Now his friends were involved and all their lives were in jeopardy. He'd only wanted to help them, and suddenly things were falling apart. He wasn't sure what to say.

"I only wanted to help you, to help Terry."

"Yeah, well Terry needs to do it for his little girl. I was doing it out of pure greed. I'd rather be homeless my whole life. At least I'll still be alive."

Masters got up and began pacing around the salon. He was breathing heavily and sweating, although the inside of the boat was quite cool. Larsen noticed a twitch beneath his friend's left eye, a twitch he hadn't seen in years.

"You're scared..."

"Of course I'm scared!"

"There's no need," Larsen began, but the agitated captain cut him off in mid-sentence.

"You should be scared too, Dan. I saw the way that guy looked at you! That could have been you out there."

"I know, Rob. But it's too late now. We're already part of this."

"I don't want to be part of this."

"It's too late. Listen, Rob. Do yourself a favor. Take some time off tomorrow. Go for a dive or something. Maybe it'll take your mind off all of this."

"That's easy for you to say," Masters was ready to leave. He reached for the door handle.

"One more thing," Larsen said, stopping him. He looked Masters directly in the eye. "Get off, and stay off the shit."

"What the hell are you talking about?"

"Oh come on Rob! It's obvious. Your eyes are all bugged out, you're all amped up, sweating like a pig and grinding your teeth so bad, you look like you're doing your own dental work."

Masters didn't respond to the charges, but simply stared at the agent with malice, his eyes squinting slightly. He opened the door and stepped out, but turned back. "I want out, Dan," he said softly. "Make it happen."

19

White House Situation Room
April 16, 1996 0904 EDT

For some people, the prospect of coming before the President of the United States was a bit intimidating, possibly a little hard on the nerves. Not so for John Macki. It wouldn't be the first time he'd met the man, and it hadn't taken him long to realize that, like all Presidents, he was just another man, a mere mortal who had simply had the balls to use his connections and political influence to get him where he was today.

Macki, Gates and the DEA Administrator Bob Constance were in a windowless room, deep within the bowels of the White House. The three sat in silence, lost in their own thoughts as they awaited the most powerful member of the Executive Branch, leader of what they all still considered a great country. The room was not huge, but large enough to accommodate twenty or so important individuals who would all be seated at the great mahogany table that occupied most of the secretive, seldom-used, subterranean space.

Gathered at one end of the table the three men felt oddly out of place, like three misguided youths who had taken a wrong turn and were now lost and unsure what to do. Macki glanced around the room, thinking about the incredible decisions that had been made in the very same chairs, decisions made over the years that had affected their country in so many different ways. He could barely comprehend the fact that they were now seated there, as if their plan warranted the consideration of the man many thought of as the most powerful man on earth. Maybe he was. If not, he wouldn't be there.

Macki watched Gates with amusement. The big man was fidgety, back straight, crossing and uncrossing his legs, cracking his knuckles. Macki decided to break the ice. "What's the matter, big fella? Little nervous?"

"Hell yes!" he burst out. "Aren't you? It's not every day I get to chitchat with the President. What if he throws us out on our asses?"

"Don't sweat it, Wes," Macki told him, sneaking a wink at Constance. "He's no better than you. Why do you think so many young people can relate to him? He's a regular guy."

"Yeah," Constance chimed in. "I saw him on Letterman! No wonder so many people voted for him."

It was a fact that the President was extremely popular with the younger generation, even if he had been slipping in the polls recently. The baby boomers had now grown up, and had been replaced by the Generation-Xers, the new brand of youth who seemed to gather most of their information from MTV.

The heavy door to the room opened and the three men jumped to their feet

A short young man with Mediterranean features entered, followed by the President, who spoke with just a slight hint of a southern accent. "Good morning, gentlemen. I assume you all know George Papandreas, my personal advisor. How are you John, Bob?" He shook hands with the two men. "And you are...?"

"Wes Gates, Mr. President. Special Agent of the DEA, El Paso. Let me say, it's an honor—"

Macki cut off mid-sentence. "Wes is largely responsible for the intelligence which we will be showing you."

Gates shook the President's hand and then reached towards Papandreas. "What did you say your name was?" While the President's advisor looked up at the big Texan, the agent nearly crushed his hand.

Macki watched the exchange with caution. He was certain that Gates knew the advisor's name only too well, and it was no secret that Gates despised him. He'd already mentioned it twice. In his slick, tailored suit, the graduate of Columbia University exuded an air of superiority that filled most who met him with contempt. The fact that he was of Greek ancestry had nothing to do with it. Perhaps it was because his dark hair, thick eyebrows and olive complexion reminded Gates of an Iraqi. No one seemed to know how he had fallen into his current position, but Macki knew it was obvious to Gates that the only action this snobby punk had seen was played out on a war game on his Macintosh.

The President broke the awkward moment. "I understand you have some information regarding the whereabouts of this Carrillo fellow. Let's have it."

Constance moved to the wall and hung up a map of the entire Gulf of Mexico, while Macki removed a stack of satellite photos from a large manila envelope. He began to spread them across the table.

"These images are ten days old. They were taken by one of our newest KH-generation recon satellites. The location is circled in red on the map, on the coast, just outside of Vera Cruz, Mexico." He referred to the wall. Macki held up a picture of the cartel leader. "This is Amado Carrillo Fuentes," he stated firmly. "And this is his fortress." He held up the overview of the compound. "Our analysts confirm it," he added. That was not true. He was going out on a limb. He had to.

"How did you find him?" the President asked.

It was Constance's turn to speak. "After our last unsuccessful attempt to capture him," he began, but was rudely interrupted by Papandreas.

"You mean the fuck-up in Juarez," the advisor said.

Constance said nothing, but glared at the short man with eyes that seemed to cut right through him.

"Please continue, Bob," the President said, and shot Papandreas a look that told him to shut up.

"After what happened in Juarez, Mr. President, we received intelligence that Carrillo might be expanding his operation into the Yucatan Peninsula..."

Constance described the operation from its beginning, telling the President about Larsen, his cover as a captain, and his success in establishing contact with Paco Herrera.

Constance himself did not know about the other captains' involvement, as Macki had conveniently forgotten to inform him of that aspect of the operation. The President, in turn, was not made aware of it and continued to listen attentively with what looked like great enthusiasm. Constance told him about Gates' recon and how Herrera had led the agent straight to the mansion and the cartel leader himself.

All the pieces seemed to fall into place after that and the President appeared to understand the current situation. But that didn't mean he liked it.

"It sure sounds like entrapment to me," the President said.

"No more than any other undercover operation," Constance argued.

"And who is officially sanctioning this operation, CIA or DEA?"

Macki finally spoke, looking at Constance. "Neither, sir. It's unofficial."

Papandreas immediately bent over and began whispering in the President's ear. Gates, Macki and Constance all exchanged glances. It was just such behavior that caused them to dislike the pretentious little bastard.

"What you're saying is that the operation is covert. Clandestine. Secret." The President looked worried.

"Yes, sir," Macki told him.

"Then it's illegal."

"Not necessarily," Macki said. "Only the extraction of Carrillo without the knowledge of the Mexican authorities."

"Why don't you just get together with the *Federales* or whoever is running the show down there, and go the hell in there and get him?"

"It's not that easy," Macki started to explain, but Constance felt the need to state his case, and jumped in.

"Mr. President, time and time again we've seen what happens when we try to cooperate with the local authorities. Carrillo is a legend to his people, a god. They want to see him caught about as much as the Colombians wanted to see Pablo Escobar taken down. Everyone down there is on the take and if Carrillo goes away, so does their gravy train. We can't afford the risk he'll be tipped about our coming. I know you're a smart man. You must understand that sometimes, covert operations are necessary for the public good. In this case, it's absolutely necessary to guarantee the success of the operation."

"I see where you're coming from, Bob, but at this stage in the game, I just can't afford to have something like this come around to haunt me. Not now, not ever." The President rubbed his face, looked down, and slowly drew his palm from his forehead to his chin before looking up again. He was clearly tired, the bags under his eyes more pronounced than ever, a man obviously under a lot of stress. His short gray hair showed his true age, but he was in amazingly good shape; a result of hours of jogging each week. He focused on Macki and spoke slowly. "If, and I repeat—if I give the green light for your little secret operation, what did you have in mind?"

Macki was quick to respond. "Nothing less than a full water-borne assault on the compound by a team of Navy SEALs. Wes?"

Gates joined Macki, spreading the close-up images of the compound across the table, and the men all stood hunched over, listening intently as the agent outlined the plan.
"The assault team will enter the compound from the water—here..."
Fifteen minutes later, Gates wrapped up what he assumed the assault would entail. The actual particulars would be determined later by whomever would be in command of the mission.

The President was still not convinced. "Now let me get this straight. The assault on the compound will coincide with the arrest of this Herrera in Key West when the boat with the cocaine comes across from Mexico. And Herrera will be on the boat."
"That's right," Macki explained. "Herrera is going along to protect his shipment. As he approaches Key West in the early morning hours, the assault will begin on the compound. We'll have real-time satellite images beamed down to us to monitor the entire operation at the mansion in Vera Cruz. The timing is crucial."
"That's what scares me. What if something goes wrong? What sort of damage control have you allowed for?" The President was no fool when

it came to covering his ass. "You realize we'll have to deny knowledge of any of this. I'll turn my back on you so fast, you won't even see which way I went."

"Nothing will go wrong, sir. It's a simple operation—the men are trained for it." Macki hoped he was right.

"That's what Ollie North told Reagan. Fortunately for him, he had no recollection of such things when that Iran-Contra shit hit the fan. Unfortunately for me, I'm too young to have Alzheimers." They all cracked a smile at that remark. "How many people know about this?"

"Very few," Macki answered.

"Good. Let's keep it that way. Don't say anything to the Ambassador or that kiss-ass Jensen. If they find out about it, they'll have my ass in a sling. And for God's sake, don't let the press catch wind of it."

The President didn't have to warn Macki about that. The intelligence man had learned from his mistake. Just a couple of years earlier, he'd gotten involved with a correspondent from ABC News, a hot little number who had turned out to be a "scoop slut"—willing to do anything or fuck anyone to blow the lid off a breaking story. She'd nearly exposed the entire Colombian operation when Macki had a bit too much to drink one night and let a little too much information slip out.

"So you're giving us the go-ahead, then," Macki said, assuming he'd read the President correctly.

"I'll tell you what, John. I know a lot of people think I'm full of hot air when it comes to getting tough on drugs. But they're wrong. I'm dead serious. It's a scourge that's ruining this country. It is a war, John, and it's going to be a long one. Any battle we can win is a step in the right direction. When we needed to put the hurt on the Colombians, I turned to you and you produced. I'm hoping I can count on you again. From what I've heard, it sounds like you've been working hard on it. I want this Carrillo bastard, I want him bad. Between you and Bob, I know we can get him. I don't care how you do it, just get it done and keep me out of it." Papandreas gaped at the President in disbelief.

"I thank you for this chance, Mr. President. We'll get him. And when we do, we'll take him alive and sweat him. He'll talk. And all the rest of those buggers, the Colombians included, are in for a rude awakening."

"I hope you're right," the President said. "These cartels are like lizards. We grab their tails and they break off. Before you know it, they've grown back. Let's get rid of them once and for all. I have confidence in you men. You can do it. Please keep me informed."

"You can count on it, Mr. President," Macki said.

"Well that's it, then. I've got a busy schedule. If you gentlemen will excuse me." He turned to his advisor. "George?"

They all stood and the President headed for the door. Papandreas followed without another look at the others. Just before he stepped out, the President turned back towards the men who had just laid everything they had on the line.

"Good luck and God bless you. The American people will be grateful." Then he turned and disappeared down the hall.

The three men in the room looked at each other with mixed emotions before Gates finally said what was on all of their minds.

"Jesus Christ," he said. "What horseshit."

Marina Puerto Aventuras

There was a place on the south side of the cut where if you were careful, you could hop across the tops of the huge jagged boulders and make it to the very end of the jetty. It was a great place to get away for a while, to just sit and stare out at the sea; the perfect place to go if you wanted to be alone.

It was there that Larsen found himself later that evening.

The dock had been very quiet when he'd walked past the boats that lined the inside wall closest to the cut, and he doubted if anyone had seen him. With troubled thoughts, the agent looked out across the vast dark Caribbean; he could barely make out the line on the horizon where sea met sky, where something terrible had happened earlier that day, something that had put into motion a dangerous turn of events. The surface of the water was flat calm; the reflection of the star-filled evening sky was incredibly clear, nearly stationary. It was quite a sight, peaceful and serene.

Everything had been going so smoothly—until Paco had pulled his foolish stunt. Now Masters and Kirchner were getting cold feet and suddenly things seemed complicated and dangerous. They were so close. If they could just hang in there for two more weeks..

A scuffing sound on a boulder behind him put his defense mechanisms on full alert. He spun quickly, his gut tightening when he remembered he was unarmed. Vulnerable.

"*Buenas noches*, captain." He could barely see the man, but his voice was utterly familiar. It was Paco. Dressed in a long-sleeved black shirt—and matching pants—he was crouched and blended easily into the surrounding boulders. "I'm sorry to disturb you."

"Are you fucking crazy?" Larsen asked. "You know, one of these days you're going to get your ass blown off, sneaking up on me like that."

"I assume you are unarmed. Please correct me if I am wrong."

Larsen didn't respond to that, changing the subject. "How did you know where to find me?"

"I always know where to find you," he answered with a smile that was lost in the darkness. "What happened to the weapon I gave you?" he asked, refusing to let the issue die.

"I've still got it."

"I strongly suggest you begin to carry it. There may be others who are aware of our little arrangement." Herrera crabbed his way down next to Larsen, and pulled a pack of smokes from his pocket. He offered one to the agent, who declined, and lit his own, cupping his hands over the flame.

Larsen looked over at him. "I wish I could praise you for your little demonstration this morning but I can't. I don't know what it was you were trying to prove, but if you wanted to scare the living hell out of my two friends, it worked."

"Good," Paco said. "Then my message is clear."

"Good?" Larsen echoed. "All you did was send the message that this whole thing is going to involve so much risk that they could end up dead. Murdered violently!"

248

"My purpose was two-fold. Not only did I get rid of a traitorous pig like Carlos, but I made sure your friends won't get any ideas." He took a long pull on the butt; the orange glow lit up his face. Larsen would never forget those eyes.

"You have about as much respect for human life as I have for the life of a *dorado*," the agent told him.

"My methods may look cruel to you and your friends, but they are effective."

"Masters wants out."

"What?"

"Masters—the captain of the *Slammer*—he wants the stuff off his boat."

"That's not possible!" Paco hissed. He flicked the remainder of the cigarette into the water.

"Yeah, well, whose fault do you think that is?" the agent said, already regretting he'd mentioned it.

"The product cannot be moved. It goes against the entire idea of keeping the load secure. You must talk him out of it."

"I think I already did," Larsen lied.

"There is no room for "thoughts" in this business. No hopes. No maybes. Only sure things!" The smuggler was clearly agitated.

"You must be sure. Convince him. Shit. I don't like this. I don't like this at all."

"Relax, man." Larsen told him. "My buddies might be scared, but they're not stupid. They saw what happened out there today. Believe me, they're not going to do anything that might piss you off."

"I hope you are right, Captain Dan. I would hate to have to hurt your friends."

Lying sack of shit, Larsen thought. The two men sat quietly in the darkness, watching as the green running light of a passing vessel headed south.

"We'll be leaving in two weeks," Larsen said.

"No sooner?"

"I don't think so. The *Slammer*'s last trip isn't until then. The *Tempest* is done in about a week, and I'm not sure, but I think my last trip might be cancelled. We'll obviously be traveling together."

"Obviously. My people are more than ready to proceed. Whatever needs taking care of on your end, set it up. But I must know exactly when we will arrive in Key West. I will coordinate with my contacts in Miami to be there. Let me know if there is anything you need." Paco stood and began smoothing the wrinkles from his pants and sleeves.

"How will I get in touch with you? Now that you've dispatched with Carlos in such a clean and efficient manner," the agent said sarcastically, "I've got no contact man."

Paco considered that for a moment, then said, "I've seen these small yellow flags some of the boats have when they first come into the marina. Do you have one?"

"Yep. It's called a courtesy flag. You fly it to show that you haven't cleared customs."

"Put it up on that pointed pole."

"The outrigger," Larsen taught him

"If I see it, I'll know to reach you." The smuggler turned to go. "Remember, Captain Dan, I will do whatever I think is necessary to protect my interests. And the cartel, of course."

"Of course," The agent repeated. He watched as Paco faded into the black.

20

15 Miles South of Puerto Aventuras
April 17, 1996 0800 Local Time

It was still early when Rob Masters and Matt Kirchner pulled off the side of Highway 307, the infamous "highway of death", midway between the resort at Puerto Aventuras and the Mayan ruins at Tulum. Their vehicle, a late model, white Volkswagen Beetle, skidded sideways briefly before it came to a halt in a swirling cloud of dust.

"Easy does it, man!" Kirchner exclaimed. "This ain't the Baja 1000."
With great effort, Masters slid his thick frame from behind the wheel and got out, apologizing. "Goddamn! They seem even smaller than ever." He kicked the door of the tiny rental "bug" and it slammed shut. For the last several years, the popular German automobiles were actually made in Mexico as well, and the whole country was full of them.

They had nearly missed it, carrying a little too much speed, but at the last second, Masters had spotted the tiny weathered sign, stuck with one rusty nail on a twisted old tree limb no more than eight feet high. Rancho San Pedro, it read: entrance to Nohoch Na chich, the longest and most extensive underwater cave system in the world.

On November 23, 1987, a hard-core explorer named Mike Madden had stopped his own vehicle in the same spot. Together with three machete-wielding buddies, he hiked the two kilometers into the dense, scrubby jungle on a narrow, often-treacherous horse trail and became the first scuba diver ever to set eyes upon Nohoch—the daddy of all *cenotes*—the Giant Birdhouse.

Throughout the Yucatan, there are no rivers and few lakes. Since nature's creation of the peninsula, the water has gone underground, hiding beneath the limestone crust, revealing itself occasionally in the form of *cenotes*, sinkholes, where the water always flowed with one destination in mind: the sea.

The Mayans had certainly lived beside Nohoch for thousands of years, but they could only dream what lay beneath the ground in the mysterious darkness of the *cenote*'s twin caves.

Madden and his dive partners had other plans. They set out, the day after, at 5 a.m. with scuba tanks and exploration reels filled with high-visibility line. On their first dive, they laid nearly half a mile of line. What they found was beyond their wildest imaginations. Once past the incredible cavern zone, the aquifer branched out into a vast cave system, its spacious submarine rooms filled with stalagmites, stalactites and giant flowstones shaped during the Great Ice Age.

Over the next eight years, Madden and his buddies would be drawn farther and deeper into the beckoning system. Teams of geologists, biologists, hydrologists, cameramen of all types, cartographers and a slew of explorers would gather in the Yucatan every October for an annual month-long push into what had once seemed the most inaccessible parts of Nohoch. It wasn't profit that drove them it was the force of the unknown, a force that lured them, and sucked them farther and deeper into the system.

It was that force which had drawn Larsen and Masters to Nohoch for the first time nearly three years earlier.

Since then, the two captains had made several dives into the incredible cave system, always escorted by a highly trained, certified cave diver. This would be Kirchner's first. When the two men had gotten up that morning, they'd originally planned to dive a spot just south of the cut known as Cedam Caves—a series of short, but interesting swim-throughs about thirty-five feet deep. But during the night, a strong high-pressure system had moved in and by dawn, the wind was honking out of the Southeast at nearly twenty-five knots. Lousy for diving.

And so instead, they'd set out for Nohoch. "It'll be a better dive anyway," Masters had said. Kirchner was nervous; he'd never been cave diving before, and was pretty sure Masters was not certified.

"How far in are we gonna go?" Kirchner asked.

"Not too far." Masters had already lifted the front hood—the storage area of all VW Beetles—and lifted out the two dive tanks. Kirchner leaned over and dragged out two bags that held the rest of their gear. "You don't have to go in very far," the captain added, "and you can see all kinds of cool shit. Check your bag and make sure you've got your light." Masters did the same, gave his mate a thumbs-up sign and slammed the hood. The two men shouldered their bags, and grabbed their tanks, slinging the heavy aluminum cylinders onto their opposite shoulder. They headed for the narrow trail that began in the brush about thirty yards away.

"You lock the car?" Kirchner asked.

"No need. What's in there to steal?"

"Nothin', I guess. How far is it?"

"A little more than a mile. And I'm not looking forward to—" He stopped mid-sentence as a figure on horseback emerged from the brush, a Mayan boy who looked to be about twelve years old. The boy steered the tired looking animal up to the two men and stopped. Up close, it looked to be a cross between a horse and a mule.

He recognized the boy as Chico, son of Don Pedro, the elderly rancher who owned the land around the *cenote*.

"*Hola!*" the youngster cried, cracking a smile. "*Buenos dias!*"

"*Hola* Chicito! *Como estas?*" Masters asked him, feigning a boxing jab at the boy's middle.

"Good, Ve-ry good," Chico replied in English, giggling.

Masters smiled. He remembered three years earlier when the boy had spoken no English at all. Now he was growing up. He already looked like the rest of the Mayans—short, black hair and dark skin. His dirty, tan, button-down short-sleeve shirt and worn brown jeans were at least two sizes too small. The captain felt bad. He was a nice kid, and Masters reminded himself to send down some clothes for him once they got home.

"And Papa?"

"Merida," Chico replied. West of Cancun, the seat of government for the Yucatan was there, and the boy's father was most likely trying desperately to hold onto his land and money. Anyone who visited the *cenote* for diving or snorkeling had to pay the rancher a small fee, and in the last few years it had become a very popular tourist spot. In a land where the average laborer made between three and six dollars a day, Don Pedro was making a killing, and the corrupt bastards in Merida probably wanted a cut. Masters realized that they should get a move on before any tourists showed up. They began loading the gear onto the bored-looking animal. He still couldn't believe their luck that the boy had shown up. How had he known they were there?

"Cap-ee-tan Dan?" Chico asked.

"Not here today, *amigo*." Masters knew that his friend was fond of the boy. "I'll tell him you said hello," he said, drawing yet another smile from the young Mayan. "*Vamonos*—Let's go!" Chico spun his living vehicle around and the three of them headed down the trail, and into the jungle.

The going was rough and treacherous, and blistering hot. Deep within the heart of the scrubby bush, there was no breeze. It wasn't that humid, but the two men were constantly pestered by angry horseflies; both Chico and his animal were impervious. The trail went up and down and snaked its way through the dense foliage as if the way had been hacked by drunks.

Within thirty minutes they arrived at the ranch. It wasn't a real ranch by any means, but more like a little group of bamboo shacks with thatch roofs that Don Pedro had put together for his family. A small pen held several turkeys that gobbled loudly as the trio approached. Another fenced-in area held several Brahma bulls, their grossly humped backs looked painful.

Masters peeked into one of the larger bamboo huts outside of which he had spied several articles of clothing strung across a thin yet sturdy piece of vine. Inside, a startled Mayan woman rose from a homemade stool, a tiny baby clutched to her chest. Two more small children ran giggling behind a dresser to hide. Masters smiled. Don Pedro had been busy these last few years. The rancher's wife responded with her own nearly toothless grin. He spotted a couple of hammocks strung up in the corner. Such simple people. He bade her farewell in Spanish, and when the captain ducked out of the fragile-looking structure, she was still smiling and rattling on in a language he didn't understand.

Outside, Kirchner was wandering around looking amused. "This place is neat," he said.

"Sure is. He's sitting on a gold mine and he doesn't even know it. Unfortunately, a lot of people are finding out about it. Pretty soon it'll be ruined by tourists, like most of these places."

"Kinda sad, isn't it?"

"Yeah. But wait until you see what's down there," Masters said, pointing into the sinkhole below. "Come on!"

Together the two men made their way down the shaky-looking wooden ladder and arrived at the water level, nearly forty feet below. Across from them on the other side of the *cenote*, Chico was busy lowering the tanks and gear to a narrow wooden dock at the water's edge. Masters knew the routine and went over to help, untying the tanks and bags.

Kirchner gazed at the crystal clear water, which extended out about twenty yards before disappearing into the cavern. Schools of guppies nipped at the surface and small bats flew in and out of the opening. "Cool," he said quietly.

"I told you, man. Look what happens when the roof falls in!" Masters explained how the ground they were on used to be forty feet above them. The southeasterly flow of the underground aquifer had finally eroded away enough soil and rock to cause the collapse and create the agricultural oasis in which they now stood. "Let's do it," he told Kirchner, and together they began unzipping their gear bags.

From above, Chico watched as the two men slid their BCDs onto their tanks and attached their regulators. Next they put on wetsuits and weight-belts and their booties and fins. Masters lifted Kirchner's tank and held it while the mate slid into his buoyancy vest, one arm at a time. Kirchner then did the same for his captain. The whole ritual amazed the boy, especially the part when the two men spit in their masks. He could never understand how they could see anything after doing that. Then the two checked their gauges, and gingerly slipped into the water.

They waited a moment, nodded to each other and each holding one hand above his head, sank beneath the surface and swam into the cavern and out of sight.

As Chico turned to go, he had a strange sensation—a feeling that he wasn't the only one watching the two Americans descend into the myste-rious water that flowed beneath the earth. He looked around: saw no one, and then scurried around the edge of the *cenote* and back to his mother.

Puerto Aventuras
That Same Day

Two hundred yards south of the cut, in twenty feet of water, a lone figure popped his head above the turbulent, foamy surface of the water. With a deep breath, Larsen inverted himself, kicked hard several times, and glided back towards the sea floor, his eyes darting left and right behind his mask, searching. Hunting.

Ever since waking that morning, Larsen had felt the urge to kill some-thing. After he and Kurt gave the boat a quick rinsing, he grabbed his snorkeling gear, spear and kill bag, and headed out towards the cut, before the wind-driven, choppy water got any worse. He'd invited his mate, thinking it would be a good time to discuss the appalling scene Kurt had not been witness to the day before. Larsen knew the mate would eventually hear about it from Masters or Kirchner, and he wanted to break the news first. Unfortunately, Kurt had declined the invitation to spear some lunch; he'd thought the water was rough, and so Larsen had gone alone.

Free diving was Larsen's specialty, a sport the agent had grown to love ever since he first learned to shoot fish in the Bahamas off Walker's Cay many years before. The northernmost island of the Abacos chain, it was only one hundred miles northeast of Palm Beach and a mecca for spearfishers. Using tanks while spearing fish in the Bahamas was illegal and Larsen was glad; free diving without them was more sporting, and certainly more challenging. The extensive reefs and coral heads that surrounded Walkers and its neighboring islands held an abundance of edible fish; among them, the hog snapper and several species of grouper. It was on the reef at Walker's where the agent had gotten his first taste of the hunt. The stalking. The killing.

He'd also learned that rough water was good water; the fish were confused, and though they could be hard to spot, it was easier to sneak up on them.

Approaching the bottom, Larsen spotted a decent hogfish, and the chase was on. He fluttered his legs very gently and allowed himself to sink down to the bottom, coming up on the orange and white snapper from behind. The hogfish was easy to identify; a snout that curved down from the eyes and tapered into a pointed toothy mouth. It had a large dorsal just behind the head that stuck out like quills and a distinctive black spot, smack in the middle of its body. It was considered by many to be the best tasting of all the snappers; white, flaky and actually very unfishy.

Larsen followed the fish very slowly. It seemed to know he was there, and stayed just far enough ahead to be out of range for a serious shot. But the agent had done this before. He continued the pursuit. Sure enough, the hogfish swam a few feet further, slowed, and began a lazy turn to the right. Larsen shifted his spear to his right hand, and held the mesh bag with his left. His weapon, a type of spear called a Hawaiian sling, felt good in his hands. Nothing more than a pointed steel shaft, with a hinged barb at the end, it slid through a short fat dowel with a piece of surgical tubing attached and functioned like a bow and arrow. He grasped the dowel with his left hand, drew back the narrow steel shaft with his right, took aim, fired and drilled the fish right in the heart, just behind the gills.

In a last-ditch effort to escape, the hogfish, shaft poking right through it, began a giant pinwheeling circle as it fluttered helplessly before crashing into the sand, where it lay quivering about twenty feet away. Larsen swam over, grabbed the shaft and headed for the surface, stuffing the dying fish into the mesh bag. A smoke-like trail of blood seeped through the tiny holes; under water, it was green due to the refraction of the light.

Once on the surface, he blew hard and cleared his snorkel, sucking in the fresh air. He then folded down the barb and pulled the shaft from the fish cinching the bag tight with its nylon drawstring.

Already successful, he'd been down less than a minute.

Breathing deeply, he continued north along the surface, ready to kill again. His muscular legs propelled him along effortlessly. Legs strengthened by long hours standing at the helm of the *Predator*.

His eyes searched the cloudy water ahead and under him, and occasionally behind; the blood he was trailing was certain to attract sharks. He'd heard the creatures were capable of detecting one part in five million.

When the outline of the mammoth Hotel Oasis loomed above him on the shore, he headed for deeper water. Once, while diving with tanks, he'd spotted a large grouper lurking in the area in about forty-five feet. Unlike the pelagic migratory species, like sailfish and marlin, groupers were more territorial and tended to favor a certain area, close to the bottom, where they could find places to hide more easily when necessary.

With a powerful thrust, Larsen dove for the bottom, and passed through the cloudy water into an environment that was remarkably clear. He spotted a jagged coral ledge, swam over, and peered underneath. Nothing.

After returning to the surface for fresh air, he returned to the same area, searching around the bottom of the coral heads, probing into the dark holes. Out of the corner of his left eye, there was movement; he turned, just in time to see a huge tail disappear into a sinister, gaping hole in the reef. He swam over to the opening and looked in. It was deep, and dark, and he couldn't see how far in it went. He felt the first tingle in his lungs as they began to burn. Cupping his hands around his mask in an attempt to make his eyes adjust to the darkness inside, he looked in again. There was something in there, he could feel it. But the alarms were going off in his head. He retreated and returned to the surface once more.

Bobbing in the rough seas, he never took his eyes off the spot even though it was difficult in the cloudy water. Sucking in the clean air in an attempt to fight off the dizziness that threatened to close in on him, the excited agent nearly choked when a wave broke over the tip of his snorkel. A violent fit of coughing and gagging created a throbbing pressure across his forehead and behind his eyes. He knew he needed to rest, but he had to get back down there!

Thirty seconds later, he'd made the forty-foot descent and arrived outside the hole; headache lost in the excitement of anticipation. He steeled himself for whatever he might find, and kicked once gently, floating— ever so slowly—deeper into the dark void in the reef. He scanned right first, and then left. The hole was huge, and extended back further than he had thought. He moved deeper, and squinted, his eyes adjusting to the darkness a little more. And there he was. One of the biggest black groupers Larsen had ever seen. With eyes as big as saucers, the monster hung there suspended, its huge pectoral fins wagging back and forth, its gaping mouth opening and closing as it forced water over its gills. Larsen's chest tightened as his pulse kicked into overdrive. His lungs began to burn, screaming for air as the gas within them changed to carbon monoxide. Together they stared at each other, hunter and prey, man versus nature. Unconsciously, Larsen had dropped the kill bag, and readied the sling. There was time for one shot. His right shoulder ached as he pulled the shaft back to the barb. He fired.

But it was too late! The fish darted away and the spear glanced off the middle of its spine, tearing a jagged, white and pink hole in the flesh.

The agent's mind screamed with a mixture of horror, fury, and frustration. He watched astonished as his target stopped only a few feet away, apparently afraid to leave the sanctuary of the hole. Where was his shaft? There!

By the time he retrieved it, he was well past his bottom time limit. He felt confused, panicked. But somehow his reflexes were still working. He drew back again, and fired.

Out of time, Larsen left everything—fish, spear, and bag—and burst from the underwater cavern with only one thing in mind. Survival. He never even felt the razor sharp piece of coral that ripped a nice gash in the top of his head as he exited the reef. He couldn't see the surface and already the dark cloud of unconsciousness was creeping into his field of vision. Somehow his oxygen-starved brain was still sending messages to his legs, and they continued to kick. Just as he surfaced, he ripped the snorkel from his mouth. He began hyperventilating painfully, and the oxygen flowed through his lungs, back to his heart and into his brain.

Nearly five minutes passed before Larsen was ready to go back down. When he entered the hole again, the fish was dead. With great effort, he left the grouper on the shaft and dragged its dead weight to the surface.

The rough seas made the going hard, and it was another twenty minutes before he reached the cut, exhausted. If there had been any sharks in the area, he hadn't seen them; perhaps the rough water had been a blessing. At the point where the large boulders began, he dragged himself from the water. With one hand on each end of the shaft, he dragged his incredible catch from the water.

Removing his fins and leaving his gear and the bag with the hogfish where he stood, he started down the dock, stumbling a bit as he went.

"Holy shit," he heard as he passed by the first boat, a 54 Ricky Scarborough, a Carolina hull. Because it was rough and the seas were expected to build, several of the boats had elected to stay in. Larsen was psyched about that.

"Goddamn," came the admiration from another.

He rounded the corner where the *Slammer* sat, deserted. He stopped for a moment, and then remembered that someone had said his friends had gone to dive Nohoch. Continuing down the main dock, he realized he was waddling like a cowboy and began laughing, which sapped the last bit of his strength. He dropped the fish with a loud slap and bent over, breathing heavily. When he stood up, his head was swimming. Out of his peripheral vision, he could see people climbing down from towers, and hopping off boats. They were all coming his way. Trying to be humble, he refused to look, but his grin gave him away.

"Pretty work, Dan" It was Terry Stanton, and he shook Larsen's hand. "Where'd you get him?"

"Out there." He pointed at the ocean, then whispered, "I'll tell ya later."

"Did you know you're bleeding?" Stanton had just noticed the orange trickle of blood mixed with seawater that ran down the agent's forehead.

"Yeah, I know. Must've hit my head. It's nothin'"

Behind them, John Flynn could only stare in awe.

Kurt came sprinting down the dock; Larsen wasn't sure if he'd ever seen his stocky mate move so fast. "Dude. You're the king!" He gave his captain a high-five. "I don't know how you do it. Either you know something we don't, or you were born with a horseshoe up your ass!"

"Probably a little of both," Larsen shot back. "C'mon, give me a hand." Each man grabbed one end of the shaft and together they carried Larsen's prize down to the *Predator*.

Kurt went on board and returned with a heavy-duty fish scale that went up to 120 pounds. By this time, several more people had gathered behind the huge Hatteras.

"Hey, nothing attracts a crowd like a crowd," Kurt said. "May I do the honors?" He leapt onto a white plastic chair with scale in hand. He was as excited as a little boy.

"Sure, man. Give me that." Larsen grabbed the scale and stuck the large stainless S-ring between the gill plate and lower jaw. He hoisted the fish off the ground and handed the scale back to Kurt.

"Sixty pounds," someone shouted.

"Ninety," another guessed.

Straining, Kurt lifted the fish yet higher. His face was red, his biceps tight. Larsen watched with an amused expression.

"Jesus Christ! Somebody check it!" Kurt looked ready to explode.

The normally shy John Flynn stepped forward and looked up at the scale. "Eighty-two pounds!" he announced. The crowd erupted and Kurt dropped the fish. There was no question about it. It was a big one.

Most of the crowd had dispersed by the time Larsen flopped the huge fish on the homemade cleaning board he and Kurt had placed across two of the shorter pylons behind the boat. A few stragglers had stayed to watch him fillet the beast, hoping to learn something from the master. Much to their dismay, Larsen decided to gut the fish only, in hopes that Masters and his mate would soon return from their dive in the jungle. Masters was a skilled free-diver as well and it would give Larsen a chance to rub it in.

With a dangerously sharp fillet-knife, he sliced the fish down the middle of its underbelly, releasing a foul odor. Before he knew it, he was elbow-deep in the viscera, which was still warm. For entertainment's sake, he removed and sliced open the end of the nearly transparent stomach and squeezed out several intact bottom fish. With a few properly placed cuts, he removed the remainder of the grouper's internal organs, and tossed them in the water.

Just then a new shadow fell across his makeshift wooden cleaning platform, and when he looked up, there she was.

The last person he had expected to see was Kym Jensen. Dressed in a short denim skirt with a matching short-sleeve blouse, open a little too far and knotted just below her breasts, she was stunning. Larsen could only stand there transfixed, speechless.

"Surprise!" she said, and just the sound of her voice made his knees wobbly; he held onto the board to steady himself.

"Oh my god," he managed. His mouth had gone dry. "What are you doing here? I mean, it's great to see you! I never expected—"

She could see he was stammering and decided to help him out. "I'm on Spring Break up in Cancun with a few of my friends. I wanted to come see you. Unless, of course, it's a bad time..."

"No, no," he told her, but the little voice in his head was screaming yes, yes. He couldn't get over the sight of her. Her hair was a little lighter and she looked a few pounds heavier, but other than that, it was as if she'd never left. "How long are you going to be here?"

"That's up to you," she said, and her suggestive smile and the devilish look in her eye made him want her. Bad.

Larsen saw her looking at the fish and told her the story.

Kym listened with great interest and praised him for his accomplishment.

"Your head," she said, alarmed. She reached out to touch the wound. "You need to get something on that."

"It's just a scrape. Doesn't even hurt."

Larsen threw the grouper in the refrigerated fish-box on the boat, and then stepped back onto the dock and used the hose to rinse the blood off his arms. "Come on," he told her, and taking her travel bag, he stepped down into the cockpit and reached up to help her aboard. "Let me get showered. Then I'll take you to lunch."

"Sounds good to me. I'm ravenous." As Larsen opened the door, she stepped inside. With a wink at the jealous guys left standing behind the boat, he followed, closing it behind him.

Nohoch Na chich
That Same Time

Back in the cavern, Masters and Kirchner had been under nearly twenty minutes, and hadn't yet explored any further than the initial cavernous passageway. Masters had instructed his mate how to move his legs carefully; short, gentle, back and forth strokes with bent knees, well above the bottom. It was easy to stir up the fine layer of silt that covered the cavern floor and most of the entire cave system; to do so would be disastrous, even deadly. As with all dives that began and ended at the same point, they'd agreed to turn back when they had consumed one-third of their available air. With the average depth of the system being only twenty feet, that would give them nearly an hour of bottom time.

Kurt was mesmerized by the incredible underwater world. He swept his light back and forth like a sword, amazed by the intricate formations of limestone icicles that seemed to drip from the ceilings and rise up from the floors of the enormous submarine rooms. Some were nearly connected, top to bottom, jagged and unsymmetrical; others were perfectly round, and hung from the ceiling only, like ancient stone chandeliers. He'd never seen anything like it, and his bugged out eyes were even more magnified through the thick, tempered glass of his mask.

A few feet ahead of him, Masters was swimming slowly, following a thin nylon line that led into the next room. Suddenly Kirchner felt a bit of apprehension. The little bit of light seeping into the cavern was disappearing as they swam deeper into the cave system itself. He focused on breathing deeply and calmly. Each exhalation of breath thundered in his ears as it rose up and bounced off the ceiling, trapped until the almost undetectable current swept it towards the sea.

Ahead, Masters swam onward, passing several rooms that seemed to branch off in all directions. They continued on for another hundred feet before his captain stopped, and then swam through a tunnel that led into the unknown off to their left. He motioned for Kirchner to follow but, before he did, the mate looked behind. And there was nothing but liquid darkness.

Deeper into the system they went, until Masters stopped and swept the beam of his light back and forth in a room to his right which he then entered.

Kirchner followed. Suddenly Masters was shouting something; it came out as more of a grunt. The inability to communicate was frustrating, but Kirchner got the idea. The room was filled with dozens of strange, purple catfish, swimming aimlessly through the beam of light as if they were blind.

Kirchner didn't like the room; there was no nylon guide-line to lead the way. Masters moved onward towards another passageway on the other side. With reluctance, Kirchner followed him. The old saying was fresh in his mind—never leave your dive buddy. In the passageway, Masters had picked up another line and Kirchner felt better. He reached down and brought up his instrument console. He'd only burned eight hundred pounds of air. After a thousand, they should think about turning back.

Every minute sent them farther into the erratic, confusing maze of the system. Kirchner felt lost. He wondered if Masters knew what he was doing. A film of sweat was building on his face; it was itchy and there was no way to scratch. His lungs felt heavy and it seemed harder to draw each breath as the anxiety descended upon the mate like a black cloud. He had to get hold of himself!

There was only one thing that could help him now. With a short burst of his legs, he caught up to Masters and grabbed his fin.

The big man turned and Kirchner pointed back the way they had come. Masters raised his console, studying it. He put his finger on his available air and held it in front of Kirchner's eyes. Then he turned to continue onward.

"No! No!" Kirchner screamed into his regulator. "Out! Out!"

In full panic, Kirchner began swimming back alone, his legs fully extended and kicking wildly, stirring up the bottom.

Masters was on him in less than three seconds. He grabbed the fleeing diver by the leg. The giant fist of his other hand wrapped around the front strap of Kirchner's BCD. "Don't panic!" he screamed into his regulator as he met his friend's wild, petrified eyes. Kirchner struggled to free himself. "No!" He shook him again and repeated, but with emphasis on each word, "Don't—Panic!"

When Kirchner had settled down, Masters slid by him and began to lead the way back. Back through the tunnels they went, following the line, losing it briefly, and then picking it back up again. Their regress was slow and deliberate, and Masters seemed to know where he was going. But after the second time Masters stopped and looked at his compass, Kirchner wasn't so sure. To him, the rooms and passageways all looked the same. He looked for familiar formations, but could find none. His sense of dread was returning.

They rounded a bend in what seemed like an extremely long tunnel and suddenly, Masters stopped. What they saw filled both of them with a sense of fear so overwhelming, they felt sick. Lying there on the bottom, clearly lit by the beam of Masters' light, was the next piece of nylon line. It had been cut.

There was no doubt.

Moments later, a muffled explosion shook the water around them. Sharp pain filled their ears.

Kirchner's panic returned even stronger. He raced past Masters, determined to find the connecting piece of what had now become their lifeline, their only hope for survival. But what he saw next stopped him dead in the water.

Up ahead in the beam of his light, a billowing cloud of thick black silt bore down on him in a relentless particle-storm of death. Before he could move, the maelstrom swept over him, blinding him instantly.

The last thing Masters heard before he turned and tried to get away, was the horrifying agony-filled scream that came from Kirchner's regulator. Not worrying about saving his air, Masters made a desperate attempt to outrun the lethal cloud of dirt and decayed matter. It was futile; he'd gone less than ten feet before it engulfed him. A protruding section of limestone shattered his mask as he plowed face first into an invisible wall, and shards of glass were driven into his cheeks and forehead. His light had been useless.

There was no hope for them now. It was over. But Masters refused to suffocate slowly. Instead, he said a prayer and ripped the regulator from his mouth, and let the dark, dirty water fill his lungs.

21

Puerto Aventuras
That Same Day

"Kevin and I broke up."

Larsen took in her words with caution. They were at the Papaya Republic and the two of them had taken seats at a tiny table close to the beach, with Larsen facing the ocean. They hadn't yet ordered a drink and already she was getting serious.

"How long ago was that?"

"About two months now, I guess."

"And?"

"And now I'm a free woman!" Her tawny hair blew across her face, and with a shake of her head, she tossed it aside. His gaze drifted past her to the reef where the breakers were jacking up one last time before crashing down in a rumbling explosion of foam and whitewater.

A waiter appeared, and set down a plate of *tatopos*—fried tortilla chips—and a bowl of *salsa*. Kym asked for a high-octane *caipirina* and Larsen ordered a Dos Equis, which the waiter informed him they did not have. He settled for a Sol and the young Mexican went off towards the bar.

"What about you?" she asked in an off-handed kind of way. "Still single?"

"Yep." The agent knew his one-word responses were driving her insane, but what did she expect? She'd burned him once and now it was his turn to play games. And so he began by changing the subject.

"How's your dad?" Larsen knew about the man but had never met the Senator. Chairman of some subcommittee that involved Mexico, he remembered. He wondered if her father had any idea what was going on south of the border.

"Oh, don't even ask. I hardly ever hear from him and when I do, he makes my life a living hell. He didn't want me to come down here. He kept saying something about a rebel uprising. Have you heard anything about that?"

"Not much." He'd heard the usual reports of the peasants' unhappiness, and the speculation about a rebellion of sorts, but there had been nothing concrete. "Your father would probably know more than I do."

"Yeah, well, he practically ordered me not to come down here, and I disobeyed him. I guess our relationship can't get much worse. Ever since my mom died..."

Larsen watched her expression change. He knew Kym and her mother had been close. He'd lost a loved one too, and could feel her pain. The image of his sister floated through his mind.

The waiter showed up with their drinks, and Larsen asked about Carlos. "Nobody knows where is Carlos," the waiter said. "Two days now he no come to work. *El Jefe* is very angry." So they had no idea. Larsen decided not to tell the young waiter that Carlos was off on a long, long vacation.

After ordering a mixed *ceviche* for a main course, which they would split, Larsen raised his beer for a toast.

"To you, Kym," he said, studying her face. "May this be your best vacation ever."

"And I'm sure it will be," she said. "But it would be nice if you would let me know how you feel." She sipped her drink and looked him dead in the eye. "Talk to me, Dan."

"I will," he promised her. "I just need to loosen up a little."

Flagging down the waiter, he ordered a *caipirina*.

It was dark when she finally came to him. He was startled and as he sprang up, he couldn't see and almost hurt her. "Shhh...Don't move," she whispered. "Lie down." Her cool hands pushed on his shoulders as he fell back to the bed.

Her long fingers soothed their way down his chest, working his muscles, then moving on, down to his waist. Her fingernails trailed across the sensitive skin and he tried to get up again.

"No, no," she said, pushing him down again. She was in control and although he loved it, Larsen didn't like it one bit.

And then her breath was next to his and he felt her hair on each side of his face. When their tongues met, he wanted her even more, if that was possible. A blind man now, he used his hands to feel her body, to find its shape as he slid his strong fingers down the moist valley in her back.

Teasing him, she broke the kiss and leaned back, moving in a way that was producing serious side effects in his body. She giggled softly, knowing what she was doing to him. And he knew he had to be careful, because he loved it too much and he was afraid to get burned again. But she was here, and he hoped there was a reason.

Kym rose off him slightly and he glided inside her. They moved together, slowly at first, then faster, their bodies colliding with more force each time they met. Kym leaned back and a low moan escaped her lips. Larsen's hands rose up, cupping and kneading her breasts, the nipples hardening beneath his touch. Her body quivered with ecstatic anticipation and then Larsen began to pick up the pace. Deep within him, something was burning, building. Grasping her buttocks, he pounded into her with a fury matched only by her own. They were really sweating now, driving themselves towards a release that could not be stopped.

It was two-thirty in the morning when something woke the agent, and at first he wasn't sure what it was. But then he smelled it; something was burning. The smell was electrical, and it was strong. He looked around the room in confusion, still half-asleep. Nothing. There were shouts coming from the dock and, in a flash, he threw on a pair of shorts and bolted out the door.

Down the pathway and onto the dock, Larsen ran as fast as his bare feet could carry him. Within seconds, the origin of the acrid fumes became apparent. Thick, black smoke poured from the engine room vents of the *Slammer*. Figures were scurrying about in the darkness, lost in the confusion like ants whose hill had been stomped on.

Larsen reached the back of the boat just as Kurt staggered out the open door, choking and wheezing.

"Who's aboard?" Larsen screamed.

"No one," his mate managed in between coughs.

"You sure?"

"Yeah. I checked every room. They never came back after their dive."

Larsen was puzzled. Where in hell had they gone? For a moment he began to fear the worst, then his mind returned to the task at hand. He turned to the gawkers and began to bark orders.

"Wake the other crews!" His shouts were directed at no one in particular, but his tone of voice spurred them into action. "Find Masters and Kirchner. And get some fucking fire extinguishers down here! Now! Now!"

They had to get the other boats out of there, and fast. The strong east wind was blowing the poisonous smoke directly into the cockpit of the boat next to it, another 61 Davis called *Reel Diamond*. Larsen knew that the owners of the vessel, a couple who were near the top of the Amway pyramid marketing scam, were in town. He looked around, but neither they nor the boat's crew were anywhere in sight.

Something burst inside the engine room of the *Slammer*. Larsen could see the flicker of flames through the engine room's side vents. The paint on the side of the *Reel Diamond* facing the *Slammer* was beginning to bubble.

"Kurt! Help me! We gotta move this one right now!" He jumped onto the *Reel Diamond* and hurried up to the bridge, firing up the twin diesels just as a Mexican security guard ran down the dock, pushing a large red fire extinguisher on wheels. He stopped right behind the *Slammer*, pointed the hose at the engine room, and depressed the handle. A pathetic stream of water pissed from the end. "Get the spring lines," Larsen shouted at Kurt. "You!" he screamed at the security guard, "Get these fuckin' stern lines." But the man only stared in confusion. "The ropes, asshole." And then Larsen remembered the words. *"Las sogas. Las sogas!!!"*

With a roar, the huge sportfisher lurched from the slip, nearly crashing into the wall on the other side. Moments later, the *Slammer*'s salon windows blew outward, showering the dock and downwind boats with hot, tempered glass. The fire had reached the fresh oxygen of the salon and now raged with new life, blazing throughout the inside and licking out the open windows and up the sides of the boat. The emergency halon fire system had done nothing.

By this time, people were pouring out of the condominiums. A loud rumbling reverberated throughout the marina as the powerful diesels of the other sportfishers came to life. Mass confusion ensued as several boats tried to leave their slips simultaneously, jockeying for position in the impossibly crowded canals. Shouts of obscenities and crunching wood and fiberglass filled the night. The scene on the dock was absolute chaos as the *Slammer* burned ever hotter.

Larsen spotted the crew of the *Reel Diamond* aboard Terry Stanton's boat. Stanton motored over to them and the switch was made. Minutes later, Larsen and Kurt were back on the dock.

"Try and find Kym," he shouted, and together they scanned the dock, with no success. Larsen glanced up at the condo and there she was—on the terrace. They jostled past the horrified throng of onlookers and jumped aboard the *Predator*, which was the last boat still tied up in its slip.

The agent shook his head in disgust at the number of video cameras he saw, and then started his boat and idled out of his slip and into the mess. Down at the end of the seawall, the *Slammer* continued to blaze alone.

"Look at that fire," he told Kurt, who had joined him on the bridge. "She's had it."

Things took a turn for the worse when the stern lines of the *Slammer* melted. With the spring lines long gone, the crews watched in horror as the boat slowly swung downwind, and sat burning in the exact middle of the canal with the bow line still attached. If the rope were to break or burn through, the fiery hulk would drift on the breeze, right into the boats that were now trapped.

The entire bridge of the *Slammer* was now aflame and Larsen weighed his options. Remain where he was, effectively trapped, or make a mad dash for the inlet, sliding by the inferno and out the cut to open water. If the *Slammer* should continue to burn and sink where she was, blocking the main artery of the marina, there would be no fishing for days. It would take weeks to remove her charred skeleton.

Seconds later, the intense heat melted the thick, aluminum legs and the entire tower came crashing down into the cockpit. Bystanders ducked for cover as the scuba tanks aboard the vessel cooked off, and the crackle of exploding ammunition sent deadly metal whizzing in all directions.

Larsen slammed the *Predator* into reverse and steered it towards the burning wreckage.

"What are you doing?" Kurt screamed.

Larsen did not answer, but just covered his face as the *Predator* slid by what was once the *Slammer* with only inches to spare. He would never forget the sight of the *Slammer*'s twin exhaust, burning as hot as the after-burners on an F-15.

Now they were upwind of the blaze, and out of harms way. Larsen's reckless stunt was the focus of the radio chatter as the other captains debated what to do. He listened carefully; there was still no sign of Masters or Kirchner. Larsen himself chose radio silence, and headed out the cut and into the darker, deeper water.

Back in the marina, two brave souls had maneuvered a small dive boat with a fairly big outboard around the front of the burning boat. Unafraid or perhaps unaware of the possibility of exploding fuel, they attached a towrope to the bow of the *Slammer* and cut the existing mooring line. Ever so slowly, the carnage began moving towards the cut.

Twenty minutes later they reached deep water and the towrope was released. The fire had nearly burned its way to the *Slammer*'s waterline.

As the crews of the *Predator* and a handful of other boats stood by watching in awe, the *Slammer* began to go down stern-first. The remaining flames rushed forward, igniting the fumes of the near-empty forward fuel tank. It exploded and with a last ball of fire that could be seen for miles, she slipped into her watery grave.

22

Marina Puerto Aventuras
April 18, 1996 0546 Local Time

Larsen was awake before dawn. Slipping out of the bed quietly, he stared down at Kym's peaceful form and threw on his clothes. She'd been full of questions after he'd returned to the room, and he'd done his best to bullshit his way around them. In truth, he didn't really have answers, and he could only guess at the underlying reasons for or causes of the fire that had destroyed the *Slammer*. He harbored suspicions that the fire had been deliberately set. But by whom? Masters? Paco? And what about the cocaine that had been aboard? The agent doubted that the Paco would have torched his own load. Or would he?

When he reached the dock, it was just beginning to get light. The only souls on the dock were two local security guards, seated beneath one of the tents, sharing a smoke. His appearance startled them and they leapt to their feet—embarrassed that he had caught them slacking. He spoke to them briefly, but their answers were as expected; they had seen nothing. He walked on.

Down behind the *Slammer*'s empty slip, someone had dragged what remained of the famous sportfisher up onto the seawall. There was virtually nothing left—a few charred pieces of the tower and its melted control box, which had fallen into the water as it collapsed. The starboard outrigger lay alongside the mess; the port rigger was still in the water. Everything else sat on the ocean floor, less than half a mile from shore, but in a depth of over eight hundred feet. The sight of the wreckage left a foul taste in his mouth, and he walked back towards the marina center. There was somewhere he needed to go, but first he would need a car.

Thirty minutes later, he was headed south in a car he'd managed to borrow from Terry Stanton. Lucky for Larsen, the captain had been half-asleep and the agent had been able to snake the keys without answering too many questions.

Just before he'd left the marina, he'd gotten a strange feeling in his gut and returned to the *Predator* for his dive equipment.

The rising sun was harsh on the eyes and lowering the visor, he cursed himself for forgetting his shades. He raced past the small town of Akumal, mashing the accelerator to the floor, swerving occasionally to avoid early-rising locals who ambled along the practically non-existent shoulder of the narrow highway.

Up ahead, he spotted smoke, and began to feel apprehensive. He rounded the last curve before the entrance to Rancho San Pedro and the Nohoch cave system with mounting anxiety. Spotting a white VW bug, he pulled off to the right, directly in front of a landscape he would never forget. Like the scarred aftermath of battle, the fire-scorched jungle smoldered as far as he could see. What had happened there?

He headed for the ranch as fast as he could, humping the dive equipment awkwardly and oblivious to the pain. He was less than halfway there when he spotted Chico approaching on foot. The boy was filthy, covered in black soot from head to toe, his blackened face streaked only by the tears that still flowed down his cheeks. When he reached Larsen, he threw his arms around the agent's waist, clutching him tightly as he sobbed uncontrollably.

"Hey, hey, Chico. It's all right, little man," he told the boy in Spanish. He hugged Chico and stroked his head; then Chico looked up at him, his red eyes full.

"Why, Captain Dan, why?"
"I don't know. Tell me what happened here."
"Two men."
"Yes. I'm looking for them. My friends. A boat captain, Roberto, and his mate."

Chico explained, the words coming in spurts between the sobs. Yes, he had seen Larsen's two friends, the big captain and the other small but strong man. He'd taken their equipment to the *cenote* and helped them get it down to the water. After watching them disappear into the cave, he returned to the ranch to finish his chores. About an hour after that, he saw the men leaving, but without their equipment. When he tried to talk to them, he saw that it was two different men, and they didn't stop. He went back to the *cenote*, and found two sets of dive equipment, but no sign of the men from the marina. Then the jungle caught fire, and they nearly lost the ranch. He had released the animals, and only some had returned.

"These other two men," the agent said, pausing, afraid of what he might hear. "Describe them to me."

"Mexicans. One with long hair. Black. Tied in the back, like a horse's tail." The boy was animated, eager to help his American friend.

"And the other?"

"Black hair, but shorter. Dark skin and a mustache. Ugly, with a big scar."

"Where?"

The agent dreaded what he knew was coming. With a mixture of fear and rage, Larsen watched as the boy drew his finger from his eye to the corner of his mouth.

It was Kirchner's body that Larsen found first, and only the fact that he was prepared for it kept him from getting sick.

The image of his friend's pale, lifeless body would join the others that had been burned into his mind in the last few weeks. Having been dead

276

for less than twenty-four hours, the mate's body had not yet bloated, and with the motionless lungs filled with water, it had simply sunk to the silty floor of the system. The eyes were wide open, bugged out in the final throes of death, looking at Larsen—accusing, but not seeing—and the agent couldn't bring himself to meet them.

Kirchner's throat was torn wide open by his own fingers, a last-ditch effort, the agent realized, to quench the fire in his burning, oxygen-starved lungs.

Finding the body had been easy. He'd simply followed the guide-line and taken the same path he and Masters usually took, the path that revealed the most spectacular views, views which he was certain were the last his friends had seen. When the line suddenly disappeared, Larsen knew what had happened.

The silt along the narrow passageway had yet to settle entirely, and shining his light further ahead through the dark, limestone tunnel, he searched for the body of his other friend. Leaving Kirchner's corpse, he swam on.

Masters body was not far. When the beam of Larsen's light sliced through the murky water and fell upon it, a lump formed in his throat and he began to weep. His shoulders shook and his breath seized in his chest. He wondered for a moment if he should just let himself die. Masters and Kirchner, two of the closest friends he had ever had were now dead, and he was directly responsible. How could he live with that for the rest of his life? Something inside him cried out, perhaps the coward, but he would never know for sure. Yes, his friends were dead, but did they die in vain? Only he could give their death some meaning, a reason they would never know but perhaps their families would one day.

Those who had murdered his friends would suffer an equal fate, he would see to it. Inhaling deeply and exhaling slowly, the agent gradually composed himself.

He latched onto the top of Masters' tank, entwining his fingers where the first stage of his regulator was attached, and began towing the stiff, awkward body of his friend towards the cave system's exit. A pang of guilt ran through him as he checked the gauge that showed his remaining air supply. There was plenty. He took a look at Masters' gauge—over fifteen hundred psi left! What had his friend done? Fighting back the tears, he followed the thin, dirty nylon line towards the entrance of the *cenote*.

When Larsen finally pulled the second body from the cavern and dragged it onto the dock, he was exhausted, and almost out of air. Chico had come down to help, and the agent was sorry such a good kid had to bear witness to what had been an ugly, truly evil deed.

Up above the *cenote*, Chico's mother held her baby in her arms, muttering prayer after prayer. Her words drifted down to the water, but were barely audible. It was an eerie sound and along with the visions, it would stay with the agent forever.

Larsen knelt to close Kirchner's eyes and was once more overcome with grief, collapsing on the wet slats of the rickety wooden dock. Chico walked over and put his hand softly on the agent's head. He too began to cry.

"Damn you Paco Herrera," he heard his captain friend say. "Damn you to hell."

Marina Puerto Aventuras

With a grunt, Terry Stanton gave the top of the last primary fuel filter one more turn. He too had been up since daybreak, and unable to get back to sleep, he'd gotten up to do some routine maintenance on the *Tempest*. The burning of the *Slammer* the night before had disturbed him, and the unknown whereabouts of his friends, the crew, had him more worried than ever. But as always, he turned his nervous energy into productivity and soon found himself cleaning the entire engine room, as well as changing every fuel filter aboard—primaries and secondaries for the engines, and the single unit for the generator. The quality of the diesel sold in the marina was notoriously bad, so even though the filters didn't look that bad, he'd put over a hundred hours on the hardworking diesels and decided to change them. Better safe than sorry.

A loud thump shook the floor as someone leapt into the cockpit. Someone opened the salon door and called his name.

Removing his glasses to wipe the sweat off his face, he awkwardly spun himself around on all fours within the cramped space. Keeping his head low, he crawled out of the engine room and onto the galley floor.

When he stood up and turned, the image of the person standing in the salon was severely blurred and he quickly replaced the thin, wire-framed specs. For a moment, Stanton was speechless. He'd never seen his friend Larsen in such a sorry state. The agent looked tired, haggard. His hair was wet, dark and matted. It framed his dirty face, surrounding his red, puffy eyes like the snapshot of a Vietnam grunt with a "thousand yard stare"— a man who had seen too much, and all of it bad. His t-shirt and shorts were filthy, covered with a mixture of what looked like mud and soot. The only part of Larsen that didn't look like it had been put through the wringer were his feet, which stood out in bold contrast to the rest of his filthy body. Stanton stood staring at the apparition, too dumbfounded to speak, and the agent beat him to it.

"He killed them, Terry." His voice was flat and monotone.

"Who killed who?" Stanton asked, finding his voice, the fear within him building. "Jesus Christ, Dan, get yourself together. Tell me what's going on."

"Paco. He killed Masters and Kirchner. Motherfucker murdered them in Nohoch..." Larsen's eyes were still out of focus.

Stanton was scared. He grabbed Larsen by the shoulders and tried to shake him from his reverie. "Tell me what happened!"

The agent looked at Stanton hard, blinking, and then frowning as if seeing him for the first time. "Everything was fine. Until Paco killed Carlos..."

For the next several minutes, Larsen described the grisly events of the last three days. Stanton barely interrupted him, absorbing what the agent told him with a mounting sense that he, also, should get the hell out.

"What did you do with the bodies?" he asked

"I buried them behind Don Pedro's *palapa*. I'll come back for them, but I'm not sure when."

"So what do we do now?" Stanton asked, glad to see that Larsen was getting a grip on himself. "I'm scared, Dan. I want to see my family again. You got us into this. Now it's time to get us out…"

"It's not that simple, Terry. There's a lot of things you don't know."

And maybe don't want to, Stanton thought. He watched as Larsen rubbed his face with both hands, smearing the dirt and dragging it in streaks down his chin and neck. The agent took a deep breath and exhaled loudly. Stanton knew Larsen wanted to tell him something. Why was he hesitating?

"We've been friends for a long time, Dan. Talk to me." Several seconds passed. Finally Larsen turned and looked at him.

"About ten years ago, my sister died of a cocaine overdose," he began.

"Yeah, I know, man. I'm sorry." He'd heard about it through the grapevine, but the two men had never discussed it, and Stanton had always assumed it was something his friend preferred to leave buried. Stanton wasn't really sure what to say. Why would a man smuggle the very drug that killed his own sister? It just didn't make sense. But then, he'd sworn to himself never to get involved with the same drug that had taken first his father, then his brother.

"Not long after that," Larsen continued, "I joined the DEA."

"That explains it," Stanton said.

"Explains what?"

"Why you're doing this."

"Well, now you know. But what's happening here is only part of it, Terry." The agent decided to start at the beginning. "Have you ever heard of a man named Amado Carrillo Fuentes?"

Stanton had not, but what he heard over the next several minutes left him feeling sick.

"I assume Kurt knows everything," Stanton said. "Who else?"

"Just him. At first, it was only supposed to be one load, on my boat," Larsen explained. "But I think when Paco saw how easily it went down, he got greedy. He demanded we do another drop, but where the hell was I going to put it? There was no one I trusted more than you guys. And now Masters and Kirchner are dead..."

"Those guys knew what they were getting into," Stanton said. "They didn't have to do it. I am. For Jessica." He thought about his little girl, and how her life depended on his coming through with the money. Suddenly, he was panic-stricken. "What's happened doesn't change anything, does it? I mean, I've got to have that money."

"You'll get your money, Terry, I promise you that. But until I find Paco, I can't say what's going to happen."

"What about the coke on Masters' boat? I can't believe Paco would just burn it."

"Me either," the agent said. "I've got a lot of questions for Mr. Herrera. But maybe I should just kill him."

Stanton hoped Larsen was kidding. Without Herrera, the DEA might not get Carrillo, and more importantly, Stanton might not get his money.

"In any case, Dan, I appreciate your honesty. I understand that it was something you couldn't really come right out with and tell me. I just can't believe it. Masters and Kirchner..."

"I wish I'd never gotten you guys involved. I'm sorry, man."

"I think it's a little late for that."

"You're right."

"You let me know, then," Stanton told him. "I'm ready to go when you say the word. I've had it with this place. I want to go home."

Larsen headed for the door. He wanted to go home too. They all did.

Along the main dock, most of the slips were empty; the wind had backed off a bit, and supposedly the bite was pretty good. According to Stanton, Kurt and John Flynn were off down the beach somewhere, bonefishing so, when he hopped aboard the *Predator*, Larsen expected to be alone. Opening the door to the salon, his instincts told him something was wrong. The feeling was confirmed when he spotted Kym down in the forward stateroom.

She was seated on the bed, her legs hanging over the edge, her head in her hands. Beneath her feet, the hatch cover for the forward bilge was open.

He approached her slowly, afraid to startle her. When he stood before her, she raised her head; the mascara that ran down her cheeks was a dead give-away. He looked in her eyes, and the sadness he saw within them tore at his heart. But in a second her expression hardened to contempt. He tried to hold her but she pushed him away.

"Why?" she asked weakly. "How could you?"

"Let me explain," he said, and reached for her again, but she pulled away and bolted up the stairs and into the salon.

"Kym, wait!" he screamed, but she was already out the door. "God-dammit!" he cursed in anger and frustration, but there was no one to hear his rage. His world was coming apart.

Kym headed down the dock in a state of emotional distress. There were several words to describe the way she felt. Yes—betrayed. Yes—she had been naive, and felt foolish because of it. But there was one word that could best describe it: devastated.

Her discovery of the cocaine hidden under the floor in the master stateroom of the *Predator* had been completely accidental. She'd been waiting for Larsen all morning, full of questions about what had happened the night before. She had not seen him since she woke up, and neither had anyone else. Stir crazy after waiting so long, she had begun poking around. It was sheer curiosity that drove her to lift the hatch that had been cut into the carpeted floor of the master stateroom.

What she had found had made her sick to her stomach. The carefully wrapped packages could be only one thing, and on further investigation, her worst suspicions had been confirmed.

She thought she knew Dan Larsen. But it was now obvious that beneath the facade, there lurked another man—one who was caught up in the world of drug smuggling and the evils that went along with it. Sharon was right. She really didn't know Dan Larsen at all.

Kym continued down the dock and past the marina office into the center, unsure what to do, or where to go. She couldn't just leave; she had to talk to Larsen and learn the truth. And if she returned to Cancun, what would she tell her friends?

She needed a drink. The Café Olé restaurant was just ahead, and they had a bar. But she could see that it was already crowded. Besides, it was too close to the boat. Larsen would surely come looking for her and she wasn't ready to confront him just yet. Maybe the Latitude 20° sports bar on the other side of the marina.

She remembered a small shuttle bus that ran from the hotel adjacent the beach to the Hotel Oasis, and crossed the street to find it.

The honk of a vehicle's horn sounded behind her. Startled, she turned to see a white Suburban with tinted windows slowly cruising towards her. The driver pulled up and lowered the passenger side window, and leaned across to speak.

"Hi. Maybe you can help me," he said with a smile. He had long hair pulled back in a ponytail.

"Maybe."

"I'm looking for some friends on a boat that is supposed to be here in the marina. It is called the *Slammer*."

"Oh my god! You didn't hear?" She walked closer to the window, leaning on the door and lowering her head to look at the man behind the wheel as she delivered the bad news.

"The *Slammer* burned up last night."

"I know that," he said icily, the corners of his mouth twisting up in a demonic grin. As Kym looked at him in confusion, a dirty hand shot out from the back seat, grabbing her by the hair and dragging her upper body through the window.

The cold metal of a gun barrel dug deeply into her neck, and she winced, too stunned to make a sound. "Now listen to me, you filthy whore," he spit out. "Get in the front seat slowly. You scream, and I'll blow your fucking brains all over this marina." Whoever was in back released her, and the driver leaned over the seat and shoved the door open. Kym was so paralyzed with fear, she could not move. "You get in here now, bitch, or I swear I'll let my friend kill you." Ever so slowly and too terrified to disobey, she did as she was told.

The last thing she saw before the blindfold turned her whole world black, was the face of the second man. It was an ugly face, a cruel face that looked like it had done bad things. A face she would never forget.

Nearly two hours would pass before Larsen would come to realize what had happened. He'd found Kym's travel-bag still in the condo, but a walk down the beach and throughout the marina in search of her had been fruitless. The last place he checked was the Café Olé restaurant. As it turned out, the only person who had seen her was the head waiter.

"Yes, I see her, Capitan. Maybe two hours ago. We very busy." He told Larsen about the white suburban. The vehicle didn't ring a bell with Larsen, and he asked about the driver.

"For sure *Mexicano*," he said, "but I no really get a good look at heem. Like I say, I no really pay attention. But I see she very beautiful and then I remember she is your woman. If not for her beauty, Capitan Dan, I don't even notice."

Larsen thanked him and walked away. He knew who had taken her.

Xpu-Ha, Three Miles South of Puerto Aventuras
Later That Day

The first thing Kym noticed about the place was the musty smell of decay and the overpowering stench of blood. The floor was dirt—that she could feel—and the wall that supported her aching back was cool and hard, like the stucco that could be found in so many of the native *pueblos* scattered throughout the Yucatan.

How long she had been unconscious, she did not know. One of the two men had struck her a savage blow when they had reached their destination. With bound hands, she gently rubbed her swollen cheek. Her mouth tasted of stale blood. Something moved on the floor in front of her and she realized she was not alone.

"Well, well," a voice taunted her. "It seems our guest has returned to the land of the living." Hands tugged at her blindfold, ripping it off, and the light made the back of her eyeballs ache. Blinking, she attempted to focus on her captors. They were the same two men from the suburban. Her first thought was that she was in some type of makeshift torture chamber, and she was absolutely right. The dried blood that was spattered and smeared on the dirty brown walls of the tiny room was a disturbing reminder that she was not the first person to have been brought there. She wondered how many had left alive.

"Who the hell are you?" she demanded.

"My name is Paco Herrera Tejeda. Say hello to my friend Raul." The man with the scar smiled at her with a vulgar display of rotten teeth. Apalled, she looked away. "And who might you be?" Paco asked.

"Kym. Kym Jensen." She included her last name as if the smuggler may have heard it before. "Where the hell am I? And why am I here?"

"Shut up, bitch! I will ask the questions here!" He moved forward, raising his arm as if to strike her. She noticed the pistol in his hand. The ugly one held an automatic rifle.

"Please," she whimpered. "Don't hurt me anymore."

Paco bent down on one knee in front of her. "Okay, we'll do it like this. I ask the questions, and you give me the answers I want to hear. If I do not like your responses, I will hurt you. Pain is just the beginning, pretty lady. My friend Raul would be ecstatic if I let him start the festivities."

Kym shuddered at the thought. She returned Paco's leering stare with a look of careful defiance. This was no ordinary trafficker. His methods and command of the English language were both excellent. Could he be some sort of rebel leader? She decided to play it safe, to play along...

"Now then," Paco started, getting to his feet. "What is your relationship with Dan Larsen?"

She knew it. Although afraid to admit it, Paco's question had come as no surprise. The wheels in her brain began turning as she quickly put two and two together.

"I'm waiting."

"I don't know," she said softly.

"What do you mean, you don't know?" he screamed. "You came here to see him. You've been staying in his condo. Eating with him. Sleeping with him. I'm sure you're fucking him." This last statement contained a hint of malice.

"I guess you could say we're lovers."

"Lovers. How nice." Paco was getting more agitated by the second. "Next question!" he snapped. "Who is he working for?"

Unsure of his meaning, she remained silent.

"Listen to me, you whore! Tell me who he is working for." Paco was on top of her in a flash, jerking her head back by her hair.

A huge knife had materialized in his hand—she could feel the blade pressed against the tender skin of her throat. "I'll ask you one more time!" he screamed.

"I don't know what you mean," she whimpered. She began to cry, her body shaking from fear. Paco looked at Raul and the ugly man shook his head.

Paco released her and she fell back against the wall.

"You see, Captain Dan and I are business associates. We share a mutual, shall we say, investment. It is my duty to protect that investment." He hesitated, not sure if she was hearing him, "listen to me!" Kym tried to compose herself and looked up at Paco, any defiance in her wide brown eyes now gone. "Lately I have been having my doubts about your "lover" and his friends. In this business, that is not possible. We deal in absolutes—what is, and what is not. The crew of the *Slammer* learned that the hard way."

Kym found the courage to speak. "You bastard. You killed them. You—"

"They had changed their minds about being part of our little investment "group". That posed a problem and problems must be solved. And it was." He did not tell her that before he had torched the *Slammer*, he and Raul had managed to remove the cocaine without being seen. It was amazing what security guards would not see when offered several weeks salary.

"What do you plan to do with me?" she asked, afraid of the response she might hear, and wondering if she should even believe it.

"I plan on using you as collateral, to make sure your lover fulfills his end of the bargain and delivers our investment to its destination, without harm coming to me or any of my associates."

"And when is that?"

"Soon. Within two weeks."

Kym could not believe her ears. She was due back in class well before then. But what the hell was she thinking? She'd be lucky if she made it back at all. What she had to concentrate on now was staying alive. And suddenly she had an idea, something that just might work.

"Do you know who my father is?"

"No. Should I?" Paco said with growing interest.

"He's Senator Thomas Jensen, and he's the chairman of the Mexican-American Relations Subcommittee."

"Imagine that. And what are you going to tell me next? That he would disapprove of your treatment?"

"No, but we're very close and I talk to him every day," she lied. "If he doesn't hear from me, he's going to think something's wrong. Then you're going to have the State Department down here looking for me, and I know you don't want that."

"And you expect me to let you contact him? Do not insult my intelligence! You call home and the next thing I know, some rescue team comes to save you."

"That is exactly what will happen if he doesn't hear from me."

"Nonsense," Paco said, but he had his doubts. American authorities poking around was something he surely could do without. He was ready to move the cocaine. Not in two weeks as he'd told his captive, but now.

And without him even knowing it, his hostage had been even more valuable than he had originally thought. No one would touch them now.

"Raul!" he shouted, without taking his eyes off Kym. "Bring me the phone from the truck!"

Washington D.C., Capitol Hill
That Same Day

When Senator Thomas Jensen had first set his sights on the ambassadorship to Mexico, he had gone after the position like a man possessed. Lately, however, he had begun to have second thoughts. The once beautiful country seemed on the verge of economic, political and environmental ruin. The people of Mexico were hurting, and the government had reached a new peak of corruption and unpopularity. The general consensus among the inhabitants of the vast area south of the border was that the *gringos* of the *Estados Unidos*—the United States—were largely responsible.

Secretary of State Johnson had really been leaning on him for answers—answers he didn't have. His calls to President Zedillo regarding the possible rebel uprising had not been returned and Ambassador LeGrone had suggested that the Mexican President was stonewalling. Jensen knew he was right.

And the DEA's hunt for the cartel leader had turned up nothing. At least that's what they were telling him. He had the suspicion they were hiding something. As of late, that seemed to be what they did best.

And so, when his secretary buzzed his office on the intercom, the Senator wasn't in the best of moods.

"Call for you on line two, Senator." The crass voice further agitated his headache.

"I thought I told you no calls," he barked.

"It's your daughter, Tom. She says it's long distance." Using his first name!

288

Jensen's mood instantly brightened. Maybe Kym wanted to come to see him after all. "I'm sorry," he said to the little black box. "Put her through. Please."

There was a bit of static on the line when he picked up the receiver, but he smiled at the sound of his daughter's voice.

"Daddy?"

"Hi honey. Where are you?"

There was silence for a moment and then she said, "I'm in Mexico."

Jensen was angry for a moment when he realized she'd not listened to a word he had said, but his anger was mixed with sadness and he made a deliberate attempt to keep the conversation upbeat. "How is it?"

"Great." Her one word answer puzzled him. Usually she was bubbly while on vacation, ranting and raving about the weather, the surf, and whatever she'd been doing.

"Where are you staying, honey?"

"In Puerto Aventuras."

"Is that captain fellow there?"

"Yeah."

"How's that going?"

"Good." Kym's voice sounded strained to him, almost frightened.

"Honey, is everything all right?"

"Yeah, Daddy. Everything's great. I just wanted to check in so you wouldn't worry."

"Okay. Well you keep in touch, honey. I always worry about you. I love you."

"Me too. And Daddy?"

"Yes?"

"Give my love to mom, too."

"What?" he asked, unsure if he had heard correctly. "What did you say?" he asked again, but the line had already gone dead.

In alarm, he nervously punched the button on the intercom.

"Yes, Senator?"

"Get me Secretary Johnson," he ordered. "And don't take no for an answer. If he's not in, find him!"

23

Seal Training Facility Coronado, California   32°39.17"N 117°13.62"W
April 17, 1996 2156 PT

Wes Gates took a deep breath and clenched his teeth as the third wave of the set hit him head on. Like the two before it, it knocked him backwards and stole the air from his lungs. Down the line, the other twenty-six men suffered the same fate. They were linked arm in arm, a chorus line of wannabe warriors, marching into the frigid surf as part of the Basic Underwater Demolition/SEAL(BUD/S) training course. Gates could barely see the other men. Fifteen minutes in, five minutes out, now it was round three. This part of the training was called "surf torture" and the phrase could not have been more accurate.

The Navy brass, particularly those at NAVSPECWARCOM, the Naval Special Warfare Command, had not been the least bit happy when Macki had demanded that Gates be a part of the team that would conduct the raid on Carrillo's compound in Vera Cruz. The SEALs were a closed unit, a secret society that only accepted men who had completed the physically demanding, twenty-five weeks of special training. But Macki had insisted. Gates intelligence—what he had stored in his mind—was crucial to the mission. Without him it wouldn't fly. Without him there would be no mission.

So now here he was. Freezing in the surf in the middle of Hell Week: the fifth week of training, the part designed to truly test a man's resolve,

290

the part that pushed a man over the brink, well beyond normal limits of physical endurance. Five and a half days of continuous training, and just four hours of sleep. They wanted to see how much pain a man could withstand. They were convinced that the human body could do ten times the amount of work the average man thinks possible. Sick bastards.

The class had begun with just over a hundred men. There were fifty-six left. The rest had either quit or been rolled back due to injuries. Those that survived Hell Week would go on to the next two phases of training—diving and land warfare. With longer runs. Farther swims.

On the rocks of the nearby jetty, the SEAL instructor barked orders through a megaphone. His grating voice antagonized the men. He was all attitude, a self-proclaimed superior being, and Gates despised him.

"I want to hear some fucking laughing out there," the instructor roared. "Get moving!"

Still arm in arm, the trainees staggered to their feet. They marched on and the next wave drove them back. Gates had never felt such cold water sweep over his entire body. He looked at the young man next to him and wasn't sure if he was going to make it. His lips were dark, his face pale, drained of the blood that had once kept him warm. He shuddered uncontrollably, muttering something Gates couldn't make out. It was obvious hypothermia was setting in. They were losing him.

The young man wriggled his arm away from Gates and the man next to him and broke for the beach. Away from the cold. Away from the insanity. Gates lunged for him but missed. The trainee continued towards the beach and Gates took off after him, struggling through the waist-deep surf. In a chain reaction, the rest of the men seized the opportunity and headed for the beach. Somewhere in the darkness an angry voice screamed as the instructor ordered them to stop. He fired blanks from an M-60 machine gun into the night sky. The sound was terrifying, yet no one stopped.

At the shoreline, the young man collapsed in the sand. When Gates reached him, he was sobbing. Gates grabbed him by the shoulders and rolled him away from the water as the trainee curled into the fetal position. Gates got on his knees and rubbed the cold wet skin of the man's arms.

"It's going to be all right," he told him. "It's going to be..."

Sharp metal dug into Gates' side. He turned, defiant.

"What the fuck do you think you're doing?" the instructor screamed. He poked him again with the barrel of his weapon. His eyes were wild with fury.

"This man is sick!" Gates shouted. "He's going to die out there!"

He turned back to the shuddering man, continued rubbing his arms and body.

The instructor hit Gates in the side with the M-60, knocking him backwards. Gates jumped to his feet and the two men squared off. Their steaming breath was visible in the darkness. The rest of the men stood watching, shivering, clenching their fists and rubbing the life back into their arms. Their teeth chattered.

The instructor leaned forward, his face so close Gates could smell his breath. "What's your name, shithead?" he demanded.

"Gates."

"Gates. Gates..." The instructor ran the name through his mind. Then it clicked. "You'll get no preferential treatment here, Gates. If it was up to me, you wouldn't even be here. I know your story, Gates. So you listen to me, and listen good. To me, you're just another squid. Just like every other lame motherfucker out here.

"In fact, your little show of concern, or shall we say, affection, just bought you and the your buddies another twenty minutes of warm, Southern California water."

Behind him, the other men gasped.

"Now remember you assholes," the instructor shouted at the top of his lungs. "The only easy day was yesterday! Now back in the fucking water!"

Marina Puerto Aventuras
April 19, 1996 1826 Local Time

"Hold on a second, Dan. Start at the beginning and explain what happened." John Macki's metallic voice emanated loudly from the tiny speaker of the high-frequency single-side-band radio on the bridge of the *Predator*. Larsen realized how important the scrambling device and secure channel was proving to be. What he was about to repeat was for his CIA contact's ears only.

"I said, first Herrera murdered our go-between down here. I saw it with my own eyes, John. Then he murdered my two friends, the crew of one of the other boats. That night the boat burned in the marina. I assume half of the second drop was destroyed along with it."

"I do remember telling you I didn't think it was a good idea to involve anyone else. Things fall apart when amateurs are involved. You of all people should know that."

"The last thing I need right now is a fucking lecture, John." Macki's reference to "amateurs" was a low blow and they both knew it. During the operation in the Bahamas a few years earlier, two Bahamian locals had been killed when Larsen had used them in an attempt to maintain his cover. And one of the DEA's best Bahamian field agents had disappeared, and was presumed dead. To blame Larsen was ludicrous. Shit happened. Period.

"I'm sorry. But I've already got my ass out on a limb, Dan. If this whole thing blows up in our faces, my career is finished! For the second time!"

"You don't understand. We're not talking about careers down here, we're trying to stay the fuck alive! This guy Herrera has stepped way over the line. He murdered two of my best friends. Friends, John. And now I have to spend the rest of my life knowing that I was directly responsible for their deaths. Not the CIA, not the DEA. It was me. I did it!" Larsen was screaming into the handset now.

Kurt came hustling up the ladder, afraid that something might be wrong. He was about to enter the bridge, but Larsen looked at him and held his hand up. His mate got the message and retreated back down the ladder.

"All right, I realize you're upset, Dan, but it won't do any good to piss and moan about it."

Larsen knew he was right. He'd always been taught to keep a secure communication short and right to the point, delivering only the most pertinent information.

"There's more," Larsen said more calmly.

"Tell me buddy."

"You know a Senator named Tom Jensen?"

"Yeah, he's Chairman of the Mexican-American Relations subcommittee. Heard of him, don't really know him. Sounds like an asshole. Why do you ask?"

"I've known his daughter for a while. She came down here to visit me a couple of days ago. Talk about bad timing. Anyway, I'm pretty sure Herrera grabbed her."

"Shit! Why would he do that?"

"I'm not sure. Probably to hold her hostage. Make sure he doesn't get busted, you know?"

"This Herrera guy sounds like a real winner."

"I'm telling you, John, I am real close to killing the bastard right now."

"I wouldn't recommend that," Macki warned.

"Why not?"

"Because this whole operation is aimed at taking down Carrillo. We need Herrera, and we'll bust him, too. We'll do it simultaneously. Remember?"

Of course Larsen remembered, but the whole operation had been planned before people started dying. They needed to act and it had to be soon. Before Paco had a chance to do anything to Kym—if she was still alive.

"I need to do something, John. I can't just sit here. It's time to bust a move. What the hell are you guys doing up there?"

"Believe me, we're working on it. I called in some favors, Dan. Big favors. A team is training as we speak, but I'm told they need a little more time. Logistics, stuff like that."

"We don't have any more time!"

"When will you be ready to get out of there?"

"I'm ready to get out of here right now. I already told you that." He was beginning to get pissed.

"I need at least three more days, Dan."

"Okay. But that's it. In three days I'm getting the hell out of here. Weather permitting. And it's gonna have to be blowing a fucking hurricane to keep me here. Pull me out, John, before I do something we will both regret. Three days."

Larsen pushed the button, ending the transmission. When he found out more, he'd contact Macki again, hopefully to finalize things. He took a deep breath and gazed out the windows of the bridge. Most of the boats were returning from a day on the rip and the dock was coming alive. He wondered if anyone would believe the scenario that had been unfolding right beneath their noses. Probably not, as he could hardly believe it himself.

It was time to bring Kurt and Terry Stanton up to speed on the latest developments. More than anything, he had to find Paco.

Right now the smuggler held the cards, and Larsen didn't like it. Sure, Paco had tested him, but he'd also underestimated him. Now the killer had pushed the agent beyond his limits. And that was dangerous.

Marina Puerto Aventuras
April 20, 1996 0604 Local Time

Paco knew that by now Captain Dan was probably beside himself with worry over the disappearance of his two friends and the girl, and he decided it would be a good time to make contact.

He wasn't sure whether the captain knew of his two friends' fate, but was certain no one had spotted the small inflatable he and Raul had used to remove the cocaine from the *Slammer*. The lone security guard who had been walking the dock that night had earned nearly a year's pay to look the other way. Paco could still remember the shocked look on the man's face when he had slipped him the cash. By the time the fire Paco had started in the *Slammer*'s engine room had begun to spread, he and Raul were halfway down the beach, headed towards Xpu-Ha.

The taking of the girl, on the other hand, had been more risky. They had snatched her in broad daylight in the middle of the street and he wasn't sure who might have seen her get in the truck. The resort was full of white suburbans, and several small agencies used them for tours and airport transfers. Acquiring one without personal identification had been

295

difficult at first, but once again, a large sum of cash had proved to be the great convincer. Paco hoped that Kym would have looked like just another tourist accepting a ride. But Paco knew that Larsen was a smart character himself, and if there was a way to find out what had happened to her, the captain would find it. It didn't really matter to the Paco if Larsen knew or not—he was prepared to tell him he had her.

When Paco pulled into the resort, it was just beginning to get light. He thought it would be best to contact the captain early, before the dock got too busy. The smuggler had become bolder about showing himself in the marina, and he knew that could only lead to trouble. Rumbling down the annoying, rocky entranceway, he noticed a fresh breeze was already building. The palms along the golf course were already bending back and forth; he thought how nice it would be to stop and play a round. But there was no time for that and he carried on down the narrow road, through the archway into the Chac-hal-al condominiums and pulled up into a parking place about fifty yards from the stern of the *Predator*. High up on the starboard outrigger, there was not one, but two yellow flags which flapped in the mounting breeze.

Paco was not surprised at the sight of the signal that the captain needed to talk. But two flags? He laughed inwardly at Larsen's sense of urgency.

For a moment he thought about just going up and knocking on the side of the boat, but changed his mind when he spotted one of the many local groundskeepers. The old man was pushing a wheelbarrow full of leaves and small twigs, his back hunched over, permanently bent in the shape that betrayed what the withered Mayan had been doing for years. The tattered straw hat that sat atop his head was pulled down low in the front; it not only blocked the rays of the early morning sun, but shut out the evil, unfair world he seemed destined to toil in for the rest of his days. Paco whistled, and the old man stopped and stared at the suburban in casual indifference. The smuggler waved him over, and as the old man approached, he quickly scrawled "meet me on the beach" on a piece of a paper bag. He instructed the old man where to deliver it, and gave him one hundred pesos; it was more than the groundskeeper would make in almost a week. Then he got out of the suburban and headed for the beach.

On the beach, it was low tide. The smell of rotting seagrass drifted into his nostrils. Paco sat down in an area of hard packed sand about thirty feet from the water's edge. Scanning the bay, he noticed four or five fly-fishermen plying the waters in hopes of catching a bonefish or permit. Scattered from one end of the long stretch of bay to the other, they were spaced almost evenly apart, and stood in water that was nearly waist deep. They waved their long poles back and forth, time and time again, in total silence. It was a ritual that was repeated every morning, but best performed when the waters were calm. Soon it would be too windy.

It was a peaceful scene, unlike the violence of the last few days, and for a moment, Paco relaxed, trying to prepare himself for the confrontation that would soon come. He would not wait long.

"I ought to kill you right now, you motherfucker." Larsen's voice was filled with malice. The cold steel of a gun barrel drove itself into the back of Paco's neck. When he turned slowly, the agent took a step back. What the smuggler saw was an expression of pure hatred, a look he had seen on several men's faces: just before he killed them. But this time it was not he who held the instrument of death, and the feeling was a bit unnerving.

"You may want to kill me, but you won't," Paco said, stalling.

"You murdered my friends. And then tried to make it look like an accident, you fucking coward." The agent's expression had not changed, but his whole body shook as the anger swirled through his veins. The gun in his hand was unsteady.

"I did what I had to do. Your friends were putting our whole operation at risk. I told you from the beginning, Captain Dan, that we are not playing the games of children here. We do not look at things in terms of right and wrong. There are only two outcomes in such an operation— success or failure. And along with these outcomes there is often an inevitable factor: that of life or death. Your friends made their decision and you passed it on to me. I did what was necessary to protect the operation and the cartel, nothing more." Paco hoped that his explanation did not antagonize the captain further. "Now why don't you put that gun down, and we can discuss our situation like businessmen."

"Not yet, you son-of-a-bitch! Tell me where Kym is or I'll blow your fuckin' head off!" He pointed the gun at Paco's face and pulled back on the slide, chambering a round.

Paco held his hands up. "Keep your voice down. Someone is going to see us."

"At this point, Paco, I really don't give a shit. Tell me where she is! Three seconds!"

"She's fine, I'm telling you. I have her in a safe place. I have not harmed her in any way," he lied.

"Where?" the agent demanded.

"At my villa in Playa del Carmen." Another lie. Kym was still in the small shack in the jungle, but Paco had considered moving her to the villa. There it would be easier to keep an eye on her. Perhaps Teresa could find out more about her, and more about Captain Dan Larsen.

"Why did you take her? She has nothing to do with all of this."

"Oh, please, Captain Dan. Just when I think you are beginning to understand me, you do or say something that makes me think you don't really know me at all. I knew you would be upset after what happened to your friends. By having Kym as my guest, so to speak, I make sure you will not do anything stupid, anything you will regret. I also guarantee that my shipment—our shipment—makes it to Florida without any problems. *Comprende, amigo?*"

"Yeah, I understand. I understand that you would probably kill your own mother if it meant protecting your precious cocaine and the fucking cartel."

Larsen's words could not have angered Paco more.

"You came to me, remember? You were the one who decided to get your friends involved. You could have taken the whole second load on your own boat. If you are so sure that we won't be searched, what difference would it have made? Because of your stupidity, we had to risk everything getting the cocaine off that boat!

"Now, I find out your girlfriend, or lover, or whatever you want to call her, has a father who is an American politician. And it makes me wonder, Captain Dan, what the connection is. Maybe you are not what you seem. Believe me, I have my suspicions about you, and for your sake and Kym's, they'd better turn out to be wrong."

"How do I even know she's still alive?"

"She's alive, and I'll prove it to you. But I will keep her with me until the end of our journey. Now get that fucking gun off me and tell me when we're leaving. I am ready to go. The longer we wait, the more dangerous it will become for us. The *Federales* already think something is going on."

Larsen lowered the gun. "We're leaving soon. Two or three days. Are you coming with me, or what?"

"No," Paco told him. "We will be going on our own boat." He had yet to find one, but with his connections and the right amount of cash, he knew it wouldn't be a problem.

"Well when we're ready, we're leaving. And I'm not going to be waiting around for you. So you better tell your people in Florida that we're coming soon. It'll take us almost twenty-four hours, so you'll have plenty of time to warn them."

Paco got to his feet, brushing the sand from the back of his pants. The two men faced each other. "I want proof that Kym is all right. Soon," Larsen demanded.

"You'll get it."

"I'd better, or else I'm going to cruise out there and dump all your cocaine in the water, and then keep on going."

"Always threatening, you Americans."

Larsen stuffed the gun down the front waistband of his pants. "This time I mean it."

24

CIA Headquarters
April 20, 1996 1042 EDT

"I want some goddamn answers and I want them right now!" Jensen screamed, and for a moment John Macki was convinced he was staring into the eyes of a madman.

Jensen had come storming into Macki's office completely unannounced. Carla had made a feeble attempt to stop the irate Senator, and had been met by the heavy wooden door slamming in her face. Although Macki had never met the Senator, he instantly recognized the man and leapt to his feet, sending his chair smashing into the wall behind him.

"Who the hell do you think you are, barging in here like that?" Macki shouted, getting right up in the Senator's face.
"My name is Thomas Jensen. Chairman of—"
Macki cut him off instantly. "I know who the hell you are, Jensen. But it sure as hell doesn't give you the right to behave like a three-year-old! So, if you'd like to sit down like an adult and tell me what your problem is, I'll be more than happy to speak with you." Macki's tough response had surprised not only the Senator, but the CIA man himself. Constance had warned him about the Senator, but he hadn't expected him to catch wind of their true activities within the Yucatan. When Larsen had told him of the possible abduction of Jensen's daughter, Macki had been alarmed and

was preparing to deal with it. Now he had the feeling that Jensen already knew. But how? He waited for the Senator to speak as he prepared for the damage control.

"Rumor has it that you and DEA have some sort of covert operation going on in the Yucatan. The Secretary passed the buck, Macki. Right to your office. Now I'm dealing directly with the spooks," Jensen accused. "And I don't like it one bit."

"I don't care what you don't like, Jensen," Macki said through clenched teeth. "First of all, this entire operation is classified. I don't have to tell you a damn thing. And the only reason I'm going to is so that you don't go charging down there and blow the whole operation."

"But you don't understand," Jensen interrupted. "It's my daughter we're talking about." The Senator had lost some of his earlier fire, and his expression changed to one of serious worry.

"I do understand, Senator. Now, if you'll let me explain, perhaps you'll see where we stand." Macki looked across at the Senator, who held his face in his hands. The man looked pitiful.

Without hesitating further, Macki continued to speak. "Several weeks ago, we received intelligence that Amado Carrillo Fuentes was expanding, and possibly shifting his operations from Juarez into the Yucatan, specifically the East Coast..."

Macki told him everything, beginning with the background information about Dan Larsen. The Senator had a hard time believing the coincidence, but Macki managed to convince him that although unfortunate, the fact that Kym had become involved in the operation was a reality.

"So you see, Senator, if you, or anyone does anything to spook this guy Herrera, we lose him, Carrillo and the whole operation. Not to mention your daughter as well."

It was Macki's last statement that shocked the Senator. He didn't care about the operation or the capture of Carrillo anymore—all he wanted was to get his daughter back. "That's the problem with you guys, Macki," Jensen said weakly, as if he were about to cry. "You play with people's lives like they were figures on a chessboard. Sacrificing certain pieces in order to capture those more powerful. You don't care who lives, or who dies, as long as you complete your little secret missions."

Macki had heard enough. "You think you've got us all figured out, don't you?" he spat, fighting the urge to reach across the desk and grab Jensen by the throat. "You politicians make me sick. You are the reason that covert and clandestine operations are a necessity. All your petty deal-making and little restrictions. You make it impossible for our law enforcement agencies to operate efficiently. These goddamn narco-traffickers are responsible for the death of thousands of young people just like your daughter! We've tried to take them down by the book, punish them in a legal manner. Are you blind? Your way just doesn't work. Do you have any idea how many good people have died trying to stop the flood of drugs pouring into our country?"

Macki was nearly shouting now and he'd risen to his feet. "We are this close to catching this son-of-a-bitch, and now you let your selfish concern for your daughter blind you! It's keeping you from seeing the big picture. If we get this guy, we can save thousands of lives. Good people have already died in this operation, Jensen. This one! Don't make it so they died in vain. Don't blow it!"

Jensen just sat there, staring up at Macki in silence. When he spoke, it was obvious the CIA man had finally gotten through to him. "All right. But what can I do? My daughter needs my help. I could hear it in her voice."

"You just sit tight, Senator. We've got it under control. We expect to take down Carrillo and Herrera within two or three days."

"I pray to God you don't create an international incident."

"So do I," Macki said. "And with your help—your silence—we won't."

"What should I do if I hear from my daughter again?"

"Just act normal. The most important thing we can do right now is keep Herrera from suspecting anything. That's what will keep your daughter alive, Senator."

"I hope so, Macki. Because if anything happens to her, I'm holding you directly responsible. You'll be lucky if you're scrubbing toilets in the Pentagon."

Playa del Carmen
April 20, 1996 2042 Local Time

It had been dark for less than an hour when Teresa heard the vehicle pull into the driveway. Bright lights played across the wall of the living room and then vanished. She heard the slamming of a car door followed by the sound of keys slipping into the lock. Her heart beat rapidly in a confusion of fear and foreboding.

Teresa gasped as Paco shoved the frightened girl through the front door of the villa and she went sprawling on the cold, tile floor. The girl was blindfolded, and now Teresa understood why Paco had instructed her to keep the outside lights turned off. The neighbors were a curious bunch.

"Meet your new friend Kym." Paco jerked the girl to her feet and pulled off her blindfold.

The first thing Teresa noticed was how much the girl looked like herself. Same thin build, blondish-brown hair and high cheekbones. But the eyes were different—soft and brown like those of a deer.

The girl raised her hand to a severely bruised cheek and Teresa's heart went out to her. There was no question who had caused the wound, either Paco or that scumbag, Raul, who was at the moment nowhere to be seen. Paco grabbed the girl by the arm, and half-dragged, half-shoved her into one of the large, overstuffed pads of a wicker chair.

"Leave her alone, you bastard!" Teresa snapped. She went to Kym's side and stared back at the smuggler. Paco raised his fist as if to strike her and Teresa shrunk back, raising her arms to ward off the blow, which never came.

"Fucking whores," Paco muttered and stomped off into the bedroom, where Teresa could hear him punching numbers into a cellular phone.

The arrival of Kym at the villa had come as no great surprise. Paco had told Teresa about her abduction and ordered her to pump Kym for information, especially that concerning Dan Larsen. She had not spoken to the captain since the night they made love and she had returned home to

Paco's savage beating and the sickening rape that had accompanied it. Almost three weeks had passed since then, and Teresa had spent a majority of that time stuck in the villa. Paco forbade her to see Captain Dan or go anywhere near the marina; if he found out she had, he promised to punish her again. He even hinted that he might kill her—something she would not put past him. And so it was fear that kept her there, that and the fact that she really didn't have any friends or anywhere else to go.

The two times she did sneak down to the marina, she was certain Paco had left town. At the marina, she had seen Larsen, but had been afraid to approach him. It was not only for her own sake, but his as well. She feared Paco's jealousy made him capable of killing Larsen if he found what he had suspected was true. She had always remained out of sight, watching the captain travel up and down the dock, cavorting with his friends behind that incredible boat, yearning to go to him, but afraid for both of them.

And now, looking at Kym so frightened and helpless, she felt that perhaps here was a new friend, someone who could share her pain and loneliness, or maybe take it away altogether. Teresa reached out and stroked Kym's cheek with the back of her hand.

"Did he hurt you badly?" she asked cautiously, afraid to ask if Paco had raped her.

"No. It was the other one, the disgusting one with the scar."

"Yes, I know him."

"What will he do with me?" Kym asked weakly.

"It is hard to say. He suspects you are involved with the captain. You realize they are working together."

"Yes."

"Then of course you realize what it is they are doing. Such a terrible business."

Kym explained how she had come to discover the cocaine, and how she had known nothing about it, and found it hard to believe.

"I also found it very hard to believe," Teresa said, pausing as she remembered the first time she and Larsen had met. "That a man like Dan would involve himself in such activities."

"You know him then? You know Dan?"

304

Teresa glanced towards the bedroom, afraid that Paco might be listening. They could both hear the smuggler's voice as he shouted angrily at whoever was on the other end of the line. "Yes." she said quietly, pausing, and Kym looked at her impatiently, waiting to hear more. "We were intimate." Teresa watched as Kym's expression hardened. "Once," she added.

"You know, I really loved him," Kym said sadly, her eyes taking on a look that was focused on something far, far away. "But that was before all this," she went on. "Before I found out he was smuggling. Cocaine, of all things. Did you know his own sister died of a cocaine overdose?" she asked, and then remembered it all might be part of one big lie. "How can I love a man like that?"

"He never told me of such a thing. I think there are many things about him that no one knows. That no one will ever know. He is not like any man I have ever met. And certainly not in this business of drugs and money and death. No, Dan is different. You can see it in his eyes. There is a kindness there, a regard for other people, you know? They are not the eyes of a killer, not the eyes of a man who is bad all the way through. Look into Paco's eyes and you will know what I mean. You will see the difference."

"Why do you stay with him? Kym asked. It was a question Teresa had often asked herself.

"I don't know. Out of fear, I guess. And desperation. I have no family. No money, nowhere to go."

"But look at you, Teresa. You're gorgeous! You can do anything. You don't need him! You just need to meet the right people..."

"Ah, Kym, thank you. You are very kind. But you do not understand. Things are different in my country. The Mexican woman is not so independent. There is a joke. 'Behind every good woman is a man'. It is nearly impossible to do anything without one. They are all the same. Paco was good to me once. Once I loved him. But no more."

"You have to get away from him."

Teresa's voice dropped to a whisper. "Yes. But I am not sure how. He is very powerful. He will find me. My advice to you now is to do as he says. Perhaps, when the time is right, you and I can both get away."

Suddenly they heard the sound of Paco's boots clicking across the tiles and they both fell silent as he entered the room. He held out the cellular phone to Kym. "Here," he said in disgust. "Talk to him. It's your lover, Captain Dan." In his other hand, he held a pistol. He placed it against the side of Kym's head. "Tell him you're alright, nothing more. If you try to tell him where you are, or anything else that I don't like, I will kill you." From the tone of his voice, both women knew he was serious.

Kym reached for the phone.

The Mansion in Vera Cruz
That Same Time

Amado Carrillo was severely disturbed when he punched the button on his own cellular phone and terminated the conversation with Paco Herrera.

For the last couple of weeks, Carrillo had been thinking only of getting out of the trafficking business for good. Although the activities of the cartel had dropped off significantly in the past two months, there was no denying the fact that he was a wanted man.

Even before his narrow escape at the warehouse in Juarez, the current American administration had been pushing hard for his capture, arrest and extradition. Although he was indicted in the U.S. under several charges, he knew they could never make most of them stick. There were only two that could really bother him, one in Miami for trying to smuggle in a small personal stash of heroin and marijuana and another in Dallas for an equally small amount of cocaine.

Carrillo knew there were several members of the American congress trying to block the annual certification of Mexico as a partner in the United States' so-called war on drugs. A de-certification could bring economic sanctions against Mexico and, with the condition his country was in, he knew its political leaders could not afford to let that happen. Even with more politicians and law enforcement officials in his pocket than anyone could imagine, Carrillo knew their hand would soon be forced, and they could not, and would not, hesitate to deliver his head to the Americans on a silver platter. The Americans' charges of rampant corruption throughout Mexico were extremely accurate, and those accused knew it only too well.

They weren't Carrillo's only problem. Since the American DEA raid in Juarez, his name had been thrust into the limelight, in Mexico and the U.S., and he had a feeling that the Colombians wanted him out of the way as well. Perhaps the current operation was their way of closing in on him, tracking him down and taking him out of the picture. Carrillo had become very high profile, and he knew that would not be tolerated. There was an unwritten law in the drug business: when a trafficker becomes a public figure, he is finished.

As he stood behind the huge picture window that fronted the Gulf, he gazed out at the rolling blue seas that stretched out before him. He thought how, in the last couple of months, he had truly come to love the ocean, to appreciate it. He only wished he could one day begin to enjoy it, free from the pressures and uncertainties that troubled him. But he was caught in a trap he'd set for himself and his family years ago, and now he had to get out. He could make it hard for them to find him, but they would never stop looking. They would always suspect that he was still involved. And they would be wrong.

He'd heard of a man in Mexico City, a man who could make a person disappear, give him a new life, in a new place. Anonymously, he'd gotten in touch with him. It was true, the man had said. But much more difficult for a family of four. It would take time and a great deal of cash. For Carrillo, the money was no problem; time was something he did not have. The man had spoken of a place in the South Pacific. Carrillo had seen the pictures of such incredible places, places where he knew he and his family would never be bothered. Places like Bora Bora, and Moorea. He dreamt of swimming in the crystal clear turquoise waters, picnicking on the tiny island motus within the lagoon and watching the waves crash along the edge of the volcanic barrier reefs. At first, it might be hard for his family to adjust. But after time, the man had said, they could be reassimilated into Mexican society if they so desired. Perhaps by then, Carrillo would be forgotten. Perhaps he would never want to return.

As he looked out from behind the window, he noticed three or four separate guards, his trusted *pistoleros*, patrolling the grounds in front of the great mansion, their weapons sweeping back and forth along with their darting eyes. He knew the scene was being repeated throughout the compound. They had been loyal and he was sorry he would not be able to thank them. One day, he and his family would leave in the car, and never return. Lucia was right; they were not living anymore: they were hiding, just barely existing. Their home was not a sanctuary, but a prison, and he and his family were the inmates. Lucia and the children were innocent, guilty of nothing but giving him their undying love and affection. He was the one to blame and he would never take his family down with him. He would free them and, hopefully, they could live a happy life together, as a family, a family with a real father, a real husband.

But now Paco's call had complicated things even more. He planned to move the cocaine into Florida in less than a week! Carrillo had hoped to co-ordinate his disappearance with Paco's trip across the Gulf. He knew that he and his family would have to be gone before Paco returned. The Colombians would try to find him and if Paco didn't know, there would be nothing to tell.

He hated the thought of throwing Paco to the Colombian wolves. Their methods of torture and extracting information were legendary. There had to be some way...

And suddenly, with just a little bit of guilt, the cartel leader realized what he had to do.

Marina Puerto Aventuras
April 22, 1996 1757 Local Time

Larsen, Stanton and Kurt stood huddled in the enclosed flybridge of the *Predator*. Larsen was listening carefully to the single-side-band radio, waiting for the six o'clock weather forecast. Stanton and Kurt were babbling about getting back home and the agent was forced to snap at them. "Shut up!" he demanded. "Here it is." There was total silence inside the bridge as the robotic voice began to forecast the current and expected conditions.

"...for the Eastern Gulf. Today, winds east to southeast, fifteen to twenty knots, seas three to five feet, swells up to seven feet. Tonight, wind becoming southeast, twenty to twenty-five knots, seas five to seven feet..."

"Shit!" Larsen cursed in frustration. "Every fuckin' time!"

Stanton and Kurt stared at him with frightened looks. The prospects of a smooth trip were dismal.

"We should've left yesterday," Kurt said dejectedly. "At least—"

"Hold on." Larsen raised his hand, cutting him off.

"...wind becoming southeast to south, twenty knots. Seas four to six feet, higher swells. Tomorrow night, wind south, fifteen to twenty knots, seas three to five feet."

"That high pressure is moving in fast," Stanton pointed out. "If the wind switches around, it'll be coming from behind us." A following sea they could deal with, even if it was big. A south wind would actually be off their starboard quarter.

"Yeah, that's if it switches around," Larsen said. He knew the weather forecasters were rarely right on in their predictions, and more than once he'd listened to them and paid the price. "I don't want to get our asses kicked for twenty hours."

"I say we go for it," Kurt suggested. "I'm ready to get the hell out of here," he added.

"I know that. We all are," Larsen told him. Over the years, he had noticed that the mate was always ready to get going; he'd felt the same way himself when he was a mate. But the mate wasn't the one who had to answer to the boss when the boat came in to port all fucked up.

Larsen shut off the radio and the bridge was once again silent. It was Stanton who finally spoke.

"So far, Dan, you've called all the shots and we've listened to whatever you said. I'm ready to see my family. Let's get the hell out of here."

Larsen looked once at Kurt and the decision was made. "All right, then. Tomorrow it is. We'll leave just before first light."

Larsen was unsure how long he had been lying there, but it must have been hours. He was afraid to look at the clock; every time he did, he stayed awake that much longer. He'd always been a light sleeper, but on this night, there seemed to be nothing he could do to fall asleep.

He was wide-awake when he heard the first tap on the salon door. Larsen rolled off the bed and stood still in the dark, waiting, listening. The tap came again and he bolted up the stairs, dressed in only a t-shirt and his boxers. When he opened the door and stuck his head out, there was no one. The dock was deserted. He was just about to go back in when a soft voice came out of the darkness.

"Hello Dan."

Larsen squinted into the cockpit, on the far side near the bulkhead. His eyes had already adjusted.

"Teresa?" he asked, astonished. "Jesus. I didn't even know you were still around!" She walked closer. "I thought you had left. I mean—"

"Ssshhh," she warned him, holding one finger to her lips. "Can we go inside?"

"Yeah, sure. Come on." He held the door for her while she went in.

They heard the sound of the door to the crews quarters opening and Kurt poked his head out. "That you, Dan?"

"Yeah, man. Everything's cool. Go back to sleep." He turned on one row of lights and quickly reached for the dimmer. He turned to look at her. She looked nearly the same, but her skin seemed paler, and she appeared frail almost, and frightened. "What's wrong? Why are you here?" he asked.

"It is very dangerous that I have come here, Dan. If Paco finds out, he will probably kill me."

"Paco! He's still here? Where is he?"

"At the villa in Playa del Carmen. He is there with your friend. With Kym."

"Oh my god! He's that close?" he asked, but didn't wait for her to answer. "How is she? Is she alright?"

"Yes, she is fine. She is frightened, but he has not harmed her more."

"What do you mean more?"

She told him about what Raul had done when they had first taken her. "Listen to me, Dan. I came here to warn you. To tell you that you are in much danger. I overheard a conversation Paco had. I think it was with his boss. He said that if anything happens to him or his shipment, he will kill you, and the girl."

"What does he expect to happen?"

"I don't know very much, Dan. I don't know much about who you are or what you really do. But I believe that inside, in your heart, you are a good man. Paco is very dangerous. If you cross him, he will kill you. I am sure of that."

"Thanks for coming here to warn me," he told her. "Can I get you anything? Something to drink, maybe?"

"No, thank you Dan. I must go." She rose from the couch and came towards him. "I only wanted to tell you this and see you one more time. I'll miss you." She reached out her arms and hugged him tightly, but briefly. Then she kissed him, once on each cheek.

Larsen was unsure what to say. He wished there were something he could do for her, only imagining what Paco Herrera had done to her in the past. "Teresa, if there's anything I can do—"

She opened the door to leave, but hesitated. She turned and looked at him once more, and reached out and stroked his cheek.

"You are a good man. May God be with you," she said tenderly. And then she was gone.

Playa del Carmen
Later That Night

Teresa had the taxi drop her at the end of the cul-de-sac, nearly a quarter of a mile from the villa. When she reached it, the lights were still off. Paco had been gone when she had left. Kym had been asleep in the room across the hall, handcuffed to the bedpost as usual. Teresa had looked in on her just before leaving; she had appeared so innocent lying there on her side. Like her, Teresa thought, she was a victim, and it only made her despise Paco even more.

Now she had had enough. When the smuggler left in the morning, she would take off for good. She wasn't sure where she could go. Maybe Mexico City. It was a huge city and maybe she could lose herself there. Or maybe she could find someone else, someone who would stand up to the evil Paco Herrera. Maybe.

As soon as she opened the door, she knew something was different. She flicked the switch for the light near the door, but nothing happened. The room was dark; the only light was that of the night sky coming through the windows and reflecting off the shiny, white tile floor. The door to the room where Kym had been staying was open. She slowly crossed the living room, went in and found the bed empty. Suddenly she felt strange, as if some evil presence hung in the air. Quickly, she turned and screamed.

"My God, Paco. Don't sneak up on me like that. You nearly scared me to death."

"Where were you?" he asked in a voice barely above a whisper. His tone was stern, accusing.

"I went for a walk", she said. Her voice was weak and it sounded like a lie. Unable to control it, her whole body began to tremble.

"A walk? At this time of night?" Even in the darkness, she could tell he did not believe her.

"Yes. I couldn't sleep."

"Where did you go?"

"To Senor Frog's."

"Who did you see?"

"I don't know. A lot of people." Teresa knew he was toying with her. It was another of his sick games and she hated it.

"How did you get home?" He approached her in the dark, crowding her against the wall. His breath was hot and foul and smelled of tequila.

"I walked," she said and instantly regretted it.

"I told you about lying to me!" He crushed her arms.

"I'm not lying!" she shot back.

He slapped her hard across the face. "I saw the fucking taxi!"

Teresa panicked, and tried to run past him towards the door. Once outside, she could scream for help. He was going to hurt her and she feared that this time would be the worst. But Paco had anticipated her move; he tripped her up and she went sprawling on the floor. He was on her instantly, pulling her hair and yanking her neck back as he dragged her shrieking towards the bedroom. His hand closed over her mouth.

"Shut up, or I'll kill you," he ordered. He threw her on the bed, and she lay there whimpering. "You went to see him, didn't you?" he asked, but she only continued to cry. "What did you tell him?" His questions were going unanswered and he was getting furious. "Answer me!"

When she looked at him again, her expression had changed. Her eyes were filled with hatred.

"I told him the truth! That Paco Herrera is a dangerous, violent and evil man. I told him that I thought that you would probably try to kill him. That is what you plan to do, isn't it?" She was committed now, and didn't even give him a chance to respond. "Oh no, you can't fool me, Paco Herrera. I know you too well. I know what you're made of. You'll kill Captain Dan and Kym and anyone else who gets in the way of you and your precious cocaine! You think it shows that you are tough, that you are strong. But you are wrong, Paco. Inside, you are weak and insecure, and you even doubt yourself. You will never be a decent man, never be as strong as Captain Dan!"

Paco reached behind him and slowly withdrew his giant knife from the sheath tucked into the back of his pants. The reflection of its huge blade was obvious, even in the dark. He hovered over her curled up figure on the bed, pointing at her with the tip of the blade, accusing. "You ungrateful bitch. Nothing but a whore. After all I've done for you..."

"All you have done is make my life a living hell. Can't you see I despise you? All I want is to get away from you!"

"You will never leave me," he said. "You don't have anyone else. You need me." He went to lie on top of her. "Now show me how much," he added as he tried to kiss her.

With all her strength, Teresa shoved him off her and onto the floor. "Get away from me!" she screamed. "No more." She got off the bed and stood over him, crying softly. But in her tears there was rage, a defiance that she could not keep locked inside any longer.

"You fucking bitch!" he said, slowly getting to his feet. "I'll give you one more chance." He moved towards her.

"Fuck you!" she whispered with as much malice as she could and spit in his face.

He grabbed her by the back of her hair, jerking her head backwards and exposing the soft, vulnerable skin of her neck, now stretched taut. With a swift motion, he drew the blade quickly across her throat, smiling sickly as the flesh separated. The wound immediately filled and overflowed.

She tried to speak, but the only sound that came out was a faint gurgle.

"Good bye, my lovely no-good whore." He stepped aside, and allowed her dying form to slump onto the floor. She would never be defiant again.

25

Marina Puerto Aventuras
April 23, 1996 0541 Local Time

Larsen and Stanton fired up their boats and, with the obvious power of several thousand collective horsepower echoing off the condominiums, the two boats idled towards the cut.

Up ahead, the first rays of the early morning sun peeked out from beneath a long flat band of clouds that lay upon the eastern horizon, turning the sky above a deep orange-red. With the *Predator* in the lead, Larsen gazed out at the scene from his position high up in the tuna-tower. The old adage about "red sky at morning, sailors take warning" popped into his mind, but he quickly brushed the thought aside. There were many more urgent reasons for him to take warning on this day and, although the weather would be a factor, it was the least of his concerns.

By Mexican law, any vessel cruising within Mexican waters, or leaving the country entirely, was required to have specific documents stating its intended port of embarkation and disembarkation. Such documents contained the specific information on the vessel itself, its crew and the reason for the journey. This time, however, Larsen had nothing of the sort. They'd left before anyone in the marina had been up and the only person he had seen was a security guard who had eyeballed them curiously as they had made their way towards the cut. The dockmaster would be alarmed when he discovered they had not cleared their departure but, by the time anyone could do anything about it, they would be back in Florida.

Staring down into the cockpit, Larsen could see Kurt scurrying around, coiling up the remainder of the dock lines and checking to make sure everything was secure before they brought the giant sportfisher up to speed. The sea was not as rough as he had expected, three to five feet at the worst, and it would be along their beam for at least the beginning of the trip. Looking behind, Larsen could just make out the form of Stanton as he stood at the helm of the *Tempest* and slipped the sleek Monterey into the *Predator*'s wake about fifty yards back.

Larsen was already halfway down the ladder and headed for the bridge when he spotted the boat.

A mile offshore and almost even with the monstrous Hotel Oasis, he could barely see what looked like the outline of a Bertram sportfish, a 46 or a 54, with no tower. He hoped it would be Paco.

He reached for the radio to talk to Stanton.

"Ya on there, T?"

"Roger that, Dan. What's the hold-up?"

"Go to the other one."

He switched to 102 and waited.

"Go ahead," Stanton said.

"Got a boat up ahead just offshore. Looks like a Bertram." The shape of the boat was a dead giveaway for its manufacturer. Boxy house with black stripe and stepped toe-rail.

"Yeah, I got it," Stanton confirmed. "You think that's our boy?"

"Roger that, Terry. Should be. I'm gonna idle over there and see. You might as well sit tight."

Larsen swung the wheel to starboard and headed towards the mysterious vessel, which sat rocking back and forth, something the Bertrams were famous for. Great downsea, but a nightmare for stability while stopped or trolling.

Pulling up close, Larsen could see Raul on the bridge. It was a Bertram 46. The Mexican stared at the approaching vessel, mesmerized by its size.

The big Hatteras dwarfed the Bertram; its futuristic lines gave it a menacing look of power and authority next to the smaller towerless rig. With a last nervous look, Raul hurried down the ladder and disappeared inside.

Larsen did the same. When he reached the pit, he sent Kurt up to the bridge.

"Bring us alongside that Bertram," Larsen told him, and as Kurt went into the bridge and put the boat in gear, Larsen went into the salon and got his automatic, which he stuffed down the back of his shorts. If Paco or his thug had harmed Kym, he might just blow them both away right there.

He peeked through the blinds just in time to see Paco come out the door. As the *Predator* pulled up, he saw the name of the boat. *Osprey*—Galveston, Texas. He'd seen the boat working along the edge, usually up to the north. It must have been based in Cozumel. He didn't know the crew. Larsen walked outside.

As usual, Paco was smiling.

"I'm not even gonna ask you where you got this," Larsen said.

"That's good. Let's just say I borrowed it." Paco looked like he was dressed for a night out on the town. He'd obviously never made a crossing before; by the time they reached Florida, his black silk shirt and matching pants would be ruined by salt.

Where he got the boat did not concern the agent. It would be more than two days later when the badly decomposed bodies of the *Osprey*'s crew would be found floating in the Gulf, west of Cuba. The sharks had already taken care of business, and the remains were unidentifiable.

"Where is she?" Larsen demanded.

Still smiling, Paco nodded with his head. "Inside."

"I want to see her. Now." Paco stepped into the salon and out of sight.

And suddenly, there she was, hands and feet bound, gagged with a dirty rag, eyes filled with fear. Raul was holding her from behind. His rotten-toothed smile signified that he was certainly enjoying himself.

"Why the hell is she all tied up like that?"

"She was being—less than cooperative." Kym tried to scream something, and struggled to free herself, but Raul held her tight. "You see?"

Paco cackled. He looked at Raul, nodded, and the grubby *pistolero* dragged her back inside.

"You don't have to treat her like that. She's no danger to you. Let her go—let her come on this boat."

"I can't do that. I already told you, she is my insurance policy."

"And I already told you," the agent countered. "Everything is going to be fine. There's no way we're going to get caught. Trust me."

"Trust you?" Paco asked incredulously. "That is something that I have found very hard to do, Captain Dan. There is something about you that I do not like. Maybe it's your lack of killer instinct."

"I've got the killer instinct alright. Enough to kill you and your boy Raul if I even think you might have hurt Kym."

Paco stared at him. "You don't need to threaten me, Captain Dan. We are business partners, remember? Now why don't you stop trying to prove your machismo and let us get on with our business?"

Larsen paused. "Here's the deal. We'll cruise at about twenty-five knots all day. Hopefully that thing can keep up. If not, let me know. We'll monitor channel 80 until we get past Isla."

The island of Isla Mujeres, directly across from Cancun, was two hours north, and slightly east. "When it gets dark, we'll pull 'em back and ten knot it. Without any problems, we'll be in Key West before daybreak. During the night, we'll monitor channel sixteen, the emergency channel. If you want to talk, call me on sixteen and we'll go to another channel."

"What course will we be taking?" Paco had no open-ocean experience and would have to rely on the Americans for guidance.

"Who's gonna be driving?"

"Raul."

"You got a GPS on that thing?"

"Yes, but we don't know how to use it."

"Great. Just stay right behind me."

The course they would be taking was fairly simple. First they would set a waypoint just east of Isla Mujeres, then fall in behind Cuba for the rest of the day and most of the night, and finally head north for the last hundred miles into Key West. Without a GPS, it would be easy to get off course, but if they stayed close enough, he figured the Mexicans would be all right.

"You'll have to fall in behind us, then. You all set on fuel?"

"Yes. The tanks are full and so are these." He pointed to the four huge plastic barrels in the rear of the cockpit. "Raul says he knows how to add the fuel to the tanks."

"Good." With no one on the bridge, the Bertram had turned broadside to the sea. A large swell rocked the boat violently and Paco slipped and fell down on the deck. He scrambled to his feet.

"Alright, then. Let's do it. Let us get going, then slip in behind us." Larsen took one more look at the Bertram, and decided that it was in pretty good shape. Hopefully it could make the trip. If Raul knew enough to check the oil and water.

"Raul! *Vamonos!*" Paco shouted and the man came out the door and headed up to the bridge after giving Larsen a long dirty look.

Look good, Larsen thought, and remember who put you away for a long, long time. As he turned to head for the bridge, he noticed that Stanton had brought the *Tempest* right up behind them. Larsen gave him the thumbs-up sign.

Kurt leaned out the bridge door. "All set, man?"

"Yep. Let her eat."

With successive roars of their diesel engines, the three boats fell into single file, heaved themselves onto a plane, and headed northeast.

Aboard the *Osprey*
That Same Day

The impacts of larger swells smacking into the front of the hull were occurring more frequently. Paco could hear and feel the spray on the windshield and surrounding eisenglass. Some of the water seeped through and fell where he lay on the padded bench, and his frustration mounted.

Suddenly the vessel lurched forward and felt momentarily weightless. Then all hell seemed to break loose as they came crashing down in the next trough. The fiberglass groaned as the entire boat shuddered.

319

"My God!" Paco screamed. "What the hell is going on?"

For a moment Raul did not respond. He was busy checking the gauges, and trying to find out what caused several alarms to go off at once. He backed off on the throttles. "We must be over the bank."

"What bank?"

"The Arrowsmith bank. I have heard about it. The water is shallow in this area. The direction of the current opposes that of the wind, and the result is a huge, dangerous sea."

Paco looked out over the bow. "I can see that," he said in disgust. The waves had grown much bigger, and their direction had changed. They were now approaching nearly head-on. He guessed that some were nearly eight feet.

"What do you suggest, boss?"

"You tell me, asshole, you're the fucking captain!"

Raul succeeded in shutting off the alarms. He then brought the throttles up to about one thousand rpms. They were making about ten knots. "I guess we'll just have to take it slow."

"How long will this last?"

Raul shrugged. "Don't ask me."

"Shit," Paco muttered. "Don't lose the others."

Suddenly the VHF crackled to life. "Yeah, the *Osprey*, this is the *Predator*. You copy?"

Paco reached out and snatched the mike. "I'll do the talking." Then he shouted into the mike with an excited voice. "Yes, *Predator*, we read you loud and clear."

"You're all garbled," came the reply. "Hold the microphone farther away from your lips, Paco."

Paco blushed at the scolding from the American. He knew he had betrayed his inexperience. Then, more calmly he said, "Okay. How is this? Is that better?"

"Roger that," Larsen said. "I mean...yes, that's better. How are you assholes doin' back there?"

"Alright. We had a slight problem, but now everything seems okay." He squinted through the wet eisenglass. He could see the *Tempest* up ahead, but not the *Predator*. "*Osprey* to *Predator*. Where are you?"

"We're right up here. We're gonna pull 'em back and ten knot it. We're on the bank and unfortunately, we've got another forty, maybe fifty miles of this."

"Okay. I read you. Ten knots."

"Just hang in there," Larsen added. "We'll be out of this before you know it. *Predator* standing by on eighty."

"Raul!" Paco barked. "Go check on everything downstairs. Give the girl some food."

Raul gave him a funny look. "You...You going to be all right?"

"Of course I am! Now get down there." Paco felt out of place in the unfamiliar role and showed his irritation.

Gulf of Mexico 20°10.06"N 94°03.74"W
April 24, 1996 0115 Local Time

Deep beneath the surface of the western Gulf, a huge black shape glided silently toward its target. Inside the *Sam Houston*, SSN609, one of the most secret submarines in the U.S. naval fleet, and secret from the entire world for that matter—the members of Seal Team Eleven were ready to strike.

The report had just come down—the seas above were three to four feet and subsiding. It was the perfect night for an insertion.

Wes Gates studied the members of the team with a keen eye. Like his own, their expressions were permanent masks of determination and intensity. Any fear or uncertainty about what they were prepared to do had been tucked away long ago. The waiting was over. The operation had begun. Gates' eyes met those of the man directly across from him. They were cold, hard, piercing unfriendly eyes.

"What the hell are you lookin' at, mate? Somethin' on that good ol' Texas mind of yours?"

"Nope. Just thinking."

"Good. You just keep on thinkin'. Maybe it'll keep that southern ass of yours alive." Lieutenant Sean McCreary, the leader of the eight-man team, was one tough son-of-a-bitch and Gates knew better than to spar with him. Not as big as Gates, but leaner and more ripped, the man was a weapon in his own right. He swam better, shot better, fought better and knew more about actual combat situations than any member of the team. He'd seen action in Grenada, Panama and the Persian Gulf and had come out of all three operations highly decorated and without a scratch. It was rumored that his body count in the Gulf alone had topped one hundred Iraqis. With his reddish hair kept high and tight, he portrayed the stereotypical naval seaman and nothing betrayed his forty-three years.

Gates shifted his gaze to the other men in the group. They were huddled together with their backs to the wall, four men on each side. The former "nukie" was crowded and there was little space for the team. There were not enough bunks for everyone on board and, since their departure from Port Everglades in Fort Lauderdale, they had been forced to "hot bunk", trading with someone who worked while they slept. They spent the rest of the time with the team, separated from the sub's regular crew. The small chamber was cramped and the lighting was dim. For the most part, they were silent with only an occasional off-hand remark about their uncomfortable conditions. They'd been briefed on the mission and were ready to execute it.

Although Gates had come to know each member of the team personally in the little time they trained together, he found it difficult to break through to them, to get close. Like all Special Forces units they were tight-knit. He was an outsider. An alien almost. And he had expected it. There was no weapon better than the man himself and the "Mark One, Mod Zero eyeball".

Although he hadn't gotten inside the compound, he had seen it with his own eyes; he knew the basic layout of the surrounding area and his intelligence had been very useful. Along with the satellite imagery, the probability of executing a successful mission was extremely high.

Gates had been on submarines before, but never one like the *Sam Houston*. Originally a Polaris-class nuclear submarine, she had been commissioned to carry sixteen nuclear-tipped missiles in launch tubes located amidships behind the sail. But as the Soviet threat diminished so did the need for some of the deadly subs and modifications had been made to the deck so that it could mount twin DDS assemblies—Dry Deck Shelters—similar to the lock out chambers found on all submarines. One of the DDS assemblies aboard the *Sam Houston* had recently been modified even further and now had the capability of launching and recovering the latest in SDV technology. The Seal Delivery Vehicle—a miniature sub—can cruise underwater at more than five knots. The SDV the team would be using was a special larger model. In addition to the two-man crew, a pilot and navigator, it could hold eight combat swimmers and, launching from a spot at least five miles from the target, it would take them well inshore, completely submerged. Launching the SDV was complicated and required a great deal of time. But Gates knew it was the best way to reach the target. If executed properly, the ingress to the shore below the mansion would be completely undetected.

For most of their journey so far, it had been difficult to gauge their speed. The sub slipped through the water so smoothly, it seemed as though they were not moving at all. But suddenly there was a sound of air being transferred between the ballast tanks, and the walls around the men began to creak. All heads snapped to attention. They were stopping.

"Sit tight, everybody," McCreary ordered. There were murmurs and some whispering among the men. Then a buzzer sounded above their heads. It was time.

CIA Headquarters
That Same Time

When John Macki blazed into the underground satellite and radio communications center, he was out for blood. His hurried gait and intense expression gave off a threatening vibe. Most of the radio technicians and other satellite and communications specialists were afraid to even look at him. They knew he was on a mission; he had no time for slackers and no time for bullshit.

He strode up behind a man who was hunched over in front of a monstrous high frequency relay system. "Anything?"

The radioman spun on his rollered chair and gave Macki a confused, dumbfounded look. "Huh?"

"I said...have you heard anything from that sector?" He asked the question slowly and sternly.

"N-No sir, nothing. But the bird is still tracking three targets, twenty-one miles northwest of Havana. Targets are moving northeast on a heading of 037 degrees. Sir." The last bit he added, not out of respect, but to keep his ass out of a sling.

"That must be them," Macki said. Larsen had told him his intended course and, according to his calculations, if the targets were the ones he expected, they were right on schedule. But he hadn't heard from Larsen in over twelve hours. Why wasn't he communicating? The E2 Hawkeye surveillance plane that Macki had convinced the Air Force to send up had been tracking the three radar blips for hours. Except for a few low-frequency chats between the vessels themselves, there had been no other transmissions. According to the Hawkeye, the three vessels had been making steady progress, rarely altering course. The Hawkeye was equipped with a high-resolution FLIR, a forward-looking infrared scanner, and was capable of tracking an object on the surface of the water as small as a human head. The crew had identified the targets.

Macki's original plan to keep the operation a highly classified secret had quickly gone down the shitter. Against his better judgement, but with nowhere else to turn, he'd been forced to call in a favor from an old friend, Admiral James Enwright, Commander of the U.S. Naval Special Warfare Command (NAVSPECWARCOM). He was the man who was responsible for the planning of SEAL missions around the globe, the development of policy and training procedures and the monitoring of current events anywhere in the world. Much to Macki's relief, he was well aware of the current narcotics situation and the flow of drugs from Mexico to the U.S. He was sympathetic to Macki's predicament.

Macki's quiet little secret had ended there. The SEAL team available, and usually tasked for operations throughout the Atlantic and Gulf of Mexico, was headquartered in Little Creek, Virginia, while all the training, specifically the BUD/S course, took place on the sunny strip of sand in Coronado, California.

From there, intelligence and other related information regarding the operation had been turned over to the man called the CATF—Commander, Amphibious Task Force—a Navy admiral whose job was to get the assault element to the beach. He, in turn, had directed his staff, the Intelligence officer and the Operations officer, to commence with the planning process. And so on.

What had started out as a small circle of men, most of whom were on a need-to-know basis, was now spinning dangerously out of control. And Macki knew there was no way to stop it.

Macki strode to another station and stared deep into the green and black display of a twenty-four inch radar screen. The three blips off the northwestern coast of Cuba were still obvious.

"C'mon, Danny," he said. "Talk to me." He took a deep breath and rubbed his eyes. The last few weeks had taken their toll. The creases in his forehead had become deep furrows. He was pale and he'd been up for hours. His short-sleeve white shirt was stained with coffee and jelly from a donut he'd scarfed down, the only thing he'd eaten all night. He was a mess.

With a crash, the heavy steel door to the communications room flew open and a young man with thick glasses ran up to him.

"Cipher from NAVSPECWARCOM, sir!" He thrust the page out at Macki. "Marked urgent, sir!"

Macki took the sheet and squinted at it in the hazy artificial light. It was nothing but mumbo-jumbo to him, a lot of numbers and letters mixed up together that made no sense. He looked at the man and gave the sheet back. What's it say?"

"Sir? It's marked for your eyes only."

"Read it, godammit!"

"It says 'Assault element in place. Operation commencing'."

Macki sprinted out the door to the elevator and never looked back.

Aboard the *Sam Houston*
0125 Local Time

Inside the Dry Deck Shelter (DDS), seated in four rows of two, the eight members of SEAL Team Eleven were packed into the SDV like sardines. Burdened by their gear and underwater breathing apparatus, they were hunched over, almost on top of each other, a position that was quickly growing claustrophobic. But they were prepared for it, and each man practiced proven mental techniques, focusing inward on himself to avoid panic. Breathe deep, hold, exhale, relax. And repeat.

"Everybody set?" McCreary asked. There were several short affirmative responses. McCreary relayed this information to the pilot of the mini-sub and he, in turn, gave the thumbs up signal to the DDS hangar supervisor and it was passed on to the rest of the deck crewmen. With a torrential roar, the hatch was opened and the chamber flooded. The impact of the water as it rushed into the chamber and SDV was startling. It was several minutes before the turbulent water settled.

The divers of the deck crew immediately got to work, and the SDV was wrestled from its cradle and slowly pushed out the open hatch of the once dry DDS. It was secured to the sub by a heavy steel cable.

Inside the SDV, the two-man crew and the members of the SEAL team were now breathing from a closed-circuit onboard system. The Mark XV computerized mixed-gas re-breather allowed them to stay down longer and go deeper than conventional open-circuit systems such as the SCUBA used by sport divers. Besides the fact that the closed-circuit system released no bubbles, The Mark XV was antimagnetic minimizing the SDV's sonar and magnetic signature. Most important: the full-face mask was equipped with a special microphone that allowed the crew, as well as the team, to speak to each other during the insertion.

Slowly, the SDV was paid out. Again they were forced to wait. Finally, the DDS deck captain relayed the final navigational information to the SDV navigator and the cable was released. They were on their way.

The SDV was driven by an electrical system that was fed by several huge batteries. The five-blade propeller system was driving them towards shore in total silence. For steering, the pilot used a set of horizontal stabilizers that controlled the up and down movement and a vertical tail rudder controlled the rear of the craft. The tiny sub's attitude and buoyancy were controlled by two ballast systems; one open and one closed. As they headed towards shore, the SDV was almost completely dark. The pilot and navigator relied solely on a computerized Doppler Navigation System (DNS) and an Obstacle Avoidance Sonar subsystem (OAS). Without a windshield, which wouldn't have done any good in the dark anyway, the pilot of the SDV was "flying blind".

Only McCreary and about half of the team had ever made an insertion in an SDV before and, even for them, it was a frightening experience. Several minutes passed as they headed for the beach. Finally, the navigator spoke.

"Course heading—one-nine-three degrees." His tinny voice came out of the receivers inside the masks. "Depth, one hundred feet. Distance to waypoint, three point two nautical miles."

They heard another voice. "Alright, everbody listen up." It was McCreary, which was obvious from his harsh, no-nonsense tone. "We're almost halfway there. Anyone got a problem?" There was no response. "Blades!"

"Sir!"

"Once we're up top, you and your boys will take the outer perimeter of the compound. From what the Sat Intel shows us, there should be at least six guards along that inside wall. Don't feel sorry for 'em, just take 'em out. The main target will be inside."

"Got it, sir!" Jack Blades, leader of Fire-Team One and the second most experienced man in the group, was ecstatic. He'd just been given a legal license to kill. As a member of the elite force for more than ten years, he hadn't put a bullet in another human being since the war in the Persian Gulf. On the outside, he seemed a mild-mannered, next-door-neighbor type of guy. But like McCreary and the rest of the team, he was a highly trained assassin.

"Gates!" the Irish lieutenant barked next.

"Here!"

"You and I will be part of Fire-Team Two, and we'll lead the assault on the compound itself. You seem to know more about the target than anyone and I have orders to take him alive."

"What about the rest of the family?" Gates voice was edged with panic. "The target has a wife and children. I'm sure they're with him."

"I...I have no such information," McCreary replied.

Gates knew better than to argue with the lieutenant, and he remained silent, inwardly seething, his anger unnoticeable in the darkness.

"Now tell me again about the man and what he's likely to hit us back with."

Several more minutes passed as Gates described what he knew about the compound itself, Carrillo and the *pistoleros*. The men of the team listened intensely, without a word or question. He knew they were eating it up. Like Gates, they were getting pumped. When he was finished, the navigator spoke again.

"Course heading, one-nine-three degrees. Depth, eighty feet. Distance to waypoint, point eight nautical miles. Speed, six knots."

McCreary was not the only one doing the time and distance calculations in his head. "Now hear this. We're going to be there before we know it. Remember, it's going to be dark as hell out there—even darker than it is in here. Follow the man in front of you. Mercer and Jackson will lead." Both men were members of Fire-Team Two and were considered the strongest swimmers.

A few minutes later the SDV glided to a halt. For the first time, the pilot spoke. "This is it, gentlemen, the end of the line. Distance to shore should be no more than six hundred yards. Hang tight while I bring this little toy up to depth." The team members waited in silence as the pilot fiddled with the ballast and steering controls and brought the SDV up towards the surface. A few moments later, they stopped again. "Twenty-five feet, gentlemen. Thank you for flying the United States Navy. We hope you'll all fly with us again." It was about the only funny thing that had been said all night.

"Now everybody take your time as we switch over to the Draegers," McCreary ordered. "Any problems, tug twice on the leg of the man closest to you. But I'll warn you right now, there's not a lot we can do about it in the dark. Stay close, stay calm, and I'll see you on the beach."

Switching over to the portable closed-circuit Draeger breathing apparatus was considered the trickiest and often most harrowing part of an SDV insertion. Removing the full-face mask and replacing it with one of the standard sport diving type—all in pitch-blackness—was not for the average diver. The fact that they already wore the Draeger equipment didn't make it any easier.

Having switched masks and regulators, each swimmer opened the oxygen bottle and blew through the mouthpiece, purging the system of air. The oxygen flowed from the bottle through the regulator and into the mouthpiece. After taking a deep breath, each SEAL would then exhale a mixture of carbon dioxide and oxygen. The mixture was recycled through a canister of baralyme where the carbon dioxide was absorbed and the purified oxygen sent back to the mouthpiece. All without giving off a single bubble. Only the oxygen actually burned by the diver's body was replaced from the tank. None was wasted. Although the system had been around for more than twenty years, it was so reliable and safe that it was still the standard.

Ready to roll, the team exited the SDV and began the swim towards the shore. For nearly an hour, they had been inactive; even in their thin, custom-fit, black neoprene wetsuits, the water had seriously lowered their core body temperature. They were glad to be moving.

For guidance, each SEAL carried an attack board, a simplistic tool that consisted of a compass, depth gauge and watch. The luminous dials of all three instruments gave off a faint light, which was the only thing visible in the inky depths. They swam along at a depth of between twenty and thirty feet, taking extra care not to fall below thirty-five feet, at which point the air inside the Draegers would become poisonous. As one, the group slipped through the water with great speed. Each man swam in a consistent way, constantly focusing on his attack board, counting each kick and judging, with fairly close accuracy, how far they'd traveled. As they approached shallow water, the topography of the ocean floor became their enemy.

Several times, they were forced to stop and veer from their intended course, avoiding coral heads and giant stone outcroppings. Yet, they were focused and pressed on; within minutes, they were in fifteen feet of water. The lead combat swimmers stopped. Waiting another minute to catch their breath, the team gathered together on the ocean floor. With mounting anxiety and exhilaration, they rose slowly and silently to the surface.

The watches on the attack boards did not lie. H-hour was coming.

The Mansion in Vera Cruz
0246 Local Time

There it was again. The shadow that moved very slowly along the wall threatened to drive him mad. Carrillo lay in his bed, heart pounding, unable to sleep. But on this night, he had an excuse. The blood that flowed through his veins was filled with adrenaline and that, along with his paranoia, left him feeling very strange indeed. To sleep would have been impossible.

Before dawn, he would be gone. They would be gone. His family meant more to him than anything in the world. His little ones, his precious Eduardo and his little queen Anna Claudia, slept peacefully in the bedroom across the hall, unaware that by morning, they would be far, far away. They were his lifeblood and he could not grow any farther apart

330

from them than he already had. Lucia lay next to him, breathing deeply, perhaps dreaming of the new land that awaited them. She had been right all along. She deserved better. His family deserved better.

All his life, he had known no other lifestyle than that of the *traficante*. Had he not done well? He'd risen from the very bottom and clawed his way to the very top. What could be higher?

As the Americans would say, he had more money than God. He'd given millions, Christ, hundreds of millions back to the community. He was a legend. They even wrote *corridos* about him!

But where had it gotten him? To a point where he feared not only for his own life, but for the safety of his family. Now he was going to change his life and it would be a change for the better.

The thought of abandoning the cartel had weighed heavily on his mind for weeks. He was the one who had built the cartel to what it was— the most powerful cartel in the country. Would it fall apart without him? Who would, or even could, fill his shoes?

Paco's desire to take over was obvious. But it was his subversive way of doing it that Carrillo despised. Paco was good, and fearless. But he was young and inexperienced, part of that new breed of smuggler, all flash and cash. He'd yet to play in the big leagues with the Colombians. They would squash him like a *cucaracha*!

Paco had the desire and his goals were, what he considered, noble, but his methods were dangerous. He often made rash decisions that lacked planning, acting on impulse alone. He killed too much in his effort to get what he wanted and Carrillo knew that would eventually come back to haunt him. He was eager but foolish, trusting people he hardly even knew. In the end, such mistakes would be his downfall.

Carrillo knew there had been others before him and others who would follow. Surely the Americans realized that! Their little "war on drugs" was a joke. It always had been, and always would be, a losing battle. As long as there was a demand for illegal narcotics, there would be someone ready to supply them. And along with the illegal trade of cash for product, there would be death. On both sides. Yes, someone would replace him, but it wouldn't be Paco.

Carrillo sat up and looked at the clock on the nightstand. It was almost time. Out by the pool, a sentry passed in front of a spotlight and the shadow passed by again. He picked up his cellular and crept quietly into the hall, startling one of the sentries making his rounds. He waved at the man to show that everything was all right and slipped into one of the empty rooms. For a moment he hesitated, but it had to be done.

With a nervous, twitching forefinger, he made the call.

Aboard the *Predator*
That Same Time

With his ear mashed up against the telephone-style handset of the single-side-band, Larsen listened impatiently to the static as whoever was on the other end searched for John Macki.

With his eyes on the radar display, he watched as the green line painted the outline of Key West every few seconds.

"Nice of you to call, Dan!" Macki's sarcastic voice was excited, and he was breathing heavily. Larsen could picture the man: a nervous wreck, running around like a chicken who'd recently had its head removed. "Secure?" the CIA man asked.

"Roger that."

"Where's Herrera?"

"About a mile behind me, I think." Larsen turned and saw the tiny white light. "Yep, he's still back there," he added.

"I've got you about, let's see...twenty-two miles out of Key West. Heading...zero-one-six degrees, speed...what, ten, eleven knots?"

Larsen was amazed. "How the hell do you know all that?" He raised his eyebrows at Kurt, who was seated next to him, bare feet up on the instrument console. The mate was silent, but had been listening intensely.

"We've got a bird tracking you."

Larsen should have guessed as much. The miracles of modern-day surveillance equipment and technology never ceased to amaze him. "You've got a satellite on us?"

"Nope, a Hawkeye. Courtesy of our friends in the Air Force."

So much for a quiet little operation, the agent thought. "What's the current situation?" he asked.

"Assault is in progress, Dan. Repeat, in progress."

It was actually happening. And then Larsen realized he'd almost forgotten something.

"Jesus! What about the diversion, John?"

"It's ready to roll. Just waitin' on you, my friend."

"Well go ahead and call it in!" he shouted into the mouthpiece. "We're running out of time and water here!"

"I'm on it. Gotta run, Dan. Don't want to miss the festivities."

"Don't let me keep you." Larsen could just imagine them watching the attack on the Carrillo compound like a bunch of kids glued to the tube. With all the shit they had at the CIA, they could probably even hear it.

"And Dan?" Macki was still there.

"Go ahead."

"Whatever happens...you done good, man. We'll take care of everything in Key West."

Larsen did not respond. He replaced the handset and stared into the blackness ahead. He switched the VHF to emergency channel nine. Within seconds, it crackled to life.

"Mayday, mayday," a voice said in distress. The Spanish accent was obvious. "This is Colombian freighter *Carlotta*. Mayday. Emergency. We have suffered serious damage from collision with unknown obstacle. Taking on water, and listing badly. Thirty-two men on board. Current position...twenty-four seventeen point four North, eighty-three zero-one point one West..."

The message was repeated twice more and then the radio went silent. The intelligence of Macki was unbelievable. Larsen recognized the name of the freighter as that of the legendary Mexican temptress. He wondered where the CIA man had come up with that one.

"Check the location of that distress call," he told Kurt, and repeated the coordinates of the position.

Kurt grabbed the big book of charts. He looked at the page they were on, but seemed lost. Larsen repeated the coordinates once more. Kurt flipped back one page. Then, using the forefinger of each hand, he traced inward until they met. "Got it!"

"Where is it?"

"Right here," he said, holding up the page for Larsen to see. "Just south of the Dry Tortugas."

U.S. Coast Guard Station, Key West, Florida 24°33.06"N 81°48.42"W
0345 EDT

"God-damn-it!" Captain Zack Stevens, Commander, Coast Guard Group Key West howled in disgust. He'd just spilled hot coffee down the front of his shirt for the third time in less than twenty minutes.

Stevens was clearly a man under a lot of stress, and he had every reason to be. It had been one hell of a night and it wasn't even close to being over. He had a collision of drunken partygoers in ski boats off Stock Island, a report of out-of-season lobster poaching off the marine sanctuary in Bahia Honda and four salvage companies bickering over who was going to pull a stranded trawler off the sea grass just in front of the dock near Mallory Square. Idiots, he thought. Didn't they know what buoys and markers were for?

And to top it off, the only chopper he had at his disposal had just reported in from the last-known location of the sinking Colombian freighter. Granted, it was dark, but they had found nothing, not even a paper cup. That had not really surprised him. The station's powerful APS-20 surveillance radar had failed to pick up any kind of return from the area even before the transmission of the distress call had terminated.

"Bastards!" he mumbled to himself and his thick, barrel chest heaved in anger. The rest of his body seemed to match. His legs and forearms were thick as tree trunks. Not a young man at fifty-three, he was of medium height, with hair so short he was often taken to be bald. He smoked filterless Pall Malls like they weren't going to make them any more and, when he put on his black-brimmed captain's hat, it was no wonder they called him "Popeye" behind his back. The only thing missing was the tattoo of an anchor on his fat, muscled arm. He was clearly not to be messed with, and every time a false distress call came in, he took it as a personal affront. If he ever caught one of the perpetrators, he swore he would kill him. But torture him first. Keelhaul him until his skin was shredded like spagetti. Hang him from the yardarm for days. Make him walk the plank in shark-infested waters. Just like the old days.

He missed the old days, the twenty years he had spent on duty at Astoria, the station at the mouth of the mighty Columbia River. In Oregon he'd found a beauty and peace-of-mind he'd never forgotten. When not pulling off dangerous rescues in the frigid, life-threatening waters of the Pacific, he often found himself traveling down I-84 into the heart of the majestic Columbia River Gorge, watching the windsurfers zip back and forth between Oregon and Washington. Yes, those were the days.

But the old lady had grown tired of the cold and, before he knew it, he'd found himself smack-dab at the tip of the Conch Republic. That had been ten years ago.

The first thing he noticed about the southernmost point in the continental U.S. was the boat traffic. Making sense of the confusion, saving lives and enforcing the laws of the sea had been a bit overwhelming at first. All the same, he'd done nothing but give one hundred and ten percent ever since and he'd been Commander of the group for the last five years.

Glancing around the large room, which was usually filled with dozens of Coast Guard personnel, he realized that what was left of the graveyard watch was nothing more than a skeleton crew. The rescue effort underway with the Colombian freighter had zapped every ranking officer of his staff. All that was left was a handful of non-rated personnel and two or three "new fish", directly out of the Recruit Training Center in Cape May, New Jersey.

Stevens focused on the huge radar display and watched as the numerous blips headed for the ghostly target. Not being directly involved in the action part of the rescues drove him up the wall. Monitoring the operation from inside the station was like watching a fucking video game, enough to make a man feel impotent. But what the hell, he thought: a couple more years and I'll be living on Easy Street, collecting a big, fat check every month, sucking down ice-cold Budweisers. Maybe take the old lady on a cruise...

Out of the corner of his eye, Stevens spotted Seaman Third Class Scott Anderson, seated at a desk, talking on the "land-line", a special telephone usually reserved for personal calls. What in hell was he doing talking on the phone at a time like this? Probably talking to his fucking girlfriend, Stevens thought. Brad Pitt look-alike or not, there wouldn't be any of that bullshit in his station. He approached the young man from behind—slowly, stalking like a jungle cat until he was right behind him, ready to pounce.

"What? Where...Who is this?" Anderson was shouting into the mouthpiece. He must have felt Stevens' presence because he spun in his swiveled, roller chair and slowly put the phone back on its cradle. The look on his face was one of complete bewilderment.

Stevens barked, "What the hell was that?"
"I don't know," Anderson replied meekly. "A guy just called and said that there were three sportfishers headed our way filled with cocaine. Said they were headed for Oceanside."
"What else?"
"That's it. Had a Spanish accent. Wouldn't tell me his name. Weird."
Stevens remained silent, stroking his chin. Thinking hard. Sportfishers? He couldn't recall any major busts involving the million dollar boats in the last few years. Probably another hoax.

Stevens ran to the radar display. And there they were. Three blips, all in a line, inside the fifth circular band faintly displayed on the screen. They were less than twenty nautical miles away. Stevens had learned a lot about the interdiction of narcotics smuggling and there was one saying that always stood out in his mind. Follow up on every tip: every fucking last one.

Stevens knew he would have to move fast. Customs would be all over it if they had been tipped as well, and they would do everything they could to make the bust, steal the glory.

Along with the glory came the much-needed federal funding, something the Coast Guard desperately needed. In the last few years, his budget had been cut drastically. He now had fewer men, boats and planes than any time in his command.

Their highly effective, high-altitude radar blimps had either been sold, deflated, or scrapped. And with Coast Guard Rear Admiral John Shkor heading the Joint Interagency Task-Force-East, based in Key West, he knew he'd better make the bust if he wanted to see another cent. And also avoid public humiliation in the eyes of his friends over at Customs.

"Anderson," he screamed. "Prepare one of the utility boats for an intercept. Crew of three!"

"Yes, sir, but..."

"But what!"

"The targets are not within the twelve-mile limit."

"I know they're not, you sorry son-of-a-bitch. But by the time you get your green asses out there, they'll be knocking on our fucking back door!" Screw that twelve-mile limit, he thought. You break the law anywhere in the ocean that I can see you, and your ass is mine. He watched as Anderson headed for the equipment room like his pathetic tight pants were on fire.

A huge man, bigger than Stevens himself, burst through the station's side door, ending Stevens' search for a boarding officer. "Jesus Christ, Mike. You're just the man I'm looking for." Mike Palance, Boatswain's Mate, was a jack-of-all trades. He could drive boats and fix boats, and handle a line better than most of the instructors at the Academy. His strength was legendary. And he had just finished a stint at the Maritime Law Enforcement (MLE) School at the Training Center in Petaluma, California. He wasn't an officer, but he deserved to be, and he would do. Stevens brought him up to speed on the developing situation and Palance hustled back out the door to prepare the utility boat for the intercept.

337

Stevens' search for a third member of the boarding team continued. He made his way to the break room and spotted Alicia DelGado. She was busy leafing through a tired magazine, and it wasn't *Cosmopolitan*.

"Miss DelGado," Stevens growled, as usual showing no preferential treatment of the female gender.

"Yes, Commander," she responded briskly and snapped to attention, saluting. Stevens studied her closely, noticing from the two diagonal bars on the sleeve insignia on her left arm that she had already made Seaman Apprentice. From the looks of her, "Chi Chi", as DelGado was known to her friends, couldn't have been more than twenty.

"Get your gear together. You're going on an intercept."

"Yes sir," she said; no complaints; no excuses. Impressive. The Commander watched her go. DelGado kept her long hair piled up in a bun. It was usually kept hidden by her blue Coast Guard-issue cap. Although he had let her slide by on the regulation length of the hair, Stevens had warned her on more than one occasion that wearing her cap backwards was against the dress code, and it set a poor example for the rest of the men. She was a feisty one, alright. Pure tomboy. She could hold her own against any of the seamen under his command—both physically and mentally—and Stevens respected that. His eyes fell on the discarded mag and he smiled for the first time all night. It was *Soldier of Fortune*.

Out on the dock, Palance was already starting up the twin diesels of the forty-one foot utility craft. The Cummins motors could pump out over six hundred horsepower each and push the aluminum boat along at a speed of twenty-five knots. They would have to hurry if they were going to catch the sportfishers before they got too close.

"You got your piece?" Palance asked Anderson, who had been busy checking the radar and setting up the GPS.

"Yeah." He patted his side holster for reassurance. Like all members of the boarding teams, he carried the M9, a nine-millimeter semiautomatic pistol. "And I brought this little baby, too." He reached into the front cabin and pulled out an Ithica 12-gauge riot shotgun.

"Good call. Hopefully, we won't need it, but you never know..."

DelGado came sprinting down the dock, her arms full of gear and they were off, headed for the channel in the gloomy darkness. Seconds later, DelGado had her hat on backwards.

Once around the bend of the island, Palance pushed the throttles to the max. The engines whined in protest.

"I sure wish these things were a little faster," Palance said when he noticed they were only doing twenty-two knots. He knew the dirty bottom wasn't helping any. "What we need is one of those Fast Coastal Interceptors."

"Right," Anderson said. "Those motherfuckers must've been bad." The high-speed "cigarettes" could cruise at forty and had a top speed of fifty knots. They had been specifically designed to intercept drug-runners off the Florida coast, but the program had been costly and, in the early nineties, most of the go-fast monohulls had been mothballed, or sold.

"I'll tell you what we need," DelGado chimed in and both men turned towards her in the darkness, eager to hear what she had to say. "We need one of those souped-up Boston Whalers. They're called Raiders. My old man told me about 'em. Said they could go more than forty knots and each one had two machine guns, a seven-six-two millimeter and a fifty cal. They slid all around the boat, wherever you needed 'em, on this metal track. Used 'em a lot in the Persian Gulf, I heard." Anderson and Palance listened with great interest. The lady definitely knew her shit.

"Anything would be better than this pig," Palance added. "But let's not forget these are sportfishing yachts we're going to check out, not Iranian gunboats."

"You ever been on one of those sportfishers?" Anderson asked Palance.

"Shit, yeah. Used to go fishing with my old man up off of Jersey. His buddy had a fifty-four-foot Egg Harbor. We used to go all the way out to the Canyon and go chunking for tuna. In the summer we'd go mako-fishing off Montauk."

"What about you, Chi Chi?" Anderson asked.

"I dated a guy for a while who used to work on one up in Islamorada. The thing was nice, but it was a charter boat, ya know...kinda beat up."

"Yeah, I hear you. The only kind I've ever been on is one of those big party boats. Didn't catch much. Everybody puked all day." Anderson went digging in the boarding bag and came up with a clipboard and pen. "What's our course heading?"

"Two-o-seven," Palance told him.

"Distance to targets?"

"Let's see..." Palance looked at the radar. "About five miles."

He noticed that Anderson was writing it all down. "Why are you doing all that?" he asked.

"S-O-P, big man. Standard Operating Procedure. Gotta do everything by the book, otherwise Stevens will rip us all a new asshole." He glanced at DelGado.

"Save it," she grunted.

Fifteen minutes later, they had the navigating lights of the three boats in sight. Palance maneuvered the boat so that they would approach from the port side. Anderson continued to make notations as the others began to suit up. DelGado came out of the cabin with three sets of soft body armor and handed a set to each of the men.

"Thanks," Palance said, "but you've got to be dreaming if you think I'm even going to come close to fitting in that."

Anderson and DelGado slipped theirs on, and all three fastened their "ballistic nylons" or equipment belts. In addition to their weapons, each belt held a can of pepper spray, an expandable steel baton, handcuffs and a flashlight. On top of it all, they put back on their bright-orange personal flotation devices. Palance's was about three sizes too small.

As boarding officer, Palance would go aboard the sportfishers and they decided that DelGado would go with him. Anderson would stay on the utility boat and communicate with the station. The frequency he would use was scrambled, as was the small hand-held unit that Palance would use to contact him at any time during the boarding.

As they neared the sportfishers, Palance got the impression that the three boats had not slowed.

"Goddamn," he said. "I can't see a fucking thing." The early-morning air was cool and thick with moisture and the windshield was covered with dew. He hit the wiper, but it wasn't much better. He swung the smaller craft in a 180-degree turn and ended up alongside the lead vessel, about fifty yards away, and matched their speed. "You may do the honors," Palance said jokingly and Anderson reached for the mike of the VHF.

"Attention sportfishing boats. This is the United States Coast Guard, transmitting on channel sixteen. Heave to and prepare for boarding." Thirty seconds passed and the three boats continued ahead, without any noticeable reduction in speed.

Anderson moved the mike away from his lips and said to the others, "Did I do that right? They must see us."

"Try it again." Palance told him. "Zap 'em with the siren first."

A loud whooping sound shattered the otherwise calm night.

"Attention sportfishers. This is United States Coast Guard Group Key West. Stop your engines. Heave to and prepare for boarding. Immediately!"

"Well how about that," he said proudly, smiling as the three fishing boats gradually stopped.

Next he demanded the names and hailing ports of the three boats. The captain of the first boat, the *Predator*, spoke for all. Anderson relayed the information to the station on the scrambled channel. He also gave their location and looked at his watch. It was four-fifteen.

"You ready, Mike?"

"Yeah."

"Give 'em hell, big man."

Anderson put the boat in gear and idled over to the lead boat. "Wow! That's a nice one," he said. He never noticed the boat that was creeping up from behind.

In a moment they were alongside. The captain of the giant sportfish had come out of the bridge to greet them. He was smiling.

Anderson keyed the mike. "Coast Guard Group Key West, be advised. Utility boat w-p-nine-one-two-niner, alongside lead vessel and preparing to board," he told the station. It was the last transmission the utility boat would ever make.

26

Vera Cruz
0256 Local Time

The SEAL team glided silently on the surface and headed for the insertion point less than fifty yards away. As before, Mercer and Jackson led, taking the "scout" positions: making their way to the beach a few yards ahead of the rest of the team. Their job was to establish and secure the BDP, or Beach Defense Perimeter, the most important aspect of the entire amphibious landing. Discovery of the team so early in the assault would be disastrous.

Once they could touch bottom, McCreary brought the team to a halt. Several tense moments passed as they waited for the signal from the beach. Small waves crumbled on the shore ahead; the sound would mask that of the team as it waded ashore. The signal came: nothing more than a quick dim flash of light. Ditching the heavy, cumbersome Draegers, the silent warriors made their way to shore.

McCreary quickly surveyed the area, and set up a "strongpoint" at the south end of the beach, behind a towering, outward-jutting section of the cliff face. As the team gathered for a briefing, they attached their night vision devices and taped their small wireless radios to their heads and ears.

With no moon, the team was nearly invisible. In addition to their black wetsuits, they wore special black custom-made assault vests, originally invented by the Israelis and popular with special operators everywhere. In the weapons department, the SEALs carried Heckler & Koch MP5 9-millimeter submachine guns with thirty-two round magazines and suppressors. For added stopping power and overall effectiveness, some of the SEALs used special Black Talon and Hydrashock projectiles that expand on impact. Under the rules of the Geneva Convention, the high-velocity rounds were illegal, but this was no regular mission. While some of the team carried an old favorite, the Sig Sauer 9mm pistol, others preferred the newer Hechler & Koch MK23, MOD 0.45 caliber pistol, specially developed for the U.S. Special Operations Command. The team also had an M-60 E3 light machine gun capable of firing 550 rounds per minute. In addition to two Benelli P7 12-gauge shotguns for close-in action, they topped it all off with a variety of flash-bang, tear-gas and explosive grenades.

When the team was ready to rock, Mercer and Jackson split off and sprinted north up the beach. There was a muffled "pop" as they fired a small mortar-like device and propelled a grappling hook up and onto the ridge above. Tiny muffled charges fired the little spikes of the hook into the ground and, within seconds, the two SEALs were up the cliff face. The two dashed for the cover of a nearby palm and set up a position, acting as flanking guards, searching the grounds for any sign of discovery.

Minutes later, McCreary and the rest of the team appeared, one by one, and gathered at the edge of the cliff, flat on their stomachs. McCreary quietly spoke into the tiny mike. "Flankers, you copy for sit-rep?"

"North end of compound secure. Got one target, armed, by the pool."
"Leave him be for now. Take the north side around the back. Give us a couple of minutes here to take the mansion," McCreary ordered. Then he sent Blades and the other members of Fire-Team Two around the south side of the compound. Glancing at his watch, he saw that it was three-fifteen. H-hour had begun.

There was no time to lose and the team sprang from their position, with Gates and McCreary in the lead. Materializing out of the darkness, they reached the pool just as the sentry spun in alarm. The look on his face was one of pure shock as a series of muffled spits from two different guns cut him down.

Inside the mansion, seated before the huge display, the chief of security thought he heard a sound. He looked up and squinted into the darkness and a flash of light swept his eyes, blinding him. He blinked rapidly and the last thing he saw, as the huge sliding door in front of him exploded, was a red dot centered on his chest. Instantly, several rounds of silent nine-millimeter death ripped through his body, tossing him over backwards. He was dead long before he hit the floor. Two *pistoleros* came from somewhere in the back, weapons blazing. With precise shots from his MP5, Gates dropped the first man, removing most of his head in the process. A loud roar momentarily deafened him as a SEAL crouched to his right blew the second man off his feet with a blast from his shotgun.

Outside in the compound, the sound of gunfire filled the night. Gates recognized the sounds of the AK-47s. As expected, the sentries had thought the compound was impervious to a frontal assault. The loud, grinding chatter of a heavy caliber weapon could be heard and the agent realized that someone had opened up with the 20-millimeter anti-aircraft gun. It went on for nearly a minute, and then a violent explosion from out back shook the mansion and the big gun was silent.

McCreary had heard it too. Crouching alongside Gates next to the security console, he raised the tiny mike to his lips, "Fire-Team Two, report."

The excited voice of Jack Blades quickly answered, "All kinds of opposition out here, sir! They opened up on us with something big! We took it out, but Jackson's been hit!"

"Shit," McCreary said to Gates. But there was no time to worry. They heard movement up the stairs and scrambled over to its right side, backs to the wall. The other two members of their fire-team spread out behind them, covering the rear. They took positions and set up what would be a deadly crossfire.

344

Without risking a look, McCreary tossed a flash-bang grenade up the stairs. Both he and Gates covered their night vision goggles as the "whump" of the device lit up the night. Waiting a few seconds for the smoke to clear, they charged up the stairs.

McCreary dove into the first room on his left, and rolled, searching for targets. Nothing.

Gates came out of the door across from him, shaking his head. Things were not looking good. They checked the next two rooms with the same result. "He's got to be here," he told McCreary. And he immediately felt the *déjà-vu*.

"He's here all right," the lieutenant concurred with a confident voice. "I can smell his fear." Together they headed down the lengthy hallway, darting into the rooms with weapons held ready at the hip, hearts pounding.

There was a movement at the end of the hallway, and McCreary raised his weapon to fire. From where Gates stood, something seemed wrong. The target was too small. In a fraction of a second, he realized the target was just a boy; he looked petrified.

"Wait," the agent cried and distracted McCreary. And before either man could react, a second figure stepped out into the hallway and unleashed a burst from an AK-47. McCreary went down as the three 7.62mm rounds stitched him deep in the chest. Before the sentry could fire again, Gates killed the man with a burst from his MP5.

"You stupid motherfucker," McCreary gasped from where he lay on the floor.
"How bad, sir?" Gates asked.
"Not bad," the lieutenant wheezed. "Not bad at all." Gates saw that there was already blood on the man's lips. He was one tough bastard.

Another figure stepped into the hallway and Gates swung his weapon from where he knelt on the floor. His finger tightened on the trigger and he stared directly into the eyes of Amado Carrillo Fuentes.

Carrillo ran to the boy and held him with his arms crossed in front of his son's body.

"Kill me if you must," Carrillo said, his voice trembling. "But please do not hurt my family." While Gates watched in shock, the cartel leader's wife and daughter joined them. They huddled together in the dark hallway, staring at the intruder with frightened eyes. Wating for him to kill them.

"We're not going to hurt you," Gates told them. "But we are going to take you out of here."

"Wha...what about my family?" Carrillo stammered.

That was a good question. Gates approached them carefully, still wating for an ambush. "I don't know what's going to happen to them," he said. And that was the truth.

Gates called for the rest of the fire team and hustled Carrillo and his family outside, keeping his weapon on the cartel leader at all times. Fire-Team Two made its way around the front of the mansion, with Jackson being carried by two of the men, his arms slung around their shoulders like an injured football player. A bullet had ripped through his thigh, but they had stopped the bleeding.

McCreary's injury was more serious. The team medic was already tending to the chest wound, and he was brought out of the mansion on a makeshift stretcher, one of the bedroom's closet doors.

The radioman sent the signal and minutes later a Special Ops version of the SH-60 Sea Hawk helicopter appeared above the compound. Engines screaming, it touched down out in front of the pool and began the extraction. The Pave Hawk, the Naval Special Warfare battlefield taxi, was an intimidating sight. With its 7.62mm machine guns, night-vision capability and insect-like windshield, it struck the fear of God into Carrillo and his family.

Crouching underneath the blades of the intimidating beast, Gates made his way to the spot where McCreary lay on the ground.

"I'm taking the family," Gates told him.

McCreary struggled to get up, but couldn't. "Like hell you are. Those were not my orders."

"I don't care. If we leave them here, they'll be tortured, then killed. Besides, they've seen everything."

With his last bit of strength, the lieutenant reached up and grabbed Gates by the vest. "I knew I never should've brought you." Then he passed out.

Minutes later, they were all aboard and, without a trace, they were gone.

CIA Headquarters
0447 EDT

"Can you believe that?" Macki remarked. He and several others had just finished watching the scenario as it unfolded at the compound in Vera Cruz. A satellite had relayed the action directly in "real time", exactly as it had happened. He'd seen images like it before, but this was one of the new birds, a sixth-generation KH spy satellite, and the video was top-notch.

Watching the assault from hundreds of miles away had been like watching a video game in which you cannot control the players. It had been highly voyeuristic; they had watched the blurry infrared images of the SEALs as they had surrounded the compound and stormed the mansion, and then they had held their breath. They'd seen the helicopter come and go, but whether the assault had been successful, they did not know. The images had not shown quite enough detail.

DEA Administrator Bob Constance was there, but so far had been very quiet, transfixed by the images on the television screen. He looked around at Macki, but still said nothing.

Now, Senator Thomas Jensen was hovering over him once again. The irritating politician had been hounding Macki all week and, although it was frustrating, he really couldn't blame him. For a while, Macki had ignored Jensen's requests to monitor the assault and the progress of the sportfishers from Cancun to Key West. The man didn't even come close to having the clearance. But Jensen had threatened to go public with the information he had and, in the end, a special exception had been necessary. At least there in Langley, Macki could keep an eye on him. The last thing he needed was Jensen hanging around Key West, where he was bound to fuck things up.

Macki looked back at Jensen and actually felt sorry for the guy. He probably hadn't slept a wink since Herrera had taken his daughter hostage. Jensen paced back and forth and he'd long since chewed his fingernails to the nub. He turned to Macki.

"What now?" Jensen asked.

"Now we wait. Why don't you have a seat?" he suggested, and Jensen took his advice.

It wasn't long before the door opened and the agency code-man strode into the room, bee-lining it for Macki.

"Read it," Macki told the man.

Adjusting his glasses, the cryptographer studied the page. "The mission has been accomplished, sir. Target now in custody, en route Langley."

"We got him!" Macki cried and the other men in the room joined in the celebration.

Constance crossed the room and extended his hand. "Good job, Mr. Macki."

"Thanks, Bob. It was a joint effort."

Behind them, the telephone rang. "It's for you, John," the satellite imagery "techie" said and handed him the phone.

Macki had expected more congratulations, but his expression suddenly turned serious. "What? When?" he demanded, and slammed the phone back down on its cradle. "Shit!" he cried in disgust.

Jensen rose from his chair with a look of equal concern. "What is it?"

Macki had to tell him. "The boats headed for Key West were just intercepted by the Coast Guard."

Aboard the *Predator*
That Same Time

"This wasn't supposed to happen," Larsen said in anger, keeping his fear well hidden.

He'd been watching the small blip on the radar ever since it appeared near Key West and headed towards the deeper channel.

At first he thought it might have been just another vessel heading south but, as it got closer, he realized it was heading straight for them. Just before they hailed him, the agent noticed the diagonal orange stripe that ran down the side, aft of the bow. Even in the darkness, there was no mistaking the Coast Guard vessel. Somewhere, somehow—someone had fucked up and fucked up bad.

Now they were telling him to heave to. He ignored them for a little while, desperately trying to come up with the right plan, do the right thing. The last thing he needed was to have the Coast Guard fire one across his bow. He backed off on the throttle and put her in neutral, and the *Predator* slowed to a stop. The water was nearly slick calm. Outside, he could see the Coast Guard vessel approaching, preparing to come alongside. The beam of their spotlight swept across the bridge.

"What are we gonna do?" Kurt asked. "What do you think they want?"

"Who knows?" the agent replied, slightly irked. How in hell could he know what they wanted? "Seems like a strange place for a routine boarding. Not a very big boarding party, either, considering there's three different boats here."

"I count only three guys. Actually, the one with the hat on backwards looks like a chick. They don't look like they've got a lot of weapons on that rig, either."

"Yeah, well they don't need a lot of guys or a lot of weapons. You can bet they'll have one guy on the radio at all times. It doesn't take long to call in the reinforcements."

"Well you better think quick, my good captain, because here they are."

The whoop of the siren split the early morning calm for the second time, and Larsen jumped at the sound. At that point, his nerves were shot.

Down in the cockpit, one of the boarding party had come aboard and was making fast the stern line of their own boat to the *Predator*'s rear cleat. Larsen noticed that it was indeed a woman. The backwards hat gave her just the right amount of attitude to fulfill what he guessed was her "tough chick" image.

"Hey, hey, will you look at that?" Kurt razzed.

"Here goes nothin'," Larsen said, opening the bridge door. "Let's see if I can talk our way out of this one." He took a deep breath and walked out.

"Good morning!" he called down. That was all he would get out.

The quiet morning erupted in a hail of gunfire, and the darkness was pierced by the tracers that followed the trail of death with eerie precision.

Larsen watched in horror as a deadly stream of heavy caliber bullets came out of the darkness behind the *Predator*, ripping the bodies of the boarding party to shreds. The girl was the first to go and she never saw it coming. The heavy rounds that tore through her back exploded out her chest and she was pitched forward onto the deck of the *Predator*. Her body armor had been useless.

The big man was caught as he moved from the utility boat to the cov-eringboard of the *Predator*. The fusillade of tracers and invisible death spun his huge frame like a rag doll, jerking him back onto the smaller Coast Guard boat. By the time he hit the deck, he was nearly cut in half. His shotgun clattered onto the deck of the *Predator*.

In a desperate attempt to reach the radio, the last man was cut down inside the small wheelhouse, which exploded violently under the barrage doing little to protect his bullet-riddled body. When his lifeless form finally crashed to the deck, a cloud of smoke and dust hung in the still air. Just as fast as it had started, it stopped, and the morning was again silent.

It had taken less than six seconds and in that time, Larsen witnessed more death than he had seen in his entire life. It was so close, so real.

In a state of shock, he made his way down the ladder, all the while staring into the evil darkness behind his boat. The silhouette of the *Osprey* was obvious. Standing at the rail, holding a heavy caliber machine gun with the barrel still smoking, Raul glared back at him with indifference. Larsen knelt down beside the girl and searched for any sign of life. There were none. He picked up her Coast Guard cap, and ran his fingers across the embroidered emblem.

She had given her life and all they had given her was Seaman Apprentice. His gaze followed the small river of blood that ran from her body, across the deck, and out the scupper.

In the distance, the whining jet engine of a helicopter was approaching.

Aboard the Dolphin HH65 Rescue Helicopter
That Same Time

The crew of the Coast Guard chopper was high-tailing it towards the indicated waypoint at nearly two hundred miles per hour. Their search for the phantom freighter had been a waste of time and now they knew they had been duped. They'd loitered around the area for too long and they were in a foul mood.

The call from the Coast Guard station had raised their spirits. The boarding crew of an ongoing intercept had failed to report in for several minutes and attempts to reach them had been answered by nothing but static.

The station had them on radar, but had lost radio contact when they had joined with one of the three vessels. The chopper had been ordered to the scene and the navigation lights of the vessels could be seen up ahead.

"Coast Guard Group Key West, this is Coast Guard Helicopter One-niner-Mike, reporting visual on three, correction—four vessels," the pilot radioed. "Dropping to five-zero feet for further verification."

Easing off on the collective and the throttle, the pilot brought the French-built twin-engine chopper down close to the water. He switched over and let the computerized flight management system control everything. Without any serious night-vision equipment, the system was a godsend. It brought the chopper down to fifty feet and kept it hovering there in the darkness, allowing the crew to concentrate more on their search than on the controls.

The crew was uneasy now, unsure what they might find. Although they had personal weapons, the chopper was set up for rescue and was unarmed. Between the six of them, the largest caliber weapon they had was an M-16. The crew was alert and tense as the 3000-watt spotlight sprang to life and painted the scene below.

What they saw alarmed them. The wheelhouse of the small utility boat had been destroyed, perhaps in some sort of collision. A man was crouched in the cockpit of one of the sportfishers. And then, suddenly, they saw the bodies.

The pilot's voice was excited and fearful when he radioed, "Key West Group, this is Dolphin Helicopter! Things here do not look good! Repeat, not good. We have what appear to be bodies on board the Coast Guard vessel, and—"

The night erupted once more. The chopper took several rounds through the starboard door, killing the rescue medic instantly. More rounds punched through the side and took off the top of the co-pilots head, spraying the interior of the cabin with gore. The chopper heeled violently to the left.

"Mayday! Mayday! We are taking fire!" the pilot screamed as he fought to control the craft. He repeated the distress call again and again, increasing throttle and trying to get the hell out of there.

The crewman looked out the door and tried to find the source of the fire, to direct the pilot away from it. Down in the cockpit of one of the smaller boats, a figure blazed away, his shots wild, tracers spewing out towards the chopper like fluorescent darts.

A second figure appeared next to him and raised an object onto his shoulder. From then on, everything became slow motion, straight out of a bad dream. The crewman saw a flash of light and, like a Roman candle firework, it reached out like a finger, headed directly for them. He had seen it before somewhere, but in his confused state, he couldn't recall where. He shouted to the pilot. And then he remembered.

The missile tracked effortlessly on the heat of the port engine. The detonation was so intense, it nearly separated the entire rotor assembly from the fuselage, which exploded in a jagged supernova of warhead and aviation fuel.

Amidst the screams of the crewmembers, who were still burning alive, the chopper fell from the sky, rotorblades twirling awkwardly and plunged into the dark unforgiving water.

Aboard the *Tempest*
That Same Time

Captain Terry Stanton had seen enough. There would be no getting out of this one. And it all seemed so unfair. He had done everything he was told, kept every secret, covered up every lie. But now there would be no money for him and no money for his daughter. *My poor little Jessica, I have sentenced you to death.* Stanton was ashamed, his grief overwhelming. He could not, did not even want to go on.

Without hesitation, he pointed the *Tempest* at the *Osprey*, and jammed the throttles full ahead. The twin diesels moaned as the huge vessel hurtled towards is target at close to thirty knots. Stanton could see the look of fear and surprise etched on the faces of the Mexicans as they spotted the approaching vessel.

Raul began blazing away with the fifty-caliber machine gun and the bridge in front of Stanton exploded in a million pieces. Next to him, John Flynn was blown off the bridge as the bullets ripped him apart. He would not live to see twenty. Raul was still firing when the *Tempest* blasted into the *Osprey* broadside.

Unfortunately, Stanton never got to see it. He, too, was dead a few seconds before the final collision.

The White House

The phone next to the President's bed was ringing. Before he could get to it, his wife had picked it up.

"Yes," she said. "He's right here....it better be good," she threatened.

The President looked at the digital display of the clock in disgust. The huge red numerals could not be mistaken; it was just before five. Something was wrong. He reached for the phone.

"I already gave at the office," the President said, and kicked himself for not being serious. It just wasn't the strongest part of his character.

"We've got a problem." It was his advisor.

"That's obvious. Have you looked at the clock? It's five in the morning. Now what is it?"

"Remember that little caper to take down Amado Carrillo? You know, with the DEA and the sportfishing boats?"

"No, I don't," the President lied. "Or should I say, 'I have no recollection of such an operation'." It had worked for Reagan. Maybe it would work for him.

"Word just came in from J-Sock." Papandreas hoped the President would remember the acronym for the Joint Special Operations

354

Command. "Apparently the sportfishers were intercepted by the Coast Guard just inside the twelve-mile limit."

"So what's the problem?" he asked in all sincerity. "Did they arrest everybody? What about that smuggler?"

"No. Coast Guard Group Key West supposedly lost contact with the boarding party during the intercept. They sent a chopper to check it out. The chopper reported taking fire and then disappeared from their radar. They think it was shot down."

"Jesus Christ." It was all the President could say. He needed time to think, and several seconds passed with no further words between the two men.

"Sir?"

"I'm here."

"What do you want to do about it?"

What did he want to do about it? There wasn't anything he could do about it. Someone else would have to do it. And he would have to give the order. Maybe he could deny it. He'd have to.

"Those boats were filled with Mexican narco-traffickers, weren't they?" the President asked.

"Well..."

"Weren't they, George?" he stressed. Sometimes his advisor could be so slow to catch on.

"Oh, I see. Why, yes, I guess they were filled with drug smugglers. Smugglers who fired upon members of the United States Coast Guard. Members of our Armed Forces."

"That's right. So I guess there's only one way to handle this."

"What's that, Mr. President?"

"Make the smugglers go away."

"Sir?"

"Blow those bastards out of the water. Terminate them. With extreme prejudice. And one more thing."

"What's that?"

"I don't want any survivors."

Aboard the *Osprey*

The severely damaged vessel was mortally wounded and listing badly to port; it would be just minutes before the *Osprey* slipped below the surface.

Larsen pulled himself over the tilted stern of the dying boat, having swum the thirty yards from where he had left the *Predator*. The vision that greeted him was not only shocking, but satisfying.

At least ten feet of the *Tempest's* bow was still deeply imbedded in the *Osprey's* salon. The collision had ripped a gaping hole in the side of the *Osprey* and from the angle of the deck, it was obvious the bilge pumps were fighting a losing battle against the onrushing water. A set of legs protruded from beneath the splintered fiberglass of the *Tempest's* starboard side. Almost the entire rear bulkhead of the *Osprey* was gone.

Removing his pistol from the waistband of his shorts, Larsen crept across the steep-angled cockpit and headed for the inside of the crippled *Osprey*. There was no sign of movement. It was dark and difficult to see, but the cockpit lighting was sufficient to display the grim sight that awaited him.

The legs belonged to Raul; his twisted body lay on the teak deck frozen in death, the machine gun still in his hands, the barrel smoking. The bow of Stanton's 58 Monterey had hit the *pistolero* nearly head-on, crushing his body and hurling it onto the deck. The collision had torn one of the thick aluminum tower legs completely in half and the jagged metal of the lower part had been driven straight into Raul's stomach, skewering him and passing completely through his body before tearing out his back. It was covered with guts and intestines. A disturbing sight, but Larsen felt no remorse.

Just inside, where the door had been, Paco also lay on the floor. He was alive, however, and it was obvious he was in great pain. The angle of his upper body suggested to the agent that his back might have been broken.

When he looked up at Larsen, his usually beady eyes were wide open. It was good to see some fear in them for a change.

"Captain Dan...Help me! I can't feel my legs!" Paco was hyperventilating and his voice was raspy, coming out in gasps. Larsen stepped over him without a second look. He had only one thing on his mind.

"Kym! It's me...Dan!" There was no response and he was overcome with panic. His legs were rubbery, his throat seizing up. Then he heard the whimpering.

With two giant steps he was down the stairs and into the galley. Kym was still bound and gagged, huddled in the corner with her back to the wall. She was frightened but, for the most part, appeared to be all right. Larsen quickly removed the gag and Kym began to cry.

In one of the galley drawers, the agent found a knife and sliced through the leather straps that bound her.

When she had composed herself, she spoke, but her voice was weak. Larsen knelt down and held her, stroking her hair as the words began to flow out.

"I...I thought you'd left me," she said, her soft voice thick with emotion.

"I'd never leave you. Never. I wanted to help you, but I couldn't. It's just so...so complicated. There's so much you don't know..."

"What's happening? We're sinking, aren't we?"

"We have a few minutes. Everything's going to be alright."

It was what the agent hoped, but he wasn't sure. He filled her in on what had happened with the boarding party and chopper, and wiped away her tears.

"Where's Paco?" she asked as he helped her to her feet. She had difficulty standing and leaned on the counter for support.

"He's up there near the door," he told her, nodding towards the spot in the salon where he'd found the smuggler. "Raul's dead."

"Good. I wish they both were. Fucking animals."

"Listen to me," he said sternly and held her by the shoulders as he looked into her eyes. "I want you to swim to my boat. It's right outside.

Kurt is there waiting. Swim to the tuna door in the back and he'll help you on."

"But I want to stay with you," she pleaded.

"You can't. There's something I've got to do and I don't want you to see it. Now get going!" He helped her cross the room and over towards the cockpit. When they reached the spot where Paco lay on the floor, she stopped and kicked the smuggler as hard as she could.

"Bastard," she said.

"C'mon! Get going." Larsen pushed her into the shattered cockpit. He watched as she lowered herself over the stern and then he returned to the salon.

Paco stared up at him and for several seconds, both were silent. Larsen pulled out the gun and considered what he was about to do. Paco was the first to speak. His breathing was still labored, his voice little more than a whisper.

"I knew about you, Captain Dan. I knew all along. What are you? DEA?"

"Good guess."

"You American agents are so stupid. You think you can hurt the cartel by arresting one man? The size of the cartels is beyond your imagination."

"No it isn't," Larsen told him. "That's why I'm doing something about it."

Paco laughed. "You and I are very much alike, Captain Dan. We're nothing but soldiers, following the orders of others."

"Maybe so, but as we speak, your boss is either dead or on his way to an American prison. At least that's a start. I'm talking about Amado Carrillo Fuentes. He is your boss, isn't he, Paco?"

The smuggler hesitated. "He was on his way out anyway. Carrillo is old. He's gone soft. Paranoid. The cartel will do better without him." Paco did not admit that it was he who had hoped to take his place. "But you don't understand," the smuggler argued. "The cartel is like a family tree, with roots so deep it could never be pulled from the ground. You break off a branch and two grow back in its place."

"We'll see," Larsen shot back. But he knew Paco's words were true.

Paco raised his head from the floor with great difficulty. "You know, I saved your life once. You owe me."

"I don't owe you shit!" he shouted and pulled back the slide of his gun. He aimed it at Paco's face and held it less than a foot away, his arm trembling. "You may have saved my life, you bastard, but you took the lives of my best friends! All in the name of your fucking cocaine!"

Suddenly the vessel lurched violently to port, and Larsen was thrown to the floor. He looked astern and saw that the water was now pouring into the cockpit. She would be under in a few seconds.

"Oh my god!" Paco screamed. "You've got to help me. You can't leave me here to drown." The water was coming into the salon and just beginning to cover Paco's legs. He reached out and grabbed the agent by the arm. The grip was tight, and Larsen realized he wasn't completely paralyzed. "Please..." he gasped. "Do not let me die like this! Please." The water was covering his chest. Larsen tore free of the dying man's grasp and scooted up the sharply angled floor.

"Go ahead, then," Paco begged. "Finish it. Shoot me, you American piece of shit."

Larsen stared into the evil black eyes and smiled at the fear that swam through them. It would be so easy to kill him, so satisfying to be the one to finish him off. But he knew that he was not a killer and to kill Paco now might free him from his demons which, finally, the agent could not and would not allow.

"No," the agent told him. "You don't deserve it. Maybe you're right, Paco. We are soldiers. But we're not alike. We're not even close." Larsen turned away and slid down the salon floor and plunged into the water. He swam away from the sinking vessel before it could suck him under. Behind him, he could still hear Paco screaming as the bow of the *Osprey* reared up and sank beneath the surface. For the smuggler, the death sentence had been handed down long ago. Finally, it had been carried out.

Now it was time to think. He swam towards the *Predator* with an uneasy feeling of vulnerability. Out there on the open ocean, there was no place to hide. Soon they would be coming and, whoever it was, he knew they wouldn't be happy.

It was just first light when the wheels of Major Jeff Saunders' F-16 Fighting Falcon left the ground at the Boca Chica Naval Air Station, just north of Key West. In full afterburner, the pilot had the sleek deadly warplane on station above the target within seconds, and he nearly over-shot it.

He still couldn't believe his ears and how quickly things had happened. Currently under the command of the Joint Special Operations staff, he'd been transferred to the smaller naval air station from his home base with the 125th Interceptor Group at Jacksonville. For the most part, his training and recent maneuvers had been dull and routine. Rousted from his bunk in the officers quarters just before dawn, all that had changed.

Apparently the Coast Guard had been attacked by a group of terrorist/drug-smugglers posing as American sportfishing yachts. From what he understood, not only had a Coast Guard boarding party been killed, but a Dolphin chopper that had arrived on the scene had been shot down. His mission: track and identify the targets and destroy them. No questions.

It had been a while since Saunders had fired at anything human, and that was part of the reason his adrenaline had him juiced to the max. But to fire on American vessels? That would be entirely different from guiding bombs to their targets with lasers, or dropping his payload on unsuspecting Iraqis in the dead of night. He had a strange feeling about this one; no wingman had been allowed. Someone was up to something, and the veteran pilot was sure it wasn't good. But an order was just that, meant to be executed and not argued. Someone was pissed off and he'd been called in to do the dirtywork.

Saunders had already fed the latest GPS coordinates of the targets into his navigational computer and according to his FLIR forward-looking infrared radar, there was indeed something down there. In a steep banking turn, he brought the F-16 down to the deck and made his first pass at just under Mach 1. So far, his Threat Warning System had picked up nothing, but he still felt better being just above the surface of the water, where his own heat signature could be lost in the clutter of the ocean swells, however small they might be.

On his first pass, the boats were no more than a blur but, as he pushed the throttles up and blazed skyward, he looked down and could make out three vessels in the grey light of the early morning. The only sign of the Dolphin rescue-chopper was a patch of burning fuel, spread erratically across the glossy surface of the water.

He cut back on the throttles and went in for another pass, higher this time, yet still careful and ready for evasive maneuvers. The images of the vessels were becoming clearer by the minute.

"*Anvil*, this is *Hammer*," Saunders radioed in, "reporting visual on three, count 'em, three vessels at given GPS coordinates. No sign of activity, no hostile action. Request further instructions, over." His anxiety was mounting and he hoped the order to destroy the vessels would be rescinded and he could continue with his career, untainted.

"*Anvil* back." Saunders did not recognize the voice, but it sounded firm, and high up chain of command. "Any sign of the rescue chopper or any other Coast Guard crew?"

Jesus, Saunders thought. It wasn't like he was sitting still, hovering over the scene. "Negative, sir. Nothing but a burning patch of fuel."

"*Hammer*, be advised. You will commence with operation as planned. Repeat, as planned." The words were as hollow to Saunders as a death sentence, a sentence he had been picked to carry out.

"Bastards," Saunders mumbled to himself, and brought his war-machine around in a one-eighty degree turn. Once again he dropped towards the water.

At one hundred feet, he centered the aiming reticle of his twenty-millimeter cannon, depressed the trigger, and opened fire. Like a dragon's breath, a tongue of flame and lethal steel licked out at what was left of the bridge of the *Tempest*; it disintegrated in less than a second. On the initial gun pass, he noticed the smaller Coast Guard vessel and the bodies. Something terrible had happened here, but what? Where was everybody?

He made another pass with the guns and destroyed the house and stern of the *Tempest*. She keeled over, within a minute, and began her voyage to the bottom. As he flew in a wide arc to survey the extent of the damage, he noticed that the larger vessel had begun to move.

Stop! Saunders mind cried out to the fleeing vessel. Why didn't they surrender? Were there Americans on board? He'd already proven what he could do. In an effort to give them one last chance, he picked up the mike and switched to the emergency channel 121.5 megahertz.

"This is United States Air Force F-16 broadcasting on GUARD. Calling sportfisher heading north on a bearing of zero-three degrees. Stop all forward movement or I will be forced to fire upon you." He listened for a response, but there was nothing but static. He repeated the warning. He would be in trouble now, that was for sure. Again, there was no reply. "You have been warned," he added and shut off the mike.

One last time, he put the jet into full military power and turned around. He flew farther away from the target this time and selected an AIM-9 Sidewinder heat-seeking missile. The missile was accurate at a range of ten miles. At less than six, it was deadly.

Saunders watched his heads-up display and counted down the distance to the rabbitting sportfisher. He armed his missile and listened for the tone.

At two miles distance, the missile lock-on diamond appeared. A loud hum echoed in his ears. The "SHOOT" designation appeared on the screen. With great reluctance and a heavy heart, he depressed the trigger. "*Hammer*, fox one," he said to no one in particular and watched as the missile took off from his left wingtip. It was nothing spectacular, just a slight whoosh, a brief glare, and then the missile was on its way. Actually, it was quite sad. Within seconds the Sidewinder had reached Mach-two.

362

It tracked perfectly, locked on to the *Predator*'s engine room and literally flew right through the cabin door. In a fiery explosion that rocked the otherwise peaceful early-morning sky, the *Predator* was no more.

Hunkered down in the life raft, Larsen, Kym and Kurt covered their ears as the screaming jet blew the *Tempest* to pieces. Within a few minutes, it slipped under. A few hundred yards away, the *Predator* slowly idled away as the autopilot did its job.

But the jet was not done. It blazed past once more and the water beneath the tiny rubber craft actually shook. The roar of the jet's powerful engine was deafening. Only Larsen saw the missile. When it reached its target, they were only a mile away. The shock wave nearly swamped them.

Larsen got to his knees and watched as the jet became smaller and smaller and the sound of its engine faded away. He struggled within himself to comprehend the enormity of all that had happened, the reality of the death and destruction that he had created. He sank down into the raft and put his arm around Kym. She was still crying. He looked over at Kurt and gave him a weak smile. His mate returned it with a thumbs up. "At least we're still alive," Kurt said.

"You think he's gone?" Larsen searched the sky.
"I sure hope so."
For the moment, it was over.

Epilogue

North Palm Beach, Florida
May 8, 1996 1315 EDT

A tired old woman walked very slowly to the side of the road to check her mail. The thin fragile shell was all that was left of Shiela Stanton. She couldn't bear to look at the For Sale sign in the front yard: one more heartbreaking reminder that her world had come crashing down around her. With Terry gone, she'd be forced to sell the house. It was a small two-bedroom and she knew she'd be lucky if she cleared enough to keep Jessica alive a little while longer. Her efforts to find out what had really happened to her husband had been unsuccessful.

Dan Larsen had been nowhere to be found and the story, so far, had been that there was a collision between two boats off Key West and both crews had drowned. She smelled a cover-up and was determined to find out the truth.

Reaching the box, she pulled out the regular assortment of junk mail; the Pennysaver, a packet of coupons and a couple of advertise-ments with pictures of missing children on the back. There was a post-card from someone, a picture of a beautiful lagoon called *Yal-Kul*. When she turned it over, she broke down. It was from Terry and it had been sent from Mexico almost three weeks earlier. She sobbed gently and, with tears streaming down her cheeks, her finger traced her dead husband's writing. "I miss you too," she cried, and clutched the card to her heaving chest, weeping openly now. It was almost too much for her to bear.

But she had to go on, had to take care of Jessica as best she could. The little girl was all she had now. Slowly she trudged up the lawn.

Back inside the house, she sat down at the kitchen table and tried to compose herself. She'd been crying too much lately, and she didn't want Jessica to see it. There was one more envelope she hadn't noticed at first, a plain white one, addressed to the Stanton family. The name and address had been typed. Just another condolence card, she figured and slipped her thumb under the flap and tore it open. Her heart skipped a beat. Inside was a check—a cashier's check—for three hundred thousand dollars. There was no note, and no return address.

That same day, just north of Singer Island in the town of Juno Beach, Dan Larsen walked along the beach, ankle deep in the warm waters of the summer Atlantic. He held a pair of extremely uncomfortable shoes in his left hand. He'd just come from his second funeral in two days. The day before he'd said goodbye to the remains of Matt Kirchner, and earlier that morning he'd laid his good friend Rob Masters to rest. The water splashed up onto the legs of his black suit, but he really didn't give a shit; the only time he got dressed up anymore was for weddings or funerals, neither of which he cared for too much.

A couple of surfers ran by with boards in hand and leashes on and plunged into the water with great enthusiasm. The waves were great—it was one of those rare summer swells, the surface of the water was glassy and the wind was light from the west and offshore. He gazed out at the sea and watched a set peel off in perfect lefts, clean and unridden. The thunder of the water on the reef was intense and mesmerizing; he nearly stumbled on a stake marking a nest of turtle eggs buried beneath the sand.

His mind wandered from the past to the future, filled with unanswered questions wherever it went. So much had happened, yet it all remained hidden like a dirty little secret. What bothered him most was that someone had ordered the destruction of the vessels and the fact that he and his friends might have been aboard had not seemed to matter one bit. Both he and Macki had tried to get some answers, but they came up against a brick wall at every turn.

The President was denying any knowledge, whatsoever, of the operation and the agent was surprised that there had been no reports of the arrest of Carrillo at all. The capture of the cocaine kingpin had been kept a secret, not only from the American public, but from the Mexicans as well.

According to Macki, Carrillo had indeed rolled over on his contacts, providing the DEA with a wealth of information regarding corrupt Mexican politicians, officials, smuggling routes into the U.S. and the re-emergence of the Cali cartel in Colombia. In return, the former leader of the Juarez cartel was given complete immunity and a new identity and life for himself and his family.

The following July, it would be reported that Amado Carrillo Fuentes had died in a Mexican hospital while undergoing plastic surgery and liposuction. It was rumored that the body on display had been made of wax.

If the President had planned to use the capture of Carrillo to boost his popularity in the polls, it had not been necessary. He was headed for re-election and, as it turned out, there wasn't anyone worth a damn to run against him. He had stated, however, that upon re-election, he planned to appoint Thomas Jensen as Ambassador to Mexico. Despite bipartisan opposition, the Senator would indeed be confirmed and, at least for Larsen and Macki, it wasn't hard to figure out why. It was good to see that someone had the balls to lean on the President once in a while, especially when his own balls were in a vise.

Larsen himself had used his own knowledge to gain a few things that he wanted. His first order of business had been to return to the jungle and retrieve the bodies of his two friends. It had been a difficult moment for him emotionally and he still carried the guilt around his neck like a ton of lead. He also demanded that a special maritime life-insurance policy be paid to the families of the two men. The check to Sheila Stanton had been cut by the U.S. Treasury from a special fund set up by the CIA. And lastly, a special memorial fund had been set up in memory of John Flynn. Each year at the Sailfish Marina, a huge trophy would be awarded to the best new mate of the winter sailfish season.

There was a shout from up on the dune and Larsen spun to see Kym standing at the top of the bluff. She waved at him and then came prancing down the wooden stairway that led to the beach. He watched her as she approached and smiled. He wasn't sure if he loved her, but he was beginning to and that was good. At that moment in his life, he really needed someone. To hell with being alone.

"Want company?" She pulled up in front of him, took his hand and gave him a kiss.

"Sure."

They walked for a while, hand-in-hand, without saying a word. They made an odd couple, she in her cut-offs and a loose-fitting white crop-top, and he in his monkey suit. He knew there had to be some eloquent words for the moment, some incredible speech he needed to give, but wherever those words were, he couldn't find them. They stopped and watched a flock of gulls circling overhead, diving and screeching, fighting over a dead crab. One of the birds grabbed it and hauled ass out to sea as the others gave chase. He watched until they disappeared and continued staring at the horizon, remembering.

"You miss them, don't you?" she asked. It was amazing how she was able to read his mind. She had seen the far away look in his eyes, the old thousand-yard stare.

"Yeah, I do." He did miss them. They had been good men, his buddies, and now they were dead. They'd given their lives unknowingly, in an effort to take down a criminal who was right now living in a mansion courtesy of the same men who would sacrifice good men's lives to capture him. It was a fucked-up world.

"It's over, Dan," she said, and held him close, looking into his eyes, searching for what he was feeling, and wishing she could help him get rid of the guilt, the hurt. "You have to let it go."

He looked down at her and smiled. "Yep, you're right," he lied, and gave her a kiss. But in his heart, it was far from over. And he would never let it go.

East of Nassau, Bahamas 25°02.45"N 77°05.63"W
May 10, 1996 2046 EDT

The sky over the eastern Bahamas had turned from purple to black and the three boys seated in the sixteen-foot Whaler were beginning to get nervous. It was an old boat, almost twenty years, and had been glassed over and patched so many times it looked like it had leprosy.

A light chop came from the southeast and rocked the boat from side to side; an occasional wave slipped over the gunwale, splashing the occupants of the tiny vessel. Not a word had been spoken for the last twenty minutes. Finally, the tension became too great and the silence was broken.

"I'm scared," the youngest said. He was fourteen.

"Hush talkin' you nonsense, boy," the motorman snapped. A couple of years older, and therefore the leader. "I done told you, it nothin'. I done it before." He smiled and besides the whites of his eyes, a mouthful of white chompers was all that could be seen. "It just a small drop. But my ol' man, he say it enough we won' be havin' t' work for a year. You gon' pitch a stink 'bout dat?" He looked at the other boy, the one who had not spoken. "Wa' wrong wi' you, boy?"

"Nothin'," he replied. Although younger, he was wiser. He'd heard the stories about what happened when you got caught with drugs. It already happened to his mother's brother. They sent him away for a long, long time, and they never saw him again. His mother told him he'd got himself killed in the jail on Fox Hill.

"You chicken, boy?" the leader taunted him.

"Nope, I jus' tink dere's better ways t' earn a livin', like fishin' or takin' crawfish from d' reef."

The older boy was quick to pounce on him. "You don' know shit, boy! Now rest your mout'."

They sat in the darkness, the little boat rocking softly in the gentle swell. In the distance, the sound of an airplane was approaching.

"Muthafucka! Here we go!" the older boy shouted, and he yanked the rope and started the motor.